Book Cover by Belle Ames Designs

Line Edits by Everly Taylor

Content Edits by The Book's Savant

First edition 2024

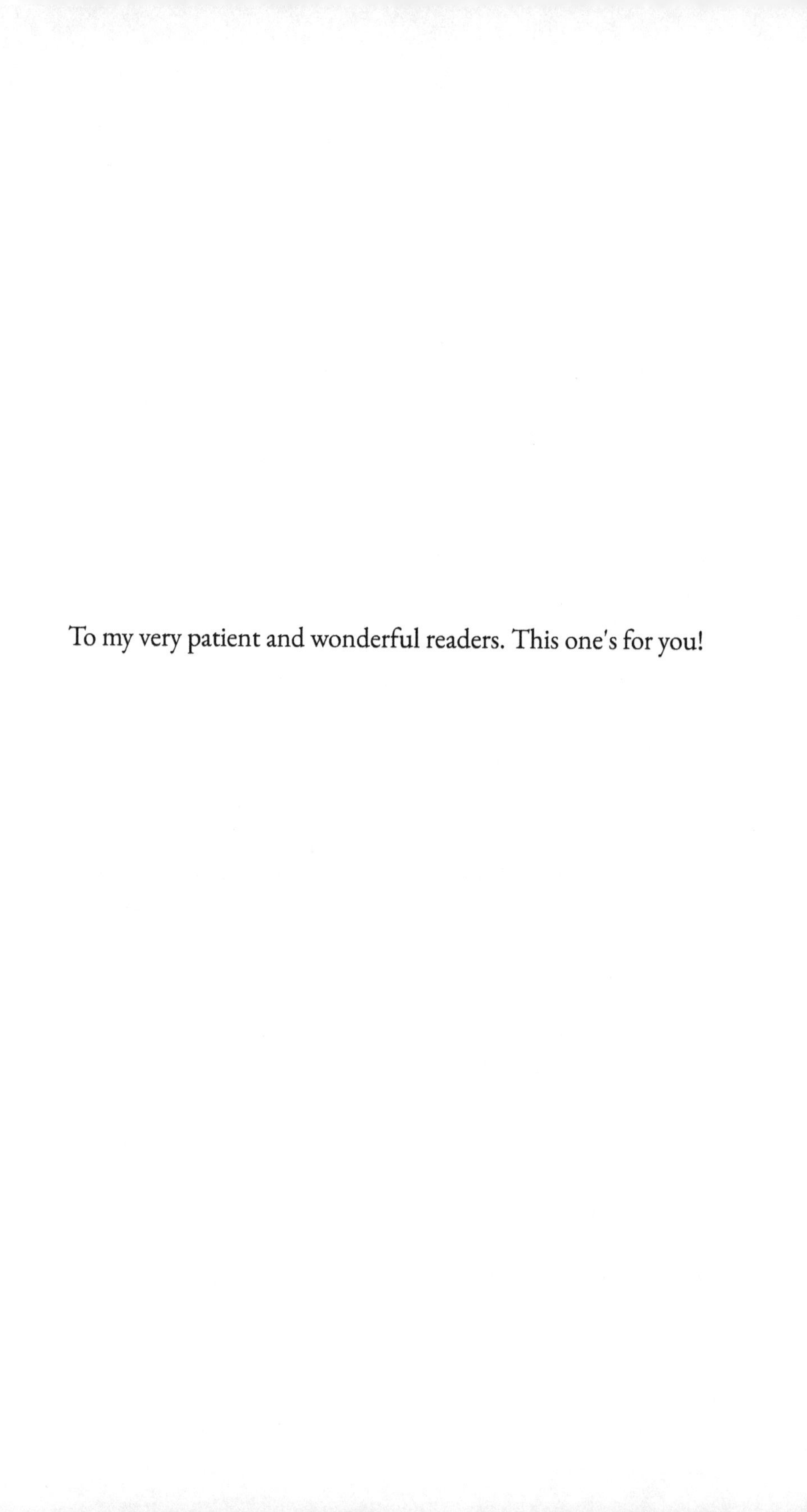

To my very patient and wonderful readers. This one's for you!

LORYN MOORE

CONTENT WARNINGS

The Darkening is a fantasy adventure story with adult themes and content. The characters have difficult experiences and backstories that may be triggering for some individuals.

- Graphic violence and death on page

- War themes

- Pregnancy loss recounted

- Sexual violence

- Sexual content

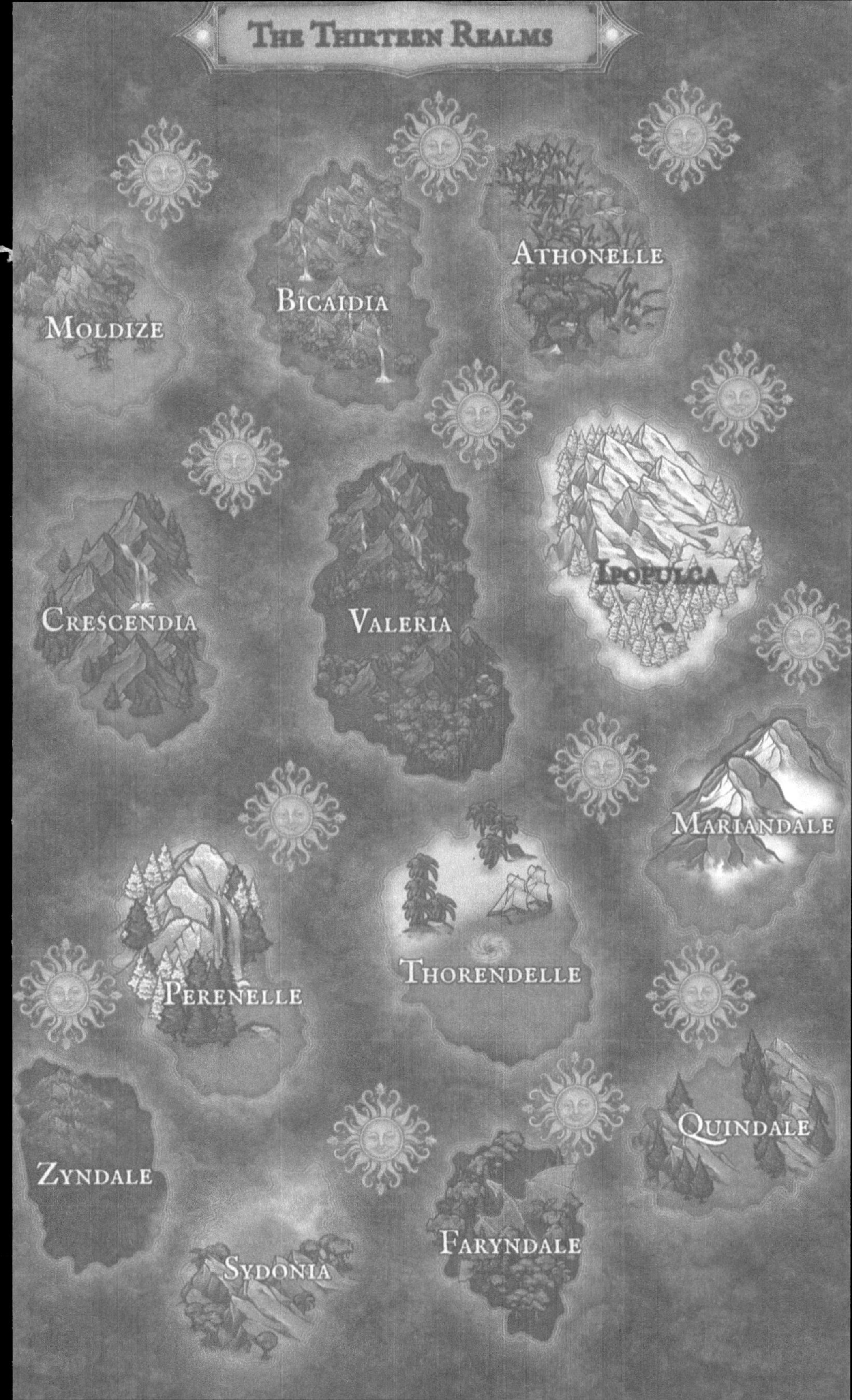

THE THIRTEEN REALMS
MOLDIZE
BICAIDIA
ATHONELLE
CRESCENDIA
VALERIA
IPOPULCA
MARIANDALE
PERENELLE
THORENDELLE
ZYNDALE
SYDONIA
FARYNDALE
QUINDALE

CONTENTS

Prologue	1
1. Monster	13
2. Secret	24
3. Imprisoned	33
4. Pain in Truth	40
5. Tormented	51
6. Delusion	60
7. Ruined	65
8. Awakening	76
9. Darkness	83
10. Trusting	99
11. Alliance	106
12. Spymaster	115
13. Memories	132
14. Roots	144

15.	Nightmares	151
16.	Orders	158
17.	Reunited	168
18.	Impossible	178
19.	Fury	191
20.	The All Powerful	198
21.	Strength	207
22.	Complicated	215
23.	Life Debts	222
24.	Turmoil	229
25.	The Hologram	236
26.	Remember	244
27.	Battle Planning	253
28.	Visitor	262
29.	Loathing	268
30.	No More Sharing	277
31.	Dangerous Hope	281
32.	Die Trying	284
33.	The Unknown	288
34.	Bad Timing	292
35.	Desperate Times	298
36.	The Escape	301

37. The Prisoner   311

38. Explosive   316

39. Valeria   325

40. Ascension   335

41. Retribution   341

42. Maximum Impact   348

43. Poisoned   357

44. Wynthorea   367

Acknowledgements   378

About the author   380

Other Books by Loryn Moore   381

PROLOGUE
Erykha

Erykha pinched the bridge of her nose, the readout of the glowing holo in front of her making her vision blur. She'd been analyzing it for days and her brain felt dull and fuzzy. Moldize had been under constant threat since her son, Arrick, and Bekka, the last creator in the multiverse, left for Bicaidia to rescue Bekka's sister.

Following their departure, the efforts to break through the Moldizean wards that protected her home world had doubled. It seemed like whoever wanted into Moldize had sensed Arrick and Bekka's power when they'd been there, and that malevolent force had maintained some level of restraint because of it.

But no longer.

She and the few other mid-to-upper-caste deities left in Moldize had kept the wards functioning and the threat at bay so far. But these new readings? Erykha shook her head, teeth biting into her cheek as anxiety boiled in her belly. They didn't have long before whoever wanted into their realm broke through.

She rose to her feet, her chair skidding across the black, marble floor with a loud screech as she rested her hand on the dagger fastened to her thigh.

Turning from the control panel, the circular, metallic table that housed the holo, Erykha strode to the tall windows that dominated the far wall. Sunlight streamed in from the floor-to-ceiling glass as she watched the city below, unable to quell the sense of foreboding that permeated her mind.

Small buildings and homes of simple but high-quality make lined the roads. She saw deities going about their business with no idea what danger they might soon face because they hadn't told them. Both she and Damion had hoped they could hold out until Bekka and Arrick returned from Bicaidia. But even if she did warn everyone, there was nowhere else for the Moldizean deities to go. They had no allies, and no other options but to wait it out and fight their way through it, if it came to that.

"We are so screwed," she groaned, staring at the bright spring day outside. The water rippled and sparkled from a turquoise sea at the edge of the city, new and vibrant against the greenery, also recently revitalized. A pang pierced through her heart as she took it all in. All their hard work these last months, all their efforts to return Moldize to some sense of normalcy, would soon be destroyed. She wasn't naïve enough to believe that whoever wanted through their wards had peaceful intentions. Piercing the protective barriers of another realm was, by definition, a hostile action.

A moment later, she heard footsteps approaching, but she didn't bother to turn around. She already knew who they belonged to—her lover, the father of her children, and her best friend, Damion. She could feel his presence as easily as the breath in her lungs, her nostrils filling with his familiar, musky scent. The thump of his boots on the ground stopped right before his hands slid down her arms.

She leaned back into his chest and let out a long sigh, a fraction of the tension she held releasing at his nearness. Gooseflesh raised along her arms as he swept the hair off her neck, pressing a warm kiss to her chilled skin. She turned and wrapped her arms around his waist, resting her cheek on his chest.

With no one around to witness her actions, she didn't feel the need to play the part of a stalwart queen. She didn't have to be the ruler with all the answers, which brought more relief than she dared to admit because it killed her to know that she didn't have them. She had no idea what came next. They had no answers, and no moves left to play. They could do nothing else but wait.

"What do we tell them all? Our people?" she asked Damion, looking up at him, despair written across her features.

Damion brushed a knuckle along her jawline. His thick beard and long, golden hair made him look like a savage warrior. She loved that about him. His wild, untamed nature. The one that drove him to hunt the very animals he cultivated, to promote life through cyclical death. A trait that he'd passed on to their son.

He paused for a long moment, considering her question with the seriousness it deserved. "The truth. That we don't have much time and we don't know what's coming, but once it does, we will do everything in our power to protect them from it."

Her eyes burned as she fought back the emotion roiling through her. She shook her head. "I don't like that answer. We need to have a plan. A strategy. We should consider all the angles, every possibility, and create contingencies for them." She didn't want to give her people a hopeless response. She couldn't bring herself to tell them they were giving up. Not after everything they'd survived these last decades.

He grimaced, looking down at her with an apology in his eyes. Without asking, she understood how much this truth hurt him. Every bit as much as it hurt her. "I don't think we have time for that, my love."

As though on cue, the holo began buzzing, then ringing, its alarm screeching throughout Castle Molo, their home. She jerked her head to the right, beyond Damion's shoulder, already knowing what she'd find there. It was the warning, the one she'd programmed to sound if the wards should ever fail. It blared, and her heart galloped in her chest in time with it, her palms sweating.

A door slammed open at the far side of the control room. The clanging sound echoed through the room, though it barely registered over the pounding of her heart in her ears.

Damion turned in response to it, hand reaching to his back where his crossbow hung, a quiver of magic-laced arrows resting beside it. He froze when he saw Lilja standing there, her white nightgown hanging about her ankles, face pale, and feet bare on the cool marble floor. Her long, blonde hair curled around her face, wild, just like her father's. She turned, searching the room, until her frightened eyes landed on her parents. "Mom, Dad? What's happening?"

Erykha rushed to her daughter's side, the alarm still sounding, not letting her forget they'd run out of time. Acid burned in her belly, as she reached for her daughter, an adolescent goddess not yet come of age, with no powers to protect herself. "Lilja, what are you doing here? You need to get back to your room!"

"I couldn't sleep," she said. "I came looking for you and then I heard that alarm and I got scared."

Erykha swore under her breath, pulling Lilja's slender frame behind her, her back to the windows overlooking the city at the far edge of the room. The control room was the most secure place in Castle Molo, and with Lilja safely behind them both, Damion gripped the crossbow at his back and pulled it free. Settling it on his shoulder, he grasped an arrow and ripped it loose. Lilja gasped behind them as the weapon blazed yellowy-white with magic, his magic. *It might not kill a deity, but it would wound one*, she thought, praying to the Ascended that it wouldn't come to that.

They surveyed the room for signs of danger; her lover and her protector, stepping in front of them both. Something felt wrong, a disturbance somewhere within the palace, somewhere close. They both sensed it, she knew, as every hair rose on the back of her neck in warning. She dared a glance down at the scanner and saw a mess of jumbled readings.

Incomprehensible.

Through gritted teeth, she hissed, "Ascended, I wish Arrick was here." His power far outweighed hers or Damion's. The instant the words left her mouth, she heard something. A crackle or buzzing coming from the far corner of the room, across from the door. She and Damion turned in unison and saw it, a ripple of power. She called her magic to her in response, the soft, red glow blanketing her skin as she prepared for whatever came next.

Their time was up.

"Mom, what's happening?" Lilja asked, her voice wobbling with terror as she stepped forward.

"Stay behind me," Erykha warned, pushing Lilja back and pulling that long dagger from the sheath on her thigh. It glowed with the same power as Damion's arrow and would provide some modicum of protection should they have to fight their way out of that room. She handed it to Lilja, who grasped the hilt with familiarity, her slim knuckles whitening with the tightness of her grip, just before a black mist gathered. It originated from a tiny point at about eye level, and then it grew, swirling and spiraling as a portal formed from that same corner.

Elation and hope sprouted in Erykha's chest so quickly it hurt. It was Arrick. He'd come home. And just in time, too. They needed him now more than ever. With a quick, hopeful look to her daughter, she rushed forward, hurrying towards her son's familiar power. But before she made it to the portal, a hand clamped down on her wrist and yanked her to a halt.

Stunned, she looked back at Damion, whose eyes remained hard, crossbow and arrow held at the ready in one hand now. "What?" she asked, a haze of confusion sliding into her mind. "What is it?"

"Don't move. I don't think that's—"

A voice, a female one, crooned through the newly formed portal. "Well, well, what have we here?" Chills ran up Erykha's spine as a goddess she didn't recognize stepped through. Her red, silk trousers and black, silk shirt rippled in the swirling mist of death magic. Her hair shone like platinum in the sunlight as her red lips stretched into a smile that was equal parts stunning and terrifying.

Erykha's stomach squeezed, her mind filling with confusion as she clenched her fists and renewed the power she'd let slip moments before. Red magic slid up her arms again, encasing her hands and forearms in a glistening sheen. *That was Arrick's magic,* she thought, her mind struggling to grasp who the hell this goddess was as she prepared her body for a fight. While she couldn't wound them like Damion, she was a goddess of physics, and she could make a mockery of all kinds of scientific laws.

Say goodbye to gravity and any normal application of force, she thought. *Let's see how well they fight in zero-G.*

A purple cloud of magic surrounded the goddess's body, lightning dancing within it. A chaos deity, Erykha knew, though the goddess in question made no move to use her power. Instead, it hovered, as though waiting for direction or for someone to make a move.

Uncertain what kind of threat she posed, Erykha hesitated for a fraction of a second as another god stepped through the portal. This one was male, and slick, with dark hair and a black suit. His blue eyes fixed on them and black mist flowed around him like a cloak, just as she'd seen Arrick's power do so many times before. So, he was the death deity whose magic had built the portal. Not Arrick.

I could have sworn I felt my son's power, his aura, Erykha thought, grasping for understanding. She'd been so sure. Rather than dwell on her mistake, Erykha steeled her spine, readying for a fight. She reached for the dagger at Damion's thigh and pulled it loose, shifting herself in front of her daughter once more, preparing for an attack. But then, to her utter and complete shock, Arrick stepped through that same portal.

Her heart hammered as confusion gripped her. Erykha took a step forward, and hesitated, forcing herself to listen to the roaring in her head telling her to stop. Where was Bekka? Or Caden and Deklan? And that was when she knew that something had gone very wrong in Bicaidia.

The portal closed then, leaving her unanswered thoughts ringing in her mind as she tried not to panic. Tried not to fixate on the worst possibilities.

She stared at her son, his moss-green eyes finding hers. Sorrow, she realized, and deep and unimaginable grief and regret shone in them.

"Son?" Damion asked. "What's going on?" Arrick looked from Damion to her, his face showing nothing but a steely determination she knew hid some fierce emotion inside of him, something she could tell he was keeping on a tight leash. Grief, rage, sorrow, she sensed it all lurking beneath that controlled surface. She knew then that whatever he had to say, they wouldn't like it.

His jaw flexed and his hands clenched into fists at his side as he moved closer to them. His muscles seemed to strain with each step, his back rigid and tense. He reached out a hand and rested it on his father's drawn crossbow. Arrick's hard gaze landed on Damion, his black power whispering at his fingertips. It was a warrior's gaze, she realized, as he shook his head and pressed the bow down harder. Shock had Damion lowering it as he stared at his son, the hard lines of their faces so similar and yet so different. Pure determination compared to absolute confusion.

"Plans have changed," Arrick said, and his voice was that of a commander, not her son. There was none of his usual warmth or humor, just a coldness that turned her blood to ice.

Erykha turned her glare on the two deities behind her son before she asked him, "Where's Bekka? Where are Caden and Deklan? Are they OK?"

"They're fine. They're safe." She watched with exaggerated care as he worked to conceal every emotion. An outsider may not have noticed it, but she was his mother, and something was wrong. He'd done something. Something he regretted, something that enraged him.

She clenched her jaw and every muscle in her body went rigid, Lilja's fingers tightening around her free hand, each bracing for whatever blow would come next.

"Arrick?" Lilja said, her soft voice a stark contrast to her brother's. Arrick cut her a sharp, pleading look, and she snapped her mouth shut. Erykha had never seen her son look at his sister like that before, and something inside of her broke.

She watched as Arrick swept his hand back in a formal gesture to indicate the deities behind him. "This is Madwyn and Riven of House Senegal, leaders of the Nefaric Uprising." Madwyn smiled again and gave them all a sickeningly charming finger wave.

Erykha hated her on sight, and with her jaw set, she questioned, "Great. What are they doing here, Arrick?" Hadn't her son left to stop these exact deities? Hadn't he been trying to get Bekka back on the Peacekeeper's seat of power in Valeria before The Rising got any worse?

"What aren't you telling us, Arrick?" Damion asked, his voice echoing from the vaulted ceilings above them.

Arrick's cool expression never wavered. "I've sworn our house to them. Moldize is part of the rebellion now." An involuntary gasp escaped Erykha's lips as she stepped back, pulling Lilja with her. *No*, she thought, *not again*. The last time they'd been a part of a rebellion, they'd gotten exiled, their realm almost snuffed out of existence, and only recently saved from that fate. What would happen if they lost again?

Damion's voice filled the silence that followed, "No. Our realm isn't my son's to promise. We'll never join you." He stepped out of Arrick's reach, raising his bow again, sighting the chaos deity with the saccharine-sweet smile. Erykha and Lilja fell into line behind him, preparing to fight.

But Arrick moved again, stepping into the path of the arrow, placing himself between the weapon and the two deities he'd sworn their loyalty to. He shook his head. "No, Father. I gave them my word."

"Move, Son," Damion all but growled, his gaze and his aim unwavering.

Madwyn stopped smiling and looked at her nails. "He did, you know, give me his word. A binding."

Erykha gasped, her reaction visceral. No, he wouldn't have. Her gaze locked onto Arrick, her mouth open in shock. "Why?" she asked. "Why would you do such a thing?" Something in her chest cracked, and she knew that he must have had a damn good reason to do something so reckless.

"I did what I had to do. I swore Moldize would support the Nefaric Uprising in the war to come. It's done."

And it was, she thought, fighting back the tears that burned at the corners of her eyes. Her son had sworn himself to the leader of the Nefaric rebels, and he'd dragged them, and the entirety of Moldize, into it along with him. Grief sliced through her as she wondered again why he would do something so insane. But no answers came.

As desperation swallowed her, she swore she wouldn't cry. She would not dishonor herself like that. Erykha was the lady of Moldize, and she understood what could happen to Arrick, to her son, if he broke any part of the binding. He could die, which meant that they had no choice but to help him because Moldize *was* his to promise. He led it as much as she and Damion did, no matter what his father had said. Sorrow burned in her chest. What had made him choose to condemn them all to this fate? Bekka, Caden, and Deklan's absence gave her some hint, and her stomach filled with acidic dread.

Erykha stared at Madwyn, who stopped looking at her nails and smiled at them all once more as she locked eyes with Riven. Something seemed to pass between them right before he dematerialized into a black mist. A second later, his body appeared right next to her. She'd barely registered his presence before he ripped Lilja's hand from hers. Lilja yelped and let out a quick shriek before he disappeared with her into a cloud of darkness, only to re-materialize at Madwyn's side.

Erykha lunged forward, a feral growl in her throat, "Let her go!"

Damion yelled something, a furious bellow of rage that Erykha couldn't make out amid the roaring in her ears. But Madwyn held up a slim, lovely hand to silence them. Riven still gripped Lilja's shoulder. Terror bucked inside Erykha, knowing what a death deity's power could do when unleashed.

Madwyn clicked her tongue, wagging a disapproving finger at them. "I can see this won't be as smooth of a transition as I'd hoped." She turned her attention to Lilja and looked her up and down, her gaze predatory.

Arrick's eyes hardened into stone. "Madwyn, that's unnecessary—."

"Silence," she commanded, and Arrick snapped his mouth shut, as though by force. Madwyn spun around, that terrifying yet dazzling smile again on her face. "Just to make sure you understand who's in charge now, we'll be taking the little one with us."

"No, you can't," Erykha shouted, lunging forward, her hand outstretched, reaching for her daughter. Lilja's eyes locked onto hers, and she saw the fear in them. But Erykha stopped short at the black magic she saw dancing along the floor, almost invisible over the black marble. An impenetrable barrier of death power lay between them, one she couldn't cross without dying. Despair and helplessness filled her every nerve-ending.

"Yes," Madwyn crooned, moving in front of Lilja. "But don't worry, she will be safe enough. So long as you do as you're told, that is. Think you can handle that?"

1
MONSTER

ARRICK

One Month Later…

I swung the black blade of my sword, slicing down hard as a deity broke through the wall of power I'd forged around myself. My blow hit home, the impact zinging through my arm as I cut through armor, leather, and flesh alike. The god gasped at the sheer agony of it, dropping to his knees, mouth opening and closing in shock. A second later, he fell forward into the mud, screaming as the toxin from my blade seeped into his bloodstream. I didn't stop to watch. Instead, I trudged forward, pushing my magic out further onto the battlefield.

Adrenaline, and the calm that came with war and death, silenced the roaring in my head. Not letting me hear the voice inside that told me to stop fighting. That I was on the wrong side. That I should let myself, and the army at my side, die.

I couldn't do that.

Even the thought of such disobedience had my arm, and the tattoo of the binding I'd made with Madwyn, burning like pure fire. So, I continued my forward march, my magic enveloping a deity whose outstretched hand aimed straight for my second lieutenant, Asthorea. Before he could release even a drop of his magic, I ripped out his soul. His face went blank before his body dissipated, ascending right before our eyes.

She spun, realizing how close she'd come to getting wiped off the field, and offered me a tight, "Thanks," before she cut through an elemental deity with her own poisoned daggers.

I gave her a nod of acknowledgment as we gained another ten feet. Ten feet closer to the Quindalean palace's thick, gray stone wall and massive gate. Ten feet further into open ground and out of the cover the treeline provided us.

The combination of the thick forest that surrounded the Quindalean palace, and Madwyn's skilled Bicaidian technology deities, had allowed us to sneak into their realm without notice. It had let us get close enough to damage their reinforced walls before we launched our full attack. But that advantage wouldn't last long.

A glance ahead told me that the gate still burned from our initial assault. I saw a small contingent of our Bicaidian elementals continuing to unleash their fire against it in a combined force. It groaned; its wards damaged almost at the breaking point. We'd be through it soon enough, and then we'd have unfettered access to the stronghold and every critical piece of infrastructure we needed to control Quindale.

The Quindalean royals hadn't been prepared for us, but they'd responded quicker than we expected. I still saw them bringing in reinforcements as deities appeared in rapid flashes of light. They burst onto the battlefield in little more than training leathers and wearing no armor to protect themselves from the poisoned weapons we wielded. A mistake I knew they'd soon rectify as well.

Fire, thunder, lightning, and wind whipped around us as water flooded the mud-laden ground we trudged through. We ignored it, advancing closer to the royals and their stronghold. I signaled, and within moments, a second regiment of our elementals started to beat back the Quindalean deities' powers.

The water subsided as quickly as it started, resulting in little more than wet boots, leathers, and an irritating puddle to slog through at our feet.

As I moved forward, a plume of fire speared straight for my heart. I spun out of its way, and it struck a demon behind me instead, incinerating it in an instant. My magic flared in reaction, and I sent out a blast of power. It hit home, spearing into the soul of the deity who'd aimed for me. I yanked it clean from her body. She dropped dead, dissipating into misty embers and ascending before her body even hit the ground.

Not pausing to think, I breathed in the scent of blood that hung heavy on the battlefield. Sulfuric and metallic, the acrid aroma of demon and deity merged into a sickening tonic. So many had died already, more than I'd expected. I observed the bodies of demons and poisoned deities alike crowding the soggy ground, creating a barricade of death between our front line and the Quindalean palace.

I looked around once more, noting the field and our position, and saw more deities and demons charging into the fight from our side, streaming in from portals hidden within the cover of the forest to reinforce us. Blasts of power rained down from the sky and I rolled to the side as a white flash of pure energy singed the deity beside me. She fell back, body convulsing before she went limp. Before I could pull her back into the protection of the forest, a barrage of explosions racked us. The ground shook, and I fought to steady myself as blast after blast slammed into the ground. Deities screamed, demons shrieked, and I smelled death everywhere. Something inside my blood sang.

I tried to get my bearings, eyes settling back on our enemy's line, and as I did, I paled when I saw what had transpired. Portals blanketed every open space along the massive wall as far as the eye could see. They sprang to life out of nowhere and through them an army charged in full armor now. Lessons learned, they ran into the battle, their bodies glowing with white power. They kept up the barrage, slamming more of those damned energy blasts right into our formations. I felt the deities surrounding me panic as the Quindalean's numbers surpassed our own. That element of surprise? It had run its course.

Our front line of demons took the hardest hit, and they fell by the dozens, unable to withstand the immense power of the Quindalean energy gods.

"Shit," I hissed. We'd missed our window. Speed and swiftness following our surprise attack had been critical to winning, to conquering Quindale's palace and its royals before they could mount a proper defense. But they'd managed to beat us back, to hold us off too long. The palace loomed over us a short distance away, that gate still burning, but the constant stream of fire we'd used to assault it was dying down. I turned and realized that not just the demons had taken heavy damage. So had our contingent of fire deities.

We continued to lose soldiers as more Quindalean deities swarmed through the endless stream of new portals. They rushed onto the field, magic alighting, and more of my demons fell. They didn't get back up. The tattoo of my binding burned as I realized that the tide of the battle had turned fully now. The Quindaleans were winning, driving forward, and shoving us back with their potent magic.

I growled in frustration and thought about Lilja, my sister. Madwyn didn't hold only my life in her hands, she held Lilja's, too. I heard a scream, and watched Asthorea drop to one knee, lightning twisting around her torso before disappearing back into the sky. Sweat slid down her face and I smelled her burning flesh. She rose, teeth gritted, and we took another ten steps back, our demons at the frontline retreating against the onslaught of Quindalean reinforcements.

I peered around, trying to determine our best path forward as ever more deities entered the Quindalean defense. I ran then, seizing Asthorea's shoulder, and spun her to face me. "Get to Riven's contingent now!" I ordered, and she nodded as she fought through the obvious pain lancing through her body from the lightning strike. But she broke into a run anyway as I closed my fist and seized three deities, charging for the weak side of my right flank with my magic. I reached inside of them and pulled their souls clean from their bodies. The godly light that surrounded them winked out, bodies dissipating.

My tattoo burned again, the pain more intense that time. I sucked in an anguished breath because I knew what I had to do to win, and I had to act fast. If we lost this battle, I couldn't bear to think about what would happen to Lilja or my parents. And if I died because I disobeyed the binding? Madwyn would know because there would be no wounds except black, burned flesh where our binding linked us.

If that happened, what kind of punishment would Madwyn exact on me, dead or not? She would never just let it go. What would she do with Moldize? To the mortals and the deities who lived there that I promised to protect? Everything inside of me hardened and my mind cleared. I understood what I had to do.

I looked to my right and saw Riven, the second commander of our first siege as an army. Asthorea had made it to him and was helping him reinforce his flank as she threw Quindalean deities through her black, depthless dimensions faster than I could count. But it still wasn't fast enough.

Madwyn fought on my left, and purple haze floated on the battlefield like acid fog pouring from her fingertips, but the Quindalean energy deities blasted it back, keeping her at bay. Trees shook, uprooting as vines snaked across the ground, spearing for us. One snapped around my ankle and yanked with enough force that I dropped to one knee before hacking down with my sword and severing it. It shriveled back and away from me, and I rose, wiping sweat from my brow.

I peered around the battlefield once more, determining the best way to do what needed to be done. Madwyn made it clear she didn't want to kill the Quindaleans. She wanted to conquer them, and she didn't want to conquer a fucking wasteland. So, I needed to end this now, before our inexperience and stupidity cost us any more lives.

The Quindalean royals stood at the back of the onslaught, near the burning portion of the gate to their stronghold. Our elementals still kept it alight, a small favor and a minor distraction we desperately needed. Unfortunately for us, the royals let their Quindalean elemental deities deal with that while they unleashed holy fury on the field. Their magic was something to behold. Rain made of pure fire and energy slammed down around us again, as the newly arrived deities speared forward, fighting their way through our front lines with surgical precision.

I needed to hurry before we lost any more ground. With resolve as hard as fucking granite, I called out, "Riven, to me!" In an instant, he translocated next to me, running through the misty, black magic we both shared.

"What is it?" He asked, turning and stabbing a goddess who charged him straight through the heart with his massive, black blade. He took a hit with pure white energy a second later and hissed as it cut straight through his leather and magic-enhanced armor, sinking to his knees in pain. Madwyn had ordered me to be their first commander, and to do everything I could to win. The binding tattoo on my wrist burned even hotter as I watched our formations crumble, and the army begin to collapse under the panic of its first battle.

I'd warned her. We hadn't trained enough for this, not yet. She'd insisted we could take them by surprise, but I'd warned her, and she hadn't listened. I wanted to fucking choke her for this, but it wasn't the time. Lightning struck down beside us and I leaped, tackling Riven to the ground and getting him clear of the blast radius. We rolled, rocks hitting my shoulders and ribs, but I didn't care. That all-too-familiar calm had come over me.

"We need to end this now," I said. Rolling to my feet, I swung my blade for an energy god who ran at me, his own magically enhanced weapons drawn. I cut him down without thinking. If I allowed us to lose any more ground, we wouldn't get out of there alive, and I would have failed in a direct order when I knew how to succeed.

And even worse, Madwyn would know it. She would punish everyone I loved if I didn't stop this, I reminded myself. Ruthless, I thought, as I watched the Quindaleans cut down more of our foot soldiers, their souls ascending before their bodies hit the ground. I had to be ruthless. I steeled myself for it, not letting myself think about what came next.

Rising to my feet, I held out a hand to help Riven up, and he grasped my forearm. I hauled him to his feet, and he tried to pull his arm away from mine, but I clamped down on it harder. "Sorry about this," I said, right before I shoved my magic through his internal shields and wrapped my talons straight into his power.

He gasped as I took a huge portion of it, ripping it from his body and pouring it into mine. More than I needed, and more than enough to get the job done. I left a small kernel of it for him, just so I wouldn't kill him. Another order from Madwyn—I couldn't kill any who served her.

I sucked in a breath, not giving myself a chance to think before I unleashed our combined power in a torrent of black mist and death. It consumed the field, our identical magic fusing. Only like-magics could be borrowed and used as I'd just done, and as it rushed across the field, coating everything in black, I closed my eyes and felt them all. The gods with lower-caste gifts, and some with upper-caste magic too. The ones we didn't need or could sacrifice to win.

I let cold calculation and the reality of what I needed to do guide me. I locked onto them, our mist surrounding them, choking them until they gasped for breath. Deities dropped to the ground, screaming, and clawing at their chests, their cries of desperation turning into horrifying keens that filled the night air. I ignored them. I took one long breath and quieted the voice inside of me, begging me to stop.

Then I ripped their souls from their bodies.

Gods fell, eyes rolling back to the whites as they dropped like stones. Their souls burned bright, bodies going dull without the celestial essence that powered them, right before they disintegrated into embers. All that remained were the most powerful energy deities, the useful elementals, and the royals, who stood a hundred feet away at the back of the front line

I'd just decimated more than a thousand in a single, devastating blow.

They gaped at us, frozen in absolute horror at what they'd witnessed. At the death I'd brought right to their front door. Everything stopped then, the silence deafening right before the screaming started.

Gods and goddesses dropped to their knees, their shouts of terror and confusion ringing out into the night sky. The ones they loved or cared for, gone in an instant, with no way or chance to defend themselves. They needed to witness what kind of destruction we could bring. We needed to break their will to fight, and I'd done just that. It was the only way to win.

They didn't need to know I'd used everything I could of mine and Riven's magic without killing us both. They also didn't need to know that if they pressed their advantage still, they might just beat us. But I knew without question that they wouldn't risk it.

Turning away from the screaming and despair, I looked down and saw the bodies of demons littering every inch of the ground at the frontline and beyond, and our own thinned army, and knew I'd done what had to be done. And yet, I grew cold inside. Darkness crept in at the edges. I felt it then, the beast inside of me that had always been there. The one I kept so carefully caged. The one that delighted in killing and death, and the one I never let free. It purred at what it witnessed as the weapons laced with the magic of their Quindalean wielders dropped.

They watched me and our army of demons, Nefarals, and Altruists, the terror clear in their eyes as the royals shouted across the field. "We surrender. Name your terms."

I'd felt the souls of three thousand Quindaleans, braced in the palm of my hand, and I'd executed over half of them. The darkness inside me basked in it. It wanted to luxuriate in the blood of the dead.

Death. I was death, and yet, I'd been so much more than that. I'd turned myself into more. Forced myself to be more, and in one instant, I'd destroyed that.

A voice behind me rose through the roaring in my ears, and I recognized it as Madwyn's. "Well done, Arrick. Ruthless, but effective."

I looked at Riven, whose arm I held. Not realizing I still gripped it, I let go, and he dropped to his knee, gasping for air after what I'd done to him. He looked up at me, his eyes wide and accusatory before he blinked, and that disbelief disappeared. His face went blank as I reached down and pulled him to his feet. He looked around, mouth dropping open in utter astonishment. I didn't know if he was impressed or horrified. Perhaps a little of both.

Madwyn walked forward, past us toward the surrendering royals, her knee-high boots and lightweight armor glistening with protective magic in the moonlight. Davendrie, her pet consciousness deity and one of only five in her inner circle, fell into step behind her. One of her Diamanti, her most trusted and most prized warriors. He turned his head and glanced over his shoulder, grinning at me as though I'd done something brilliant. As though I hadn't just killed over a thousand deities in cold blood.

As they slipped from earshot, Riven stared at me once more. His face twisted into an expression I didn't recognize. "How many?"

I swallowed down the bile that burned my throat. Pushed down the stain that I'd wear on my soul forever. "Just shy of fifteen hundred."

He looked at me like I might be a monster, and for the first time in my entire existence, I thought he might be right.

2
SECRET
ARRICK

A few hours later, Davendrie clapped my back, grinning as he leveled a finger at my face. "You saved our asses out there, Commander. What even made you think to do that?" His bronze face looked joyous, like I hadn't just murdered over a thousand deities and broken the spirit of a thousand more on that damn battlefield.

My throat tightened and my blood heated as I remembered what it felt like to hold so many souls in my hands at one time and to decide their fate with no consideration beyond winning, but I kept my face impassive. I didn't know what to say to him. At last, I answered, "It was the only way to win."

"You are one cold-ass motherfucker," he replied, guffawing. "To the Moldizean!" He cried out, holding up the glass of god's-ale to the rest of the army. Everyone lifted their glasses in response, repeating, "To the Moldizean!" We toasted in the Quindalean royal palace then, the remains of our army eating their food and drinking their god's-liquor. Everything about what I'd done, what we'd all done, sat like a stone in my gut. And yet ... if we'd lost?

My sister's youthful, innocent face flashed in my mind, followed by my parents, and my realm—I imagined them all burning if I'd failed. Oh yes, Madwyn had every bit of leverage she needed to turn me into her personal killing machine. But I would never again let our army get into the position we'd found ourselves in on that battlefield. The next time we fought, we'd be prepared, and I'd make damn sure I didn't let her rush me into battle with a half-assed plan like she had that day, regardless of the fucking binding.

"To Arrick! Thank you for saving my pretty, little ass out there before you saved the rest of our asses!" Someone else in the crowd shouted, and I turned my head to see Asthorea standing on a large wooden chair, booted foot propped on the wooden table as she raised her glass and grinned down at me. Her battle gear was singed, but she appeared otherwise unharmed.

I grabbed one of the dozens of full mugs from the long table at the center of the banquet hall, and held it up in solute to her, dipping my head in acknowledgment, just as a god from the crowd yelled, "And what a nice ass it is too!"

Asthorea doubled over laughing before she raised her glass again and said, "Damn straight!" Everyone burst into a roar of laughter, and I joined in despite myself.

When it died down a little, I yelled to Asthorea and her admirer alike, "You're welcome!" Before I sipped my god's-ale.

A little while later, I felt a hand slam down on my shoulder and a squeeze. "There's our hero." Riven, I realized, and my muscles tensed. The room shouted, "Here! Here!" Riven repeated the chant, grabbing another full mug of god's-ale from the table and holding it up. He clicked his glass to mine so hard that my drink spilled over the edges. Then he began singing, a victory song that must have been Bicaidian. I'd never heard it, but the rest of the army sang along with him, shouting the words and swaying with a drunken post-battle high.

When the sound reached a fever pitch, he leaned in and said so that only I could hear. "If you ever strip me of my magic without my permission again, I'll have you burned alive. Do we understand each other?"

I eyed him, brows lifting, schooling my reaction. I couldn't help but be impressed with the venom in his words. "We do." His face drew taut with rage, and I didn't know if it was because I'd insulted his masculinity or because of how many I'd killed with our combined power. I supposed I never would know.

At last, Madwyn's voice rang out above the crowd, and Riven stepped away from me, striding to his sister's side as she entered the crowded banquet hall. "Friends!" she said, sweeping into the room in a blood-red dress that fit her body like a glove. She'd washed her skin until it shone, and her hair fell in a straight, glossy sheet on either side of her face. A small, golden circlet sat atop her head, and I couldn't help but think she looked like the regal queen she wished to be. "You've accomplished much today! We've conquered Quindale! We now have full control over all of its resources! Our position grows stronger, and soon the Valerians will have to face us. They will have to bargain with us, and they will have to give us what we want! They'll have no choice! At last, we will be free to live our lives, free to use our power, and free to pursue whatever we wish!" Everyone shouted their excitement, banging their glasses on the long, wooden tables that filled the room. God's-ale and god's-liquor sloshed and spilled, soaking the lacquered surface. "There is one deity who made our victory today possible. Do you all know who that is?"

"Arrick, Arrick, Arrick," I heard them chant, quietly at first and then louder until my name roared and echoed within the banquet hall.

"That's right," Madwyn said, her voice once again rising above the shouts. Everyone quieted for her as she asked, "Arrick, come up here, would you?" She stood at the head of the main table, where a large wooden chair, that could only have been the Quindalean king's, sat. I felt the burn of the tattoo on my arm and realized she'd meant that as an order. So, I did, winding my way through the crowd of soldiers, each of them clapping my back as I passed.

"Arrick did something that took real bravery today." I didn't know how to react to that. Bravery? What I'd done had required nothing akin to bravery. It had been more like determination to save the people I loved, and I hadn't hesitated for a moment. I'd chosen them over those 1,500 deities without even thinking about it. Simple as that. But that didn't matter, because an approving rumble went through the room as she continued. "He showed true resolve and quick-thinking in the face of danger. Without him, we'd have lost. I want to honor his heroism right here, right now." She scanned the room, and everyone went quiet, and I realized what she planned to do before she did it. "First my ally, and now a member of my elite warriors." She looked at me, a wicked, disarming grin sliding over her lips. "From today forward, Arrick, you are a full member of my Diamanti, with all the benefits that this station entails."

A collective gasp swept through the room, and I wondered if she'd lost her damn mind. The only reason I served her was the binding, and she wanted to make me a member of her most trusted, elite soldiers?

"For what you did today, for the ruthlessness, the brutality, and the necessity of it. You're now in full command of my armies, reporting only to Riven and me. You'll make sure we are ready for our next conquest. And when the time comes, we will win as an army, together." She laid a hand on my shoulder, leaned forward, and kissed either of my cheeks as everyone cheered. The spot where her lips pressed against my skin burned like poison, and I resisted the urge to wipe away the feel of it.

The crowd kept cheering. They cheered for the suffering, the pain, and the terror I'd caused. They cheered because in trying to save my family, I'd saved them. I'd saved my enemy and the enemies of the goddess I loved. The one they kept imprisoned and refused to allow me to see.

By killing over 1,500 in one breath, I'd made them more powerful than ever before, and that decision had been as easy as breathing. I tried to remind myself that many more would have died if I hadn't done it. Most likely more than I'd killed, if the battle had continued. I'd done what I did so that we could win. So that I could save my sister, my family, and my realm. A long time ago, I'd told Bekka that I'd sell my very soul to save them. It seemed I'd lived up to that promise.

I stayed and drank with the soldiers and celebrated with my lieutenants for as long as I could stomach it. It kept me from thinking too much, and it built the relationships I knew I'd need to survive in this den of vipers. So, I'd play the part of their fearless commander. But when night threatened to turn into day, I excused myself from the merriment. I spared a quick glance at Madwyn, who was playing a drinking game with her other Diamanti and the common foot soldiers, laughing as she won a round.

Even I had to admit, she had charisma. The army loved her and the Nefarals respected and trusted her. She believed in what she was doing from the core of her being. It was why she fought. She would make a tough enemy, I knew.

I'd be lying if I said I didn't understand her cause, but that didn't mean I agreed with her methods. She was insane, reckless, and would destroy everything in her effort to carve out a small slice of the realms for herself. With that thought in mind, I slipped out of the banquet hall and into the darkened hallway that led to the chambers we claimed for sleeping.

We'd sealed off the entire palace, the royal family imprisoned in their rooms until we could determine what to do with them. Until Madwyn sent Davendri to go to work on them. Revulsion pulsed through me at the idea of that worm of a consciousness deity crawling around in my head, just before someone called my name.

A voice I'd know anywhere; Madwyn's voice. I turned, the darkened corridor lined with exterior windows. I could see the sun beginning to paint the sky purple, and I focused my energy on not growling in irritation as I waited for her to hurry down the hall and catch up with me. A few seconds later, she fell into step beside me. I realized she'd taken off her shoes, and her head barely made it to my shoulder as we walked down the hall together.

She peered up at me and I saw weariness on her face for the first time. "I miscalculated," she said, her voice calm.

Looking down at her, I raised my eyebrows in surprise. I'd never heard her admit fault before, so I waited for her to continue, interested despite myself.

"Our army wasn't ready. You were right."

"Obviously."

She pressed her lips together, and I could see annoyance flash in her eyes. "I've never led an army. I need your help, and that's why I made you a Diamanti tonight. The army, my people, they need to listen to you so that when we go into battle next time, we win outright. Without the kind of death we exacted today. We lost precious resources when you did that."

My ire rose, but I clamped my jaw and spoke through gritted teeth, "You left me no choice."

She waved a hand. "I know, and I accept full responsibility for that."

"Good," I said, knowing that when she spoke of wasted resources, she meant the powerful energy and elemental deities I'd killed. I'd tried to keep the upper-caste deaths to a minimum, but I needed them to fear me too. So, not all of them had made it off the battlefield. But I assumed she'd be furious with me for it. For squandering the very resources that made Quindale worth conquering. Instead, she was giving me a gentle rebuke. At least she understood how close we'd come to losing.

"Alright," she said, nodding her head. "Oh, and what I'm about to say next is an order." The binding burned over my wrist as her expression hardened back into ice. "You're to tell me the moment the army is ready for its next conquest, you're to give me the best advice to win every battle we fight, and you're not to steal my brother's power again. That last one is from him. He didn't like that at all, and after what happened with Ellarah, I owe him."

I'd heard of Ellarah. Whispers flew around Bicaidia about strife brewing between brother and sister over Riven's injured lover. Healers visited Riven's chambers day and night, tending to the mysterious Ellarah, who'd yet to wake from a deep stasis sleep. The healers were mostly Bicaidian deities who'd chosen to serve Madwyn rather than die at her hand. Just like most of the other non-Nefarals who served in our army.

I looked down, focusing my attention on Madwyn as she gave me one long, harsh look, waiting for me to acknowledge her words. I did, giving her a curt nod. Seeming happy enough with that, she turned and padded back down the hall to her army.

I could feel the pulse of the tattoo on my wrist, the sting of the orders, and I wanted to cut the thing from my body. Carve it straight out of my skin and feed it to her. Not that it would do any good. Bindings were permanent. They couldn't end until both parties agreed, and something told me Madwyn would never let me go.

As she stepped through the glowing light of the open door and into the banquet hall, I pressed my hand against the exterior stone wall and closed my eyes. I inhaled and exhaled, breathing through the rush of pain that assaulted me as the secret I'd kept for five long months surfaced without my permission. The same secret I'd kept since I'd bound myself to Madwyn, since Bekka and I became soulfused, and our powers had merged.

It was that new magic that flowed through me. Bekka's magic. That same creation gift that had transferred from her to me that day in Bicaidian hell. It vibrated just beneath the surface of my skin, aching to get free, and I clutched at my chest as I fought to keep it down, to keep it hidden.

Madwyn could never know about it, and I swallowed hard at the intensity of its urgency to be released. It grew worse each day. I wondered for the millionth time how long I could keep it a secret, how long before Madwyn found out. Before I wouldn't be able to contain it with brute force and iron will anymore. It only grew more insistent, and without a release, I would eventually crack. And once I did, I could only imagine what kind of horror Madwyn would release on our world.

If she found out, I would just have to make sure she never got the chance to use it.

3

IMPRISONED

BEKKA

Three months later…

My stomach growled as I stared up at the ceiling of the prison cell I'd occupied ever since the day Arrick traded his fealty to the Nefarals for my life. Otherwise known as the single worst day of my life. Or maybe it was a tie between that and the day my grandfather died, but not before gifting his power to me. *It's a real toss-up*, I thought bitterly.

I closed my eyes against the bright lights that never turned off and sighed. It had been four months. Or at least, I was pretty sure it had been. It was hard to keep track with no windows and the constant hum of too-bright lights for company. At what I thought was night, I prayed to the Ascended for darkness. That way, maybe I could get just one night of decent sleep. But alas, it wasn't to be.

Instead, I remained stuck in this prison, on the razor's edge of torture, never quite tipping over it, with no discernable way out. Fatigue and hunger gnawed at me as I pushed myself into a sitting position on the firm bed. I pressed my back into the cool stone wall, yet another discomfort this place offered. No blankets, no softness, no warmth. Only cold stone, despite Bicaidia's warm climate. I could only assume that this was another method meant to wear me down.

Because you see, I had yet to do what they wanted me to. I refused to give them the satisfaction, and I never would. No matter what they did to me, I would never send a holo to my parents begging for peace or for Valeria to surrender. It would never happen.

It didn't help their cause that I knew that this meager, albeit uncomfortable, attempt at torture was the worst that they could do to me. After Arrick agreed to the binding, he and Madwyn had set the terms.

I remembered the pain that split through my chest as Arrick made the bargain that would seal his fate forever. In return for his fealty, obedience, and Moldize's support, Madwyn had promised that we'd remain alive and physically unharmed while in her care, and she had bound herself to that promise. But she hadn't allowed Arrick to negotiate us out of this dungeon, no matter how hard he'd tried to convince her. Though, on the plus side, she still couldn't kill us. So, all the threats and intimidation they'd thrown my way made zero difference. They couldn't fool me. I remembered the words of that binding as though they'd happened yesterday. How could I forget?

I still saw it in my mind's-eye and heard it in my waking dreams every single night I spent alone in that damned cell.

"How did everything get so completely fucked?" I asked aloud to no one in particular, thumping my head against the wall. I did that a lot. Talked to myself. After all, who else was there? I thought, fingering the outlines of the tattoo they'd inked on me before they'd taken off the shackles. It glowed gold on my skin, an intricate rune, ancient and old. Illegible.

I might not be able to read it, but damn if it wasn't effective. No magic, no strength, and way slower accelerated healing. I'd learned that the hard way when I tried to punch a hole in the wall in a fit of rage during my first week in prison. It hadn't ended well.

A healer had mended my broken bones, but they remained stiff and achy. Something told me they'd wanted to teach me a lesson, and it had worked. I decided not to punch any more walls after that. Flexing my stiff fingers, I groaned in frustration, feeling a now-familiar helplessness I didn't much care for.

My head jerked toward the door as I heard the locking mechanism slide, and I struggled to my feet. The hinges creaked just before the precipice swung wide. A demon skulked inside, its sulfuric stench suffusing the room. Glaring at it, I wished like hell I had my godly strength back so I could take it apart with my bare hands. Or maybe dematerialize it with my magic. Ooh, or maybe turn it into an adorable, fluffy bunny as I pointed and laughed at it.

The options were limitless, I thought as I stared, my expression stoic, waiting for it to tell me that I needed to make a hologram. At which point I would refuse. Then I wouldn't get food for at least a full day. Or what I counted as one with what little time indicators I had. It had become a routine. Mundane and boring, just like everything else in this place. The truth was that, at that point, I'd grown used to not eating. And despite the lack of mirrors, I could feel how thin my body had become. My pants sagged off my hips and my bones felt sharp to the touch.

It couldn't be pretty, I knew, but then what difference did something that trivial make? It wasn't as though I had to host a dinner party or look sexy for someone. No one came to see me. *Not even Arrick*, I thought, trying to tamp down the pain thinking about him caused.

Instead, I focused on the moment in front of me, and as the demon's hulking form stepped to the side, I sucked in a surprised breath. Behind it was the goddess who'd come with Remi to hell. I racked my brain, trying to remember her name and failing. We hadn't properly introduced ourselves when we fought for our lives in Bicaidian hell together. I blinked as I stared in shock at her.

Her face had grown angular and drawn, her curls frizzy and dull. *She looks about as good as I feel*, I thought, knowing that I wasn't in any better condition.

Questions assaulted my mind in a barrage of confusion. What was she doing here? Helpfully, the demon spoke, its hissing, monstrous voice like nails across my ragged nerves. "This one stays here now. No more private suites. Her Grace's orders."

I looked at the toilet at the far edge of the room. It didn't have a door. Then I looked at the bed; a single cot. Just when I thought this place couldn't get any worse. Of course, I should have known better. If the last year had taught me anything, it was that things could always get worse. Often, they got that way even when you tried to make them better.

We stared at each other; my suspicion evident in every line of my face. Why now, why her, and why not Remi? Was this some kind of trick? Or a trap? Had she turned on us? Was having her in here with me a way to get me to make one of those cursed holograms? I couldn't see how, but then my brain function wasn't what it used to be. Lack of food, water, and stasis sleep did that to a deity.

The door slammed shut, the disgusting smell of the demon still lingering despite the creature's exit. Neither of us moved an inch. We each continued to glare at the other, an epic showdown with equal measures of distrust. I had the nagging thought that if she were a spy or a traitor, she had a funny way of getting me to trust her.

Eventually, I sat back down on the bed, pressing my back against the wall again. She didn't budge, just eyed me like I had three heads that spewed fresh piss from all orifices. Sadly, that wasn't an exaggeration. I looked over at her, pointed down to the bed beneath my ass, and said, "Dibs."

She looked even more annoyed by that declaration, though it was hard to tell. The goddess had an air of authority about her that I found more impressive than I cared to admit. Breaking her death glare with me, she strode to the opposite wall and sat a few feet from the toilet, pressing her own back against the cold stone.

The room was a small square, just big enough to fit two, maybe three, but not comfortably. She stretched out her legs in front of her and rubbed her wrists, worrying at the rune tattoo we both had there.

"So, you're the creation deity who was worth causing all this trouble over," she said. Not a question, but more of an assessment. Judging by her expression, I came up shy of her expectations.

"Yep, that's me. I definitely planned for all of this to happen. Get kidnapped, get my grandfather killed, then get captured by Nefarals and stripped of my powers. I had a big checklist, just making sure I didn't miss a single point because Ascended forbid that anything go right." I thought about the prophecy, predicting that I would be the most powerful creation deity to ever exist, and it seemed like an eternity since I'd learned of it. In reality, it had been less than a year, and I couldn't help but notice that someone had really screwed that one up.

Pushing that thought far from my mind, I looked down my nose at her, letting her see just how fucking ridiculous I found her statement, in case my sarcasm wasn't clear enough for her already. When she just stared at me, I continued, "So, who are you anyway? That psycho Madwyn said something about an organization, right?"

She scoffed, shaking her head. I saw a flash of white teeth and realized that she was smiling, though it looked more like a grimace. "You wouldn't believe me if I told you."

I shrugged my shoulders, indifferent. "Tell me anyway." It came out as a command, which impressed me, considering how drained of energy I felt.

Her gaze locked onto mine, and I saw an element of surprise there. As though she found me a little less disappointing now, and to my astonishment, she answered, "My name is Emorie, and I was the leader of the Nefaric Uprising before that psychotic bitch Madwyn hijacked my movement, my organization, and my plans, and destroyed everything."

I narrowed my eyes at her, confusion, disgust, and suspicion warring for dominance in my mind. Why in the Twelve Hells had Remi conspired with her then? As though she could sense the direction of my thoughts, she held up a hand. "Listen, Princess, there's a lot you don't know. And let me be clear—I didn't want any of this to happen. This was never what our movement was about."

I leaned forward, my voice a hiss of anger. "What do you think an uprising is then, sweetheart?" I could hear the malice dripping from my tongue, a reaction to her Princess comment, but I didn't care. "Whether you wanted this to happen or not, you were playing with fire starting a movement like that, and you're not even a Nefaral!" I shouted, recalling her science power that day in hell.

Emorie seemed to vibrate with anger as she looked me up and down. "It wasn't about the Nefarals. It was about the governor chips, the ones your family implanted into hundreds of thousands of unknowing deities. At least half of whom weren't Nefarals at all."

As her words landed, everything inside of me froze.

4
PAIN IN TRUTH
BEKKA

I blinked in shock. What she said hit me like a punch to the gut. The Peacekeeper's council and the royal families had chipped Altruists without their knowledge? I couldn't believe it. Everything in me rebelled, but she pressed her advantage and kept talking, "They've been suppressing deities' powers for years, and not just Nefarals. They've kept the caste system intact through the generations and used consciousness deities to wipe the memories of their victims. Haven't you ever found it strange that no one in the middle or lower castes ever ascends beyond that?"

"But that can't be—" I sputtered, "They wouldn't—"

Emorie's smug expression made me want to slap her. "They would and they did," she said, her tone brooking zero argument. She said it as a statement of fact. The sky is blue. That wall is stone. Nothing more, nothing less. "I started the movement to expose the truth. We wanted freedom. We'd gained allies across the Twelve Realms. Our goal was to force your grandfather and the rest of the leaders of the Twelve Realms to end the practice. I thought that if I could gather enough of us, and we had enough political power, they'd have to listen. The Nefarals were just a natural ally, the most obviously disaffected population. After all, they all had governor chips, forced to pay for the transgressions of their parents for almost a millennium." She shook her head then. "I should have known we couldn't control them." Her gaze broke away from mine as she looked into the distance.

My mind reeled, spinning, my brain trying to make sense of everything she'd just told me. The trouble was, I couldn't process it. I'd always known my family to be fair. I'd seen no signs that they would be that heartless, that morally bankrupt.

"You must be mistaken. They wouldn't—" I started, but then Emorie cut me off.

"Funny, that's what your sister said. At least, until I showed her the evidence of the chip in her neck. After that, she believed me just fine."

The blood drained from my face as the full meaning of Emorie's words soaked in. Remi had a governor chip? But how? How could my family do that to their own daughter?

I thought about the lengths I'd been willing to go to keep Arrick's neck free of that same device. I couldn't imagine the damage this information would do to Valeria, my family, and all the other leaders in the Twelve Realms. The sheer wrongness of it. The invasiveness. It would be devastating to the stability of the already crumbling peace, not to mention the pain it would cause anyone who'd been violated in such a way.

"Remi knows, then?" I asked, and Emorie nodded, her face drawn and tired. Dumb question, I knew, but I could imagine how she must have felt when she found out the truth. That would have devastated her. "How?" I shook my head, not able to understand in my weary state. "Why?"

She shrugged her shoulders. "I can't say why. You'd have to ask your family about that."

Nausea crawled up my throat. "How? When?"

"Right after the required power assessment tests, after we all come of age."

"Shit," I breathed, unable to articulate anything more eloquent. This was so bad, so very bad. I licked my lips and trained my eyes back on Emorie. "Did you have one too?"

Emorie rubbed her hands on her grimy trousers and nodded her head. "I did."

"How did you find out? How did you learn about any of this?" Governor chips were undetectable by anything other than royal-issued scanners. The royals kept them under lock and key in each of the palaces. The practice had never struck me as odd before. It had just been the way we did things, but considering Emorie's revelations, I was starting to realize how secretive and strange it was.

She rubbed her hands over her face, and I could see the same exhaustion that dogged me in her. "It's a long, long story."

I deadpanned her. "Well, if you haven't noticed, all we've got in here is time."

Emorie lifted her shoulder in tacit agreement just as two trays of food slid through the slot at the bottom of the metal door. She didn't move, her head lolling over to stare at the food, as though she wished she could translocate it to her without having to get up and grab it.

Sensing her reluctance to move, I rose from the bed and walked over to the trays, picking them up. I settled mine on the cot and handed the other to Emorie. A small olive branch, but something.

She took it with a nod and muttered her thanks. We each dug into our plates in silence, neither willing to take the time or energy to talk between bites.

When we finished, we each kept our own counsel. I assumed she'd dismissed my question, so I blinked in surprise when she broke the silence. "I found out a few years ago, about my governor chip, I mean. I'm from Mariandale, and you know about the phenomenon there, I'm sure?"

A shiver ran down my back and I nodded. Mariandale was an eerie place, one I'd learned about growing up but had never had the displeasure of visiting, thank the Ascended. Centuries ago, before the War of the Nefarals, a dimensional deity soulfused with a death deity, merging their magic as Arrick and I had. But, in the surge of power that followed, the barriers between the metaphysical and human dimensions broke down. So, the dead walked in the human world, as did the demons and the angels from heaven and hell. The word disaster didn't begin to cover it.

Emorie continued her story. "I'm a science deity, specifically an engineering goddess. I have a talent for inventing sophisticated technology, always have. Before I knew I had a chip, I was a middle-caste goddess, working on a project with a few other deities. We wanted to build a scanner to evaluate the barrier between the metaphysical and human realms. We aimed to reverse the damage done by magic with new technology."

She paused, taking a sip from the canister of water allotted to us for the meal. After a brief pause, she continued, "Everyone else had gone home for the evening and I stayed behind at the lab, working on that damned scanner. I knew we were getting close to something, and I just couldn't let it go. You see, other deities had families or friends. But me? I had my work, and I was married to it. Always have been. Anyway, I had a breakthrough that night, only it wasn't the kind that I was expecting. Without realizing it, we'd built a scanner that recreated the internal physical systems of all living creatures. I realized it after I tested it on a hotspot of the phenomenon in a forest near the lab. It scanned a tree and showed me every tiny molecule that compromised it. The scanner read out all irregularities straight down the list. I realized that while this wasn't what we intended, it would make a useful medical tool for communities that lacked an upper-caste healer.

So, excited, I turned it on myself and started a scan. That's when I saw it. The chip in my neck. I couldn't believe it. Nor could I explain why I would've had something like that. I'm not a Nefaral. It made no sense. So, I stayed up all night each day over the next week, building a replica of the scanner. I didn't tell anyone, not even my partners, about what I'd found or about my test run and the scanner's true function. When I'd finished the replica, I sabotaged our original so that no one else would see what I did. Then, I took my new prototype home from the lab before anyone saw it. I'd made some improvements and turned it into a handheld device that I could use discreetly. After that, I started scanning people without their knowledge, keeping data, and running models. I realized that over thirty percent of the Altruist population had governor chips. You can imagine my surprise when I discovered that."

She looked at me, her gaze a little sharper, more intent now that she'd eaten. I shook my head in disbelief. "Thirty percent? It's that high? They did it to that many deities?"

She nodded. "After I realized the extent of the problem, I left my post in Mariandale and traveled the realms, posing as a technological consultant. But really, I wanted to discover if this was only an issue in Mariandale or if it crossed all Twelve Realms."

"I'm assuming it did?" I asked, though I already knew the answer.

She nodded, "Worse in some places, close to forty or fifty percent, and less prominent in others. Lower-caste deities seemed to be most affected, though it spanned across all the castes. The more of them I uncovered, the angrier I got. I realized I needed help to sort this out. That's when The Rising began. I recruited deities under the radar, afraid the royals or the Peacekeeper would kill me if I came out too soon, without the proper support. After a while, I told people I vetted and knew I could trust what I'd discovered. Together, we built a network of spies and deities dedicated to finding the truth. And after a long time, we did. We had all the evidence we needed to bring the Peacekeeper to the table. We wanted to know why he did this to us, and we just wanted it to stop. Our movement was about to use its influence to force him to meet with us, but then—"

She trailed off, and I knew what she was going to say next. "He died," I finished for her, my throat constricting with emotion as I remembered the last time I saw him, and what he'd done to save me. Gifted me his power. With my body so close to death, he'd had no choice but to give it all to me. And once a deity did that, they couldn't come back from it.

She pressed her lips together, and to her credit, I could see sympathy in her eyes. I wouldn't have expected it, considering what my family had done to her and so many others.

She sighed, continuing, "I think that's when everything I'd built started to fall apart. I was just too blind to realize it. After he died, we began hearing rumblings within our ranks. The Nefarals we'd worked so hard to recruit and get on our side started to question the plan. There was no Peacekeeper anymore, you see. We knew he had an heir. Twelve Hells, after your sister's wedding, everyone across every realm knew about you. But you were gone, disappeared from thin air, and out of the picture. And with no one to claim the Peacekeeper's mantle, they wanted to know why we couldn't just take what we wanted. I thought I was holding it together, keeping those radical opinions at bay. I cautioned reason and restraint, but I should have known better."

I sighed, running a hand down my neck to ease the tension forming there. "So, then my sister tried to open a portal to Bicaidia from Moldize to help me get home, and the Nefarals took their shot, right? After that, everything imploded?"

Emorie's eyes burned bright with passion. "Yep, that's right. I never thought it would go this far. And I never wanted it to go this way either. I just wanted answers, and to be free. To know what I'm capable of without that damned chip. Well, I guess I got what I wanted." She thunked the back of her head against the wall and rubbed her hand along her neck. "Madwyn and Riven destroyed all the governor chips in Bicaidia, you know. Too bad they slapped this damned rune on my wrist before I got the chance to really test my magic out."

We sat in silence for a long minute, before I said, "It's not your fault, you know. What happened ... It isn't your fault. Madwyn, Riven, and everyone who followed them are to blame; not you. They would have done this with or without your help."

Emorie shook her head. "But I provided them with the network, the means to coordinate their assault, and the intelligence to burn it all down. And that's what they did, and what they will continue to do." She dropped her head into her hands, rubbing her temples. "How could I have been so blind?"

I thought back through the last few months. The chain of events that had led us to this point. I couldn't help but think that some fucked up puppeteer was using us as marionette dolls in his or her sick game. Some long-ascended deity laughing at our plight.

I sighed, shifting on the bed, my body stiff and exhausted. Though I hardly knew her, I had to admit that I felt a strange pull toward the goddess sitting next to me. Maybe it was the pain I saw etched in every line of her face. Or maybe it was the guilt she bore, something I could relate to all too easily. Either way, I knew then that she wasn't a spy or a traitor, and I couldn't help the gratitude I felt for the company, despite her life-altering revelations.

I could talk to her and share the sheer mundaneness of my days with inside our hell-hole prison cell with her. Without warning, the ever-present lights dimmed a shade or two overhead, which I assumed meant it was nighttime. I wished again that I could see outside, see the sky for just one moment.

Emorie's voice broke me from my thoughts. "I know it's late, but I have an idea."

I perked up. "What kind of idea?"

"You know how to fight, hand-to-hand, right?" Slowly, I nodded, wondering where she was going with that. "Think you could take those demons standing guard out there?"

I scoffed and gestured down at the sorry state of my body. "Not like this, I can't. I'd need to be at full strength, and I'd need some kind of weapon. In case you haven't noticed, we don't have our godly muscle, thanks to this little beauty." I gestured to the tattoo, the disgust I felt towards it plain on my face.

Emorie licked her lips, and rose to her feet, the effort the movement took her apparent based on the grimace she bore. She moved closer to me, her steps slow and careful, as though she feared she may falter at any moment. Settling onto the foot of my bed, she looked into my eyes. "What if you had enough food to regain that strength? And what if I could devise some kind of weapon for you?"

I raised my brows in surprise. "How would we manage either of those things?"

She rolled her eyes and shook her head. "Look, they made a tactical mistake putting the two of us together. Nefarals are inherently selfish. Their gifts don't let them see the lengths that someone like me might go to make them pay. You want to make them pay, right?" I bristled a little at the inherently selfish comment, thinking of Arrick. The Nefaral who sacrificed his freedom to keep us all alive, but I didn't argue. It wasn't the time.

Instead, I said, "I do, but again, how do we plan to do that?" I was growing suspicious of the gleam in her eyes. She had a scheme. I could almost see it taking shape in her mind, and I wasn't sure I was going to like it.

"Two plates of food are enough nutrition for one person a day," Emorie stated, her tone matter of fact. I blanched, knowing what she'd say next. "What if I gave mine to you? Do you think it would be enough to regain your strength? I mean, I'd need at least a little each day, just to sustain my mental faculties so that I could devise a weapon. You might have to forge it since I'm already weak enough with the half-meals we've been getting, but I could tell you how."

I stared at her, dumbfounded. "You can't be serious. If you give me your food, you could—"

She shook her head, her frizzy, matted hair wobbling with the vehemence of the gesture. "What? Die? Not likely, Twelve Hells, not even possible."

I narrowed my eyes at her. "You might not die, but you could drop into stasis sleep before we even get the chance to get out of here."

She lifted her slim shoulder. "It's a risk I'm willing to take. Like I said, they've underestimated how far I'm willing to go to fuck them over, good and hard."

I gnawed on a lip, weighing her plan. I didn't like the idea that I would get healthier and more vibrant while she wasted away right in front of me. But, if we were going to get out of our prison cell, I knew we needed to make some sacrifices. Probably a lot of them. I just didn't love that someone else would make those sacrifices besides me. "I don't know," I hedged, shaking my head.

She scooted closer to me and wrapped her already bony fingers around mine, drawing my attention to her. Her intensity made my voice catch in my throat. "Bekka," she implored. "You're the only one of us trained in combat. Of the two of us, you're our best shot at making it past the demons guarding us. Please, let me do this. I want to do this."

I stared into her eyes, a cat-like yellow, almost gold, and imagined that when she wasn't frail and haggard from weeks of borderline starvation, she would make a formidable goddess. A force of nature, and as much as I hated to admit it, she had a point. If I could get my strength up, and if I had a few weapons at my disposal, I might be able to break us out of there.

Might being the operative word. Though it was a long shot, it was worth the risk.

At last, I nodded my head. "What do you need me to do?"

5
TORMENTED
REMI

Remi sank to her knees and let out a cry of pain, her hands bunching into her hair as she yanked against her scalp. "No, no, no," she moaned, tears threatening at the corners of her eyes. "Not again." She rocked back and forth from her knees to the tips of her toes, sobbing.

Unseen fingernails scraped across her defenseless mind before securing their grip on it. Whispers seemed to drift through the surrounding air.

They're all going to die. It will be your fault. You can't save them. They'll all die.

"Leave me alone!" she screamed, her voice breaking just before the images assaulted her. One after the other, they battered her. Bekka's lifeless eyes, staring up at her from a sea of blood. Thayne's throat slit from ear to ear, his skin gone chalky and veins inky from the poisonous black blade protruding from his chest. Valeria, set ablaze, overrun by demons and Nefarals, humans in their once flourishing mortal realm, dying in the streets.

She slumped to the floor, her body limp and drained, sweat slicking her skin. As the images faded and the claws released their grip on her mind, she stared, glassy-eyed, at the ceiling. Her whole body ached, her strength flagging. She didn't know how much more of this she could take.

Even though she knew it was a consciousness deity named Davendrie, one of Madwyn's lapdogs, who showed her those images, she still couldn't separate the emotion from them. It wasn't real, of course. The binding with Arrick had guaranteed all their physical safety while under Madwyn's care.

However, it seemed Madwyn had woven a loophole into that binding. She'd promised them physical safety, but she'd said nothing about mental safety. Peacekeeper law prohibited breaking through the mental wards of deities to torture them. *That law even protected prisoners*, she thought, as her tears dried in streams of salt down her cheeks. But she needed to remember that there was a new law now, one that didn't give a shit about what the Peacekeeper thought.

Doing her best to calm her racing heart, she stared at the bright lights on the ceiling for what felt like hours. The cool stone of the floor helped anchor her mind back to her body. No more visions, no more pain, and after a long time, she pressed her palms to the stone and rose to her feet.

Her legs wobbled beneath her. Part hunger and part fatigue, she knew, as she shuffled over to the small, lone sink in the cell. She turned the handle and water poured from the faucet. Cupping her hands, Remi let them fill with the cool liquid, then splashed it over her clammy face.

She couldn't imagine how terrible she looked. Months without regular showers and without so much as a hairbrush didn't lend itself to pristine hygiene. Remi had given up finger-combing her red mass of waves long ago. Instead, she'd ripped a thin strip from her bed linen and secured the matted mess on top of her head.

Running her fingers over the bun, Remi realized that she'd pulled it loose during that last episode. Groaning in irritation, she untied the strip, gathered her tangled strands, and re-tied it. Better to get it out of the way for the next episode, she knew.

Sighing, she ambled back to the bed and settled her weight on the firm, thin mattress. No pillow, no blanket, just a fitted sheet she'd almost destroyed during a particularly bad session with Davendrie. Rips adorned the fabric, leaving the springy mattress beneath exposed.

She reached for her water canister, the only modest comfort allotted to her, and pressed it to her lips. Cool liquid slid down her throat and she sighed in relief.

She'd had no visitors during her time in the prison, except for the demons. They came every day at Madwyn's behest. Or at least, that's what she presumed. They wanted her to make a hologram, begging her parents to surrender or some other nonsense. She couldn't be sure. Remi hadn't bothered to listen to the details.

Instead, she'd refused them outright. She didn't need to know the specifics.

It would never happen. She'd never let her family come close to surrendering to Madwyn. After everything that bitch had done? Remi would rather dance naked on the surface of the sun. It didn't matter how many visions Madwyn sent to her. The chaos deity had given up far too much of her leverage when she'd struck that deal with Arrick. There was only so much she could do to Remi, or any of them, for that matter. Neither Madwyn nor her allies could kill any of them while they remained in this dungeon.

As her hands grew steadier and her body calmer, she heard the lock on her cell door disengage. She didn't bother to move. It was probably just her demon guard, coming to command her to do the holo. She would say no, of course, and it would fuck off back to whatever useless task it did when it wasn't annoying her with its idiotic demands.

She heard footsteps fill the room, but she didn't bother to turn her head. "I'll save you some time. My answer is no. It will always be no. So, can we please stop doing this little dance every day?"

"But you haven't even heard what I have to say yet." Remi's eyes widened, and she straightened, turning to survey the source of the familiar voice. Anxiety hummed over her skin and her gaze settled on the last person she expected to see: Riven. *What the hell is he doing here?* She thought, hatred filling every inch of her body.

He held a tray of food in his hands. It contained just enough to feed a child—her normal fare. But she spent minimal time eyeballing her meal before she fixed her gaze on his face. His cool blue eyes looked passive and emotionless as he strode forward and extended the food to her.

Remi hesitated before she reached out and took it from him, setting it on the foot of the bed, not daring to touch it. Eating felt too vulnerable around him, and vulnerability was the last thing she wanted to feel in his presence. She might not be able to control that perception, but she wouldn't give into it any more than necessary.

So, ignoring the tray, she watched him with wariness as he linked his hands behind his back. His dark suit and hair looked slick as ever and she wondered again what he wanted from her. The silence felt heavy and thick between them as that loathing she'd nurtured over the past four months made her mouth twist into a sneer. "What do you want, Riven?" she asked, at last, the bite in her words unmistakable. "Did you come to gloat? To enjoy what you and your sister have reduced me to? To torment me some more?"

His smooth expression didn't waiver while he rubbed a hand over his chin in thought. His answering silence had Remi's entire body on edge as she ran through all the possibilities. Maybe they'd found a way to circumvent the binding with Arrick. Maybe Riven was there to kill her, along with her friends and sister. Chills ran down her spine, but she kept her gaze steady, refusing to let him see the fear that gripped her.

At last, he shook his head. "No, I came to talk to you about Ellarah." Remi tried to search his expression, to get some hint of what he wanted to say about her friend, but she found him unreadable.

"Is she—" Remi cut off, swallowing hard, unable to say the word that had haunted her ever since Madwyn plunged the dagger into her friend's belly. At last, she worked up the courage and finished the sentence, "Dead?"

Riven stayed motionless for a few gut-wrenching beats before he gave his head a curt shake. "No, she's not. No thanks to you and your friends."

Remi blinked in surprise before she rose from her bed in anger. "What the hell is that supposed to mean? We did everything we could to save her."

He shook his head and looked away from her, a tick in the muscle of his jaw the only sign of his agitation. "It means that I gave Ellarah the antidote, which she would have g a lot sooner if you hadn't taken her from me that night at the travel depot. Now, though—" His jaw flexed again, and Remi could see a flash of concern flicker across his face. "Her recovery is in question. She is still weak, unable to access her power, and bedridden.

The one small mercy I have is that she doesn't remember what happened to her. So, she doesn't have to relive the trauma on top of everything else."

Remi scoffed then, rolling her eyes. "How convenient for you, Riven."

He glared at her, and she met his gaze head-on, stiffening her spine and squaring her shoulders. "So prideful still," he observed, crossing his arms as though she amused him. She ground her teeth, wishing she had access to her power. She'd fry him the instant she got it back. A goal that she had every intention of achieving.

Remi interrupted him before he could continue his assessment of her character. "You know, the minute she finds out what you did, she will despise you. She'll never forgive you for it. You'll be lucky if she can stand to be in the same room as you."

At that, Riven's composure cracked. Black misty magic flared around him in angry wisps before he extinguished it with a clenched fist. Remi wanted to smile, happy to have cut him, even if only a little.

"I didn't come here to debate my actions with you," he sneered, as though her opinion were the least important thing in the Twelve Realms to him. "I came here for Ellarah. She's ... unable to get out of bed for long periods of time right now, and she's asked to see you and Thayne. I've held her off as long as I could, but she's getting suspicious."

Remi laughed that time and it was a bawdy thing. She threw her head back and roared with it. "And what? You thought you'd just saunter in here and ask me for a favor? You disgust me." Remi prowled closer to Riven, refusing to let her frailness show. She looked him up and down, as though he were the vilest creature in the multiverse. "I won't help you deceive her or add to your ability to keep her as your prisoner."

No matter how much it hurt to turn down a chance at getting out of that cell, to give up the possibility of seeing the sun or the Bicaidian moons and stars again, she couldn't do what he asked of her. It would betray her friend's trust. So, it didn't matter how much she longed to see Ellarah healthy again.

"It's adorable that you think you have a choice," Riven observed, a dark gleam sliding into his eyes. She'd never seen him look like that, a small ripple of desperation visible in his otherwise polished exterior. Magic seeped from his body, winding around his fingertips.

Gooseflesh raised along her arms in response to it, but she held her ground, unwavering. He stalked around her, arms crossed and looking her over in an assessing manner. "Oh, Remi, you think you've had it bad in here the last few months?" He clicked his tongue. "It could get so much worse for you, or more specifically, for your sister."

Spinning to face him, she snapped. "What about my sister?"

He shrugged one shoulder, as though disinterested, still circling her, toying with her like a bird of prey did with a mouse. "She's had a pretty comfortable stay here, at least compared to you. You see, my sister doesn't have quite the same disdain for her that she does for you. So, Davendri has left her alone. But it doesn't have to be that way. I could, I don't know, put in a word, ask for a favor, issue a command of my own. And then she could join you in that personal hell you call your mind. How does that sound? Is that incentive enough for you, Remi?"

Everything inside Remi rebelled in reaction to his threat. *He wouldn't*, she thought, already knowing the ridiculousness of that. Of course, he would. Bekka meant nothing to him. She was just a means to an end. She should have known that he wouldn't take no for an answer. That he had a plan to make her do what he wanted. She clenched her teeth and spoke through them, "What do you want me to do, Riven?"

He let the smug expression of victory slide over his visage. "Tomorrow morning, you'll bathe, make yourself presentable, and dress in the clothing I send you. I'll be back around lunchtime to collect both you and Thayne. You will not try to escape or defy me during this visit. And, most importantly, while we're there, you will not tell Ellarah anything about what happened in the travel depot or since. Do I make myself clear?"

Remi swallowed the bile that rose in the back of her throat. "Fine. You have my word." She felt every piece of her being vibrate with fury and guilt. But she would do what he asked if it meant saving her sister from the torment she experienced every single day. She could only hope that Ellarah would understand and forgive her if any of them ever got free.

"Your word isn't good enough, Princess," he hissed. His magic oozed faster from his fingertips then and slipped further up his arms. "I'll require a binding." He repeated his conditions, and Remi listened to them with rapt attention, unwilling to agree to anything more than a single visit. If he tried to exact control over more than that, her sister would have to suck it up, just like she had.

When they agreed on the terms and the verbiage, she held out her hand, blinking and feeling like a complete imbecile when she remembered she couldn't ignite her own magic. Riven took advantage of her momentary surprise, along with her agreement to the terms, and gripped her hand. His power flowed around her wrist, inking her like a tattoo.

Leaning in, he whispered as though it were a secret, "Bindings don't have to go two ways. I can still get what I need from you, even without your power. You just have to agree." With that, he stepped back from her, turned, and exited her cell.

Stunned, she stared at the cell door and into her empty room. Had that really just happened? How could she be so stupid? Remi looked down at her arm, with his magic inking up her wrist, and knew it had. She'd lost her edge. *I never would've agreed to that bargain if I was in my right mind*, she thought, hating her fragility.

If only she could have left him with more than a stunned look on her face. Like say, a reminder of what a pathetic rat he was.

It seemed that would just have to wait until tomorrow.

6
DELUSION
REMI

"You're not here," Remi said, leaning back against the stone wall as she opened her eyes to stare at the apparition. It had first appeared three days earlier and then reappeared after Riven's departure. And despite her best efforts to ignore it, it wouldn't go away.

Instead, the hallucination sat across the cell block from her, looking at her with a shit-eating grin on her face. "Does that really matter, though?" It asked, its voice so damn familiar and soothing that it made her heart squeeze.

Remi stared at her delusion, the detail of it uncanny. If she didn't know any better, she'd think it was real. Unfortunately, she did know better. And as a result, she knew it wasn't Bekka sitting across from her. Not really. Instead, it was her own screwed-up mind playing tricks on her.

"It does if it means I'm going crazy," Remi muttered in response, rubbing the heels of her hands to her eyes as though that could wipe away the delusion. She knew Davendrie had done some damage to her mind, but apparently, he'd done more than she could have guessed. Because now she was seeing, hearing, and even feeling things that weren't there.

Fucking perfect.

"Honestly, Rem, what difference does it make?" Not-Bekka asked, pulling herself into a standing position. She wore a thin, flowing chiffon skirt and a tight tank top. The attire was the height of Valerian fashion before Remi's wedding. Her blonde hair gleamed like a golden sheet, and she looked beautiful, just like she had in the before-time, as Remi had taken to calling the world before their grandfather had died and everything had gotten so completely messed up.

Not-Bekka strode over to her and sat beside her, and Remi could swear that she felt the warmth from her sister's body seeping into her skin. Not-Bekka spoke once more. "Why does it matter if I'm real? It's better than being all alone in here, isn't it?"

Remi closed her eyes, considering that for a moment. She could feel Not-Bekka looking at her. Actually feel the eyes of her hallucination on her face. *How is this so real?* She wondered again, trying to fight against her senses and stay in reality.

But even as she ran through the potential causes of this delusion, she already knew that it couldn't be Davendrie. Remi had decided that yesterday, after her last nightmare. She hadn't been sure until then. And when she'd curled into a sobbing mess, Not-Bekka had stayed with her, stroking her hair, soothing her ragged nerves, and saying nothing. She hadn't tormented or taunted her or done anything like what Davendri's hallucinations usually put her through. So, it couldn't be him. It had to be her mind, desperate for solace. Or at least, that's what she told herself.

At last, Remi opened her eyes and turned toward her sister. "What are you?"

Not-Bekka shrugged, her toned shoulders flexing as she did. "Again, does it matter?"

"I guess it doesn't." Looking ahead again, Remi raked hands through her hair to snap herself out of her hallucination, tugging hard at the scalp. Sadly, no such luck.

Rather than disappear, Not-Bekka asked, "Hey, do you remember that time Mom and Dad took us to Thorendelle for that diplomatic visit?"

At the rush of memory her question brought, Remi couldn't stop a bubble of laughter from escaping her lips. She didn't miss how unhinged it sounded, considering her current predicament. "Which time?" she asked, feigning innocence.

Not-Bekka nudged her with her elbow and chuckled. "You know which time."

Remi's mind flashed back to the visit in question. Thorendelle was a beautiful sea realm with crystalline blue water and white, sandy beaches. It was the only realm with a booming civilization of merpeople living in its pristine seas. Whenever her parents needed time away from their responsibilities in Valeria, they would visit Thorendelle. Well, there or Ipopulca, her grandfather's original homeland.

"Oh, so you mean the one where we got into that fight with the high prince of Thorendelle?" Remi asked.

"That would be the one," Not-Bekka said, smiling as she turned to face her. Despite her best judgment, Remi turned too, looking into the smiling eyes she knew so well. Something inside her loosened, relaxed just a little as she grinned back. "I still can't believe what you did to Kazik."

"What?" Remi said, feigning innocence. "He should have known better than to tangle with a Valerian."

Not-Bekka laughed and shook her head, her hair tossing back and forth with the movement, the shiny gold of it glistening in the harsh light of the room. "I will never forget the look on his face when you dared him to go to the mortal realm and skinny-dip with the merpeople, and then when he got far enough out to sea, we stole all his clothes and took them back to the palace. He had to make the trip back to the immortal realm butt-ass naked." Her eyes watered with tears as she recalled the all-too-familiar story through snorts of laughter.

Remi laughed too, unable to stop herself, then asked, "Do you remember Kazik's bare ass? It was so pale compared to the rest of his tanned body. I like to think I did him a service. That booty needed sunshine something fierce."

Not-Bekka doubled over then, giggling, Remi joining in with her. After a few moments, Not-Bekka wiped tears from her eyes and asked, "Well, I guess you showed him who was boss, didn't you?"

Remi shrugged, also brushing the tears of her own laughter away with her thumb. "Kazik was mean to you, remember? He called you a baby giraffe with the style of an eighty-year-old human man, and everyone teased you the entire time you were there because of it. He deserved to suffer."

Not-Bekka's face turned contemplative as she straightened against the wall beside Remi. "You know, no one ever fucked with us again after that. Not a single other royal kid."

Remi nodded, scooting closer to the apparition that was becoming more like the real Bekka and less like Not-Bekka. She even smelled like the real Bekka. "Damn straight, sister."

Not-Bekka smiled and turned the full force of it on Remi. "I'm not sure if I ever thanked you for that. So, in case I didn't, thank you."

"Don't mention it," Remi said, as Not-Bekka draped an arm around her shoulders.

To her surprise, Remi let her. She could feel the warmth and weight of that arm on her shoulder and marveled at just how damn real it felt. When Not-Bekka spoke again, her voice was whisper soft. "Do me a favor and remember that feeling, Rem. That feeling when we won. Don't let go of that, no matter how hard it gets in here. Don't forget who we are. Who you are."

Remi exhaled, letting a little more of that weight she'd carried around these long months drop. She looked at the vision of her sister. "I'm trying, but I don't feel like that person anymore. I feel hollowed out, sucked dry."

Not-Bekka shook her head. "You have more strength left, Remi. Don't question that for one second. You're going to get out of here, and you're going to be free again. But until then, remember who you are."

Remi opened her mouth to protest, but the apparition rested her slim hands on either side of Remi's face and pulled her attention to her. "Promise me," Not-Bekka said once more.

Remi held her gaze for a beat before she squeezed her eyes shut, remembering that day on the beach when she'd taken Kazik down. A bit of light-hearted riffing, but also a message. You didn't screw with the Valerian princesses. She recalled how she and the rest of the kids in the palace had laughed at the jerk who'd humiliated her sister.

Then she thought about her current situation and absorbed what Not-Bekka was trying to tell her. After so much suffering and pain, she had forgotten what it felt like to win, and she needed to hold on to that if she had any hope of getting out of her cell without fracturing into a thousand tiny pieces. So, after a long moment, she said, "I promise. I won't forget."

7
RUINED
Thayne

Soft fingers traced a slow, agonizing path up Thayne's inner thighs. He could feel sumptuous lips and a hot mouth, sliding along that same path, moving closer to the throbbing between his legs. His hands wound into silken hair, as he groaned with pleasure.

He could feel the heat of a fire nearby and hear the soothing crackle of it in the back of his mind. Beneath him, he felt the press of a soft bed, its satiny sheets drawing on the warmth of his and his companion's body.

At last, after what felt like an eternity, a gentle hand closed around his erection and milked him with long, languid strokes. He twisted his fingers deeper into the thick locks, and when she took him into her mouth, he cursed at the sheer pleasure of it.

Opening his eyes for the first time, he looked down at the goddess who gave him such unimaginable ecstasy. Their gazes locked, and he felt a jolt of recognition, a sensation he couldn't quite pinpoint coursing through him. But before he could place it, she removed her mouth from his hard length and raked her nails down his abdomen, crawling up the bed until she sat astride him. As she straddled him, he could see the bare perfection of her creamy skin, the full roundness of her breasts, and the icy blue of her eyes on his.

Raising her body above him then, she removed her hands from his chest and gripped the sheets beside them. She swirled her hips in a circular motion, stopping with him just outside her entrance, teasing him as her hands dug further into the blankets, leaving his cock pulsing with anticipation. She tilted her head back, the column of her throat exposed as she moaned in apparent desire. Then, just when he thought she'd take him inside her, she raised her hands.

All thoughts of pleasure and sex evaporated as he saw what she held in them.

A black dagger, its dark, vicious blade pulsing with magic. She smiled a radiant, feral grin, and every memory, every feeling of visceral hatred, came rushing back. "Madwyn," he growled. He tried to move his hands but couldn't. They'd been welded to his sides by some unseen force. He fought, struggling to kick and buck, to shove her off him, but it was no use. He couldn't move.

His eyes darted around the room, and he saw it then. Blood stains marred the white rug, the floor littered with the corpses of dozens of deities.

He saw his parents' unseeing eyes among them, both of their throats cut, black veins spreading over their bodies. He saw Ellarah, her skin also marred with inky, black veins. Then his gaze fixed on Remi's body, a gaping hole in her chest, and her heart ripped out. Blood dripped from either side of her beautiful, full mouth.

His head pounded with fear and rage as his eyes locked back onto Madwyn, the goddess who'd given him such pleasure only moments before.

Now though, she smiled down at him, the weapon held poised, ready to kill him. It couldn't be real. It had to be a dream. Another damn nightmare, he told himself, just before she plunged the dagger into his heart.

Thayne bolted upright, gasping for air, hands scrabbling at his chest. When he found no wound there, he let out a sigh of relief. His heart thundered as he took in the cool, semi-damp cell around him. Four other gods slept nearby, none of them disturbed by his sudden awakening.

They'd all grown used to it; he knew. What did he expect? The nightmares had become a nightly occurrence since Madwyn imprisoned them in the dungeons of what used to be his home. He dragged a hand over his face and rose from the threadbare mattress on the floor. A slick sheen of sweat coated his skin, but he could already feel his nerves settling, his body recovering quicker than it had at first, when the dreams were new.

He stalked over to the single window, the only comfort afforded them, and looked out at the rising sun. The pink and orange hues of early morning stretched over the red, high desert of Helverta, and he scrubbed a rough hand over his thick beard. He breathed in the fresh air, the golden glow of the warded bars over the windows not lost on him.

Back when they'd had hope of escape, he and Pietyr had tried to pry them loose. It hadn't gone well. The bars' protective magic had knocked them both into stasis sleep. It took three days before Rackham and the demigods could wake them.

He tried to focus on that memory, any memory other than the dreams, as he watched the sun make its ascent into the sky. He sucked in a long breath, trying to calm the turmoil inside his mind. Grief sliced through him like a blade as he closed his eyes and saw his parents' lifeless faces once more.

While he knew that Ellarah and Remi still lived, protected by the Moldizean death deity's bargain with Madwyn, he also knew that his parents hadn't survived. Was that how they'd died? Sliced throats and poisoning from a demon's blade? Thayne wondered, shame at his unwitting part in the attack on Bicaidia damn near overwhelming him.

He shook his head to clear the image away, but more came. He'd watched his parents die so many times, in so many nightmares, and in so many different ways. But he had no way of knowing the truth about their end, only that they'd died on inauguration night, when Madwyn and Riven had betrayed them all.

Staring out the window, his nerves settled while he considered the nightmares for the thousandth time. He knew they had to come from Madwyn. He just couldn't understand why she always had to mix sex with them.

It always left him feeling sick, nauseated by the prospect of being touched by the goddess who'd murdered his family, and so many of his people, and thrown them all into prison. And yet, she always aroused him in the dreams. He couldn't make sense of it, and he didn't want to.

They'd fucked more times than he could count in real life when they'd been together, and it hadn't just been sex. It seemed she liked to remind him of that, because there was always a moment, before she allowed him to remember the truth, that he felt that tenderness and trust toward her. After all, he'd loved her before everything had gone to hell.

He tried again to push the disturbing thoughts from his mind, fingers rubbing at his wrist as the rune tattoo there flared, suppressing his magic. Thayne frowned at it, wishing he could cut it from his skin as exhaustion tugged at him. Looking up into the sky, he said a silent prayer to the Ascended for just one hour of uninterrupted rest. Just a few blissful moments without Madwyn's torment, because truth be told, it was fucking with his head. Every time he derived even a moment's pleasure from her mouth or her hands or her body in those damned dreams, it felt like a betrayal.

Not just to himself, but to Remi, to his parents, and to his entire realm. It made him question every shred of honor he thought he had. But then, that was probably why Madwyn chose such a punishment for him, and why she mixed the pleasure in with the raw horrors. To rip his soul to shreds. She knew him well.

It was the only thing that explained why she kept muddling their past with the present, blurring the lines between his current reality and the one that had preceded it. And now, he felt like the resolve that had held him together since inauguration night, the desire to win back his realm and avenge his family, was beginning to wane. Instead, he felt fucking impotent. Useless and caged.

It would be better if she just killed him outright. Instead, she'd reduced him to a weak-willed prisoner who couldn't even slay his enemies in his own dreams. Who instead took his pleasure from them.

His fist clenched, and he swore under his breath, right before he felt a presence loom behind him. Turning, he saw Deklan leaning against the wall, arms crossed over his chest, staring at him. He looked unimpressed, but that seemed to be the demigod's default expression, and Thayne couldn't disagree with the sentiment.

"Another night terror?" Deklan asked, staring down his long nose at Thayne.

Thayne nodded, still staring out the window. "Every time I close my eyes." The sun had crested the mountains at last and light filled the cell.

As it grew brighter, Deklan remained silent, considering Thayne's response. A moment later, rustling sounded from the other cots that rested on the floor in the room. Thayne turned his head and saw Pietyr sit up and then stride over to the single toilet in the room to piss. Then the rest of them stirred too, Rackham rolling away from the light streaming in from their window, groaning in annoyance as Caden rose to sit on the edge of his bed, rubbing the sleep from his eyes.

Five male bodies in close quarters didn't make for the most pleasant aromas, and Thayne leaned closer to the window, attempting to drag in some fresh air, hoping it might clear his mind.

A few minutes later, their demon guard shoved small plates of food through a slot in their prison door. They all ate in silence for a while, each trying to savor the food rather than wolf it down. They'd learned to expect modest portions, and they each tried to make their single daily meal last as long as possible.

Rackham swallowed a bite of nutty bread and then gestured with the rest of it as he spoke, "I've been thinking—"

In response to that proclamation, a collective groan swept through the cell. Rackham had been relentless in his pursuit of escape. The rest of them had all but given up. They'd tried every damn thing that any of them could imagine. Granted, their imaginations hadn't been as vivid because of the lack of food, magic, and restless sleep, but still. If there'd been a way out of the cursed cell, they would have thought of it by then.

"No, Rackham," Pietyr said, glaring at the time god, as he licked sloppy stew from his fingers. "No more schemes."

Rackham set the bread down on his plate. "But you haven't heard my plan yet."

"I don't need to because I already know it won't work," Pietyr argued, fed up as all hell.

"You don't know that. None of you do."

"Yes, we do!" Pietyr snapped, the sharp sound echoing off the adobe brick walls. He pushed to his feet and took two quick steps to stand before Rackham, as the time god rose to his feet and glared at him. The two eyed each other, as though an all-out brawl would start at any moment.

But to his surprise, Rackham took a deep breath, as though to calm himself, and dropped his voice lower. "You don't understand. I am onto something, and I know it. This could be the solution we've been looking for. You see, the door is made of—"

"For Ascended sake, Rackham, give it a rest," Thayne growled, cutting into the argument and rising from his own cot to stand beside Pietyr, his plate of food forgotten. "We're stuck in here until Madwyn decides to release us, which will never happen. No one ever opens that door for us, and no one ever will. The sooner you accept that, the better." He'd grown just as sick of Rackham's constant schemes as Pietyr. They never worked, and most of the time, one of them ended up unconscious for days on end after they tried them.

Rackham's lips pulled back in distaste. "You too then, high prince? You've decided to give up and let Madwyn and Riven win? You've just accepted this as your fate?" He glared at Thayne with distaste, then said, "You're a fucking disappointment."

Thayne's eyes flashed, and he stepped closer, right into Rackham's space, going toe-to-toe with the young god. "Say that again."

"And you'll what?" Rackham all but snarled.

Caden moved between the three gods, raising his hands, and trying to diffuse the situation. "Everyone, just settle down. Now isn't the time to be at each other's throats." Thayne and Rackham glared, neither deity moving an inch.

Deklan snorted, and they all turned to see what he found so amusing. He waved a hand. "No, please, continue. I could use a good old-fashioned brawl." He cracked his knuckles and showed his teeth in what might have been a smile, if it hadn't looked so lethal.

Caden looked down his nose at his brother, an expression they shared. "Now isn't the time to stir the pot, brother."

Ignoring Caden's attempts to settle the situation, Pietyr stepped into the showdown and dropped his voice low, the warning in it apparent, "Just one day, Rackham. I would kill to go just one day without another one of your fucking plans."

"Better one of my plans than accepting defeat like a damned coward," Rackham snarled. That was when Pietyr snapped. He lunged, gripping Rackham's shirt in his fists, charging forward and slamming his friend's back into the wall. Cocking his fist, he planted it in Rackham's face. Everything seemed to slow down then as Thayne took in the melee. He felt like an observer looking on rather than a participant, despite his proximity to the brawl. Pietyr slammed a jab right into Rackham's face, who cried out, bones crunching. Caden rushed over to stop it, while Deklan's eyes gleamed with delight, hurrying into the melee and throwing punches of his own at will.

Rackham followed Pietyr's blow with a devastating kick to the groin. *Low blow*, Thayne thought, wincing in sympathy, as Pietyr sunk to his knees. Fists flew with no sense of logic as they all snarled and spat like wild animals. Thayne sighed, stepping back and pinching the bridge of his nose. This was what they'd been reduced to, he realized. Squabbling over whether they could change their circumstances. Calling each other names rather than banding together and fighting back, and he was no better than the rest of them. Hadn't he just been in Rackham's face one second ago?

Just as Deklan landed an elbow into his brother's nose, a pulse of light shone over Caden's skin. Thayne blinked then, and sucked in a surprised breath, but found no air to greet him. He gasped, fighting to get oxygen into his lungs, and watching in absolute shock as Caden rose to his feet and everyone else clutched at their throats too. As gods, they didn't need air to survive, but without their magic and normal healing abilities? They'd drop into stasis sleep in seconds if they couldn't breathe.

Thayne sank to his knees then, darkness creeping in around the edges of his vision. He could see the other gods gasping for air as well, the confusion on their faces plain. Then, another pulse of light, and the ground rumbled, shaking beneath their feet. Thayne tried to focus his eyes, to stay conscious for just a moment longer, and landed his gaze on Deklan and Caden who stood nearby. Vines, unnoticed by Caden, sprouted from the stone itself and speared for Caden's feet as Deklan's face turned damn near purple from lack of breath.

The corded plants tightened around Caden's leg and yanked him to the ground. He hit the floor hard, chin slamming into the stony bricks and teeth clicking together in an audible snap. In an instant, the light that had suffused him dissipated and a rush of air-filled wind whipped through the room.

They all gasped in unison, gulping in greedy breaths of the returning air as Deklan's light also diffused. After a solid minute, Thayne's vision cleared, and he pushed back to sit on the floor, trying to get his bearings.

Everyone stared at the twins, the demigods, in utter stupefaction. They had magic, he realized with astonishment.

They had magic!

Madwyn tested them when they'd first arrived and hadn't bothered with a rune on their wrists. They'd registered no magic at all, and given their watered-down godly blood, she and her allies hadn't considered them a threat. They'd been inconsequential, only kept alive by the grace of Arrick's binding with Madwyn.

But now—Thayne's eyes locked on Pietyr's and then Rackham's, as a new blaze of hope shone in all their gazes. They had magic. It wasn't powerful, but it was enough, and far more than any demon would have. They could use it to get out of there.

But before anyone could say a word, a loud clanging in the mechanisms of their cell door drew their attention. Someone was at the door. The first time they didn't want someone to open it, and of fucking course, it was happening. Noticing the vines laying on the floor, Thayne hurried to cover them with a cot. He'd just dropped the mattress in place when the door swung open.

To his astonishment, Riven stepped in, narrowing his eyes in confusion at the chaotic scene inside the cell. All five of their chests still heaved, as though they just finished brawling, which they had. So that would be a simple explanation. And when Riven's gaze settled on Caden's black eye and bloody lip, a smile spread across his lips. "No, please, don't let me interrupt. Continue beating the shit out of each other."

Everyone remained silent as Thayne glared at him. "What do you want, Riven? Why are you here?"

"You, actually," Riven replied, eyes locked onto Thayne's. "The rest of you can carry on tearing each other apart for us. That would prove helpful, since we can't do it ourselves."

Without further preamble, Riven grabbed Thayne by the arm and pulled him toward the open door. A demon stood at the precipice, its sharp, yellow teeth horrifying against its milky white skin. Thayne ripped his arm out of Riven's grasp. "I can walk on my own, you prick."

"Very well, have it your way," Riven said, gesturing for Thayne to exit the cell first. With one last glance at his companions, whose mouths remained open in shock, Thayne stepped out into the hallway.

They would discuss whatever the hell had just happened when he got back. Maybe, just maybe, they could plan a way out with it. After all, if they had magic, then maybe escape wasn't as impossible as it had seemed that morning.

8

AWAKENING

THAYNE

"What do you want, Riven?" Thayne asked as Riven led him to one of the many interrogation rooms within the prison block. Rather than answer, Riven opened the door and gestured for him to enter. Thayne could hear a steady pulse in his ears as he tried to compose himself. The shock of Deklan's and Caden's sudden power surge had become a nagging specter in his mind, but he pushed that aside for the moment. He couldn't afford to think about that. Not when he considered what would happen if anyone other than his cellmates found out about it.

"Why don't you sit down?" Riven asked, his tone conversational. It reminded Thayne of how things used to be, back when they'd been friends. No, more than that. They'd been like brothers their entire lives. At least, until Riven betrayed him and took everything he'd ever loved from him. That betrayal still tore at Thayne's chest, a gaping wound that would never heal, even if he got his revenge and ripped the death deity's throat out.

"I'd rather stand," Thayne replied, crossing his arms as he remained at the doorway, glaring at the death god.

"Suit yourself," Riven answered, striding into the room ahead of Thayne. He moved to the circular metal table at its center and sent a pulse of his magic into the holo, turning it on. It whirred, emitting a puff of hot air right as the demon behind Thayne shoved him forward. Surprised, he lurched into the room and was about to turn and swing at the creature when the door slammed in his face.

Fuming, he spun back to Riven and watched as the readout from the holo streamed data. He knew what they used that holo for—to divine the truth of a matter. It made the need to push the revelation about the demigods far from his mind even more urgent.

He doubted the questions Riven had would center on the demigods and their magic, but he still needed to be careful. Thayne couldn't give him any reason to look deeper into his psyche. As he continued to eye the readouts, he could hear the mechanisms inside the machine whirring as it assessed his baseline statistics.

Riven propped a hip on the table and crossed his arms, training his ice-blue glare on Thayne. As he did, Thayne's rune pulsed in his wrist, and he wished he had just one fragment of magic left. Something he could use to kill the friend who'd destroyed him and his realm. Because honestly? That was the one thing he wanted most in the world. Vengeance. He would do anything to get it and pay any price to achieve it.

But rather than wrapping his fingers around the death deity's neck and squeezing, he asked, "Why did you bring me here, Riven?"

Riven continued to eye Thayne just before he glanced at the readings on the holo. After a long beat, where he waited for the data stream to cease, Riven replied, "I didn't bring you here for me. I did it for her. It's what she wants."

"Who? Madwyn?" Thayne asked, raw emotions bubbling to the surface at the mere taste of her name on his tongue. The primary ones: loathing and contempt. Secondary? A pulse throbbing between his legs that had him clenching his jaw with self-loathing. He hated her for that pang of lust. She'd turned him into little more than an animal, unable to control his base desires.

"No, Ellarah," Riven corrected.

He opened his mouth to continue, but Thayne interrupted. "You mean Ellarah's awake? She's conscious?" He stepped forward then, dropping his arms to his sides as his eyes searched Riven's expression, trying to discern whether he was lying. Seeing nothing deceptive there, he scrubbed a hand over the ever-growing thickness of his beard, trying to process it.

"Of course she's alive, you imbecile. Though she wouldn't be if we hadn't overthrown Emorie's compound. You know you almost killed her, right?" Riven asked, bitterness lacing every word he spoke.

"I almost killed her?!" Thayne shouted, balking at Riven in disbelief. The god was delusional if he believed that to be true. "I'm not the one who shoved a poisoned dagger in her gut, as you may recall. You have your sister to thank for that."

Riven bristled. "Madwyn had her reasons. She knew we had the antidote and never intended to kill Ellarah. She just wanted to make a point."

Thayne shook his head and looked at the ceiling, praying to the Ascended for patience. "If you believe that, then you're the imbecile."

"Enough!" Riven shouted, slamming a palm down on the table and shattering the holo, the clang of the impact rattling off the stone walls. "Like I said, this isn't about Madwyn, it's about Ellarah." He lifted his hand, rubbing his fingers together as though the blow had stung. Judging by the large dent in the table and the obliterated holo, it had. *Now, if only it had broken every bone in his hand*, Thayne thought darkly. "She wants to see you."

Thayne raised his brows in surprise. "See me? She wants to see me?" The casual way Riven said that gave him pause. He surveyed the death god, his mind working for a moment just before realization hit him. "You haven't told her, have you? That you've imprisoned me. She can't know, because if she did, she'd want to do a lot more than see me. Am I right?"

Riven's ice-blue eyes flashed, a mirror image of his sister's, and the un-welcome memory of that morning's dream popped into Thayne's mind. He closed his eyes and forced the images out of his head, that unwanted throb still beating low in his abdomen.

Riven's voice helped draw him back to the present, "She remembers nothing that happened on inauguration night."

Thayne blinked, stunned. "And you haven't bothered to tell her, have you?"

His jaw ticked. "I couldn't afford to risk her recovery. She isn't strong enough yet."

Thayne laughed then, but the sound held no humor. "You're despicable, and you're lying to yourself. You haven't told her because you know she'll hate you. She'll never forgive you for what you did."

Riven snarled then, fisting his hands into Thayne's ragged shirt and lifting his feet off the ground, giving him one violent shake. "You don't know what you're talking about. Ellarah loves me, and I love her. She'll understand why I did what I did once I explain it to her. She'll understand." He sounded like he was trying to convince himself as much as Thayne.

Thayne let the pity show in his face, an intentional slice of a knife. "So, is that what you tell yourself? Is that how you sleep at night?"

Riven let go then, shoving Thayne away as though in disgust. "My personal life isn't up for discussion. Ellarah wants to see you, so you're going to visit with her, and it's going to be on my terms."

Thayne brushed a hand down his shirt, unruffled despite the show of force, and scoffed. "Like hell it will."

Black mist seeped from Riven's fingers, an involuntary reaction to his anger. He always had trouble controlling his emotions, a weakness Thayne planned to exploit one day. "You'll do it because it's the only way you'll leave that cage. And get a shower, a full meal, and ..." he paused, leveling a gaze on Thayne. "You'll get to see Remi. She's already agreed."

Thayne's heart hammered in his chest as he thought about his wife. He hadn't seen her since they'd dragged them all out of hell in shackles. He recalled the night before their capture. When she'd come to him, sought him out, pressed her near naked body onto his, all soft curves and creamy, glowing flesh. If she did that now? He might have a different reaction.

But he couldn't change the past. As her face flashed through his mind, he remembered every small moment with her before this prison. They'd fought together, grieved together, and confided in each other during those weeks of uncertainty in Emorie's compound after Madwyn's betrayal.

Riven had calculated the incentive well. He wanted to see her, burned for it even. But then he thought of that nightmare, and the hundreds of others like it, and nausea crawled up his throat. He didn't deserve her, not when every night in his dreams, he betrayed another small piece of the trust they'd built. He hated himself for it.

Then there was Ellarah to consider. Could he lie to her? Leave her in the dark over everything that had happened? He shook his head. "I won't lie to one of my best friends."

"You will if you want her to recover," Riven said. "I told you, she's still ill. She couldn't handle the truth right now. It would break her, and it would be your fault. Think about what's best for her." He rested a hand on Thayne's shoulder, trying to make his case.

Thayne shrugged Riven off him, stepping back out of reach. "She's that bad still? Even with an antidote?" he asked, skeptical. He would have expected the effects of a godly antidote to work immediately. What in the Twelve Hells was that black poison if even an upper-caste healer's antidote couldn't fix it?

"She is. She needs stability right now. Anything else could push her recovery back weeks."

Riven settled his hands back at his sides, sliding them into his pockets as Thayne observed him. He could see the tension in the death god's shoulders and the sincerity in his eyes. Whether Riven told the truth, he couldn't say, but Thayne knew he believed it.

The thought of getting out of there, showering, and sharing a meal with Remi and Ellarah? Well, the comfort and the familiarity of it dragged at him. Riven may not allow him to tell Ellarah the truth, but maybe he could do a little recon of his own. It might be the opportunity they needed. A way for them to find an escape from the palace. A chance for him to discover a weak point they could exploit. He knew his home better than anyone, so if someone could find a chink in the armor of its new inhabitants, it was him.

"Fine. I'll do it," Thayne said, feigning reluctance. Even if he found nothing to aid their escape, at least he would see Remi and Ellarah again. And whether he deserved that reprieve or not, he wanted it more than his next breath.

"Good," Riven replied. "I knew you'd see reason." With that, he held out his hand and black mist swirled around it. "Now, I'll need your word."

Thayne reached out then, grasped Riven's hand, and hissed in pain, knowing what would come next.

A binding, and it would be one-sided.

The bastard had him.

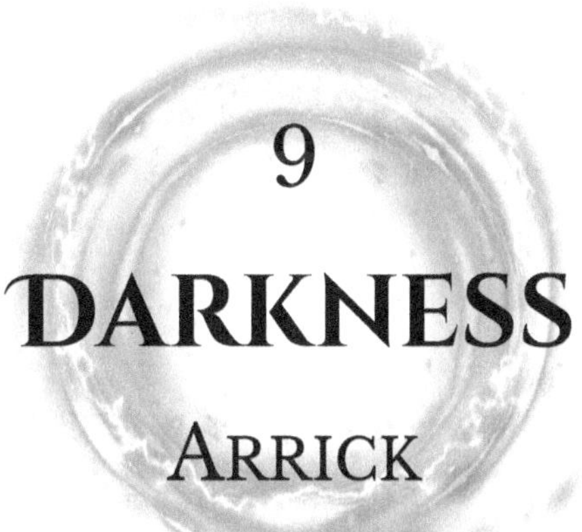

9
DARKNESS
ARRICK

"**M**oldizeans! Flank them now! Move!" I shouted, commanding my legion of demons to surround the army of Perenelleans. "Close the gap!"

Some of the Perenellean soldiers tried to break free from the main body of the army, but I couldn't let them. We had to keep them in front of us and encircle their ranks. It was our third battle, our third conquest, and three months had passed since the first. Three months since I'd taken over the training, strategy, and command of Madwyn's army.

As expected, my demons obeyed me without question, their broad feet thundering against the muddy ground of the once grass-covered meadow. At my back and on my sides, we closed the gap together, cutting down any deity who tried to break through with our black, poisoned blades, and shielding magic. I didn't look at the bodies of the injured or the dying. I only pressed forward, eyes scanning the field for any other breaches.

Relentless rain fell from black, ominous clouds overhead. I felt as much as heard it clinking against my spelled armor as my demons and I advanced, tightening our stranglehold on the Perenelleans' position. Across the field,

I heard deities scream and drop to the ground in waves and knew Daven-drie had secured the position we'd strategized.

I sent my magic out in a pulse, trying to get a read on the rest of my army's positions. As it twined around bodies, providing me with the rough location of our allies, I could sense that Asthorea had secured her post too. Good, they'd done their jobs, which meant that the battle would end soon.

We pressed forward then, pushing the Perenellean army inward as they hurled their magic at us. They fought harder, pushing back as they realized what we were doing, as they noticed the vice closing in around them and cutting off any chance of escape.

A second later, a bolt of vicious lightning struck the ground next to me, a jolt of electric pain searing through every single nerve in my body. I hissed, dropping to a knee and growling, rage building inside me faster than I could stop it. My chest heaved as I tried to breathe through the agony, through the killing fury it unleashed. All around us, the lightning kept striking. It scattered demons and cooked them alive as a few more agonizing jolts lanced through me.

I groaned, struggling to stay on my feet, when a massive wave of water flooded the field. It slammed into my thighs, its murky depths threatening to pull me down beneath its raging surface. I could feel my bloodlust rising, and I roared as another jolt of lightning struck, sizzling in the water and killing more of my demons. As I fought to stay upright against the whip-ping current that swirled against my legs, growing deeper by the second, I assessed the battlefield. We needed to find that fucking water deity.

The segment of our army positioned on the eastern edge of the circle, struggled against the speed of the rushing water. As they fell prey to the sweeping currents, our elementals worked around our edges to mitigate the damage. They'd have to use a shit load of magic to contain the rising tides. Especially considering how condensed the battle grew as we continued to press inward, our lines converging on top of the Perenelleans.

A few of the weaker deities from our front lines washed away, slamming into my demons, taking them down with them as their heads disappeared beneath the muddy water's surface. Until, at last, I found what I sought.

I saw him. A deity stood at the center of the Perenellean army, brows drawn down in deep concentration as he stared at the rushing water, directing it with his outstretched hands. Without giving myself a chance to think, I unleashed my magic. It burst from my palm, dancing across the water as black mist jetted toward my target. I couldn't help but smile as my power wound around his leg and penetrated his warded armor. He gasped, dropping to his knees and clutching his chest.

I sent my magic deeper, seeking the soul of the damned deity. Another strike of lightning next to me sent pain searing through my entire body, but it didn't matter. I had hold of his soul, his celestial essence, and without a second thought, I ripped it from his body. The torrent of water disappeared. A heartbeat later, I found the lightning deity and ripped his soul clean from his body, too.

"Back to me!" I shouted, wasting no time. "Back in formation!" The demons and the deities who'd gotten washed into my ranks from Asthorea's and Davendrie's regiments rose from the ground, coughing and sputtering, and rushed to my sides. Together we strained forward, slamming hard into the wards and magic-laced weapons of our Perenellean adversaries.

No one doubted my lead as we surged forward, everyone following without question, closing ranks, firing off magic, and slicing with their poisoned weapons. I could see the terror in the Perenellean's eyes as we continued our march inward. Then I heard screaming and shouting behind their front lines, followed by bright flashes as some attempted to translocate before we trapped them in our vise.

Pushing our advantage, I gained another ten steps with my battalion, my black blade singing like a song in my hand and my power dancing free, pulling souls from their bodies at a steady pace, ensuring that we won, but without the kind of damage I'd done in Quindale. With every death, I ensured that my tattoo never burned with disobedience. A routine I'd grown accustomed to.

In truth, unleashing my magic felt like pure ecstasy. My blood burned for the battle that I was born to wage. I'd fought my entire life to keep that part of me in check—that blood lust, that yearning for death. But when a blast of pure energy flew at me like a bomb, grazing my shoulder and searing straight through the flesh of it, I lost control. I roared in pain as a violent pulse of my magic ripped from me, and the entire front line of the Perenellean army fell, two dozen bodies dissipating into shining mist on the wind as they ascended.

I clenched my teeth as that other gift, the one I kept guarded and hidden, burned too. Bekka's magic awoke like a sleeping beast inside me, drawn to the dissipation of my own magic, begging to be released in kind. I gripped my chest, dodging a blow from a sword laced with golden godsbane, a paralytic poison used in wartime by the Twelve Realms, and tried to remain steady on my feet.

Tightening my grip on my blade, I lunged, stabbing that same deity straight through the shoulder and kicking him square in the chest. My demons took care of the rest, slashing with their weapons as he fell to the soggy ground.

I struggled to shove Bekka's power down and lock it away again as we advanced, squeezing the Perenelleans into each other until they could barely move.

They fought harder, struggling to break free as they recognized just how tight the noose we'd closed around them had become. More flashes of power blinked from within their cramped circle of fighters, upper-caste deities translocating to escape what came next, taking the coward's way out. Rather than push myself harder though, I reigned in my death magic and pulled my control tighter. I needed to be careful. I couldn't let myself loose again, not with Bekka's power so close to the surface.

Just then, a Perenellean deity held his godsbane blade high, charging me, and I swung my own poisoned sword, cutting him down with ease. He looked young, too young to die on a battlefield. With some effort, I tore my gaze away from him and tried not to think about who I killed. More gods and goddesses from Perenelle translocated into the fray, replacing the cowards who'd fled, appearing in the middle of our flanks, only to be swarmed and killed within moments by our demon foot soldiers.

We kept fighting, cutting through each other, clashing swords and magic roaring throughout the killing field, the sound of it hideous and thrilling all at once. The Perenellean weapons glowed with amplified magic and ours swirled with black poison, the blades looking almost sentient as we sliced them through our enemies.

Just as I raised my sword for another strike, blood and mud splattering my face and coating my tongue, a blast of fire hit me from behind. It cut through my magically reinforced armor and sent me stumbling forward. I used my momentum and balance to spin, hands raised, and ready to use my power in a controlled burst. Before I did, I prayed to the Ascended I could keep it under control and that I could keep Bekka's power concealed. But I hesitated when I saw the young goddess standing before me. Her strawberry-colored hair flew in the wind, her scalp coated with the same mixture of mud and blood as mine, fire dancing at her fingertips.

My power guttered as we stared at each other, locked in a moment of silence amidst the chaos. Her face looked childish, too young, her eyes widening with terror as she registered the black gift of death I held in my palm. My focus narrowed to that moment; our gazes transfixed on each other. She looked like Lilja, with her freckles and green eyes. She couldn't be more than a handful of years older than my sister. I lowered my hands, resolving right then to walk away and let her live, but before I could, a long, black blade plunged through her back, sliding out from her chest.

Her face went ashen, fresh, red blood oozing from the wound as the wielder yanked the blade back out. Her eyes stayed locked onto mine as she coughed, a fine mist of blood spraying from her lips. She sank to her knees, mouth opening and closing in shock. I remained frozen in place, unable to say or do anything to help her. The aloofness, the song of death in my blood, ceased. She was just a kid. A teenager at most, probably still new to her gifts.

She slumped forward, falling face-first into the bloody mud and something splintered inside of me. I kept my face impassive, eyes hard as death as they locked onto the deity who'd attacked her. It was Davendrie. He smiled at me then, a gleam of elation in his eyes. He'd enjoyed the kill.

Before I could say or do anything more, the bastard turned and raised his hands. My eyes flicked in the direction he held out his fingers and watched as two Perenellean gods turned their magic on one another, destroying each other in the blink of an eye.

Davendrie strode back toward his post, walking through the crowd then, lost in the heat of battle, and I snapped back to myself as a magic-laden arrow hurtled straight for me. I leaned back, dodging it, just before it could bury itself in my eye. Despite the shock that had overcome me, I felt the binding tattoo burn, so I pressed forward and kept fighting. I'd made a promise, and I had to keep it. I had no choice but to lead our army to victory. Madwyn had given me orders, and I couldn't disobey them.

After that, the battle went quickly. Our soldiers cut through the unprepared Perenellean force like a warm knife through butter, our regiments squeezing them into immobility while Madwyn's science deities wrought havoc on their infrastructure. We encircled them and closed in on them, giving them no quarter on the battlefield, and the hackers ensured they'd no way to call for aid. It hadn't taken long after that for the royals to surrender.

In the conquest's aftermath, I stared at the ruined meadow around us. Trees lined either side of the once peaceful landscape. Blood soaked deep into the soil, both demon and godly. It smelled of warm iron, sulfur, and shit, mixed with the sickly sweetness of the pine trees nearby.

Before me, knelt what remained of the royal family and upper-caste deities of Perenelle. We'd secured their hands behind their backs with the same golden shackles they'd used on Bekka that night in Bicaidian hell, when I'd sold my freedom for her life.

Demons trained their black, poisonous weapons on the Perenellean queen, awaiting my orders. Or, more specifically, Madwyn's orders. She owned me, I thought, grinding my teeth as the image of that young, strawberry-haired goddess flashed in my mind. I'd killed so many today, and I hadn't hated it, hadn't given it much thought. Not until that moment had snapped me out of my killing haze. What did that make me?

Uninterested in confronting that question, I turned my attention to the matter at hand and surveyed my demons for any signs of flagging. Their deep, black skin, and razor-sharp teeth were coated in mud, fiery red eyes burning with the desire to kill, to maim, and to torture. It reminded me just how out of place they were here. They belonged in hell, their true home and the place they were made for, where they served a noble purpose. Yet in the immortal realm? They were little more than mindless killing machines, obeying orders without question.

Davendrie stood next to my demons, along with Asthorea, and me. Madwyn's other two Diamanti, Crellen and Brielle, didn't join us during this campaign. Instead, Madwyn ordered them to maintain control over Quindale and Crescendia, the other two realms we'd conquered. And as for Riven? She left him in charge of Bicaidia, while she led the science deity's infrastructure attack on Perenelle, outside of the battlefield.

The other Diamanti standing at my sides may have trusted me as the commander of their army, but I was under no delusion that I had any true control. They watched, scrutinized, and reported my every move. So, no matter how much they tried to befriend me or feign comradery, I understood the reality of my situation. They only trusted me to win the battles, and nothing else. Should I step one toe out of line, they'd report it back to Madwyn. And then I would get punished.

"Well done today, Arrick. Madwyn will be pleased," Davendrie said, and the mere sound of his voice made me want to punch him in the throat and watch him choke for sport. But that would disobey a direct order, and I didn't feel like screaming in agony.

So, rather than open my mouth and risk murdering him, I inclined my head in acknowledgment. I knew battle. Understood it intimately. I'd been doing it since before I'd come into my power. All part of living in a place like Moldize and spending as much time as I had in the mortal realm there.

But Madwyn's war was unlike any I'd ever led or fought in before. In Moldize, I'd been protecting my friends, my adopted family, and keeping Itoriah safe. Here though? It was all about accumulating and solidifying her power. I tried not to think about that and not to let the guilt of my role in it gnaw at me.

As much as I hated myself for it, I enjoyed war. I liked the clarity and the fighting—hells, I liked all of it. But the shame I had for that innate bloodlust I couldn't seem to curb anymore sat like a stone in my gut. It didn't matter that I would never choose to fight for Madwyn, if it weren't for that damned binding. It didn't matter because the darkness that festered inside of me grew with every life I claimed, with every terrible thing I did.

Before I could sink further into the self-loathing that followed every battle, I felt the wind rustle at my neck and a static charge prickle the air. *Strong magic,* I thought, turning my head and shielding my eyes from the too-bright sun. The sky had cleared since the battle, all traces of Perenellean power gone, so the sudden appearance of full-force magic could only mean one thing. Swirling purple smoke laced with lightning caught my eye just before Madwyn walked through a portal. I clenched my jaw, preparing myself for what came next. For the show I would need to put on, for the role I had to play. The one I'd played for months.

I removed my hand from the hilt of my sword and laced my fingers behind my back, straightening my spine in a posture of respect right before my sister, Lilja, walked through the smoke behind Madwyn. My muscles stiffened as a quiet roaring built inside my head. I didn't dare breathe, lest I excoriate Madwyn for bringing my sister to a damned battlefield. Neither did I dare to move, lest I shove my sword into her gut for the simple pleasure of watching the light in her eyes wink out.

I scanned the surrounding field, stomach burning with anger as I took in the dead bodies of my demons and the swaths of injured deities, bleeding and broken, covering the field. It was no place for a young goddess, even one brought up in Moldize.

Yet, there she stood; beside the deity I hated even more than I'd hated Gabryel. My discerning gaze traveled the length of Lilja, checking her for injury or fear, but I saw no sign of either. Her blonde hair, wild and untamed, whipped in the warm wind that blew through the valley. She dressed in the standard attire of Bicaidia; loose, silk trousers and a tank top cropped at her waist. *Despite that, she still looks like home,* I thought, my stomach lurching.

Unfortunately, I'd seen my sister only a handful of times since Madwyn abducted her from Moldize. Madwyn wouldn't allow it. She may have already held my fate in her palm, but she'd still taken my sister to control me further. As though she'd known that my life wouldn't be enough to own me. An astute observation considering how willingly I'd offered it to her in Bicaidian hell to save Bekka, Caden, and Deklan, along with the others I didn't know. But with Lilja here too? Well, I would never risk her life.

My jaw tightened then as my sister's green eyes landed on an injured deity sprawled on the ground next to her. Raised, black lines traced through every vein in her body, and blood trailed down either side of her mouth. She coughed and misty red spurted, Lilja's face blanching as she jumped back, avoiding the spray. Madwyn only laughed at her obvious alarm, looping her arm through my sister's and pulling her along.

Lilja looked at Madwyn's hand where it touched her and sneered for a split-second before she schooled her features. *Good*, I thought, relief filling me. It brought me some comfort to know that my sister saw through Madwyn's charm and to the insanity, the cruelty that lurked beneath it. Just then, when they were mere steps away, my sister looked up, her eyes finding mine, and I could see the sadness and fear in them. My gut burned, and my fists flexed to the point of pain behind my back.

Another second passed, and they stood in front of us, Madwyn's eyes gleaming with triumph. Davendrie stepped forward, inclining his head in a show of respect, "My queen, the conquest was a success. The prisoners are yours to do with as you please."

Madwyn's face split into a feral smile, and she fixed her attention on me. She eyed me up and down, the pleasure in her gaze clear and repulsive. She stepped closer to me, trailing a red polished nail across the seam of the armor along my chest. I tried not to react. "You did well today, Arrick. Thank you again for your service."

I could feel Lilja's wide, doe eyes on me, watching as the chaos deity touched me without my permission. While Lilja may not have known the full extent of my connection with Bekka, she knew enough. And she'd know just how much I would be itching to snap every single finger Madwyn laid on me. So, I didn't dare look at her. I didn't want to see the sympathy I knew would be in her expression. Not after everything I'd just done. I didn't deserve it.

So instead of acting on my violent instincts, I remained silent, and dipped my head, accepting Madwyn's acknowledgment. I needed to be smart and bide my time. And I would, I thought, as the chaos goddess stared at me, lingering for a beat too long before she stepped past me and went to survey her prisoners.

As Madwyn moved further away and closer to the Perenellean royals, Lilja slipped her hands into her pants pockets and stepped closer. Her presence beside me filled me with warmth and the familiar scent of her skin. I wanted to reach out and pull her into my arms. To tuck her head against my chest so that I could shield her from the horror that surrounded us. But I couldn't. Not then, not with so many eyes on me.

Lilja whispered, her voice so soft I could hardly hear it. "Arrick, are you OK?" I cut her a sideways glance and saw that she stared straight ahead, at the kneeling prisoners and the wasted field. Her golden skin had paled, but she'd lost the doe eyes, and I couldn't help the pride I felt at how quickly she'd controlled her emotions. But, with that, I still noted the worry in her voice. I knew what she must be thinking. I was a Nefaral, prone to the allure of the natural darkness inside me. A death deity surrounded by death. Was I getting lost in it?

Honest answer? I didn't know.

I wanted to promise her I was still me. To reassure her that despite what she saw on that field, I would never choose that kind of vicious slaughter. But the claws of Davendrie's magic snaked down my neck then, and I stiffened. He'd been trying to worm his way into my mind since day one, despite the victory I'd handed them at Quindale, and I gritted my teeth, hardening my mental defenses. With my sister there, he must have sensed my distraction and tried for an opening. Facing straight ahead, I whispered. "I'm fine."

Before Lilja could say more, Madwyn's voice rang out, echoing across the valley and between the mountains on either side. "The choice is simple. Swear your oath, swear your people and your resources to our cause, and live. Refuse, and die." She shrugged her shoulders as though it mattered little to her which they chose.

For a long moment, no one spoke. Everyone just stared. And then Madwyn motioned. All her Diamanti stepped forward, the three of us moving in unison like we'd choreographed it. The warm scent of my sister disappeared as Davendrie and Asthorea flanked me on either side.

Without her having to ask, we all let our magics off their leashes until our powers rippled across our fingertips and trailed up our arms. I heard Lilja gasp behind us, whether in surprise or horror, I couldn't say, and didn't want to know. The deities who knelt before us had been stripped of their powers already, rendered helpless by the golden shackles on their wrists, and yet we threatened them with death, insanity, banishment, and more. I hated our side.

And with how much I loathed this, I couldn't help but wonder what my sister might make of it all. Lilja had been young during The Burning, a child conceived after almost a decade of my parents wanting a sibling for me, another child of their own. We all loved her, but we'd kept her sheltered from the worst of what happened in Moldize. She'd never witnessed anything this brutal before, and I fucking hated that she had to see it now.

In response to Madwyn's ultimatum, the high queen of Perenelle, Rhona, glared up at her. Rhona's silver armor gleamed while her dark eyes filled with hatred. "You'll have to kill us. We'll never join you."

Madwyn paused, staring down her nose at the queen goddess. "Very well then, Davendrie, if you'll do the honors?" A sly grin spread across the consciousness deity's lips in response to his mistress's request, his black eyes bright with excitement. He lifted his open hand, palm up, and slowly closed his fist. The queen screamed, the shrieks echoing off the surrounding hills of the blood-riddled meadow. She twined her fingers into her hair, ripping out thick strands as blood seeped from her eyes and nose.

Lilja sucked in a horrified-sounding breath and covered her mouth as she stumbled forward, her hand gripping the leathers on my arm. As though she needed to hold on to me for stability. I turned then, feigning annoyance at the disruption, a charade for my peers. I pulled her hand from my armor and held it in my grasp. To an outsider, it would look like a rebuke. But I kept my grip soft, and murmured, "Close your eyes, Lili. You don't need to see this part."

She lifted her terrified gaze to me, just before she shut her eyes, obeying me. Moisture pooled at the corners of her lids, but to her credit, no tears escaped.

I released Lilja's hand, just in time to turn back and see the queen's body slump, striking the soft ground with a muffled thump. She was dead, and Davendri looked gleeful, wired with the thrill of a fresh kill, and I wished I could rip that black, twisted soul from his body. I wished I could pass judgment on the gods as I did with mortals and send him straight to hell. But I couldn't. That kind of power, I didn't have.

Madwyn held out her arms then, as though welcoming her captives home. "So, who's next?" A murmur of fear rippled through them all as they stared at their fallen queen. I could see the tide turning already.

The high prince rose to his feet then, Rhona's only living son, his face white and splattered with his mother's blood. "We'll fight with you, Madwyn. Just please, don't kill them." He gestured behind him, and I followed his hand to where his wife knelt, all but cowering at his back. Their two eldest children were there as well, young still, likely with powers only just formed. He may have brought them to the battle to fight, but he wasn't willing to sacrifice it all now that they'd survived the worst of it, unlike his mother. As I thought of what I'd done to save Bekka and her sister, to save Caden and Deklan, and now what I did to keep Lilja alive, I couldn't say I blamed him.

At that, Madwyn gave him a curt nod. "Good," she said, smiling and striding over to him. "Let's settle the details, then, shall we?"

I felt cold inside as the high prince nodded his agreement. Perenelle, Quindale, and Crescendia had all fallen within a matter of months, and Valeria hadn't even put up a fight to save them. I wondered how many more realms would fall before they realized the severity of the threat Madwyn posed and got their shit together. Without Gabryel to lead them and with

Bekka imprisoned, I didn't like the answer. For the sake of all thirteen realms, I could only hope they wouldn't be too late.

10
TRUSTING
BEKKA

I awoke with a start, gasping as my hand flew to my chest. I half-expected to find a gaping wound there. Instead, felt nothing except old, tattered clothing and my unmarred flesh. The warmth of Emorie beside me and her voice anchored me to the present.

"Bekka," she whispered, as I gulped down air in the pure darkness. "What's wrong?"

I shook my head, trying to calm my racing heart and my ragged breathing. But then I saw it again, the dream replaying in my mind. I could see her eyes, the pale strawberry-blonde hair, and then that sword cutting through her chest, blood exploding from her mouth like a fine mist.

The coldness that lanced through me had cut me to the quick. It had all felt so real. A battle, and death, so much death. And in the vision, I'd seen a black, misty power I knew all too well. It skirted the field, slithering along the muddy ground like a sentient fog, and when it touched anyone, they fell, ascending within a heartbeat.

I knew instinctively that the fog was Arrick's death magic. But I hadn't just witnessed the scene as a third party, I thought, raking my nails over my scalp to center myself. I'd been in it, and I'd felt it too—a powerful, intense bloodlust as his magic felled deity after deity. It couldn't have belonged to him, could it? I squeezed my eyes shut and tried to make sense of it.

I knew he had some darkness in him, every Nefaral did, and he'd told me as much himself, but he'd also told me that everyone had a choice. That just because he was a Nefaral didn't mean he had to choose the darkness. He had proven himself honorable, good at his core, and a true protector. Not a murderer, never a murderer. *He didn't relish or enjoy killing, did he? I thought. No, it had to be a dream. No, correction, a nightmare.*

Chills prickled up my arms and down my spine from the cool, dank temperature of the prison, or at least that's what I told myself. I didn't want to think about what else might be causing the icy trail along my back as I sucked cool air.

After a few more steadying breaths, my heart rate slowed and my mind settled.

Until at last, I answered Emorie's question. "I don't know. A nightmare maybe?" I chafed my arms, trying to create some semblance of warmth. Deep down, I knew it hadn't been just a dream, despite my best efforts at denial, and I could still feel icy fingertips tracing a trail down my spine.

I'd had a week of full meals and had started to get my strength back. The more of it that returned, the more intense the nightmares got. They grew more vibrant, and I felt more from them with each passing day. As I settled, I faced the question that plagued me every waking hour now: Were they Arrick's actual memories? Was I seeing what he saw? Feeling what he felt? Or were they just nightmares?

Deep down, I already knew the answer to that question. I just hated what it meant. Madwyn was forcing him to kill and to fight for her, and I knew why he did it. He'd sworn himself to her to protect us … to protect me. I tried to tamp down the despair and worry that threatened to overwhelm me, but it didn't work.

I needed to get stronger faster, and I needed to get out of this damned cell. Because with every dream and every step into Arrick's memories and experiences, I could feel that kernel of darkness growing.

"These nightmares have been happening more often lately," Emorie observed, and even though I couldn't see her in the pitch black they'd kept the cell cloaked in for at least two days, I could still feel her scrutinizing me. Not that I would complain about the darkness, it was a reprieve from the constant light of the last months. But I wanted to see her face, to read her expression, and decide if I could trust her. I wanted that more than I cared to admit. Emorie gave up her food for me as the first step in our plan to escape. She had held up her end of the bargain there, but could I take a leap of faith and tell her the truth about Arrick and me?

Soulfused mates were rare in our world, and I knew what it would mean for our fight if we escaped. I was no longer the only creator in the multiverse. Arrick could wield that power too, alongside his death magic, and Madwyn had him in her clutches. She owned him because of me.

How long could he fight the buildup of pressure he must be feeling from my power? How long could he keep it a secret? My magic combined with that inherent darkness inside of him must be killing him inside, and what would happen if that kernel of darkness continued to grow? To fester as the cold fury I felt every time I slipped into one of those dreams grew along with it?

I chewed on my lip, knowing that our power had to be used. If we didn't, then it would consume the deity who suppressed it. Usually in the most spectacular way possible, and while leaving a hell of a lot of damage in its wake. And that would be an enormous problem for anyone in the same damn galaxy as him. Because my power? Well, it could take out a planet, or a whole damned solar system, if either of us let it build up too much.

I chewed on my lip as I dropped my head into my palms, trying not to think about the devastating consequences if he risked releasing any of that pressure. The outcome would be just as bad, maybe even worse. The Twelve Realms traced the use of all major gifts. Our technology would pick up even the smallest fraction of creation magic within any of our realms. It was one of the ways my grandfather had maintained order so well. He'd made it his business to know who wielded their magic in his realms and when any major new gift popped into existence.

So, the instant my creation power so much as sparked in Arrick's palm, someone would take notice, and while they may not trace it back to him right away, it wouldn't take long before they figured out our secret.

Emorie whispered again. "What are the nightmares about, Bekka?" The words sounded heavy, as though she sensed my trepidation despite the lack of visibility in our cell. As though she could feel it rolling off me in waves.

I sighed, rubbing my eyes. Despite my desperate desire for it to be otherwise, I knew deep in my belly that my dreams were tied to the real world. They were his actual experiences, and he was in serious trouble. I slid a hand down my tangled braid and turned my head to where Emorie sat. Could I trust her? Could I tell her?

The lights flashed on without warning, and I hissed, wincing as I covered my eyes. Fireworks exploded beneath my lids as my vision struggled to adjust. I hated prison, I decided. I mean, I'd already decided that, but I hated it even more than usual at that moment. After a few more seconds of rapid blinking and colorful cursing, my eyes adjusted. They fixed on Emorie, who sat beside me on our tiny cot, the one we'd taken to sharing for warmth.

Even with the near-blinding, I could see the empathy and concern in her expression. Hard to say if she just worried that my lack of sleep would prevent us from escaping or if she genuinely wanted to know what was wrong with me.

"Bekka, you can tell me what's happening," Emorie said, her voice soft and reassuring. I wished again that I had some way to know for certain that I could trust her. If I made the wrong decision, would she betray me?

Without giving myself a chance to consider further, I said, "If I tell you what's going on and you breathe a word of it to anyone, I swear on my grandfather's immortal soul, I will get out of here. And when I do, you will be the first person I kill."

"Ruthless," she said, nodding in approval as a grim smile slipped over her lips. "I like it. We'll need that if we hope to fight our way out of here and save the Twelve Realms."

I watched her then, a gleam of hardened certainty in her eyes, and something inside me told me I was making the right choice. Maybe that was foolish, but I wanted to trust her. I needed an ally, and she was my best option. OK, so she might have also been my only option, but that didn't make her a bad one.

So, decision made, I let out a long breath, and told her everything. As the words poured from my lips like a confession, her mouth dropped open until her bottom lip damn near rested on the mattress.

"Ascended, Bekka. You're telling me he's a creator and a death deity?" Emorie dragged a hand through her matted hair, fingers sticking in the knots. She yanked herself free, curly, tangled strands ripping out as she did. Her annoyed scowl spoke volumes, and I could have kissed her for lightening my mood, even if just a little. Then she turned her serious expression back on me.

Uh oh.

I nodded, a tiny spool of dread winding its way through me. "It's bad, right? I know. It's bad." A dumb question with an obvious answer, I knew. Even so, I'd hoped in the light of day and from someone else's perspective, it might be less terrible.

"You think?" she asked, sarcasm dripping from her tongue. "It's a damned disaster." She chewed on her lip as she contemplated the full ramifications of how bad it could get. "You don't think he'd tell Madwyn, do you?"

I shook my head, my tangled braid whipping back and forth with the intensity of my denial. "Never. He'd never risk us. He'd never risk me." I knew that because the very idea of putting him in danger made fire ants crawl under my skin and dread burn in my throat. It felt like every cell in my body rebelled at the thought, and I knew it must be the soul bond.

"OK," Emorie said, and I could tell she didn't fully accept my answer. "But he can't use your magic without getting tracked ..." She trailed off, and I knew she'd come to the same conclusion as me.

"I know. We don't have much time."

"That he's lasted as long as he has is damn impressive. We need to move faster. I'll cut my food portions more, you'll train more. Then once we're ready, we hit them hard and—"

"If you cut back anymore, then you'll be no good to me when we leave," I interrupted. "You need to be ready to follow me out, and we don't even have a weapon yet, anyway." A look of determination slid over her features, and I knew what she'd say next. Leveling a finger at her, I glared. "I'm not leaving you behind, so don't even think that."

"You just need to make it out, then you can come back for me. It's not like Madwyn can kill me while I'm here. You'll be in way more danger than I will." When I just shook my head, she rolled her eyes, treating me like a teenager would an irritating parent.

"You're coming with me and that's final." I wouldn't let her stay behind, not when my escape could bring a full-scale war to Bicaidia's doorstep. Madwyn may not be able to order her dead, but that didn't mean she couldn't get killed in all the destruction that would follow.

And in the fog of war? All it would take was a little creativity to find a loophole in that binding, and she'd be dead and ascended before I could say anything about it. But rather than voice any of that, I appealed to her practical side. "I know nothing about Helverta. I've only ever been to the palace here. If we're going to escape and actually get away, then I'll need your help."

After a lengthy stare-down, which to my astonishment, I won, she let out a resigned sigh. "Fine. We cut my rations in half again for a week to speed up your recovery. Then back to my regular portions. We need to make sure we're ready the next time that door opens. Deal?"

I nodded then. "Deal."

11
ALLIANCE
ARRICK

It had been a long, grueling battle in Perenelle followed by an even longer day afterward. I'd just returned to Bicaidia after overseeing the surrender of the Perenelleans, and all I wanted to do was wash the mud and blood away before I collapsed into stasis sleep.

Also, I wanted to forget.

Slipping into my room in the palace-turned barracks for Madwyn's army, I felt exhaustion weighing down every limb and muscle. I shut the door behind me and scanned the space for anything that looked suspicious. Despite the privacy I'd received from the other Nefarals, I still didn't feel comfortable enough to trust that no one tampered with my shit while I was gone.

As I assessed, I noted the four-poster king bed and the large, raw-edged, wooden desk across from it. Nothing looked out of place. I turned my attention to the balcony doors, peering through the floor-to-ceiling glass that overlooked the sparkling Synbue River below and the surrounding red-rocked mountains. Next to the desk was the door to my bathroom, where a shower beckoned.

I unclasped and untied my weapons, along with the armor and leathers I'd worn into battle, depositing them onto the desk. Sweat, blood, and mud coated the onyx-colored armor, my under-clothing, and my skin. It smelled pungent, earthy, and metallic, but something else lurked beneath it. Death, I thought, a scent I knew all too well.

As I inhaled it, contempt and regret dogged me, but I couldn't escape what I'd done. Instead, I tried not to think about the faces of those I'd killed. I pushed that young, strawberry-haired goddess that Davendri had stabbed through her too-young heart from my mind, rubbing my arm where she'd burned it with her magic. The bright red wound still felt raw, since I hadn't bothered with stasis sleep or a healer yet. Others needed both more than I did.

My fingers tested the painful singe as I thought about that cough of blood and the shocked look on her face. Without warning, the anger I had kept concealed surged to the surface.

Madwyn had taken my sister onto that battlefield. I ground my teeth as I pulled the thin, linen shirt I wore under my armor over my head, and shoved the leather pants down as well. I slammed open the door to the bathroom, striding inside as it hit the stone countertop with a loud crack.

I didn't care.

Turning the shower to scalding, I stepped inside, the water washing over me. I let it burn away the dirt, the muck, and the blood. I stayed under the hot stream for a long time, hoping to sear the grime from my very soul. But it was no use.

I already knew that everything I'd done for Madwyn would leave a stain. It didn't matter that I had no choice. What mattered was that, despite that, a part of me fucking enjoyed it.

I pushed that thought away, wishing it hadn't been true. But it was. Even after everything I'd done to turn myself into something more than a bastion of death, it didn't matter. Not anymore. I liked the killing, the calm and stillness it brought me. I didn't want to think about what that made me.

Squeezing my eyes shut, I tried to push the faces of the dead from my mind again, fighting like hell against the innate darkness that lived inside me. But even with my best efforts, I could still feel it creeping in further around the edges.

I needed to focus on the light, on the reason I'd sworn myself to Madwyn in the first place. People were counting on me to keep them safe, and I had to remember that. Bekka's face flashed in my mind then, her smile broad and her laughter ringing in my ears.

Goodness lived inside her, and she'd given some of that to me when our souls fused. As though summoned by my thoughts, her gift hummed, heating my skin again, and I sighed, pushing it down and forcing my dark power to swallow it.

I thought of her silken skin, and of trailing my fingers over it again. I remembered her full lips and what it felt like to sink my teeth into them. Between my legs, I could feel myself stiffen at the thought of her beautiful body, smooth and soft.

I imagined what she would say if I could speak to her again. I remembered how she could make light of even the darkest situation, of how she disarmed me and got me laughing, no matter how bleak I felt. She was my light in the shadows, my beacon, and the reason I had to keep pushing forward. I needed to hold on to that if I had any hope of getting through this with my soul intact.

I rested my hands on the dark, river-stone wall of the shower, and as the water hit my back, I let the pain of our separation overpower the rest of it. A few minutes later, I was done. Exhaustion tugged at me, my shoulder burned with pain, and I knew I needed stasis sleep. Turning the faucet off, I grabbed a towel from the hook outside the large, walk-in shower. I dried myself with it, my hair still dripping as I wrapped the towel around my waist.

I pushed open the solid wood door to my bedroom and froze. Everything inside me went still, and my expression went blank.

It was her. Madwyn.

She sat, perched on the edge of my bed, legs crossed, body leaned back to rest on her palms, assessing me. "You did well again today, Arrick. Less theatrical, but more efficient and strategic. Nice work."

I crossed my arms over my chest and leaned on the edge of the bathroom doorway as though I hadn't a care in the world. The picture of unruffled calmness. "You said that already." I didn't move, just watched her with a mild hint of amusement to cover the irritation I felt at her sudden appearance.

"Well, I just wanted to tell you again." I remained impassive as she raked her gaze over my body, the gleam in her eyes unmistakable. I'd seen human women and deities look at me like that before. It had never disgusted me the way it did then, but I didn't dare show it.

Instead, I just dipped my head in acknowledgment of her gratitude. "Thank you. But, in the future, I'd appreciate a knock. I'm not exactly decent." I let a feral, almost threatening grin tilt up the corner of my mouth before returning to neutral.

Her lips twitched then as she locked her eyes onto mine. "You know, you should stop fighting me. Stop fighting this—" She lifted a hand to gesture between us and smiled broader. "It would make things a lot easier on you." Rising from the bed, she prowled closer to me as though we had all the time in the world. It took everything in me not to step back in distaste.

"I'm not interested in easy," I answered, arms still crossed, letting my meaning sink in. She may command me on the battlefield, but I'd be damned if she made me fuck her. My boundary on that was crystal clear.

But rather than take offense at the slight, she tilted her head back and laughed. As much as I hated to admit it, she had a good laugh. The sound was both charming and disarming, but in reality, it was all a deception. She shook her head, the blonde strands of her hair rustling in the mid-morning sunlight. "I know you think I'm the enemy, but you're wrong. I made you a member of my Diamanti. Do you want to know why?"

"Because I killed over 1,500 deities for you during our first battle and you conquered Quindale as a result? Or is it because without me, you'd all be dead?" The memories tasted bitter as I tried to swallow them down.

"Partly. But also because, like it or not, you're one of us. A Nefaral; and I know you think you're better than us, but you're not." She eyed me, daring me to disagree. I said nothing, and she continued. "If they'd forced you into a cage, you'd rebel too. I can see that in you as plainly as I see your pretty, green eyes."

"You know nothing about me or what I'd do."

"Oh, I think I do. You try so hard to be good. To be noble and fair, but the darkness that follows me, I can see it dogging you, too. And you may think you love Bekka, but you can never have her. Her family would never allow it. They would never accept someone like you, someone with all that black in their soul, into the fold. They think you're beneath them."

She eyed me, still waiting for a reaction. When I gave her nothing yet again, she continued. "Join me. I mean really join me, and I can change that. I can give you what you desire most." She paused again, and I held my tongue, just to see what she'd say. Interested in what she thought I wanted. "When I'm done, everyone will respect us. Everyone will accept us. Not just that, but we will rule it all."

She swept her arms around the room, the gesture meant to encompass all the thirteen realms. I understood her then, the kernel at the center of her rebellion. That desire to be treated as an equal and not as an abomination just because of her magic. It made sense, but the path she'd chosen would lead to nothing but pain and suffering. If she succeeded, she would turn every single realm into a graveyard and call it peace. If she failed, though? Our kind would never breathe free air again.

I kept my face blank. "I fight, kill, and bleed for you, Madwyn. What more do you want from me?"

"Your loyalty. A true alliance." She observed my face, as though trying to examine me for any hint of what I might be thinking. She'd get nothing from me that I didn't want to give.

At last, I pushed off the wall, stepping around her and striding toward the armoire. I opened it, grabbing the more casual clothing customary for the Bicaidians. Thin, loose tan pants, and a white linen shirt. Chucking them on the bed, I turned to face her. In the past few months, I'd given her no reason to either trust or distrust me, though no one would dare call me warm. However, I had won her battles and earned the respect of her army.

But then again, she'd ordered me to do so, and the binding had ensured my obedience.

"I'll consider it," I said at last, schooling my expression into a contemplative mask. What Madwyn didn't understand about me was that I didn't give a damn what the rest of the Twelve Realms thought about our kind. I'd grown up in Moldize, ostracized and loathed from the moment of my birth. Nefaral or Altruist had little to do with it. But rather than voice that, I said, "But before I do, answer one question for me." I slipped the shirt over my head and slid the pants on beneath the towel before dropping it to the floor.

Her eyes never left my face. "Ask away."

"Why do this? Why start a war? There were other paths to take, ones that would have been a hell of a lot less bloody and maybe even more effective."

"A death god complaining about death? How ironic," she mused, shaking her head and chuckling as she drew closer to me. "Riven was never so squeamish."

Ignoring the barb, I replied, "If I'm to give you my loyalty, then I need to understand your goals for this conflict, your reasoning for what you've done, and what you will do next. You can force me to obey you because of the binding, but I will not give my full allegiance to anyone blindly. Bound Diamanti or no."

The smile that spread over her mouth was all teeth and ferocity. "It's simple. Revenge, Arrick. I want revenge. I want to make them pay."

"So, what? You burn it all down? That won't leave much behind to rule, and do you think anyone left will follow you after that? That they won't rebel in kind?"

Her expression darkened. "Now that I control five of the thirteen realms, I don't have to burn it down. I just need to strike a match and set a few small, contained fires. Then they will do the rest for me, once they know the truth about their precious Peacekeeper."

"What are you talking about?" I asked, allowing confusion to sweep over my expression. Gabryel had a dark side, that much I knew since I'd seen it firsthand. He'd been willing to let my family die, along with everyone in the Moldizean realm, rather than lift a finger to help us. But it would be to my advantage to let her think she could sway me. To let her think she could tell me something that I didn't already know about him.

She smiled, looking triumphant then. "You see, Gabryel and his royal allies have been oh so naughty. In their quest for total control, they made an egregious error."

I said nothing. Instead, I used the silence to let her talk. I'd noticed that she was the type who enjoyed filling those silences. She strolled to the window and looked at the painted, sunset sky, before she continued, as predicted, "You see, they didn't just put governor chips in the Nefarals. They chipped thousands of Altruists, too. Manipulating the power levels of everyone who dared to rise above their family's caste or whose power proved the teensiest bit too difficult to control."

I had to clench my jaw to keep it from dropping. *Fucking hell*, I thought. *They couldn't have, could they*? I understood why they'd done it to the Nefarals, and to some extent, I understood Gabryel's hatred of Moldize. But they'd chipped other Altruists? Their allies? What a reckless thing to do, stupid even. What had made him think they wouldn't get caught? Madwyn had calculated the situation correctly. It was the kind of secret that could implode the entire system, and a chaos deity had it in her grasp.

I let my surprise show then, schooling my expression to portray just the right amount of it. "If that's true, then why not just tell the truth and watch it crumble from afar?"

She turned back to face me, her arms crossed over her chest. I could see the shadow of sadness cross over her features before she smiled. I noted that flash of truth beneath the mask, wondering what might be at the root of it. If it wouldn't be useful for me to find out and use later. Because I couldn't continue to let things play out as they had over the last four months. I needed to fight back, to find a way out before she figured out my secret.

After a quiet beat, she said, "All in good time. I just need to make sure that I release that information when it will cause maximum impact." With that, she strode to the door, her heels clicking on the terracotta floor. As her hand reached for the doorknob, she turned back to me. "Consider my offer. I think you'll find it's better than anything the Altruists are willing to give you."

With that, she opened the door and strode out.

12

SPYMASTER

ARRICK

I awoke to a loud banging on my door. Irritated, I groaned, "Piss off!"

A laugh sounded behind the precipice. Female and one I didn't recognize, and more banging followed it. A male voice shouted, "Get your ass up, Arrick! We're going to celebrate our victory today, and we need our commander to join us!" That voice, I recognized. Davendrie, I thought, and anger hit me. The last thing I wanted to do was to celebrate what he, or any of us, had done in Perenelle that day.

"Come on, Arrick," the laughing female crooned, and I could tell who else had disturbed my sleep—Asthorea. "It's time to stop brooding and enjoy the perks of being on the winning side."

When I didn't answer, another voice spoke, smooth and cultured, "We won't take no for an answer. So, come out before I order you to." Riven. I clenched my teeth and rubbed the heel of my hand over my forehead in frustration. He outranked me, and Madwyn had given me orders to obey him. Fucking perfect.

"Fine. Give me ten."

"We'll give you five," Riven said. "Meet us in the grand hall, and then we're going into the city."

I listened as their laughing and talking faded down the hallway. When I could hear nothing but the sound of my own breathing, I rose to my feet. *The city?* I thought, wondering what they meant by that. Most of Helverta had suffered severe damage on inauguration night, and while they'd made some repairs, Madwyn hadn't treated the city's reconstruction as a top priority. But it didn't matter what I thought. Riven ordered, and I obeyed.

I ground my teeth as I pulled on a casual, lightweight shirt, pants, and a pair of soft, leather shoes. No blood, no gore, but also no strategic benefits to the clothing should I need to defend myself. Just soft, pliant material, nothing like what we wore in Moldize. It reminded me again of how pampered things had become in the Twelve Realms, and how they'd hurtled themselves into war without thinking through the repercussions. Almost like it was a game to them. Like the Nefaral's freedom and lives didn't hang in the balance if they lost.

I opened my door after four minutes and then strode into the hallway, calling my magic. It formed a portal ahead of me in a black misty sheet, and I stepped through it. A second later, I stood in the grand foyer of the palace, the trio who'd interrupted my rest not ten paces ahead of me. All of them were dressed in formal, fancier Bicaidian fare than what I'd selected. Dark, slick suits for Davendrie and Riven, and a slim, navy, silk dress for Asthorea, with a deep slit up one bronzed leg.

"There he is. Four minutes and forty-five seconds. Well done," Riven called, shouts of celebratory revelry ringing out from the nearby banquet hall.

"I aim to please," I replied, keeping my voice light, and I heard him chuckle in response.

"No, you don't," he said, but I could hear the humor lacing the words. "But I don't give a shit as long as you obey."

I ground my teeth, and they all laughed, grinning as Davendrie opened the palace's main entry door wide, and cool night air swept inside. They breezed out, and I followed them, walking along the grand entrance lined with manicured plants, most of which had made it through the battle on Remi's inauguration night. I would never understand how. But as we cleared the palace grounds, I couldn't say the same for the city itself.

Businesses, government buildings, and homes stood in various states of either disrepair or destruction. Some structures crumbled, looking like they'd melted into the ground. Others appeared singed merely at the edges, or had small chunks taken out of them, and were still habitable or, at a minimum, usable. We entered one such building, only two blocks from the palace entrance.

Davendrie slapped Riven on the back and Asthorea howled with laughter at something he'd said as I followed a few steps behind them. I paid little attention to their conversation, my mind too focused on the city and its residents. The deities who occupied the city but did not belong to Madwyn's army, looked terrified by our presence. They hurried to cross the streets, desperate to get away from us. As they did, they cast furtive glances beneath their lashes at me, and I realized I was the one making them uneasy.

I'd heard them whisper about me, of course. The Moldizean death deity. A cold-blooded murderer who led Madwyn's army into victory after victory. They said that I came to destroy the Twelve Realms after Gabryel's death, to seek my revenge on them. Too bad that couldn't have been further from the truth. Instead, I'd tried to stop it, but war had found them anyway.

I slid my hands into the loose pockets of my pants and reminded myself that at least I'd kept Bekka alive and safe. I'd accomplished that much for them, and while I couldn't assist her, see her, or talk to her, it left them all a chance. They had a creator, and the heir to the Peacekeeper's mantle. She just had to break free, and I trusted that she would figure out how to make that happen.

As my three companions walked inside the large building, I followed them, grabbing the door, and crossing the threshold. The music hit me first. It was loud, and the deities sang along with it in loud, bawdy voices. As though they knew the song well, something famous from their world. I'd never heard it before. I didn't particularly care as I squinted in the dim lighting, eternal candle flames burning on candle sticks hovering in the air above us. Large tables dominated the center of the room, forcing a sense of community that everyone seemed to enjoy a little too much.

Riven strode to four empty chairs at a table and pulled one out for Asthorea. She smiled sweetly at him, tossing glossy, black hair over her shoulder as she sat. "Come on, Arrick," Riven said, waving me over to an empty chair beside her. I obeyed, not missing the burn on my wrist at the casual order he delivered as I sat beside her. Riven grinned, his pale face and blue eyes brighter than usual, the contrast with his near-black hair stark. "I'll get the first round."

He sauntered to the bar, and I noticed that my companions' formal clothing stood out among the mixture of battle armor and more casual clothes around us. I scanned the room and realized I'd been mistaken. This wasn't just a place to drink, and I cleared my throat in surprise as I saw the near-naked goddesses with serving platters. Others gave lap dances, while still more led revelers into back rooms. Dosing drugs pulsed with vibrant light, surging with energy as people partook, drank the god's-ale and god's-liquor, and tasted the servant-caste deities who worked there.

But before I could get up and leave, a chair screeched beside me and a young goddess settled next to me. "Arrick, right?" she said, her voice low and husky. I didn't want to look. If she was naked and sitting next to me, I didn't want to see it. I'd been burning for far too long without Bekka, and the idea of seeing a naked goddess who wasn't her made me want to break something.

I trained my eyes forward, watching as Riven gathered pitchers of mixed god's-liquor and four glasses. "Yes, that's right," I replied, keeping my tone cold.

Davendrie grinned then, his teeth too white against his bronze skin, and his eyes too bright, considering their depthless black color. I wondered if they'd all been dosing, amping up their magic, and getting that rush that came with it. It wouldn't surprise me. "You know, Sylennia, I don't think he likes you."

Asthorea chuckled, leaning onto the table to peer across from me, her bare arms flexing with toned muscle beneath her smooth skin. "Don't take it personally. He's kind of a broody asshole, but we like him anyway."

Davendrie chuckled, and I turned my back to the newcomer, arching a brow at Asthorea. "Broody asshole? That's the thanks I get for saving your life? How many times has it been now?" I had to keep a baseline level of familiarity with the other Diamanti, aside from Riven. They needed to trust me to some extent. They needed to obey me on the battlefield, so I reminded myself to play the part.

She shrugged her shoulders, her features sharper in the low-light. "I call it like I see it."

I clenched my teeth and prayed to the Ascended that those drinks would arrive soon. I needed something to take the edge off, lest I rip the soul from my irritating companions and, in the process, commit unintentional suicide.

Forcing my gaze to Sylennia, as Davendrie had called her, I fought back my surprise. She was stunning. Beautiful in a way I'd rarely seen before, and she stared at me with an intensity that it made me uneasy. Beautiful and deadly. I could sense it on her right away, like recognizing like. "Who are you, and what do you want?" I asked.

She leaned back in her chair, and a sultry smile spread across her lips, dark hair curtaining her shoulders. "Riven mentioned you'd be here tonight. I've heard so much about the Moldizean death deity who's won all our battles, and I just had to see him for myself." She peered at Asthorea then. "He might be a broody asshole, but at least he's pretty."

Despite myself, my lips twitched. "Pretty?"

She cocked her brow and tilted her head to the side. "Maybe a little too pretty."

"One could say the same about you, Sylennia," I observed.

She threw her head back and laughed, the sound like a bell, and I realized that she must curate everything about herself. It was all meant to reel you in, and when it did, I would hate to see what happened next.

She leaned in, letting her leg, bare beneath her short, black dress, brush against mine. I resisted the urge to curl my lips back and snarl at her. "Oh, come now, I've been told I'm just the right amount of pretty."

Riven arrived then, saving her from my temper as he set the pitcher on the table along with the glasses. Dark magic swirled around his finger before he launched a small swatch of it at Sylennia's hands. It struck her golden-tanned skin, and she sucked in a breath, rubbing it and glaring at him. "Ouch."

Riven grinned at her. "Don't play with your food," he admonished. He waved over one of the half-naked servers to ask for a fifth glass. "Glad you could join us, Sylennia."

"Why did you invite her again?" Davendrie asked, clearly annoyed as he poured himself a drink from the pitcher and took a sip.

"You're just bitter that she shut you down last time she came into town," Asthorea said, following suit and getting herself a drink. Davendrie scowled, looking like he might take her mind apart for daring to mention that, but he restrained himself.

I came next, pouring myself a drink before passing the pitcher to Sylennia. She retrieved a glass from the servant-caste deity and beamed. "So, tell me all about Perenelle. I heard it was a complete and utter victory, full surrender, and full access to all their resources."

They obliged her, recounting every, single detail, while Riven listened and smiled with pleasure. I downed my drink faster with each word they spoke. Every moment I relived was another opportunity for renewed self-loathing, and more time to contemplate everything Madwyn had forced me to do that day.

Riven slapped his palm on the table then, and I could see the red creeping up his neck, the flush of drunkenness. "We're going to win this war. With Gabryel gone, we're going to win and free our people. We'll have a place where we can live without shame or supplication. For once, we're going to call the shots." I listened to the impassioned speech, and I could feel the rest of them nodding, and for the thousandth time, I wished I could go back in time and throttle Gabryel and the rest of the Peacekeeper's council for its stupidity. For its short-sightedness.

It made no sense to keep the Nefarals chained like animals. Especially not for so long after the war, let alone chipping the Altruists. They'd sown the seeds of this rebellion, and now they'd reap it.

A raucous cheer roared behind us, and I turned as a door to the outside rolled up along the back wall. A small patio sat just beyond it, adorned with large boards painted with bull's-eyes. Knives lined the brick walls of the entire thing, suspended by some unseen magic and waiting for someone to grab them. I saw Asthorea grin. "Want to play a round?" she asked us, excitement gleaming in her eyes.

"Let's do it," Riven replied, sucking down the rest of his drink and slamming it on the table. He stood on the chair as Davendrie, and Asthorea rose too, the crowd of deities cheering for one of their fearless leaders.

His voice rose above all the singing, shouting, fighting, and fucking. "Who thinks they can beat the Diamanti in a game of skill? We'll take all challengers! The winner gets a free round of —" he raised his brows at the half-naked servant deities, male and female. "Whatever your pleasure might be, on me!" Shouts of approval rang out, and a crowd of deities followed them out the door. Only Sylennia and I remained.

"What, you don't want to play?" she asked, peering at me over the rim of her glass.

Looking her dead in the eye, I said, "I don't play with knives. I kill with them."

She chuckled, undeterred, as she scooted closer and placed her slim hand on my thigh. I tensed in reaction.

"What are you doing?" I asked through gritted teeth, unsure what signal I'd sent that made her think I wanted her to touch me.

"Play along, will you? We don't have much time."

I stiffened further, staring at her as I tried to read her. "Time for what?"

"You need to relax. I need you to pretend that me touching your leg isn't the most distasteful thing that's ever happened to you or else this ruse won't work, and I need to talk to you."

Curiosity piqued, I forced my body to relax, to turn toward her. I placed my elbow on the table and leaned closer. I let my eyes grow hooded, and she smiled in approval. "Much better."

"Whatever you have to say to me, do it fast."

Shadows trailed over her fingers as she took her other hand and ran a dark-polished nail down my forearm. Right where the binding tattoo inked my skin. I knew she couldn't see it, so I stared at her, my expression giving away nothing.

"Is it true? That you're bound to Madwyn? That you don't serve her willingly?" Her eyes looked up into mine and I could see that gaze vibrate with intensity.

I paused, debating what to say next. Was this some kind of test? "What makes you say that?" More shadows spilled from her fingertips, giving me an idea of how she might have accessed that information. Taking a guess, I said, "I don't think you're supposed to spy on your queen."

Sylennia's jaw clenched, her eyes hardening before returning to the coyness she'd manufactured for this conversation. "I'm not supposed to do a lot of things, and yet, here we are." She trailed her fingers further up my thigh, and I narrowed my eyes at her in warning. She chuckled, fingertips stopping their perusal as she leaned closer to my ear. "And she's not my queen. She was my friend once, but then she overthrew the government and didn't give me much choice. My options were to serve her or die in prison, so I did what I had to do to survive, just like you did, from what I hear."

I clenched my teeth, biting down the retort that sprang up. My bargain with Madwyn didn't serve my interests. I'd have died happily before serving her, but I couldn't condemn Bekka to that fate, nor Caden, Deklan, and Remi. Instead of reacting, I kept my face blank, betraying none of my thoughts. "Get to the point, shadow spy."

"I've been in Quindale for three months. Riven tasked me with running our shadow spies, but something's wrong there. Something's wrong in all the conquered realms. Riven brought me back here to monitor things for a while. He's concerned as well." She stared straight through me then, her eyes haunted. "Ever since we took away the governor chips, things are getting worse. Some of the deities who had them are losing it. It's like—" She paused, as though trying to put a finger on it, her palm still resting on my thigh. "It's like they can't control themselves, their emotions, or their gifts. I've made eighteen arrests in just the last three weeks. They all ended up bashing their own heads in while they awaited trial in prison."

I raised my brows in surprise, unable to hide my shock. I thought about the amount of effort it would take to do that. A deity would have to slam their head into a wall for days to accomplish it. A chill crawled down my spine. "Why would they do that?"

"I have no idea," she said, shaking her head. "And when I try to investigate or get our healers involved, Madwyn gets angry. She insists nothing is wrong and that it's just a means of rebellion. She's in denial. But if we don't figure out what's happening, I'm worried it will only get worse."

I flexed my jaw, my teeth clenching. "Why are you telling me about it? If I'm bound to Madwyn, then how do you know I'm not required to tell her about this conversation?"

She leveled a serious look at me. "Are you going to?"

I hesitated, waiting for her to look away. She'd been rash to approach me. She didn't know me at all and had no clue where my allegiances might lie, and yet she'd confided in me. A risk I found insane, reckless in the extreme. Her eyes never left mine, and I was impressed despite myself.

At last, I relented. "No."

"Then my sources are right. I've heard she gives you a long leash. She wants you to join her willingly."

I resisted the urge to scoff. She'd given up any chance of that happening when she imprisoned Bekka, Caden, and Deklan, and kidnapped my little sister. But rather than elaborate, I asked, "So, you've been spying on me too, then?"

She shrugged, the picture of flirtatious nonchalance to any outsider. "I look into anyone I might count as an ally, should I need it, and I have the sense I'm going to. Riven's leeway will only extend so far. He won't go against his sister, not fully."

Her gaze landed on mine again, as though looking for my input. Rather than respond, I let the silence linger between us. After a long beat, she filled it. "Look, Bicaidia is my home. A lot of the deities who live here are my friends. I'm Riven's spymaster. It's my job to protect them, even from themselves." Her eyes darted to the patio over her left shoulder, and her expression softened at whatever she saw there. I took a chance, glancing in that direction too, and found it. Riven. He laughed, throwing knives, and hitting the bullseye three shots in a row. I filed that apparent soft spot away for future use.

"Again, what do you expect me to do?" I asked.

She glanced up at me and trailed her hand down my arm again, threading her fingers through mine. I felt a smooth, small orb pressed between our palms. "She sends you to Moldize, right? To gather more soldiers, and to keep your parents in line?" I looked down at her hand and gave her a slight nod. "Take this, and give it to your mother, the lady of Moldize. I hear she's a talented science deity, so she should know what to do with it."

"What is it?" I asked, and her eyes turned earnest.

"Everything I know about what's happening. All the data I could gather without getting discovered. You need to give it to her, and soon."

I dipped my head in acknowledgment. "I'll consider it."

"No, you need to do it," she insisted, and a frantic look crossed her features before she could school them again. "We don't have much time. You can't say no."

I arched my brow. "Can't I? How do I know this isn't some trick? How do I know you won't betray me? I'm not as quick to trust a stranger as you are."

"You want me to prove I'm not lying?"

I shrugged, a wicked grin sliding over my lips, keeping up the ruse. "It's the only way I'll consider doing what you've asked."

She ran her tongue over her teeth, as though in thought, then her eyes snapped to mine. "I've met your sister, you know. She's a sweet little thing."

Everything in me went cold and a thread of magic seeped from the tips of my fingers in warning. "Are you threat—"

Her hand tightened on mine, and she shook her head. "No. I'll take you to see her. Tonight, if you agree to do what I've asked. But we leave right now, before the others decide it's time for the celebration to end."

She jerked her head toward the outdoor patio, where a cheer of raucous laughter sounded. When I followed her lead, I saw a knife sticking out of Davendrie's thigh, and everyone roaring with hilarity as they shouted and pointed. My lips twitched too, disappointed that I hadn't been the one to lodge it there.

Not one to be ashamed, Davendrie shouted, "Is that all you've got?!" Before he laughed with surrounding the crowd.

"I only wish that hit him a bit higher. Perhaps in a more sensitive area," Sylennia observed, and a low chuckle rolled out of me without my permission. I couldn't help but agree.

Then I grew serious again. "You'll really take me to see her?"

"Have you been forbidden to go?"

I shook my head. "Madwyn keeps moving her. She hasn't forbidden it, but she makes it hard for me to find her. It's like it's some kind of game for her."

"Then, you have my word. I'll take you to her tonight," Sylennia said. "Now, let's go."

I considered her offer, but already knew what I'd say. She found a weak spot, something I wanted enough to take the risk she presented to me. I needed to shed the darkness that had enveloped me these last months, and seeing Lilja would remind me why I fought and obeyed. She knew the real me and would center me in that knowledge. It didn't hurt that I'd get to make sure she remained unharmed too.

Knowing she had me, Sylennia pushed up from her chair, keeping her hand locked in my own, the orb still fitted snugly between our palms. I rose as well, and we started for the door.

"Arrick, Sylennia! Where are you two going?" Riven shouted, Asthorea and Davendrie stopped to stare as well, the knife still protruding from the latter's leg.

Asthorea winked at us, grinning as she gripped the knife and ripped it out. Davendrie let out a stream of curses, which resulted in more laughter. Riven roared with it too, and his eyes went even brighter with a different kind of amusement when he saw our clasped hands.

"Oh, I see. Have fun, you two," he shouted after us. "It's about time you enjoy some of what we have to offer, Arrick." I could still hear them laughing when we reached the door, letting it slam shut behind us.

We arrived back at the palace minutes later, and Sylennia didn't let go of my hand as she led me up the stairs to her chambers. For all the world, we looked like lovers, stealing a private moment. I hated the ruse, but I couldn't see a better way to provide the cover we needed to avoid any prying questions. I would do whatever I needed to do to see my sister again. To have one moment of warmth and light. One moment with someone who reminded me I wasn't a monster.

I kept that thought in mind as we climbed a few flights of stairs and stepped into an internal hallway not too far from my own. The rooms on Sylennia's wing of the palace also overlooked the river, a sign of status within our army.

After passing about a dozen doors, she reached the one she sought. She pressed her hand against the center and sent a pulse of shadow magic from her free palm. The lock opened, and she turned, grinning at me as she pressed her back into the door.

Three deities, lower-ranking officers in Madwyn's army, who I knew without asking would be on the other side of the hall in less elaborate quarters, passed us. They eyed Sylennia and me, offering us approving grins as she grasped the front of my shirt in her fist and tugged me inside.

I let her drag me in, shutting the door behind me with my foot. Once closed within her room, she released my shirt and spun, sauntering to the balcony, and drawing the thick, forest-green curtains. The thin straps of her silk dress slid down her arms with the motion, and I wondered if I'd made a mistake following her there.

"You never know who might be watching," she tossed over her bare shoulder.

But she turned then, sliding the straps back into place as I watched her transform from a flirtatious goddess looking for a night of pleasure into the shadow spy she claimed to be. Illusions were her trade, and apparently, she had mastered them.

"Your sister," she said, her face deliberate and serious. "You're right. Madwyn moves her around every couple of nights, but I managed to locate her earlier this evening before I left to meet you at the lounge."

"That's what we're calling whorehouses now? Lounges?"

She chuckled, the sound darkly amused. "The Nefarals are in charge now. What would you expect?"

"Some modicum of self-restraint would be nice."

"You're funny, you know that?"

"Only funny? I've been told I'm hilarious."

"Right," she said, lips quirking up just before shadows exploded around her. Shadow magic was one of the few powers the sensors deployed throughout the Twelve Realms couldn't track. That was the main reason our royals had chosen them as spies. They also tended toward inordinate beauty, a trait Sylennia embodied. That beauty had a way of granting them access to all kinds of situations. Add to that, most of the shadow spies I knew had mastered the art of seduction.

She stepped forward, getting closer as the darkness of her power folded in around us. And then, without a word, we soared through the shadows, wind whipping around me. The translocation felt more abrupt and tumultuous than my magic. Faster and more urgent. A few seconds later, we appeared in a room. Smaller than mine, girlish, lavish, and comfortable. I stared at the four-poster bed, and the slight form sleeping under a light purple bedspread.

Breath catching in my throat, I stepped out of the faint veil of Sylennia's magic and moved closer, keeping my footsteps silent. As I drew nearer, I saw that Sylennia had told me the truth. It was Lilja, and relief flowed through me at the sight of her.

I dropped my hip onto the mattress and tried not to disturb her. Seeing her, peaceful and asleep, after everything she'd witnessed that day, gave me some small hope that maybe one of us could get out of this with our soul unscathed.

I glanced back at Sylennia, shadows gathering darker around her. "Thank you," I whispered.

She inclined her head. Then, as she faded away, sinking into the shadows, I said, "I'll give this to my mother when I go to Moldize next. You have my word." I slid the orb she'd let me keep out of my pocket and held it out so she could see it.

A smile bloomed over her still-visible lips. "See, I knew you'd be a useful ally. I'll return in an hour to retrieve you." And with that, she vanished. I didn't bother to say that I had every intention of making her a useful ally as well. All in good time, I thought, shifting my focus back on my sister. I watched as she slept, her pale face sprinkled with freckles. She looked angelic. A small, eternal flame burned at her side table, hovering inside a glass jar on her nightstand—a common nightlight for children in all thirteen realms.

"Lili," I whispered, brushing my hand through her untamed hair. She stirred, her eyes opening into slits just before they flung wide.

"Arrick?" She asked, her voice louder than I'd have liked. I pressed a single finger to my lips, and she stilled, quieting as she stared at me.

"You're here? You're really here?" she whispered, watching me as though I were an apparition.

I nodded, and I saw her lip wobble. Something cracked inside me as she sat up and launched herself into my chest. As she wrapped her arms around me, squeezing tightly, I held on to her too, breathing in the scent of home.

13
MEMORIES
REMI

Remi felt clean for the first time in ages as she left the isolation of her prison cell with Riven leading the way and a massive, milk-white demon in tow. She could feel the ghost of its blackened sword at her back and took care not to make any sudden moves. She didn't want to give it a reason to nick her with the pointy end of the poisoned blade, accidentally or otherwise.

As they wound their way around the cell block, she glared daggers at the death god's neck, imagining all the terrible things she'd like to do to him and his sister. She found, as always, that these dark machinations brought her a tiny sliver of joy.

Despite her hatred for him, her belly fluttered with butterflies because she would get to see both Ellarah and Thayne tonight. Excitement at the prospect of being with two deities she cared about and who cared about her made her feel giddy in spite of her situation.

Even knowing that she'd have to lie to Ellarah through her teeth, she couldn't help but feel relieved. She'd gotten out of that cell and would have the chance to talk to someone other than herself or Not-Bekka.

As they walked, she stared at the dull, adobe floor of the prison, her sandals clicking on the stone. Her loose-fitted forest green trousers flowed around her legs and a snug, blank tank top fell just above her navel. Riven had given her golden cuff bracelets to hide the runes tattooed there, beautifully detailed things that would look like a fashion statement rather than the deception they were. She looked like her old self once more, if one ignored the weight loss and the dark rings embedded in a semi-permanent circle under her eyes.

After a few moments, they passed a break in the thick metal doors and took a right. A few steps later, they stopped at another cell. *This has to be Thayne's room*, she thought, staring at the metallic, reinforced entryway. Her pulse quickened with anticipation and anxiety. What would it be like to see him after so long? Would he be as damaged as she was? As torn up with invisible wounds that no one else could see? She hoped not, doing her best to stand up straighter and square her shoulders. She might feel those things on the inside, but she'd be damned if she let anyone see them.

Riven grasped the handle, pulling out a large ring of keys. *Sometimes, the old ways are the best ways,* Remi thought, remembering her grandfather. Harder to tamper with or trick than magic, Remi watched the intricate teeth of the key as it slid home. A moment later, the locking mechanism sprang free, and he offered her a curt, "Wait here," before he slipped inside and left her with her demon guard.

Unfortunately for her, he'd never leave her unattended. The demon exhaled and stepped to her side, its rank, sulfuric breath making her cringe as it stared at her. The way the creature eyed her made her feel like its next meal. Probably not far off the mark, she knew. But then, did demons eat deities? Surely not.

At last, the door clicked open and Riven appeared. Curiosity had her tearing her gaze away from the terrifying demon and back to her true captor. A second, larger god walked through the door and Remi's eyes locked onto her husband's, her heart seizing in her chest. All fear and anxiety fled her, and she rushed forward to meet him. Within seconds, she crashed into his large, firm body.

His arms wound around her waist, and she slid her hands up to his neck, her fingers twining into his hair. She could feel him hesitate just before he wrapped his fists into the fabric of her shirt, gripping it as though he didn't want to let go. She understood the sentiment.

He smelled like his normal blend of fresh rain and petrichor, and she breathed him in, letting the last two months of isolation slip away. She'd seen him die so many times in her nightmares that just having him there, being able to touch him, felt overwhelming. It felt like coming home.

He buried his face into her neck and breathed her in as though she were his anchor. She understood the feeling as he pressed a kiss to the sensitive spot between her neck and collarbone, making everything inside of her shutter. "I've missed you so fucking much, Remi."

Remi opened her mouth to reply, his words a caress on her ragged nerves, a salve that she wanted to bathe in. But before they could say or do more, Riven cleared his throat. "That's enough. Let's go."

Without ceremony, he turned and walked down the hall, clearly expecting them to follow. Remi pulled away from Thayne and looked into his eyes for one more moment before she turned to follow. In that single unguarded second, Remi could see the pain that etched its way through Thayne, and she knew without having to say a word that he hadn't had it easy, either.

She wanted to talk to him, to press her cheek into his powerful chest, and let him comfort her, to let them both comfort each other. But she knew Riven would never allow it, and deep down, neither would she. She couldn't give in to the weakness, at least not yet. She had to stay strong if she had any chance of surviving this hell with her mind intact.

So, instead, they moved through the familiar palace halls and grand ballrooms, silent as specters. She saw gods and demons milling around, and every so often, the raucous shouts of a celebration rang out.

She inhaled, smelling god's-ale, god's-liquor, and roasting meat. Her mouth watered in response. Remi would kill for just one bite of something that didn't resemble slop or bread, or one sip of something other than stale, tepid water. Chancing a glance at her husband, Remi saw him watching her, eyes bright with a different hunger.

Her cheeks flushed as they strode past the grand dining hall and toward the courtyard where the beginning of the end had started. Breaking his stare, she closed her eyes and let the fresh air bathe over her clean skin. The warm, floral scents of the open courtyard blended with the savory smells of the palace kitchens and made her feel weak-kneed with appreciation. She tried not to think about the fact that this moment wouldn't last. Sooner than she'd like, she'd be back in that Ascended-forsaken cell, alone with her tormented thoughts and hallucinations.

The rounded arches and pillars breezed past them as they reached a grand staircase that led to Ellarah's chambers. The new ones her friend had gotten after Remi had incinerated her old one during her first week in Bicaidia.

She hurried up the steps behind Riven, sad to leave behind the fresh air, but she could feel Thayne's steady presence behind her and felt bolstered.

Maybe, just maybe, they'd get a moment alone together. A second to be together, but she quashed that hope as quickly as it rose. She knew better. There would be no reprieve from her loneliness. At least, nothing aside from the dinner she promised to Riven. She shouldn't get her hopes up, she knew, pressing her fingers to the place Thayne had kissed on her neck. It tingled beneath her fingertips, and she closed her eyes for a brief moment to savor it.

Finally, they reached the rough-hewn, wooden door, an iron knocker anchored at eye level. Riven turned to face them and gave them what she assumed must be his best warning glare. "Don't forget about our bargain, and don't do anything stupid. Remember, your time down there could always get worse."

The threat hung in the air like poison before he turned and grasped the metal knocker, tapping it three times on the door. They waited until a soft, "Come in," sounded from inside.

Ellarah's voice, Remi registered, and unexpected relief swept through her. Of course, she knew Ellarah was awake and in recovery, but hearing it for herself lifted a tremendous weight from her shoulders as Riven opened the door and gestured for them to enter.

They strode inside, and Remi's eyes locked onto her friend. She sat on the four-post bed, propped up by an array of fluffy pillows, her legs tucked under a soft-knit blanket. Her face looked paler than usual, and her cheeks drawn, as her lovely golden eyes lit up when they landed on the three of them.

"Remi, Thayne!" she said, her excited voice raspier than usual. "You came! I've missed you guys so much. Riven has been way too protective of me, but you know how he gets. He wants me to rest after the accident."

She rolled her eyes in that familiar, teasing way, and Remi had to fight to keep the tears from falling.

Remi swallowed the lump in her throat. "Hey," she croaked, blinking a few times to keep her eyes clear. "It's so good to see you awake. We've been so ... worried about you," she finished, choosing her words carefully. She hoped that Riven didn't notice their awkward cadence.

"Yeah, I know. I can't believe what happened! Was it crazy? Tell me it was crazy, because—" she blew a raspberry. "I don't remember a thing about it."

Thayne and Remi exchanged an uncertain glance before Riven cut in. "None of us could believe it when the portal arch malfunctioned. We're lucky that no one else got harmed in the explosion."

So that's how he'd tricked her, Remi thought darkly. She wished she could tell her friend the truth. She hated seeing her so cheerful, so oblivious to the direness of their situation. And as for Ellarah? She was a prisoner, too. She might not know it, and Riven could deny it all he wanted, but if Ellarah knew the truth, she would never stick around.

Thayne's voice seemed as stilted as her own when he said, "He's right. We got lucky, though I wish you'd made it out unharmed too." He strode over to the bed, and even with all the months he'd spent in a cell, he still carried that powerful self-confidence that drew her to him. He sat on the edge of the bed and pulled Ellarah's hand into his, looking down at it with a tenderness that made Remi's heart squeeze. "I'm sorry for what happened to you, Ellarah. Remi and me—we didn't expect it to go that way."

Remi could feel the sincerity of his words as Riven stiffened beside her. He eyed Thayne with a predatory glare, but they both ignored him. Understanding the double meaning behind his words, Remi walked around

Thayne and sat on Ellarah's other side. She pulled the blanket onto her own lap and scooted closer to her friend, soaking in the nearness of another person. A real person.

"You couldn't have known. I don't blame you for this," Ellarah said, shaking her head as Remi settled beside her. "And look at me, I'm fine … or at least, I'm on my way to fine." Remi's gaze locked with Thayne's, his handsome, angular face strained with emotion, and she squeezed her eyes shut, leaning her head on Ellarah's shoulder, trying not to let the guilt she felt show.

But before she or Thayne could say anything else, Ellarah continued, "I made Riven promise to bring lunch for us." She rolled her eyes. "He thinks I'm too fragile for long visits, but I told him I at least wanted to share a meal with my friends."

Remi's mouth watered and she tried to tamp down the eagerness she felt at the prospect of a full meal. She lifted her head then, eyes scanning the room, taking it in for the first time. To the right of Ellarah's bed stood an oversized set of glass, double doors, and a massive, covered balcony. The arches and pillars broke up the stunning view of the red mountains beyond.

In the middle of the terracotta tiled room sat a plush, teal rug with a small table and four chairs in the center of it. The table had four place settings, a bottle of sweet wine, and a jug of water on its surface. Struggling to tamp down her excitement, she turned to her friend and gathered her other hand into her lap. "That sounds great. Are you sure you're up to it?"

"Of course I am!" Ellarah said, shaking her head like they were crazy to suggest otherwise. "Riv, where's the food, anyway? We made the arrangements hours ago. Can you go check on it? Please?"

Riven straightened, and Remi could almost see the wheels turning in his mind. Then he said, "I'm not sure that's such a good idea. I don't want to leave you alone in here—"

She looked at him like he'd lost his mind. "I'm not alone. Thayne and Remi are here. They'll keep an eye on me." She beamed then, looking between the three of them. Seeing her like this, so happy to have the gang back together, made Remi's chest ache. Deep down, she wished Riven's version of events was the truth. The world would be a lot less complicated and terrifying if it was.

Still hesitating, Riven looked from Ellarah to Thayne and then to Remi, apparently trying to figure a way out of doing what Ellarah asked him without looking suspicious as fuck. A few more seconds and he looked resigned. "OK, I'll be back in just a few minutes."

He turned on his heel, pulling the door open and striding through it. Then he gave Thayne and Remi one last warning look before he shut it behind him. Alone in the room, Ellarah sighed in relief, her whole body seeming to relax.

"Everything OK? Remi asked, picking up on the change in their friend's mood.

Ellarah's expression turned serious, all traces of cheer vanishing. "I don't know, is it?" She scrutinized them both then, as though trying to read every single line of their expressions.

Thayne's sharp cheekbones and onyx eyes betrayed nothing. and Remi did her best to compose her features too. At last, Thayne asked, "What do you mean? Why wouldn't it be?"

Ellarah exhaled, an irritated sound slipping through her lips, and narrowed her eyes. "Look, we don't have much time to dance around whatever the hell is going on here. He'll be back any second and if there's something you need to tell me, you'd better do it, and quick too. You have no idea how much convincing it took for me to get you guys here. Nothing makes sense anymore." Remi stopped breathing, hope blooming in her chest without her permission.

Thayne cleared his throat and shook his head, locking eyes with Remi for a moment before refocusing his attention on Ellarah. "What do you mean? What do you think is going on?"

Ellarah crossed her arms over her chest, a look of utter confusion sweeping over her. "What in the Twelve Hells is that supposed to mean? I don't know what's going on. That's why I'm asking you guys." She paused, looking between them again, head whipping in time with her glossy hair.

"It's not that—" Remi said, and sucked in a pained breath, an electric current shooting through her head. She pressed a palm to her brow and tried to steady her breathing. She'd come much too close to breaking her binding with Riven. The mind-numbing jolt was a warning, lest she go too far. She breathed through it before continuing, "I'm sorry Ellarah, but there's nothing to tell."

Ellarah's mouth dropped open, going slack for a minute before she snapped it shut again. "Why is everyone lying to me? First, Riven lies to me and now you both do too? Thayne," she said, turning her scowl on him. "I've always trusted you, always told you the truth whether you wanted me to or not, and this is how you repay me?"

Thayne's jaw ticked and she could see him swallowing his words. "We can't, Ellarah."

"Why?"

"Because there's nothing to tell," he said, trying to smile at her, but it looked forced as hell.

Ellarah huffed in frustration. "I was so damned excited to see you two today and finally get some semblance of truth, and yet, here we are." With that, she tossed the blanket from her legs and scrambled off the foot of the bed, avoiding both Remi and Thayne. "What is so bad that you can't even talk to me about it? I'm not that damn fragile, and I'm tired of everyone treating me like I'm made of glass. Because guess what, I'm not. I'm a middle-caste energy goddess for Ascended-sake, not some frail weakling! So, just tell me, I can take it."

Remi had to bite her tongue to keep from blurting out everything she wanted to say. She wanted to apologize, explain, and get Ellarah out of that bedroom and away from Madwyn. Riven too, for that matter. Because whether he loved her or not, he wasn't good for her. He was lying to her face and keeping her close to the deity who'd stabbed her in cold blood.

When she and Thayne both held their silence, Ellarah stepped back to the foot of the bed and leaned forward, resting her hands on it. Remi could see the instant that realization hit her face.

"Oh, I see. You can't tell me," she said, a hesitant guess at first, and though neither Remi nor Thayne reacted, she continued as connections seemed to click in her mind, "Twelve Hells, you really can't tell me. What happened?" She chewed on a lip, calculating, and then shook her head. "Are you guys OK? Are you ..." She peered around the bed, checking the door. "Safe?"

Remi felt the blood drain from her face. She could also feel a small tingle of hope dancing in her mind. At last, she moved from the bed to join Ellarah at the foot of it. Remi rested her hands on her friend's shoulders, praying that what she said next wouldn't break the binding, only skirt the edges of it.

She'd had a shitty past few months, but that didn't mean she had a death wish. "You need to remember that night, Ellarah ... on your own." She widened her eyes to emphasize the importance of what she said.

Ellarah's tongue moved over her lips to wet them before she nodded, seeming to understand Remi's meaning. "I wish I could, Rem, but it's all small flashes and then utter blackness." She chewed on her lip, her eyes laced with concern before she leveled her gaze on Thayne.

Thayne shook his head at the question in Ellarah's eyes. "Remi's right. You have to remember. That's the only way you'll know. Though, say nothing to anyone about your suspicions, OK?"

Ellarah's brows wrinkled in confusion, her expression shifting to worry, and then resignation, before she nodded. "OK, I'll find a way. I don't know how, but I will. I swear it, and when I do, I'll come looking for you."

Remi smiled, the light of it reaching from her eyes to her very soul. "Good. We're counting on it." Remi couldn't know if Riven had used Davendri to pluck the memory from her mind, or if the injury had done the work for him. But if it was the latter, then they still stood a chance. "Remember, and ..." Remi pressed her finger to her lips, the universal gesture to keep her mouth shut.

And with that, they heard footsteps outside the door, followed by the knob turning. Before it opened, Remi kept that finger resting on her lips, staring at Ellarah, indicating that she wanted Ellarah to keep that promise between the three of them. Ellarah nodded, and Remi hugged her just before the door swung open. Her eyes locked onto Thayne's, and she could see emotion moving in his eyes too, and everything inside her heated with anticipation.

As Riven entered the room, an array of servants carrying trays of food following in his wake, Remi prayed to the Ascended that maybe Ellarah would remember. Then, if the stars aligned just right and she managed not to get caught, Ellarah might just be the one to save them all.

14
R☾TS
THAYNE

"How'd it go?" Pietyr asked when Thayne returned from his dinner with Ellarah and Remi. The demon had allowed him to keep the clean, new clothes, which was more than he could say for the rest of his cellmates. They all looked dirty and beyond disrepair, but it didn't matter because they had magic. They wouldn't be in that cell much longer, not if he could help it.

Thayne shrugged in response, heading toward his cot. He didn't tell them that holding Remi, pressing that kiss to her neck, had damn near broken him. Nor did he mention how badly he wanted to snuff Riven out of existence for not allowing them a single moment of peace together.

Instead, he strode over to his mattress while the four of them lay on their backs, hands behind their heads, staring at the ceiling. They all looked bored. They'd discovered Caden and Deklan had magic and had immediately started planning and practicing. Unfortunately, that couldn't fill an entire day stuck in a small cell with nothing else to do.

"Come on, Thayne. You've gotta give us something," Rackham said. "Did you get to eat real food? Something other than slop? I haven't had a proper meal since...Ascended, I don't even know anymore."

"Before we went into hiding with Emorie, after inauguration night?" Pietyr offered.

Rackham chuckled. "That sounds about right. But then I guess I'm sort of used to shitty food. It sucked in Mariandale too, what with all the hell and heaven collapsing into the mortal dimension. Hot fucking mess."

Pietyr laughed in response and Thayne couldn't help but smile, releasing some of the tension he'd held onto during the entire meal with Remi and Ellarah. While it had felt damn good to see them, it hadn't been easy. He would have given anything for just one unguarded moment with his wife, to anchor himself in the knowledge that he wanted her. Not Madwyn, but her.

Pietyr's voice pulled him from his thoughts. "Mariandale is a giant pit of despair. I still don't understand why you all stayed there and didn't just abandon it. But then, if I hadn't served my term there, I never would have met you or Emorie and joined The Rising."

"Yeah, but would that have been such a bad thing? It hasn't exactly worked out all that great for us," Rackham replied.

Thayne grinned despite himself, settling into his mattress and laying down. He braced an arm under his thin pillow and thought that truer words had never been spoken.

Before he could answer Rackham's question about the food, which had been fucking incredible, Caden asked, "What's Mariandale? And what do you mean, heaven and hell collapsed into the physical world?"

Deklan pointed at his brother. "What he said."

"It's pretty much as shitty as you would imagine," Rackham replied, before launching into the details of the phenomenon. When he finished, the brothers grew silent, contemplating it.

Then Deklan said, "We lived in a wasted hellhole our entire lives, and even if we had the option, we wouldn't have left either."

Rackham pointed at Deklan, not looking at him. "See, he gets it. That shit is home, and when it's your home, you don't have a choice. You don't just abandon it because things get fucked up. You try to make it better. And that's what we've been doing ever since it happened. We've been trying to fix it." He turned to look at Pietyr and Thayne then before he asked, "You two planning to abandon Bicaidia just because it's shitty now?"

"No," Thayne and Pietyr replied in unison.

"There you go," Rackham said, gesturing with his hands.

After a long pause, Caden broke the silence. "You know, Bekka fixed our world. If Arrick hadn't kidnapped her and brought her to Moldize, it wouldn't exist anymore."

Everyone went silent in surprise. The demigods never spoke about what happened in Moldize before they arrived in Bicaidia. Based on his observations, Thayne knew Caden and Deklan were warriors, but not much else.

Thayne asked, food inquiry forgotten as a weight settled in the room, "What happened in Moldize?" But he left out the question he really wanted to ask. How did Gabryel die there?

Caden sighed and rubbed his palm over his forehead as though he could wipe away a memory. He and Deklan shared a look from the space between their cots. At last, Deklan nodded, and Caden told them the entire story. They all listened in rapt attention as he explained who Arrick was to them, how he lived among the mortals for months at a time, bringing them food and supplies, doing his best to protect them while the world burned up around them.

They told them how he'd brought Bekka back to their mortal home-world, pretending she was his wife. And how it had shocked all of them to see him with a woman. He'd never taken an interest before, and it seemed like total bullshit, except it wasn't. Something happened between them, Caden explained, and they'd grown close since Arrick brought her into the fold.

Thayne already knew that. Arrick may have traded himself for all of them, but it would've taken an idiot not to see the real reason he'd done it. The way he'd looked at Bekka in Bicaidian hell. Like she was the only thing in the Twelve Realms that mattered, and like he'd cut out his soul to save her.

Unfortunately for the Moldizean, he probably had, Thayne thought, wondering for the thousandth time what was happening in the realms, and what Madwyn would do with two powerful death deities, as well as all of Bicaidia's resources at her disposal. None of the possibilities seemed good to him.

Caden continued their story. "She got trapped in Itoriah, with us humans, by accident. One of the malicious tribes we warred with off and on attacked us, and she ... disintegrated them with her power, and exposed herself to us as a deity."

"Damn," Rackham breathed. "How many?"

"Dozens," Deklan replied, voice cool as ice.

"Why would that trap her, though?" Pietyr asked, voicing the same question that had popped into Thayne's head.

Caden answered, "Because of the wards in Moldize. They didn't allow the gods to use magic in front of mortals. They didn't allow magic in the mortal realm at all. But somehow, Bekka could do it, and when she gave us proof of divinity, Arrick insisted the only way to get back home and save our world was to kill us all. She refused to do it, and we all found another way out instead. None of it would've worked without her, though." They all waited as Caden paused, and Thayne glanced in his direction. He could see the tightening on the demigod's face. Grief, worry, and concern traced every line.

"Bekka is a warrior at her core," Deklan said, as though he sensed his brother's hesitation. "If we can get her out of here, she'll defeat Madwyn and Riven, and the rest of the rebels. She won't stop until she does."

They all remained quiet, letting the demigods' words soak in, and then Thayne asked a question that weighed heavily on his mind. "What about Arrick? Do you think she can defeat him?"

Without skipping a beat, Caden said, "She won't need to, because we're going to free him."

A long silence swept through the room then, so quiet Thayne could hear his heart beating in his chest.

At last, Pietyr said what he knew they'd all been thinking, "Bindings are permanent. There is no saving him." He spoke with finality, but Thayne didn't miss the note of apology in his voice.

Deklan rolled onto his side in response, his eyes cold as he glared at Pietyr. "You better pray to your precious Ascended that you're wrong. Because there is no fucking way Bekka is going to leave him to Madwyn, and neither will we."

Deklan glared at all of them, daring any of them to refuse the challenge he tossed at them. Oddly, he and Caden could kick their asses any day of the week in their current condition. They might not be full deities, but they had magic and their full strength without the runes. The rest of them didn't.

At last, Rackham let out a long sigh. "Don't worry. We won't leave him here to rot, either."

Pietyr's bed cot rustled as he turned to glare at his friend. "Don't make promises you know you can't keep, Rackham."

"Come on, Pietyr," Rackham said. "He sacrificed his entire existence to Madwyn for us. The least we can do is to try to repay him."

All of them sat up then, seeming to sense the seriousness of the moment as their feet thudded on the stone ground. They stared at each other. It was on the tip of Thayne's tongue to argue, to tell Rackham that Arrick hadn't done a damn thing for them. He'd done it for Bekka, and maybe Caden and Deklan too, but not them. Only, did that matter? The result was the same. He'd brought them all into the bargain, too. He hadn't needed to do that, but he'd done it anyway.

Pietyr's jaw flexed as he considered. "Fine. I pay my debts. If there's a way to break a binding, we'll find it."

Deklan nodded, eyes locking onto Thayne's. "And you, Prince? Will you help?"

Thayne let out a long breath and shrugged his shoulders in resignation. "I suppose we owe him our lives. I'm in."

A pact made by five unlikely friends. One that Thayne wouldn't take lightly, no matter how simply they'd made it.

Then Rackham turned bright eyes on him. "Hey, you never told us about that food or what happened with Ellarah and Remi."

Thayne chuckled despite himself, thinking that Rackham had a one-track mind. With that settled, they all laid back on their cots as the lights went out at the same time they always did. Like clockwork. Thayne spent a long time describing each delicious morsel for them, and then he told them about Ellarah, and how she might be starting to remember inauguration night.

They all fell silent after that, contemplating what it might mean to have more magic at their disposal and an ally on the outside. However, he could sense that none of them dared to hope too much for that. They all knew Riven or Madwyn could snatch it away if Ellarah made the wrong move. Davendrie could pluck out any inconvenient memories, now that she'd healed enough to withstand his probing. If he hadn't already done just that.

And as the silence dragged on, he heard the heavy weight of their even breathing fill the room.

He closed his eyes, and the world went dark for just a few blessed moments before his tormented dreams started anew.

15

NIGHTMARES

THAYNE

Only they weren't like the dreams Madwyn had sent him into every night for months. Instead, damp air hit his face. Thayne blinked, looking around in surprise as his vision cleared and the world came into focus. He stood in a bathroom, but not just any bathroom. The one in his old royal suite at the Bicaidian palace. He could feel the dark, stone floor, cool and a little rough beneath his bare feet.

He heard a sound then, muffled beneath the noise of a running shower. Water streamed from overhead onto the pebbled floor and natural stone walls of the shower's enclosure. Uncertainty pulsed through him, and he moved closer to the opening in the wall.

He rested his hand on the edge of the entrance, bracing for whatever might come next. When his gaze landed on the source of that muffled sound, everything inside of him went still.

It was Madwyn. She sat on the pebbled floor, her clothes soaking wet, and her knees tucked to her chest. Her shoulders shook with racking sobs. Cool water sheeted down her blonde hair, long back then, and just how he remembered it on that day so many years ago. She shivered, her body shaking so hard it looked like she might break apart with it.

Then, he knew what this was and everything inside of him went rigid with it. A memory; one he hadn't thought about in years. He clenched his fists as he tried to steel himself against it, to fight through the visceral pain that day dredged up inside of him.

He wanted to close his eyes and turn away. To leave that room and never go back. But he couldn't do any of those things. She and Davendrie wouldn't let him. So instead, he watched Madwyn cry, her thin frame looking so damn fragile in that shower that his heart ached with the pain he knew she felt because he felt it too.

A moment later, he heard his own voice calling for her outside of the door. Then he heard the knocking, and he already knew what came next. Time seemed to slow as he opened the door, and he saw the male he'd been before Madwyn had shattered him into a million fucking pieces. He watched as the old him saw her, sitting there broken and in despair.

He rushed to her, dropping to his knees beside her in the cool spray, hand landing on her shoulder. Thayne touched her as though she were the most precious thing in the world to him. And as that day played out before him, he remembered a time when she'd been just that.

He heard himself ask, "Maddy, baby, what is it? What's wrong?"

Madwyn looked up at him, her long, dark lashes spiky with water, her normally vivid blue eyes dull and gray. She blinked them, and he watched her tears mix with the water. She never cried. He remembered thinking that at the time. He'd never seen her cry before. "I'm sorry. I'm so sorry. I tried. I tried. I tr—" She broke off, moved her arm, and brushed her hand through the water, sweeping it over the stones. She held it up to show him, and that was when he'd realized what had gone wrong.

Blood coated her fingers. Thin and light, but more of it than should have been there, given the hard flow of the shower above them. He stared down at her hand, and that same sick feeling that had washed over him that day hit him just as hard.

He could feel his eyes burning as the old him, the one that had loved Madwyn more than anything, wrapped his arms around her. Cool water washed over them both as he pulled her onto his lap and let her cry into his chest.

They stayed like that for a long time, Thayne adjusting the water to a warmer temperature after he'd wrapped his arms around her. Then, when her shoulders had stopped shaking, and the sobs had given way to a quiet stillness, he helped her to her feet. She stood like a ghost, eyes unseeing as he peeled off her clothes, took the soft sponge from the stone ledge at the far end of the shower, and poured her lavender-scented soap onto it. She stood, stone-faced and still as a statue as he washed her clean, blood still trickling between her thighs as he went. Then he turned off the water and grabbed a soft, thick towel. He wrapped it around her, gathered her into his arms, and carried her out of the bathroom.

Something cracked inside of him at the memory, and he tried to fight back the emotion. Because that was the day that Madwyn had lost their child. It had been over five years since it had happened, and yet, the wound still felt so damn fresh. He pressed his fists to his eyes to stem the flow of emotion reliving that moment dredged up inside of him.

He had never forgotten how it felt when she'd told him she was pregnant. There had been so much joy, so much hope and expectation for their futures, and for the future of their son. They hadn't told anyone. It had been too early, but it had been a boy. Something tightened in Thayne's throat as that memory hit him, and as he saw through the vision just how broken Madwyn had looked. How damned fragile. Nothing like the goddess he knew now. He tried to swallow as his eyes burned but found that he couldn't.

Then blackness surrounded him, and he spun, trying to get his bearings. Wanting the fucking dreams to end. He didn't want to remember how things had been before. He didn't want to think about how much he'd loved the person who'd destroyed everything he cared about, who'd destroyed him.

He yelled, "Get the fuck out of my head! You bitch!" But even his words came out strained, as though he were fighting back tears. It had been so long since he'd thought about his son, their son. Pregnancies within the immortal realm were difficult enough and risky as hell. It took some couples centuries before they had a successful union. Humans could breed like rabbits, something he'd often envied them for, but deities couldn't.

Sure, some had luck or good genes, but most? They had difficulties, and even though he'd known that ... even though they'd both known that, that loss had broken them. It had been the beginning of the end of their relationship. A slow death that had taken years, and only the betrothal to Remi had finally ended it.

His hands balled into fists at his side, and he could feel his magic flare right before the runes suppressed it. Anger, resentment, and despair boiled like poison inside of him as Madwyn appeared. She stood before him, but it wasn't the Maddy he'd known back then. It was the one he knew in the present world. The one who'd betrayed and ruined him. The one who had killed his family for power and a chance to control their world.

He glared at her, jaw clenched so hard he thought his teeth might crack from the pressure, but her gaze never wavered from his face. No trace of humor, laughter, or love danced in her eyes, just emptiness.

"Why are you doing this? Why are you in my head? And why did you show me that?" he asked through those gritted teeth.

She let the silence hang for a while, then said, eyes never leaving his, "Because you're not allowed to hate me, Thayne. I won't let you."

"You don't have a say in that," Thayne replied, his voice dangerous and low, anger boiling inside him.

"You loved me once," she replied, turning her head to look at something beyond him. He followed her eyes and saw nothing but the pure blackness. Davendri must have created a bridge for them, a way to speak mind-to-mind. As for what she could see on her end of the bridge? He had no idea. She let out a long sigh, rubbing her arms as she retrained her attention on him. "And no matter how angry I am at you, or you are at me, I won't let you forget that."

"Angry with you? You think I'm just angry with you?" He prowled forward, closing the short distance between them, and fixed a menacing stare on her. "Anger doesn't even begin to cover it! You killed my parents and conquered my kingdom, and you played me for a fool to do it! You used my trust and how I felt about you and you betrayed me!"

Her demeanor shifted then, eyes flashing with rage. "And you didn't betray me? You left me! After that day, you abandoned me!" She threw her arms wide as though to encompass the loss she'd just forced him to relive. "You started taking your assignments with the shadow spies, and you abandoned me. You hunted those traffickers in Valeria, knowing damn well you might come home with a new betrothed, and when you did? You didn't even think twice about tossing me to the side for that Valerian bitch, even after everything we'd gone through together. You broke me. Ripped me apart, burned everything inside of me that mattered. I just returned the favor."

"So, this is about me? You did all of this to get back at me?" he yelled, the utter disbelief of it wrapping around him as he tried to process what she'd said. Revenge? Against him? Everything she'd done? Blowing apart the Twelve Realms? No, it didn't make sense. There had to be more to it than that. She couldn't be that insane.

She shrugged. "No, I did it because it needed to be done. We couldn't keep living that way forever. But I'll tell you what, you made it a hell of a lot easier to betray you when you betrayed me first." She shook her head, hair swaying as she considered her next words. "And I thought I could do it and not look back."

He glared at her, not missing the fact that she couldn't seem to leave him the fuck alone with his guilt and his shame. She had to keep adding to it. "And how'd that work out for you?"

"It's harder than I expected," she admitted, hesitating as she ran her tongue along her lips. She wrapped her arms around herself again, and for the first time in a long time, she looked young. Almost vulnerable. "I hated you for so long. But now—" she trailed off as she turned back to look into his eyes once more. "Now, you're not allowed to hate me because even though you think you do, I know you don't."

"You don't know a damn thing."

"But I do, Thayne," she said, ignoring the first part of what he said. "I know you better than you know yourself. You've just forgotten that."

His eyes flung open then, consciousness rushing to his mind, as though he'd been trying to wake for a long time. He shot up from his bed, gasping for air like he was choking for it. His hands clenched into fists, gripping the threadbare sheets. She'd released him from the bridge, from the dream she'd shown him, and yet that bone-deep sadness still clung to him. That despair mixed with his anger, and it weighed heavier on him than he cared to admit.

He turned his head and looked out the window. It was still dark outside, and he laid back on his mattress, head resting on the cot. He stared up at the ceiling, thinking about everything she'd said.

After a long moment, he decided that she was wrong. She really didn't know a damn thing because he hated her more than he ever had before. And when he got out of that cell, he would make her pay for everything she'd done to him and the people he loved.

16

ORDERS

ARRICK

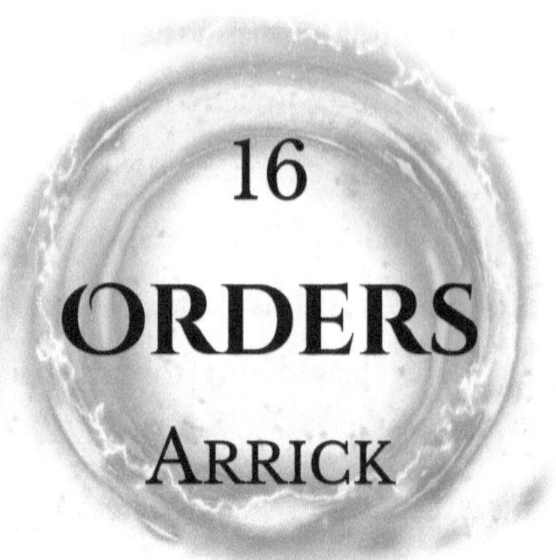

"**G**ood, now pivot. Don't forget your footwork," I said to the young pestilence goddess who swung her dull practice sword up to deflect a downward blow from her opponent.

The pair stopped sparring, and she nodded at me in response, her face flushed, dark hair tied in a high ponytail. I strode over to her and demonstrated the right steps. She watched me with keen eyes as I moved, and then I gestured for her to try again. She did, and I nodded in approval at the improvement. "Much better. Keep practicing," I said, stepping away and surveying the full range of the training grounds.

The progress of our new and seasoned warriors impressed me. Their weapons' mastery had improved and so had their hand-to-hand combat skills. They moved as a unit and obeyed orders without question during drills.

It helped that after Madwyn had released the intel on the governor chips in Perenelle, Quindale, and Crescendia, she'd recruited large numbers of deities to her side. So, she had a formidable force at her disposal with

"

all kinds of gifts to wield, should it come to an all-out war against the remaining realms. Something we'd somehow managed to avoid so far.

We also learned that a small contingent of war deities had survived our conquest of Crescendia, which surprised me. Not that they'd survived, but that they existed at all. War and combat were rare gifts, its necessity having fallen into disuse in the Twelve Realms. So, I put them to work in leadership roles and training positions within our contingent.

All eight of them stood in small groups, teaching their skills to our army. Crossbows, knives, swords, daggers, and the magic-enhancing projectiles our Quindalean and Perenellean allies had helped us create in direct opposition to Peacekeeper law. All had practice stations. The warrior deities split themselves into groups based on their strengths and trained Madwyn's army according to that breakdown.

The Diamanti also participated in our exercises, working with deities of like-magic, helping them master their gifts at whatever level possible. As a result, the army grew stronger and more skilled every day. I'd done what Madwyn ordered me to do. But I was also biding my time, looking for a way out while trying to build the relationships I needed to survive when I figured it out.

The truth was that I feared what my progress meant for the rest of the Twelve Realms and Bekka's family in Valeria. Because that's where Madwyn had turned her sights to next—Valeria. She'd been trying to initiate peace talks with Bekka's parents for weeks, but they continued to ignore her. Something that infuriated Madwyn to no end. She'd spent the last two weeks brooding about it, and everyone was avoiding her dour mood.

As I moved closer to the castle, watching the magic projectile weapons practice, dark shadows gathered a short distance away. They solidified, and I felt a familiar presence loom just before Sylennia stepped into view. I watched her stride toward me, sending me a flirtatious grin, which I returned. All part of the ruse we'd fabricated.

According to rumor, I spent every night in her bedchamber since we'd met at the lounge. Everyone *knew* we were lovers, but that wasn't reality. Instead, she snuck me into Lilja's room every night, giving me that precious time with my sister. Sylennia gave me the opportunity to protect her, while Lilja reminded me I still had a soul. That I wasn't the monster everyone thought I was.

I shielded my eyes from the bright sun as she approached. "What brings you here, spymaster?" I asked her.

She lifted her shoulder. "Madwyn wants to see you. It seems it's urgent."

I pressed my lips together. "Do you know why?"

"I'm not sure, but something tells me you're not going to like it."

"Any guesses?" I asked, but before she could answer, a scream ripped through the palace grounds. It echoed from the walls of the nearby travel and communications depot and the looming palace behind us.

I spun on my heel, unsure what to expect as my eyes landed on a frail, young goddess. Her hands gripped either side of her head and she screamed again. Her face turned deep red, on the verge of purple, as her shouts grew raspy from lack of breath. A slither of blood snaked down her nose and her ears, as I realized the problem. Not hesitating, I sprinted forward, Sylennia on my heels.

Davendrie had his eyes fixed on the young deity. He looked murderous with rage. I'd never seen him like that before. At least, not outside of the heat of battle. He looked wild, out of control, unhinged as he unleashed his gift on our ally. I knew he was a sadistic fuck, but never with his own army, only his enemies. I reached him in a single breath, and without thinking, I drew back my fist and slammed it straight into his jaw. As I did, the goddess collapsed into unconsciousness, blood dripping from her ears.

His head snapped to the side with the blow, and he turned on me. I didn't miss the feral look in his eye nor the scrape of his magic down my spine, trying to break through my defenses, attempting to tear my mind apart next. I let my magic dance up my arms, snaking it across the ground. I ran its sharp edges over his skin, and he paled in response, shaking his head as though to clear it. His magic subsided, and he looked around, blinking, his confusion obvious to anyone with half a brain.

"The fuck are you all looking at?" he asked, realizing that the training had stopped, and everyone's eyes had fixed on him in shock. A few deities rushed forward to help the goddess he'd injured. Blood coated the sides of her face and dripped from the top of her lip down to the bottom of her chin. A god and goddess hauled her up, looking panicked as they carried her to the palace, toward the makeshift barracks staffed by our healers.

"What the hell was that, Davendrie?" Asthorea snapped, abandoning her training post to stand beside me.

Another confused look crossed his face, his expression hardening. "Nothing, I'm fine. Nothing to see here. Get back to work."

My gaze trailed him as he stalked off the field. Riven stood at the edge of the trees, atop the hill that led up to the palace. As Davendrie drew closer to him, Riven fell into step beside the consciousness deity right before they disappeared into the gardens.

Everyone's attention landed on Asthorea and me, looking to us for some hint at what they should do next. I cleared my throat, rubbing my knuckles, the spot where I'd hit Davendri still warm. Almost as though his skin had scalded it.

I raised my voice to be heard across the grounds. "Go back to your training. I will inform you of any updates on ..." I scanned my memory and latched onto the name of the injured goddess. A promising consciousness deity with upper-to-middle-caste powers. "Nireen's injuries. I'm sure she'll be fine."

With that, a small, hushed whisper went through the regiment, and they all returned to their exercises. I looked between Asthorea and Sylennia. Asthorea's face appeared ashen and shocked, while Sylennia looked worried but not surprised. Remembering Sylennia's reason for being there, I turned my attention to Asthorea. "Madwyn needs me. Can you finish up here?"

She nodded absently before shifting her attention back to our army. "I'll take care of it."

"Thanks," I said, already trudging back up the grassy hill that led to the palace. Sylennia kept up with me, walking at my side. When we got out of earshot, she whispered, "Did you see his face? His eyes? That's how the ones who bashed in their skulls looked just before they did it."

I nodded, fists clenching and unclenching as I tried to work out the tension in my knuckles. "What the hell was that?"

"I don't know, but that's what I'm hoping your mother can help us find out." Sylennia chewed on her lip as we drew closer to the palace. More deities loitered around the exterior courtyard, and we slowed our steps. "Do you know when you'll get sent to Moldize next?"

I shook my head. "Madwyn hasn't ordered me to go back in months."

"Shit," she whispered, linking her hand with mine. A pretense, and another way for us to deceive our true motivations. I did my best not to pull away. I didn't want her to touch me. But I needed to nurture this alliance. I didn't have many true ones, and I couldn't afford to alienate her.

For Sylennia's part, when we drew closer to the palace, she stopped talking. She knew as I did that prying ears hovered nearby, and we walked the rest of the distance to the command room, where we planned all our battles, in silence.

We had to be careful inside the palace. As Sylennia liked to say, we never knew who could be watching. When we passed the banquet hall, large wooden tables lining the inside, we peeled off to the right, down a private hall where only leaders of the rebellion went; Madwyn's Diamanti, her high-ranking shadow spies, and her lieutenants. I approached the large, wooden door of the command room and pressed my palm to it, sending a pulse of my magic through the sensor.

I looked at Sylennia, dropping her hand before I entered. She strolled in behind me, and I peered at the large, wooden roundtable with the holo at the center. Streams of data poured from it as Madwyn's highest-ranking science deity, Preva, analyzed it.

We'd recruited her from Quindale. Her governor chip had capped her magic thirty percent below her true capabilities. Freeing her had motivated the goddess to join Madwyn's cause and fight back. Again, I wished I could choke Gabryel for his idiocy.

Because that same anger and bitterness could cause the rest of the Twelve Realms to fracture if they ever found out the truth. I wondered yet again what the Valerian royals and the Peacekeeper's council had been thinking to do something so fucking reckless. None of it made any sense, not even Gabryel's role in it, despite my low opinion of him.

But that was a problem I wouldn't solve any time soon. So, instead, I focused my attention on Madwyn. She stood at the table, leaning over it, as she and Preva spoke in low voices, pointing at various readouts throughout the long streams of data. I couldn't make out what they said, and I tried to focus on the numbers and letters, but they went dark when Madwyn waved her hand over the holo.

"Thank you, Preva. You're dismissed." Preva nodded, her head angled down in deference to Madwyn as she tried to stay as far away from me as she could manage. The Bicaidian Nefarals and their Bicaidian allies may have considered me a hero, but they'd lived with a death deity in their midst for decades. In the other realms, however, their deities had either seen me in battle or they'd heard the stories. They all treated me the same way. Like I was some wretched creature to be feared.

Ignoring her apparent distaste, I sauntered further inside, hitching a hip on the table at the center of the windowless, interior room, and crossing my arms over my chest. Madwyn had chosen the room for the privacy it offered, and the lack of unwanted interruptions. I knew enough about Madwyn at that point to know that she valued secrecy and the element of surprise above pretty much anything.

"Did you need something, Madwyn?" I asked and tried to tamp down the dread I felt. She'd never called me there for an enjoyable reason, and I had no cause to believe this time would be different.

Her eyes fixed on me as she rose to a standing position and walked closer, a sly smile in place. "Sylennia, you can go too. What I have to say is between

Arrick and me," she said, waving a dismissive hand in the shadow goddess's direction.

Without a word, Sylennia melted into darkness, and Madwyn spared her a quick glance before returning her focus to me. Likely to ensure that the goddess had truly left.

Madwyn wasted no time, getting right to the point. "I need you to do something, and I already know you won't like it. So, we're going to skip the part where you tell me you hate me and refuse out of that misguided honor you have and go straight to you obeying me. Because, if you don't, I will not hesitate to burn everything you love to the ground. Starting with your sweet, little sister, and ending with Moldize. And since I've claimed most of Moldize's eligible fighting deities and I have your sister in this very palace, I don't think I'll have much trouble accomplishing either task."

My jaw clenched, and I did my best to control the rage that boiled inside of me at having my friends and family threatened. Madwyn had ordered the Moldizean fighting force to Crescendia, under Brielle's command, which left my home world damn near defenseless.

Deciding that my best move was to throw her off balance, I asked, "Have you ever considered asking nicely before you threaten me?"

She narrowed her eyes. "This is a special request. One I want to make very clear that you shouldn't bother trying to refuse, and one I don't want to waste my time arguing about with you."

I clenched my fists to keep from choking her. "What is it, Madwyn?"

"That's it? Just 'what is it'? No angry seething or threats?"

The muscle in my jaw ticked. "You've left me little choice. So, tell me, what is it you want from me? What are my orders?"

"You're to go see Bekka in the dungeon," she said, examining her nails before she looked back up into my eyes. I waited for the other shoe to drop, because getting to see Bekka? It sounded like the answer to my prayers, not like something that required threats. So, what did she want me to do to her?

I waited as dread built up inside of me, and at last, she continued, "And you're to convince her to make a holo to her parents. We need them to negotiate with us, and I need to prove that we have their daughters. Remi and Bekka are the only bargaining chips we have, and the only way we can move forward with my plans."

"Move forward with what plans?"

She let out a long-suffering sigh. "I already told you, Arrick. You just haven't been listening."

I thought back to that night she'd visited me in my chambers and asked me to join her in a true alliance. "Revenge? So, what? You're going to kill them all?"

She lifted a shoulder. "I never said that."

I rose to my full height, looking down at her. "What are you going to do, then?"

"Didn't I say I wanted to avoid all these pesky questions? Didn't I just give you no choice? So, can we skip the whole domineering death god bit and get to the part where you do as you're commanded?"

The tattoo burned, and I could see the black ink squirm before growing starker on my skin. I glared at her, fists tightening further. "You're willing to just let me see her? After all this time, you've ordered me to stay away, and to stop asking you about her? But now you're just going to send me into her prison? Alone?"

Madwyn nodded. "I think you'll be most effective that way. You're to tell me what she says about the holo. You can tell her whatever you want about my threats, whatever convinces her to do it. But you're to tell her nothing of my plans for the realms or her family, or anything that I've accomplished so far. Do you understand?"

"I know nothing about your plans, Madwyn. You haven't exactly been forthcoming."

"Oh, but you know enough, and enough in the hands of someone smart is far, far too much." With that, she rose from her chair and waved a hand over the holo, turning it back on. "You're dismissed. Let me know as soon as it's done."

I felt the binding burn. A casual order, but an order, nonetheless. So, I turned and strode to the door, my fists clenched so tight that my knuckles hurt. But her voice stopped me then, "Oh, and Arrick, please let me know how she feels when she finds out you've moved onto greener pastures here. I'm sure she'd love to hear about Sylennia. So, you're to tell her all about it."

I stopped in my tracks, hands gripping the doorframe, the order ripping its way through our bond. Everything inside me went rigid, and Bekka's magic burned. I could feel its anger on my behalf, but I suppressed it before I said, "I doubt she'll even care."

Then, I opened the door and left.

17
REUNITED
BEKKA

A full week had passed since I told Emorie about my connection with Arrick, and about the power he'd gained as a result. Neither of us had spoken of it since, but I could tell that she worried over it.

Since that night, she'd doubled her efforts at forging weapons for us. I'd also been training harder, preparing myself for what came next. It felt more urgent than ever that we escape, and as I laid on the floor, staring up at the ceiling, I could hear the steady rhythm of Emorie's breathing in the cot next to me. I'd given up the bed a couple of days ago and slept on the floor instead.

The way I figured it, she deserved whatever comfort our little slice of hell had to offer. After all, she had to deal with the constant nag of hunger, and unfortunately, I was no stranger to that kind of suffering.

Not anymore.

With a sharp inhale, I rolled onto my stomach and started the training regimen I performed twice a day. I learned the exercises from Deklan and Caden when Arrick had left for the Moldizean underworld to give us both space after my grandfather's death. Back when I'd needed them for a distraction and to stop thinking about the look on my grandpa's face when he died. But now, I used the regimen to prepare my body for what came next. For the moment when we would get our opportunity to strike and finally escape.

They didn't let us out often, so we needed to be ready the second those doors opened. We couldn't afford to waste any opportunity we got.

I counted fifty pushups and rolled onto my back to start my ab movements. My muscles flexed as I sat up, feet pressed to the floor. While I moved, I could feel the pull of my pants against my flesh, a new sensation. *Having enough food really does work miracles*, I thought, a pang of sympathy shooting through me for Emorie.

As though my thought summoned her, her voice called out, gravelly from sleep, "Just hearing you do that makes me tired."

I let out a hushed chuckle. "You may have mentioned that once or twice before."

She yawned and the fitted sheet rustled. "When you're done with that, I need some help with the weapons."

Weapons were a strong word for what we had. Unfortunately, she couldn't do much fabricating given the limited materials available in our cell. The only viable option wasn't the easiest thing to make happen. Would it be an effective tool when the time came? Maybe. Was it easy to get? Nope.

"Are you sure?" I asked, exhaling a groan as I rose to my feet and started my leg routine. "My body might be the only weapon we'll need. I'm getting ripped, you know."

Even in her starved state, she snorted out a laugh. "Uh-huh. Right. Because being ripped means you can defeat a poisoned sword with your bare hands."

"Your sarcasm is noted, and also unappreciated," I replied, chuckling under my breath. "I'll get to it as soon as I'm done here, I promise." A few more minutes passed, and I finished my exercises, a thin sheen of sweat glistening on my forehead. I couldn't imagine that I smelled good. Our last shower had been just one day after Emorie had joined me in our cell weeks ago.

I swiped my brow with my forearm and asked, "Do you think they're ever going to open that damn door? Or is all this work just a waste of time?"

Emorie shrugged her thin shoulders, her dull, brown hair frizzy around her face. I could see some pieces of it starting to mat and I knew my hair didn't fare much better despite the braid I forced it into every few days. "Someone has to come in here, eventually. We have to assume they'll let us shower again at some point."

I nodded, allowing a small rush of hope to spread through me. "We'll be ready when they do," I vowed, opening and closing my fingers into fists. I'd been through a lot in the past few months. First kidnapped and squirreled away to Moldize, then trapped in the apocalyptic Moldizean mortal realm, followed by getting trapped in Bicaidian hell, and now locked in the Bicaidian dungeons. I wished I could say I'd grown used to pain and suffering. But I couldn't.

I longed for the soft comfort of home, of Valeria, more than I cared to admit. I wanted to talk to my parents, to hug them, to grieve my grandfather's death with them without feeling the weight of the Twelve Realms on my shoulders. I wanted to return to Castle Molo and remember what it felt like to have Arrick's arms around me. Thinking about him made me wince, the wound of our separation an ever-present ache in my chest. It was better not to let my thoughts linger on him, because when they did, it shattered me.

Besides, before I could even hope to see him or my family again, we needed to get out of this damn dungeon. Ascended knew how much longer I would have to wait before we could be together again, or if we ever would be. I tried not to think about his deal with Madwyn and the hopelessness it made me feel.

One step at a time, I thought, moving over to the cot and sitting next to Emorie. We'd escape and then we'd come up with a way to free him. It didn't help that I knew of zero ways to break a binding. But that didn't matter. I refused to accept defeat. I'd find a way.

"Alright, I'm ready," I said, and she rose to a sitting position and wavered for a moment. She closed her eyes, pinching the bridge of her nose as though fighting a dizzy spell. I reached out and supported her elbow to steady her. "You OK?"

She inhaled and exhaled slowly before she opened her eyes. "I'm alright."

She eased off the bed and shuffled over to sit by the wall. She pressed her back against it, sliding down the cool stones. I knew she had little energy, and I worried we might not make it out in her current condition, despite my insistence that she take more rations.

But she was a proud goddess, so I said nothing. Instead, I sank to my hands and knees, then to my belly, and crawled under the mattress. Under the cot stood a welded metal bed frame. Several steel poles ran the width of the bed, and I'd pried one off so far. I'd also loosened one side of the second pole, and now I just needed to free it.

Though the rune tattoo sapped all our power, it left us some level of our godly strength. Not all of it, as I'd learned before with the whole fist and wall fiasco, but enough that with some time and effort, I could break these shitty welds.

Working hard, I used a combination of the free pole and leverage to pry the second side of the pole off the frame. As I grunted and huffed from the effort, Emorie watched.

I couldn't see her, but I could feel her eyes on me. After about an hour of pulling, I pushed my body out from under the bed for a break. It was getting close to mealtime, and I didn't want the demons to catch us by surprise, in case they happened to peak through the delivery slot for our food.

I moved over to the wall where Emorie sat and scooted beside her. We sat in silence, Emorie's eyes heavy as she dozed off once again.

When the demons shoved our food through the slots, as they always did, I rose, grabbed the plates, and brought them back to us. That time, rather than scooping most of her food onto my tray, I handed her the full one. She looked up at me, surprise showing in her yellow-gold eyes, "No, Bekka, we said—"

But I waved my hand in dismissal. "No, Em. You need to eat something. I can go one day without both portions, but if we keep denying you most of your food all day every day, I don't think you'll be able to follow me out of here, even if you didn't have to fight. You can barely stand, and besides, we already talked about this. You're coming with me."

Her hollow eyes stared into mine, as though debating the wisdom of my statement. Of course, it was the smart thing to do. She needed some semblance of strength, or else both of us would be screwed. At last, she reached out her hand and wrapped her fingers around mine, squeezing. "Thank you, Bekka."

A few hours later, I pried the second pole from the frame. I danced a little celebration around the cell that probably made me look like a complete idiot. But I didn't care because I had two thick, arm-length poles with serious heft. Deklan and Caden had taught me to fight with swords, and I figured I could wield these in somewhat the same way.

With one in either hand, I started practicing with them, just before the lock to our cell door clicked. Emorie and I shared a look that had my heart rate rocketing into my throat and straight to my ears.

This was it. Our chance. It was too soon, but that didn't matter. Ascended only knew when we'd get another opportunity.

Emorie rose to her feet on less shaky legs than she'd had moments before and I took three running steps over to stand beside the door, back pressed against the wall. I had both poles in my hands, my palms sweating, and I prayed I could keep my grip. That my skill with them would be enough to fight our way through whatever demons guarded our cell. I just had to be fast and take them by surprise.

Breathe in, breathe out, I thought, closing my eyes as another lock clicked. I looked at Emorie, who'd moved to stand on the other side of the door. She needed to take shelter using the massive metal sheet, or she could be injured in the melee in her weakened state.

The handle creaked and clicked, and the hinges groaned as the door swung open. A god stepped through and before I could overthink it, I launched myself at him. I lunged forward with the metal baton, swinging down hard. He dodged the blow, dancing to the side, and my pole hit the ground, the reverberation of the metal singing up my arm.

Ignoring the pain, I raised my second arm, but he caught my wrist. I fought him as I heard the door slam shut behind us. A second later, he had both of my wrists pinned in either hand and pushed me back, trapping me against the wall. I twisted, trying to kick out, but he blocked my attempts with his knees and then stepped closer, pressing his full body against me.

Somewhere in the recesses of my panicked mind, I heard a voice. But I was too terrified, too desperate. I had to fight. This was our chance, likely our only one, and I'd just blown it. I snarled, gnashing my teeth and bucking. It wasn't until he dropped my wrists to grasp my face between his hands, steadying my head, that any logic or words broke through the haze of fight or flight that consumed me.

"Bekka, baby, it's me. It's me," he said the words over and over until I heard them, and recognition hit me.

"Arrick?" I asked, my body going quiet with a sudden, indescribable combination of relief and shock. My eyes locked onto his and everything else faded away. I dropped the poles, fingers going weak, and the metal clanged on the ground as I wrapped my arms around his neck.

Tears sprang into my eyes as I melted into him. I dug my hands into his hair and pressed my mouth to his without thinking. It was the first time I'd seen him since we'd forged our bond. Since he'd bound himself to Madwyn to save us. And with him there, so close to me, I could feel everything

I'd felt the day we'd made that connection. Right before everything went sideways.

Arrick groaned, tilting his head to the side and sliding his tongue into my mouth, taking the kiss deeper. He pressed his firm body even closer to me, pushing his thigh deeper between my legs, and I moaned into his mouth, wanting nothing more than to be with him right then and there.

He was my anchor, the person I cared most about in the entirety of every single realm. I carried a piece of his soul inside me, and he carried a piece of mine in him. Forever linked. Forever inextricable. My hands roamed over his back, found their way under the fabric of his shirt, and I raked my nails down his smooth, solid skin. I wanted him closer, and I wanted more, and I could tell he did too as he groaned into my mouth with pleasure.

Then, Emorie cleared her throat. "I'd say get a room, but—" she broke off and I felt like someone had struck me at the reminder of her presence. I wanted to drag Arrick onto that damn cot and do all kinds of naughty things to him, but as usual, the time wasn't right.

We would have a witness, and that would be awkward for everyone. Arrick's heated gaze still speared me to the spot, and then, growling with disappointment, he extricated himself from me and slid a hand down the braid of my dingy hair. He didn't seem to notice the matted tangles of it. Instead, he looked at me like I was a miracle, like he'd never seen me before, or like he never expected to see me again.

Then I noticed the distress in his eyes. But he composed himself, as though realizing it too, and my heart squeezed. He stepped back, grabbed my hand, and pressed it to his mouth. His lips traced fire on my skin. "You have no idea how much I've missed you."

I smiled, despite the despair I saw lurking just beneath the surface of his controlled expression, my eyes stinging with a combination of joy and sadness. "I think I have a pretty good idea, since it's probably about as much as I missed you. But ... what are you doing here? Are you OK?" I stepped forward and pressed a hand to his chest. I could feel his heart pounding beneath it, and I knew that something wasn't right. Despite the kiss and the raw passion, I could tell he needed something that had nothing to do with lust. I could sense it. My thoughts turned to the dreams I'd had about him, and I looked up into his face, trying to read it.

His eyes grew serious under my scrutiny, the green in them intensifying. He dropped my hand and ran his own over his neck. A sure sign of distress from him and my belly clenched.

"What is it? What's wrong?" I asked, trying to search his expression for clues, as though I might read his mind. Instead, I felt a sharp tug of resignation and a depthless well of dread and suffering. Surprised at the sudden presence of them, I realized the emotions had to be coming from him.

So, I couldn't just see and touch him; I could feel what he felt. Which meant that soulfused mates could feel each other's emotions. No one had ever told me that. But then, soulfused couples were a rare enough bond that I'd never met another pair. I only knew that it had nearly killed my grandpa when my grandmother died. Or at least, that was what I'd been told my entire life. That, and that they'd been inseparable, a union so powerful that everyone thought them unbreakable. At least, until they'd broken.

I stared into Arrick's eyes as he answered my question, and as the words fell from his lips, I could feel as much as see the self-loathing that accompanied them. "You need to make that holograph for your parents, Bekka."

My mouth dropped open in shock and then shut again, like a fish sucking air. "No. And why would you even ask me that?"

He swallowed as I stepped away from him, out of his grasp, shaking my head. "I can't do that. You know I can't. I won't help them. Whatever Madwyn plans to do with it, I can't trust that it won't destroy what's left of my family."

Arrick squeezed his eyes shut and tried to reach for me. But I stepped back, the sting of betrayal simmering beneath the surface. When he spoke, everything in him seemed to strain. "I know, and I'll do what I can to protect them. You have my word. You need to trust me and make the holo." His pain cut through me as though it were my own, and his guilt threatened to swallow him whole as he asked me to do this for him. It didn't matter, though. He was still asking.

"Why are you doing this?" I demanded, shaking my head. I didn't want to refuse him. The bond that solidified in our souls tugged at me to help him, but how could I do that to my family? I didn't trust Madwyn, and I knew whatever she had planned for Valeria wouldn't be good. She was conniving ... pure evil. She'd already proven that, and I didn't buy for one minute that she wanted a truce with Valeria, no matter how many times her emissaries insisted on it.

His shoulders sagged in resignation then. "Because Madwyn gave me an order. And if you don't do it, she'll kill Lilja, and when she's done with that, she'll destroy Moldize."

18
IMPOSSIBLE
ARRICK

Bekka's eyes popped wide as she swayed under the weight of that revelation. Catching her elbows, I held her steady. Turmoil roiled inside her, the conflict over what I asked her to do pulsing through our bond. The bridge I now had to her emotions surprised, but also comforted me. Feeling what she did felt right somehow, and it didn't hurt that I understood her current emotions, because the same conflict churned inside me.

The problem was, I didn't know for certain what Madwyn planned to do with the holo once Bekka made it. But judging from her desire for revenge, I didn't have hope for civility. Instead, I expected mayhem.

But what choice did I have? If I failed to get Bekka to agree? I didn't want to think about it because Lilja's life and the lives of everyone I protected back home were at stake. I couldn't just let them all die.

But I also didn't dare to let myself consider what damage might occur in Valeria, because it wouldn't happen. I would help her family. I needed to remember that I had an ally in the palace, and maybe I could convince Sylennia to assist me. But my instincts bucked as I thought about asking her to commit treason. She might be willing to take me to see Lilja, and look into the strange happenings in the ungoverned, conquered realms, but would she help me save the Valerian royals should it come to that? I had no idea.

What I did know was that what I asked of Bekka put her in an impossible situation, and if she refused, Lilja's death would be immediate. However, if she made the holo, it would take time for Madwyn to enact her plans for Valeria. Time that I could use to our advantage.

Bekka's expression morphed from shock to anger and then a sad resignation. At last, she lifted her eyes to me. "How can I choose between your sister, my Moldizean friends, your family, and my family?" The inherent goodness, the positive innocence of true optimism that made her who she was, faltered. I hated myself for it. I wanted to drink in that goodness, bask in the glow of its warmth after all the icy darkness I'd experienced these last months.

I didn't want her to lose that. She was everything I wasn't, and it killed me that everything she'd gone through might damage some of what made her so damn amazing. It didn't help that I knew that if I hadn't kidnapped her and brought her to Moldize, then none of this would have happened.

She would have stayed happy and safe in Valeria, with her grandfather alive to protect and teach her. She'd never have known me, and as much as I hated to admit it, she would have been better off for it. I'd brought her nothing but misery and suffering since I'd come into her life. I wished I didn't have to face that fact, but I couldn't escape it.

After what felt like an eternity, I reached out, brushing my thumb across her cheek, "Madwyn commanded me to ask you, so I had to. She can't command me to create certain outcomes, so you can refuse my request if that's your wish." I felt the sharp jolt of terror at that prospect, but I schooled my expression and held her gaze. She seemed to sense it anyway, the same way I could sense every emotion radiating from her, too.

"But your sister would die and so would your family," she said, reaching up to brush my hand on her cheek. The words, the cold reality of them, hit me once again. I'd have to find another way to save them if she refused.

"Madwyn doesn't make idle threats, though she would lose her only leverage that isn't tied to the binding we made. If you choose not to, we might call her bluff. But—"

"We'd be playing loose and fast with your kid sister's life, and every life in Moldize. I can't do that," Bekka said. She stepped away then, turning to pace around the tiny cell, and I could feel her realizing the same thing I already had.

So, I gave her all the information I could. That way, she could see the situation clearer. "Moldize is weak right now. Most of the fighters we could muster are with Madwyn. If she attacked my home now? We couldn't mount a defense. They'd be helpless to stop her. But Valeria is still strong. They might be able to keep her at bay, and if they can't, I swear I will do everything in my power to ensure your family's safety." Sadness pulsed from her, and fear for what came next. I hated to draw that comparison, but she needed to understand the landscape. Valeria stood a chance. They could stop Madwyn if she struck. But Moldize? They wouldn't make it out alive, and something told me that Madwyn would force me to take part in its destruction as punishment.

I watched as she continued to pace and took in her appearance for the first time. To my immense relief, she looked healthier than the last time I'd seen her. Small swipes of dirt covered her arms and face, and her godly sheen seemed dimmer somehow. But she'd gained some weight back and the muscles of her arms flexed beneath her skin.

Before either Bekka or I could say more, the other goddess, who I recognized from that night in Bicaidian hell, spoke, "Bekka, I hate to break it to you, but your family's getting dragged into this fight no matter what you do. That's just a matter of time. His kid sister and Moldize, though? You have a chance to save them." The goddess, her name a blank spot in my memory, pushed off the wall she'd been leaning against, and her legs wobbled.

I scanned her, realizing she looked ready to drop into stasis sleep at any second. I looked back at Bekka, noting the differences. Why did Bekka look healthy, but the goddess she shared her cell with didn't? A thought hit me then, but I pushed it down and tried to wipe it from my mind. I didn't want to know.

Forcing my attention back to Bekka and the matter at hand, I said, "She's right. Regardless of the holo you make, they won't avoid this fight. Madwyn will see to that no matter what you do. But I have an ally inside. Her name is Sylennia, and I think I can convince her to help me."

Bekka's shoulders dropped, and she ran a hand over her tangled braid just before hope sprang into her eyes. "An ally? Really? How have you kept that a secret?"

I considered Madwyn's order to tell her everything, and knew I had no choice but to do just that. "Madwyn thinks we're lovers, so she commanded me to tell you about her. She wanted to cut me, and make me hurt you, too."

"Lovers?" Bekka asked, her eyes narrowing, and I recognized the jealousy there, felt it sticky and hot as it pulsed through her. "And why would she think that?"

I stepped closer, resting my hands on her shoulders to reassure her. "It's a ruse, Bekka. They think we sleep in the same chamber, but she takes me to spend time with Lilja every night. Otherwise, I'd never see her either, and I need that. I need something aside from—" I sighed and ran a hand down the back of my neck, as a little guilt that I hadn't let myself feel about the arrangement with Sylennia surfaced.

Bekka seemed to sense the despair that swallowed me, and her eyes softened, all traces of her initial jealousy gone. "I trust you, Arrick. I just want to be out of this damn cell and see you whenever I feel like it. I want to—" She let out a long breath. "I want so many things." We let the silence hang for a minute, because what was there to say? None of it was possible. Then she refocused on the matter at hand. "You're sure you can get her to help us?"

"No, but I'll do my damned best to try, and if she doesn't, I'll find another way. You have my word."

She hesitated, watching me, and I could see her mind working. Then she replied, "Ascended be damned, I'll make the cursed holo. But I have to ask, why now? Why didn't she give you this order before?"

I opened my mouth to reply, but hot, lancing pain shot through my brain and I remembered Madwyn's order. "I can't—" I shook my head to clear it and sucked in a breath, pressing the heel of my palm to my brow to staunch the agony of it.

A gentle hand touched my shoulder, and another brushed over my cheek. "Arrick, are you OK?" Bekka's voice sounded distant. Madwyn's order not to divulge any of her plans or conquests burned through me, and I knew I couldn't answer Bekka's question. Even without Madwyn's order, I couldn't help as much as I wanted to because I didn't know what she planned to do next. No one did, except maybe Riven.

But despite the pain, Bekka's question stuck in my mind. Why hadn't Madwyn commanded me to do this earlier? I thought I knew the answer. The Rising had conquered four of the Twelve Realms, plus its alliance with Moldize. She'd waited until now because she wanted to negotiate from a position of strength. A sound strategy, and that was the problem. Twisted and evil as she might be, Madwyn understood strategy on a political level, if not a military one.

I exhaled as the last of the searing pain subsided. A little taste of what would come should I ever break our deal. When it retreated fully, I threaded my fingers through Bekka's and held her hand between mine. "I'm fine. I can only tell you that she wants to arrange a truce negotiation with Valeria."

The other goddess spoke then, "And you believe that?"

I didn't answer for a long moment, just stared into Bekka's eyes, allowing myself to fall into them, to soak in the light that radiated from her despite everything she'd been through. After what felt like an eternity, yet not long enough, I chose a non-committal response. "I couldn't say."

Bekka's cellmate rolled her eyes and scoffed, and I took in the contrast of their appearances once more, and that time I looked them over more thoroughly, not letting the emotions I felt for Bekka cloud my judgment.

As I did, I noted their bedraggled clothing, the state of each of their bodies, and the pipes Bekka had tried to brain me with, and then I realized what they'd been doing. It clicked into place without my permission, despite my efforts not to overthink things, not to over-analyze them.

"Shit," I hissed, pressing my palms to my eyes in complete frustration. "I can't be here. Dammit! I can't know about those weapons." I flung a hand at the discarded metal pipes on the floor. "I can't know that you're trying to break out. A blind human could see that you two have something planned. You don't understand, my mind isn't safe. She can make me tell her anything."

Bekka rushed forward. "But that's not what we're doing." I scoffed at the ridiculousness of that statement and raised my brows in disbelief. She'd just lied to me, and I could feel it as plain as if I'd told the lie myself. But even though she must know I would sense the falsehood, she continued, "The bed, you know, it broke all on its own. And I was dancing with the batons earlier, keeping Emorie entertained. Oh, and that's Emorie by the way," she flung a hand to her cellmate before she continued. "You walked right into my interpretation of a Valerian battle dance. I mean, you know how clumsy you are, and Emorie, she's just sick. So granted, we haven't showered in weeks and it's freezing in here and the lights don't turn off, except for those few days of total darkness we had about a week back. But that's beside the point. She needs a healer, sleep, and a little washy scrubby, and she will be ship-shape in no time. We are not thinking about escaping. I just—I don't even know where you'd get a cra-azy idea like that."

I examined her as she talked and pressed my lips together. The humor I felt as I watched her brought me so much pleasure, I couldn't put words to it. But she needed to be more careful, especially around me. And as everything she told me sank in, not about the Valerian dance battle or my nonexistent clumsiness, but about the constant light, followed by total darkness, and the lack of showers, simmering fury boiled inside me.

I looked past her, at the single bed and toilet, details I hadn't noticed before. I'd been too distracted, but I saw it now, and that rage burned. The cot was filthy, with no covers, pillows, or blankets. The room was cool; no, it was cold, and the lights. They were too bright and … she'd said they never turned off. Except for when they kept her in darkness for days?

The anger surged then, so white and hot that I had to fight to control it. Black mist seeped from my fingertips as I struggled to master myself, Bekka's magic burning beneath the surface too. My soulmate hissed in a breath then, and I knew she must have felt just how furious I was.

Bekka shook her head, stepping closer. "No Arrick, it's not your fault. I'm OK. Really."

I felt the lie as easily as if it were my own once more. "Damn her, she's been keeping me—" another pain shot through my eye, another bitter reminder that I didn't own my tongue. I clenched my jaw. "I've been otherwise engaged, and haven't been able to come here. But it's clear Madwyn isn't holding up her end of the bargain. She's getting around her obligations, and I don't know how."

Emorie, as Bekka had called her, exchanged a look with my soulfused mate, like they knew something I didn't.

I debated the wisdom of asking for more detail, but before I could decide, Emorie said, "We've had a lot of time to think about this one. We aren't being tortured, not technically. They care for us, in the most basic sense. And the binding didn't guarantee that we live in the lap of luxury for all eternity."

More anger, deeper and darker, snaked its way through me, cold and black, just before my magic slid up my arms, the coolness of it doing little to soothe my raging temper. Emorie was right, and I was an idiot. I'd been exhausted, half-starved, and on the edge of burnout when I agreed to the terms of the binding. I thought I'd guaranteed their protection, but I hadn't considered how much room my words left for interpretation. At least, not until now.

The darkness of my magic flooded the space beneath my skin, freezing my blood to ice. Then Bekka's magic rose, forcing its way to the surface. It felt like millions of fire ants biting beneath my skin, trying to eat through me. I clenched my fists and willed it back down. Bekka's hand laced through mine, anchoring me back to my body. I'd needed it, I realized, as the feel of her fingers in mine soothed that fury.

"Arrick, you're angry. I can feel it, and my magic ..."

I dropped my forehead onto hers and squeezed my eyes shut, letting the pain wash through me. "You can feel your magic, can't you?" I asked, my voice a whisper so the other goddess wouldn't hear me. I didn't know what Bekka had told her.

"Yes," Bekka said, hands tightening on mine. "You have to keep it secret."

"I know," I groaned, holding onto her. "Don't worry, I can handle it."

Under control again, I opened my eyes and saw her wide, coffee-colored ones searching mine, and I didn't miss the disbelief in them. "I'm going to get you out of here. I swear it, Arrick." Her lack of agreement that I could keep it under wraps didn't surprise me. She knew what her magic felt like better than anyone, and it was only a matter of time before my control slipped.

But rather than dwell on either of our false hopes, I took a step back and shifted the topic of conversation to more important matters. "I'll talk to Madwyn about all of this. It seems she and I have very different definitions of 'cared for'."

"No," Emorie interrupted, shaking her head, matted hair whipping. She seemed to wobble on her feet and Bekka pulled out of my grip, reaching out a hand to steady her. "Say nothing. We don't need her poking around in here or asking questions."

I considered Emorie's request, but something didn't sit right. Madwyn sent me there, knowing what conditions I'd find. It had to be a test. It was the only thing that made sense. "If I say nothing, it will only raise her suspicion. She'll know I'm hiding something."

Emorie groaned, hand gripping the matted curls at the top of her head. "We can't let them move us to another room."

"She's right," Bekka added. "This is the best room for dancing." She raised her brows conspiratorially at me, and that description had my lips twitching once more despite everything.

Her hand squeezed tighter on mine and that desperate hope evaporated as I looked at her again. "A compromise then. I'll demand more food, a second cot, blankets, pillows, access to a shower, and that she turns the lights off at night. I won't ask for more. And we'll fucking hope she doesn't ask me if you're making plans to escape."

Emorie and Bekka shared a look then, and each nodded their consent.

Bekka cleared her throat and asked, "When do I make the holo?"

"Tomorrow morning. Someone will come for you then."

"You?" she asked, her eyes looking up at me with hope.

"I'm not sure."

She nodded, disappointment swallowing her, as though understanding that it wouldn't be my decision.

But then she looked at Emorie and something passed between the two goddesses that caused my back to go rigid. I leveled a serious look at both of them, the one I used as a commander. "Try nothing tomorrow while I'm there. Bekka, promise me you'll make the holo and walk out." When she didn't meet my eye, I gently grasped her face between my hands. "I mean it. Promise me you'll do nothing but make that holo tomorrow." Fear encircled that fury I felt. I couldn't let her do anything that would jeopardize Lilja. Or herself. Her safety from the binding only lasted as long as she remained under Madwyn's dominion.

But when I looked into her eyes, I could see the light of defiance in them. I could feel it burning in my belly, as it must be in hers. "Arrick, this will be the first time I'm out of the cell, away from the dungeons. It's an opportunity I can't—"

Without hesitation, I rested my fingertip on her lips and shook my head. "You must, and you will forgo it. I can't be there when you ... dance. There's more at stake than you realize."

Bekka stared at me then, trying to gauge what I could mean by that. I watched her expression shift from determined to uncertain. "What is it?" she asked.

I let out a long sigh. She needed to understand the truth. She needed to know what would happen. "If I'm there when you decide it's time to dance, she'll force me to stop you, then punish me through Lilja for not telling her about your plan. Madwyn will never believe that I didn't suspect something. So, whatever you do, I can't be there."

"You don't understand. We never leave this place. We won't have another—"

I reached out and squeezed her hand, and she paused mid-sentence.

"You will get another chance. Trust me. She'll grant my request for more frequent showers. Believe me, I've earned it. But until then, you need to understand that Madwyn knows what buttons to push, and she's not afraid to do it. She is chaos, Bekka, a master manipulator and strategist. I can't say more than that, but don't underestimate her resolve. She believes she's liberating the Nefarals and everyone chipped against their will. She wants to rule the next world order, and for her, the ends will always justify the means. So, you have to be smart, all of you do, and the first part of that is steering clear from me. You must keep me in the dark. Always. I already know too much. Madwyn made an error, or maybe she got overconfident, but she didn't ask me to report on what you're doing down here. That doesn't mean she won't when I return. I'll do what I can to keep it under wraps. But like I said, we'll just have to hope she doesn't ask me about it."

Pain flashed across her face then, and I could feel everything she did. Despair and loneliness, longing, worry, and fear. I sighed, dropping my forehead to hers. I'd promised once that I would always be by her side, no matter what came. I wanted nothing more than to fulfill that promise and help her. To get her out of that damn cell and back home to Valeria, where she would have a chance at safety and happiness. More than anything, I wanted to be with her there. But I knew I couldn't. I was a liability. A risk that she couldn't afford to take. So, I could only hope that she would make it somewhere far away from me. Somewhere far away from what Madwyn would force me to do to her, should she ever get free.

She tilted her head up and pressed her lips to mine. Heat spread through me, and I wanted to pull her into my arms and slide my hands over her beautiful body. When she pulled away, I could feel the heat radiating from her too, a dull ache in her heart that mirrored my own. "We need to get you out of here, Arrick."

I wanted to tell her we'd find a way. I wanted to say that I would do whatever it took to break the binding, and I would, but I didn't want to give her false hope if I never found one. So, rather than speak useless words, I trailed a knuckle over her smooth skin just under her jaw and brushed my lips over hers, the sweetness of her mouth making me want to lose myself in her, to fall into that bright light that always seemed to emanate from her. Instead, I pulled away and looked into her eyes. "Make the holo, Bekka, and walk away."

She swallowed and then nodded her head. "OK."

19

FURY

ARRICK

As I left Bekka's cell, I struggled to contain my rage. I wanted to break every bone in Madwyn's body, to rip her soul free of it and watch her waste away. I wanted her dead. The cool mist of my power pooled around me, swelling inside the prison hallways. Prisoners screamed as it slithered under locked doors and ran claws over their skin, but I didn't care.

She hadn't let me see Bekka and the others, not once, and now I understood why. Though she hadn't tortured them, she'd only cared for them to the minimum degree possible. I recalled the words of my binding after we'd unsheathed our magic, and how I'd allowed her to put Bekka and the others in the dungeon.

Madwyn had promised they would remain physically unharmed, but that they must remain in prison. She'd refused to negotiate that point, and I didn't have the leverage I needed that day in Bicaidian hell to make her change her mind. But that didn't excuse my stupidity for giving her too much leeway to circumvent the bargain. 'Cared for' and 'physically unharmed' while in her custody left far too much ambiguity, and she'd capitalized on it. I felt like a damned novice.

I wanted to hit something, to kill someone, I thought, as I stormed up the stairs and out of the prison, back through the gardens, and toward the palace. I knew who I sought. Who would bear the brunt of my ire.

Madwyn.

My magic burst from me then and I stepped through it, translocating into the great hall, not breaking stride for an instant. The order to report back to Madwyn and my desire to rip her throat out coalesced into a deep burning that seared through my arm. I didn't care about the pain. I stormed down the hall, expecting to find her waiting for Bekka's response.

But before I could reach her, I felt a presence beside me as a hand closed on my shoulder. It squeezed hard, and I all but snarled, wrenching myself free and turning to face Riven. He positioned himself in front of me, his posture casual, but blocking my path to his sister.

"Get out of my way," I said through gritted teeth.

"I need to talk to you," Riven said, eyes boring into mine.

"And I need to speak with your sister, so move." I damn near growled at him when he didn't budge.

Riven sighed. "You look more like you're going to rip her limb from limb than talk to her. So, why don't you take a minute to cool down, lest you get your hand slapped. Or worse. Madwyn isn't in the greatest mood right now. It's not a good time to test her."

My fists clenched as I resisted the urge to slam his head into the wall. I debated all the ways I could kill him. He wouldn't stand a chance if I took him down quickly. But the tattoo on my arm burned, the pain shooting straight into my eye at my imaginings. I sucked in a breath, the agony sobering. "Fine. What is it, Riven?"

He hesitated, hands slipping into his pockets as his face went contemplative. "It's Davendrie. He collapsed after the incident at training today. He's healing now, but ... he had a nosebleed and a fever that the healers couldn't explain. It took them hours to staunch the blood flow."

I stared at him, wondering what he expected of me. I gave zero shits about Davendrie. He was a sadistic bastard who enjoyed preying on anyone weaker than him, especially young females. But then I thought about Sylennia and what she'd said about those other deities. And he got a nosebleed that the healers couldn't stop right away? We didn't get nosebleeds or fevers without an obvious cause. Injury, consciousness magic, pestilence, poisoning—all sound reasons and easily detected by a healer. But bleeding for no reason?

"Why are you telling me this?" I asked, unsure why he felt compelled to talk to me.

Riven leaned a shoulder against the white, plaster wall. His black suit looked tailored and crisp, mismatched with his disheveled hair, unusual for him. After a long pause, he replied, "Have you seen anything else like that before? At training? Davendrie said he didn't remember hurting that goddess, and from what I could see—" he swallowed, as though trying to find the right words. "The incident should have left an impression, at least."

My mind fixed on what Sylennia had told me. About the other deities who exhibited similar symptoms in other "freed" realms. How many more deities had had similar incidents that had just gone undetected? In Bicaidia, we'd been living in wartime. Brutality and cruelty ran rampant and were necessary to win a war. I remembered how Davendrie stabbed that strawberry-haired deity through the back. I recalled the delight he'd taken in it. Had something been wrong with him then? Or had he always been that bloodthirsty?

I shook my head, unable to think of anything I'd witnessed like what had happened on the training grounds. I debated confiding in him and telling him the details of Sylennia's concerns for one second before I shot that idea down. She said he sent her to look after things, but she only trusted him so far. So, telling him more? That would need to be her call. "I've seen nothing else like it."

Riven nodded, his face going thoughtful. "Davendri will be awake soon, the healers assured me of that. We'll need to monitor him. I'll ask that you report anything unusual you see to me. With him, or anyone else."

An order, not a request, I thought as my tattoo hummed. "What about Madwyn?"

He shook his head, thumb brushing over his lip. "She has enough on her plate. I don't want to worry her. We'll tell her once we know more." With that, he pushed off the wall and sauntered past me. "Enjoy your chat with Madwyn. I'll be in my chambers, spending time with Ellarah, should you think of anything."

Another brief mention of the goddess he kept locked in his room, I thought, wondering who the hell she was.

"She's awake?" I asked, a little surprised at that. The last I heard, she remained in stasis sleep, healing from her injuries. Those injuries and how she'd gotten them had been the topic of much conjecture among the Diamanti. The prevailing rumor was that Madwyn had stabbed her during the inauguration night attack, but again that was hearsay.

But if she was awake? I knew no one had seen her in the main palace itself and I couldn't help but wonder why not? Especially if she'd woken up.

He turned for a moment and offered me a nod, face still somber. It didn't look like the happiness I would have expected from him, given his lover's improved condition. I noted his reaction, curiosity piqued, but he turned and walked through his magic, leaving me alone in the hall.

My anger had settled into a low simmer, and rational thoughts had returned. I supposed I had Riven to thank for that, I mused, before I walked into Madwyn's situation room a moment later and readied myself for a different battle.

The kind that would require some stealth and a little more finesse than my usual fare of late. So, I sent a pulse of my magic into the sensor on the door and pushed back the rest of the fury. It buzzed open, and I stepped inside, glaring at Madwyn.

"Arrick, what a pleasure to see you back so soon. I hope your visit went well. Did you succeed?" I glared at her, and she laughed as two servant-caste deities saw the dark expression on my face and scurried out the door. Smart, I thought, keeping myself on a tight leash.

I shut the door with a firm click behind them and turned, moving closer until I towered over her slender frame. She straightened, rising to her full height as though sensing my suppressed ire, but still had to crane her neck to look up at me.

Only then did I speak. "She agreed, but for once, you're going to shut your mouth and you're going to listen to me." Her lips twitched, her eyes sparkling with amusement, though her face remained impassive. "You will provide my friends with ample food and sanitation, including regular showers, fresh clothing, and fresh linens. You will also give them another cot. That single one is far too small for two people, and you know that. They will have blankets, pillows, and simulated day and night. That is what 'well cared for' means, at a minimum. They will not be half-starved and freezing in that damned prison for another second, or I swear on all I hold precious, I will burn everything you love to ash. I may be bound to you, but I also know how to inflict maximum damage, and I will do it before you or the fucking binding can stop me. Do we understand each other?"

Madwyn paused, looking at me blankly before she broke into an amused grin. "Such dramatics," she said, staring up at me still. "Don't you ever think about asking me before you threaten me?"

I recognized the words I'd said to her earlier but didn't react to the slight. Instead, I just stared at her, letting her know just how serious I was. I couldn't go against her for long before the binding consumed me for my disobedience, but I didn't need long to exact immense damage, and that time, I wasn't bluffing.

At last, she relented, waving a hand and stepping away from me. Turning back to the table, she swiped through images on the holo. "Fine. You've held up your end of the bargain. I will ensure the improvements are made. You're dismissed."

Her command burned, but I fought it. I needed to say one last thing before I left her. "I will collect Bekka for the holo tomorrow, and I expect the improvements to be in effect by then."

"I will see to their accommodations, but as for your other request? The answer to that is no," she said, eyes flashing. "You don't get to threaten me and get whatever you want in return. I'll let you see her cell when it damn well pleases me. Now, you're dismissed," she said, waving me off, the command burning up my arm and down my side. I all but growled at her as I walked out the door, resisting the urge to slam it shut behind me.

As I left, I couldn't help but grin. My strategy had worked. The anger and rage had taken her off guard, and she hadn't asked me a damn thing about Bekka, aside from whether or not she agreed to the holo. I could only hope that my luck would continue.

20

THE ALL POWERFUL

THAYNE

"You both need to dig deeper," Pietyr said, eyeing the demigods as they struggled and failed to summon their newfound power. "Your magic is still too weak."

Caden's brow shone with sweat as he clenched and unclenched his fist. Deklan, meanwhile, looked furious, eyes closed and mouth grim. Thayne ran his hands through his hair in frustration as nothing but a small breeze shifted in the room, followed by a slight rumble beneath his feet.

At last, Deklan opened his eyes. "It's no use. I can't seem to do what I did that first time. I don't have that kind of control."

Caden sighed and swiped a forearm over his brow. "My brother's right. Besides, how do we know that our experience with magic will be the same as yours? We have generations of human blood pumping through our veins."

Pietyr shook his head, a look of pure determination sliding over his features. "It doesn't matter. You're part god, both of you. You just need to find your access point and how to channel more power into it."

Rackham stood shoulder-to-shoulder with Pietyr, nodding his head in agreement. The discovery of the twins' magic and the promise to free Arrick had put them all on the same side again, united them with a shared purpose. *But we've hit a wall,* Thayne thought as Rackham continued Pietyr's explanation, "You just need to find that thread of power and pull."

"There is no fucking thread," Deklan sniped, and Thayne could see the frustration in the normally unflappable god's face. "I'm telling you, I don't feel an access point. The first time, I just reacted to Caden trying to kill us."

Caden jumped in, his expression grim. "How many times do I have to tell you? I didn't mean to do that. It just happened. Besides, I'd say you got your revenge," he muttered, rubbing his jaw. A large purple bruise had formed on it from smacking against the floor.

So, they had magic, but slower healing powers, Thayne had noted, which put their power ranking somewhere in the lower-caste. That the jaw had broken at all informed his assessment. It didn't matter how quickly it healed. Deities with higher caste rankings didn't get broken jaws from falling on stone. But mortals also didn't heal in a matter of a few weeks.

So, that meant that they had a decent level of active magic lingering beneath the surface. He agreed with Rackham and Pietyr. The brothers just needed to figure out how to control it.

Thayne stepped closer to them and raised his hands. "I know you're frustrated, but the deeper pool of your magic is there. These two don't understand elemental gifts, but I do."

"Understand it?" Deklan asked, looking at Thayne like he'd lost his damned mind. "What do you mean? Pietyr said to harness it. Like it's just ripe for the taking, but I assure you, it's not."

Thayne nodded his understanding. "I get it. I'm an elemental too. My power is unique because I control multiple elements, but it's the same concept." He watched as Pietyr and Rackham rolled their eyes at each other behind the brothers' backs. How could he help it if they only controlled one thing while he had three?

Pietyr stepped back, raising his hands. "Go right ahead, Thayne the all-powerful."

Rackham snorted with laughter. "Yeah, we wouldn't want to impede your greatness."

Thayne raised a brow at them, lips twitching. "You two done yet?" When they said nothing, he turned his attention back to the demigods. "The lower-caste gods in our pillar need to tap into the element to use it. Caden, you're an air deity, and judging by the show of your power, somewhere in the middle of the lower-caste. You probably have the strength of your family's bloodline to thank for getting that high in the rankings, considering how many generations removed you are from Afryel." After significant probing, the demigods had admitted where their power came from, and Thayne was still reeling from the shock of that revelation. A creator procreating with a human? He'd never heard of such a thing.

Pushing that thought from his mind, he said, "Deklan, you're an edaphopath, commonly known as a land deity. I'd guess your power ranking is on par with your brother's."

"And that helps us how?" Deklan asked, glaring at Thayne like he wanted to start cracking skulls.

"The last time you used your power, either anger or fear overwhelmed you. Caden had just been elbowed in the face, and Deklan, you couldn't breathe. It was fight or flight. But now, you need to use it when you're not either furious or panicking. Because if we are going to break out of here using lower-caste gifts, our plan needs to be methodical."

"You're not explaining how we do that," Caden said, frustration lining his face. "Trust me, I want this to work as much as you do. I just don't know how to make it."

"Close your eyes," Thayne said, feel the air, breathe it in, exhale it. "You're a lower-caste air god, which means you can't create air. So, don't try because it won't work. What you can do is manipulate it. That's how you sucked it out of the room before. So, first, find the element. Then keep it simple. Move the air bit by bit."

Caden nodded his head, closing his eyes in apparent concentration.

Thayne left him to it and turned to Deklan. "Same situation for you. You can't create plants from nothing. Not any more than Caden can create air, and for the same reason. But these adobe bricks are made from soil. They have the roots of dead plants in them. Your magic revived them and pulled them from the stone."

He gestured at the ground where the vines sat discarded. They'd turned greenish-brown, dying from lack of water and soil. The places they'd sprouted from the stone had cracked, but not enough. Reinforced stone still lurked beneath it. If they planned to use his gift to escape, then he would need to delve deeper.

Pushing that thought from his mind, he said, "Lay your hand on the stone, like you did before. Remember? You were kneeling, hands on the stones, when you accessed your stronger magic."

Rackham's eyes gleamed as he stepped forward. "Of course. Lower-caste elementals can't create, but they can manipulate and control. We should have thought of that earlier."

He punched Pietyr's arm, who grinned and shook his head. "I guess the cocky bastard did have something useful to contribute."

Deklan sunk into a crouching position and rested his hand on the floor. "This feels ridiculous," he complained before he closed his eyes.

Thayne tried not to grin. They did look ridiculous, but he refrained from mentioning it. Instead, he said, "Now, focus, both of you. Try to feel the element you're looking for, and when you find it, open your mind to it. Connect to it. Wrap your very consciousness around it. Bend it to your will."

As he watched them struggle, Thayne could feel his stomach clench in anticipation. This was basic elemental instruction, long forgotten from his early years of training—at least until now. It should work. He looked from Pietyr to Rackham, who both seemed excited and anxious. They needed the brothers to come through. They would play a central role in whatever plan came next.

After a long pause that had them all holding their breath, a strong breeze whipped through the room. Caden's eyes shot open, the gleam of excitement in them clear. He raised his hand and made a stirring motion with his fingers. Within seconds, the wind took on a gentle, but firm circular motion. A broad smile stretched across the demigod's lips and his white-blonde hair flew in the breeze around his face. The light that shone from him just two days earlier skittered across his skin once more, glimmering in a godly sheen. Only visible when he used his power, it seemed.

Then, not to be outdone by his twin brother, Deklan slammed his fist to the ground and let out a growl of frustration. Seconds later, the floor rumbled. Adobe stones cracked, a fissure running the length of the room.

Pietyr and Rackham stumbled, their backs hitting the wall as they jumped out of the way to avoid the rupturing stones.

"Yes! That's it!" Thayne shouted, his heart a beating drum in his chest. "You've got it!"

Caden's grin grew wider when he closed his fist, and the wind fell silent around them. At the same time, Deklan placed either hand on the floor and drew them closer. The fissure closed, the stones reforming into perfect, unmarred adobe blocks.

All five of them stared at each other in a mixture of astonishment and excitement. The demigods had done it. Granted, the magic wasn't as powerful as he'd like, or the ideal type to escape from a Nefaral-filled palace teeming with demons.

But it was a start. And it was a hell of a lot better than nothing.

Later that night, Pietyr, Rackham, and Thayne sat huddled in a tight circle. The brothers had fallen asleep earlier than usual. The hours they'd spent practicing had exhausted them. So, while they slept, the three remaining gods whispered in hushed tones.

"You two are the expert strategists here. You're the ones who ran all those missions with the shadow spies. So, how do we want to do this?" Rackham asked, looking from Pietyr to Thayne.

Thayne rolled his shoulders, releasing some tension as he listened to Pietyr's reply. "We need to keep building their strength and get their power amplified to its maximum because if today is any indication—" Pietyr jerked his head at the snoring demigods. "Then we have work to do. We also need to plot out the best path for escape, one where we are least likely to get intercepted. That's where Thayne comes into play. He's the only one of us who's left this cell since they locked us in it."

"Agreed," Thayne replied, rising to his feet and gathering whatever objects he could find, which included torn strips of clothing, bedding, and their tattered shoes. Once compiled, he laid them out on the stone floor, creating a rough approximation of the prison. As he built the model, he walked them through it. Pietyr had some level of familiarity with the layout, but Rackham didn't, so Thayne took the time to explain and answer questions.

"What about the palace? What did you see when you were inside?" Rackham asked, eyes scanning through Thayne's prison model.

"A lot of demons and a lot of deities. It looks like Madwyn has transformed the palace into living quarters for a small army," Thayne replied, shaking his head.

"Fuck," Pietyr breathed. "So even if we get out of the prison, we have to avoid ... how many?"

"Let's just say we can't afford to be spotted. We need to stay hidden and get the hell off the palace grounds as fast as possible. The best way to do that is along the far edge of the gardens and closer to the river. We can keep to the shadows as long as we make our move at night."

Rackham paled. "That's all well and good, but it doesn't answer Pietyr's question. How many deities and demons are we talking about?"

Thayne leveled a hard gaze on him. "More than enough to stop us. That's all you need to know. Any more, and it'll get in your head. You can't let it."

Rackham nodded, chaffing his legs as though amping himself up. "OK. I trust you. Or at least, I think I do. Mostly because I have no choice. But you know what, fuck it, let's do this."

After that, they strategized until they had the workings of a plan. Though, Thayne recognized it for the long shot it was. Even with the demigods' powers, they would have to get through damn near a mile of palace grounds before they reached a safe place to jump from the cliffs into the river. They couldn't afford to risk too far of a drop, not in their weakened states. Not with the runes on their wrists suppressing their healing abilities.

"Then there's the wild card," Thayne said, rubbing a hand over his beard in thought.

"What wild card?" Pietyr asked, narrowing his eyes.

"Ellarah," Thayne said, and both Pietyr and Rackham winced.

"What?" Thayne asked, looking between them. "She could make a useful ally, if she remembers what happened on inauguration night."

Another shared expression passed between his companions. "What is it you're not saying?" Thayne asked.

Rackham replied, rubbing a hand over his messy hair. "Look, I won't pretend like I know Ellarah all that well, but isn't she in love with Riven? You don't think she'd give him a chance to explain if she does remember? Then if she tips him off, who knows what he'll do to keep her with him? They have Davendri on their side, and he'll rip into her mind the second she doesn't fall into line."

"Ellarah isn't stupid—" Thayne argued, but Pietyr cut him off.

"No, Rackham has a point. Love makes you do dumb things. You know that, Thayne. We don't know which way she'll swing in the end."

They fell into silence and Thayne chewed on his cheek as he considered. Their opinions mirrored his own, though he didn't dare voice that. The idea of a higher-powered ally outside the dungeons gave him a sliver of hope, but that hope dangled on the razor's edge. He didn't think Ellarah would risk his life and Remi's by giving Riven a chance to explain. She wouldn't be that emotional or that reckless, would she? Pietyr had a point, though. *Love makes you blind*, he thought. He was the perfect example of that.

He pushed the unwelcome thought from his mind as Pietyr said, "Look, we can keep Ellarah in our back pocket. She's a wildcard that we can't control unless you get to see her again, which may never happen. So, let's focus on what we can control."

Thayne nodded his agreement and as they settled back onto their cots, exhaustion tugged at him. But despite Pietyr and Rackham's concerns, Thayne prayed to the Ascended that Ellarah would remember. Her presence on the outside as an ally, or as someone who could create a distraction for them, would be invaluable because their plan was risky as hell.

Unfortunately, he still had to acknowledge that Pietyr and Rackham had a point. They couldn't rely on her. They'd have to use what they had at their disposal right now, and he could only hope it would be enough.

21
STRENGTH
REMI

Remi awoke, screaming from the nightmare. Her heart raced and her blood seemed to boil as she rose to a sitting position in the dark cell. She didn't know if the dream had come from Davendrie or her own mind. It lacked some of the venom of Davendrie's typical ministrations, but it still tormented her as she squeezed her eyes shut and tried to block out the images of her family, dead.

A few seconds later, she opened her eyes. No lights shone in the cell. A new thing she hated even more than the constant brightness that had been her existence before the lunch with Ellarah. But in that black cell, she could feel Not-Bekka sitting beside her on the stiff, narrow cot.

A hand reached out and squeezed hers, and she marveled again at the realness of it, at the feel of the weight next to her on the mattress.

"Another bad one?" Not-Bekka asked.

Remi swallowed, her mouth dry and her throat raw and aching from her screaming. She pressed her palm to her clammy forehead and groaned. "Yes."

The silence hung for a while and Remi soaked in the comfort she felt from Not-Bekka's hand in hers.

Not-Bekka's voice broke through it, "Don't worry, Remi. You're going to get out of here. We all will. Remember what I told you. We are Valerians, and you don't mess with the Valerian princesses."

Remi had told her about the lunch with Ellarah, and how Ellarah might remember what happened soon. Not-Bekka had been so certain that Ellarah's memory would return, and she'd rescue them from the Bicaidian dungeons. But for Remi, that tiny sliver of hope had been dashed on the rocks of reality and despair.

Because the more time she had to think about it, the more time doubt had to creep into her mind. Who knew if or when Ellarah would remember? *Or if she even could remember*, Remi thought, chewing on a nail. She wouldn't put it past Riven to have that memory stripped. But then again, that could be an invasive process and Ellarah may have been too weak. But if she showed signs of her memory returning, would he do it now that she'd recovered?

Remi dragged a hand down her face and sighed, mind shifting to the other things she'd seen that day. She recalled the hordes of demons, feasting in the palace as though celebrating a victory. She couldn't imagine what terrible triumph that could have been, or how many more would come before they escaped. If they ever managed it. And if they did, would it be too late?

"You're going down a despair spiral again," Not-Bekka observed, and Remi squinted to try to make out her face, but couldn't. The problem with Not-Bekka was that she wasn't Bekka. Instead, she was a figment of Remi's imagination and thus always knew what Remi was thinking. It irked when she wanted privacy.

"I can't afford to get my hopes up," Remi said, moving her legs to toss them over the side of the mattress and press her bare feet against the cool stone. "Because if I end up stuck here for months or years, and I let that false hope run wild, then I don't think despair spiral would even begin to cover the level of emotional turmoil I'll feel."

Not-Bekka turned to position herself next to Remi, shoulder-to-shoulder. "You can't let your mind go to that dark place. It won't do you any good."

"What difference does it make? It's not like happy thoughts are going to solve anything."

"You're stronger than this, Remi."

"Am I though?" Remi asked, turning her head and wishing to hell she could see her sister's expression.

"The Remi I know is," Not-Bekka replied, and the certainty in her voice made something in Remi pull tight as a flash of anger pulsed.

"Well, maybe I'm not the same Remi you used to know," she snapped, rising to her feet as she stalked across the floor to the tiny bathroom sink and metallic mirror. She stared into it as though she might see her reflection despite the lack of light. Even if she could, she wasn't sure she'd recognize it anymore. Yet she stayed there, waiting for Not-Bekka to say something, to argue with her. When she didn't, Remi clamped her hands on either side of the sink, fingers gripping hard. "Maybe I'm tired of being strong all the time. Maybe I want someone else to shoulder the burden, even for a fucking microsecond because this weight, Bekka? It's too damn much. I can't take it anymore."

A hand landed on Remi's shoulder, and she couldn't help but stiffen in surprise. She hadn't even heard Not-Bekka move. Every inhale and exhale of breath was an effort as she tried to fight through the anguish she felt.

Not-Bekka turned her then, as gently as their mother used to, and wrapped Remi into her arms. Remi let her, pressing her cheek to her hallucination's shoulder. How did it feel so real? "You're going to get through this, Remi. You can carry this for just a little while longer. Don't think about months or years. Think about days. It's always one step at a time. One minute, one hour, and one day at a time, OK? And if Ellarah doesn't figure something out, then we will. I'll help you."

Remi wished with everything inside her that this moment was real. She inhaled the familiar scent of Bekka and tried not to let the tears that threatened to overflow slide past her eyelids. If she started crying, she feared she'd never be able to stop, and any remaining strength she had left would disappear. But despite the agony, resolve tightened around her. One minute, one hour, one day. That she could do.

"Alright," Remi said, her voice low. "One step at a time."

Not-Bekka let out a long sigh, the sound relieved, just as Remi heard an unfamiliar clang against the cell door. Remi whipped her head to stare at it as the metal slab flung open and the lights flashed on. She blinked hard, her eyes struggling to adjust to the abrupt change. Not-Bekka had disappeared. She could feel that more than see it because her eyes stung like hell as they watered against the brightness. They burned for longer than she liked before she could focus on who had entered.

Madwyn.

Hatred burned up her throat and as she straightened to her full height. Her fists clenched at her sides, and she called her fire magic to her in rote memory. Of course, nothing happened. The damned rune on her skin flared as she tried to access her power. She wanted to fry the bitch where she stood, but that would never happen. Not with her trapped in that cell and her magic trapped inside her, too.

"What are you doing here?" Remi ground out through her clenched teeth.

Madwyn smiled as though she hadn't a care in the world and strode over to sit on Remi's cot. "Come, sit, Remi. Let's talk like civilized goddesses."

What the hell is wrong with her? Remi wondered, glaring at her through her lashes. "You're insane if you think that's possible."

She shrugged a toned shoulder. "Well, what can I say? I'm an optimist."

"A nihilist, more like," Remi muttered, glaring at the deity she'd once called an ally. Someone she'd even considered a friend. *Murderous, traitorous bitch*, Remi thought, nails biting into her palms.

"Oh, come now," Madwyn said, admonishing, "No need for nasty names. Besides, if you don't do as I ask, I can always have Davendri root around in that head of yours a little more."

Remi's belly tightened, her back going ramrod straight in a visceral reaction to the threat. She wanted to slap the lips off Madwyn's smug face but couldn't risk it. Whether she liked it or not, Madwyn's threat hit home. Her mind already felt like it was coming apart at the seams. So, Remi strode to the bed, sat beside Madwyn, and resisted the urge to strangle her. "What do you want?"

"Well, off to a rocky start on the civility front, but I guess I can't blame you there."

"Stop talking about stupid bullshit that neither of us cares about and tell me what you're doing here."

Madwyn's lips twitched upward, amused rather than angry. What would it take to get under this bitch's skin? She'd never seen anyone accomplish it, and she swore to herself right then and there that she would find a way. Maybe not soon, but someday she'd claw through that placid exterior and to the black soul that lurked beneath it.

"Tomorrow, a demon will collect you in the morning. You'll shower and make yourself presentable. Then it will take you to make a holo to send to your parents. It's about time we started our negotiations with Valeria, don't you think?"

Remi scoffed, a bitter laugh escaping her throat. "In what multiverse do you think I'd ever agree to that?"

Madwyn's face went cold as ice then, the gleam in her eye unmistakable. "The one I'm making, my dear. The one where Bekka has already agreed to cooperate." She rose and strolled back to the door as Remi's brain short-circuited. *Bekka agreed?* She thought, unable to believe she was hearing.

"You're lying," Remi said, rising to her feet. "She'd never." Her chest rose and fell, and no small amount of panic seeped in.

Madwyn's hand lingered on the door handle before she turned back and offered Remi that devilish grin that had once seemed so appealing. "She did. It seems Arrick helped her see the light. Good thing too, or else things would have gotten ... dicey ... for him and his entire family. Well, his entire realm, really." She paused on the word dicey, and Remi's mind slipped back to Bicaidian hell. To when Arrick and Madwyn had made the deal that protected them all.

"I don't believe you," Remi said again, the denial ringing hollow.

"You don't need to. You just need to do as you're told, Remi dear. If you won't for your own sake or your sister's and Arrick's, then do it for Ellarah's."

Remi could hear the blood rushing in her ears. Ellarah, her friend and the only person she could call an ally in Bicaidia who wasn't trapped in its dungeon. *The only one who might be able to help us escape, if she could just remember what happened on inauguration night*, Remi thought, before she tamped down that hope yet again. One day at a time, she remembered.

"You wouldn't," Remi said, composing her features to hide her shock. "Riven would never allow it. If you did something to her, he'd never forgive you." As much as she loathed him, Remi knew Riven loved Ellarah. She couldn't imagine that he'd allow her to get hurt, or killed, for that matter. Madwyn may have some sick hold over her brother, but if she killed Ellarah? Remi suspected that hold would break and Madwyn would lose one of her most powerful leaders.

Madwyn raised her eyebrows and shrugged. "Her recovery is so tenuous, you know. Keeping her from the antidote as long as you did—" she clicked her tongue in admonishment. "No one will blame me if she succumbs to her injuries."

"You're sick, Madwyn. You would do that to your own brother?"

"I would. There's no price I wouldn't pay for this revolution, Remi. It's time you learned that." A memory flashed in Remi's mind, and the horror of it washed over her. Madwyn sounded like her grandfather, her parents.

Whatever it takes.

Those words hummed through her mind like a song, and she tried to block it out. She didn't want this twisted goddess to bear any resemblance to the family she loved. To the people who'd raised and cared for Remi her whole life. Despite all their missteps, they were good deities, weren't they? She looked at Madwyn then, feeling nauseated as she considered that question, and found she didn't like the answer.

"So, do we have an agreement?" Madwyn asked, as though Remi had any other choice. Refuse, and something terrible would happen to Ellarah, and to Arrick or his family. From that brief time in hell, Remi knew that something had happened between Bekka and Arrick, that their relationship had been more than just one of convenience. Her sister's keening screams when he'd promised himself to Madwyn still reverberated in Remi's ears. Something told her that if she allowed Madwyn to harm him, Bekka would never forgive her.

"I think you know the answer to that," Remi said, her voice as cold as ice. She might be forced to agree to this fool's bargain, but she didn't have to give Madwyn the satisfaction of hearing the actual words.

"Good, that's what I thought," Madwyn said before she opened the door and disappeared into the hall beyond.

22
COMPLICATED
THAYNE

*Y*ou're not allowed to hate me.

Those words had echoed in Thayne's mind ever since that dream. They replayed each night when he slept because the dreams hadn't stopped. Instead, every night a new memory came to him, and a mental bridge with Madwyn followed it.

Sometimes she spoke to him. Other times, she would just look at him in a way that made him feel like he might come apart at the seams.

At that moment, though, he didn't feel like he would tear himself apart. Instead, she'd dropped him into a memory that fixed his full attention on her, something she did often.

His gaze swept over her face as he slid his hand up her bare thigh, hitching it higher, and settling his weight between her legs. Her chaos magic crackled over his skin, stinging as it bit. *It feels so damn good*, he thought. Just like it had the time they'd fucked in the lush garden at her family's estate, etched into the red cliffs of Helverta. The memory of that night poured over his senses because she hadn't made him an observer this time, but an active participant, just as he'd been that night fifteen years before.

You're not allowed to hate me.

He loosed a little of his lightning, sending a slight jolt between her thighs that had her gasping right before he plunged himself inside of her. "You're so fucking wet and warm," he whispered, lips brushing over the shell of her ear as he groaned with all-consuming pleasure. *It feels like coming home,* he thought, the mirror of the same one he'd had that night so long ago. Everything felt quiet inside her, and he'd known in that moment that he wanted to be with her forever.

She moaned, and he covered it with a rough kiss, fastening a hand around her throat as he moved. In and out, all the way to the tip, and then slamming back inside her to the hilt. Nothing about them had ever been easy or gentle, he remembered, as she raked her nails down his back, hips bucking up to meet his thrusts.

He felt her breasts, soft and full, pressed beneath his weight and he remembered thinking that he would burn the world for her and offer it to her in the palm of his hand if it would give her the tiniest ounce of pleasure. A clap of thunder boomed, and a bolt of lightning struck the ground beside them, shaking the soft, grassy ground beneath them. She gasped in surprise, clenching around him as her hair rose with the electric current.

He looked down at her, her eyes bright with surprise and pleasure, and remembered thinking she was the most beautiful thing he'd ever seen. He never wanted that feeling of belonging to each other to end.

You're not allowed to hate me.

The image faded away as abruptly as it had started. Thayne looked around and saw a burning city, smoke clogging his nostrils. Scanning his hands and body, he saw that he wore the same tuxedo he'd worn on the night of the inauguration ball. He could feel cobblestones beneath his knees and rose to his feet, turning to take in the surrounding destruction.

Then his parents appeared, their eyes milky and lifeless as they stared at him. They looked like they were made from clay, nothing like the deities they'd been before Madwyn had killed them. They stared at him with those unseeing eyes, as though they could see straight into his soul.

Then all the memories came flooding back as agony, unlike anything he'd ever felt before, washed over him. He stared in disbelief as he realized that, for a moment, he'd forgotten everything else, lost in the pleasure he'd found between Madwyn's thighs. But how could he forget?

It was his fault. His choices, and Madwyn's betrayal, had caused his parents' deaths and Bicaidia's fall. Shame swallowed every single inch of him. How could he blank out everything that had happened? Why had she done this to him, to all of them, at all? Why was she doing this to him now? All he'd done was try to be a good high prince for his people and form an alliance that would benefit them all. Even Madwyn, whether she could see it or not. Because he'd planned to use that relationship with Remi to change things through Gabryel.

Even though his romance with Madwyn had ended, their friendship hadn't. He thought it never would, and he never would have abandoned his promise to help the Nefarals or to help the energy deities, both causes that he cared about because of Madwyn and Ellarah.

"I'm sorry," Thayne said, staring at the shadows of his parents. "I'm so sorry." There was nothing else to say, and they didn't speak as they looked at him with the kind of accusation he knew would burn into his soul for the rest of his miserable existence. And then, they disappeared.

When they faded, he saw Madwyn sitting on a deep green, wing-backed chair in front of him, and he recognized this new place for what it was. The mental bridge she'd formed every night since she sent him the memory of their son. Thayne hadn't told the others about it. They knew about the dreams, of course. He couldn't hide them when he woke sweating and shouting most nights, but they didn't know about the conversations.

He could already imagine what they'd say if they did. Pietyr would call him an idiot and tell him to refuse to talk to her. Deklan would agree. Those two, whether or not they admitted it, had an anger inside them that burned hotter than the sun, and they carried resentment like an eternal torch.

Caden and Rackham had calmer dispositions, and they'd probably try to get him to pump her for information, to trip her up, or get her to divulge a way out of the palace dungeons. But they didn't know her the way he did. He couldn't trick Madwyn into anything. She always thought through her moves, and she wouldn't let her emotions get in her way, not when she cared this much about something, and he couldn't afford for her to go poking around in his head any more than necessary. Not when they had magic, and not when they were so close to finding a way out.

So instead, he stared at her face and noted the beauty of it. But that softness, that happiness, and the glow she'd had while she writhed beneath him all those years ago were gone. Thayne looked around then, taking in his surroundings, and noted the utter blackness of the mental bridge. He stood before her, a cloud of sheer dust appearing. It solidified into a chair before his eyes—a mirror of Madwyn's.

"Am I supposed to get comfortable or something?" he asked, exhaustion, shame, and a sick loathing tugging at every inch of him. He could still feel a pang of arousal between his legs, as though even his own body would betray him. He hated her so fucking much.

"If you want," she said, waving a hand. Deciding it couldn't hurt him more than she already had, he dropped into the chair, sagging in relief. It felt comfortable. Though he knew it wasn't real, he relished the softness of the cushions beneath him.

"I don't want to talk tonight, Madwyn. Leave me alone," he said, but his voice lacked the usual venom he managed to muster for her. He was too tired, and he didn't have it in him to fight or argue anymore. He wanted peace for just one day.

Ignoring him, she asked, "You remember that night, right? The first night we made love? It was in the garden of my family estate. You told me you loved me, and we couldn't keep our hands off each other after that." She let out a long sigh, her blue eyes shifting to look down at her hand as she smoothed her fingers over the carved, wooden armrest.

"Why are you doing this?" Thayne asked. "Why can't you just let it go?"

"I told you," she said. "You're not allowed to hate me."

"Why the hell not?" Thayne asked, anger rising, replacing his exhaustion. Madwyn had a talent for bringing out the worst in him. "What difference does it make? I'm trapped like a rat in a cage, so why does it matter what I think of you?"

"Because despite everything, I don't hate you, so you don't get to hate me either. We're in this together. Always have been," she said, fingers gripping those armrests so tight that her knuckles whitened. Thayne looked at her then, really looked, and saw the light in her eyes. *Brighter than usual,* he thought, bluer ... and something about her seemed different.

She stared at him with an intensity he didn't recognize and as he considered her words, realization hit him hard. She would never let him escape her. The sex dreams that left him raw and aching hadn't been enough for her. She wanted to see him and talk to him after. As though she knew just how fucked in the head it would make him. She wanted that. She wanted him pulled apart at the seams because she needed something from him. What though? He couldn't begin to guess. He didn't even bother to guess. She'd always played things close to the vest, and he had no reason to think she'd change just because he asked nicely.

When he didn't respond, she continued, "I know you don't understand why I did what I did, but our world? It needed to be burned down, Thayne. The Twelve Realms needed to change. They hurt too many deities for too long and kept the Nefarals down even longer. Most of us didn't even fight in the war, and they still controlled us, watched us, and caged us like animals. I struck when I did because another opportunity never would have happened and no one else had the guts to do it. So, I stepped up."

"Stop trying to justify what you did, Madwyn. You had me, you had Remi, and you had the new creator, who you would've helped bring back to the Twelve Realms, all on your side. Everything could have gone differently. You would have had a seat at the table, and with all of Emorie's information, there would have been more than enough leverage for you to drive actual change. But that wasn't good enough for you. So, you can say this is all about the common good and freedom, but this is really about you. It's about power and your desire for control. You killed my family and ruined my realm. Ascended only knows what you've done since." He thought about the demons and deities he'd seen celebrating in battle gear in his banquet hall when he and Remi went to see Ellarah all those weeks ago.

She let out a long sigh and rose from her chair, shaking her head. He could tell that nothing he said landed. Not a single hit. She'd put up a wall against any criticism, any truth, and nothing could permeate it. *A defense mechanism?* He wondered. *Or something else?*

"Think what you want, Thayne," she said. "But I'm not your enemy. I never was and I never have been."

"You're wrong, Madwyn. You made yourself my enemy, and you can't undo that no matter how hard you try."

She shook her head then and turned, disappearing into a wisp of wind and dust. As she did, he heard her voice say, "You say those words enough, and maybe you'll start to believe them too. But I think we both know they're lies."

23
LIFE DEBTS

ARRICK

I made my way to Sylennia's chambers, needing to talk to her after everything that had happened. I sent a pulse of my magic through the sensor, and the lock sprang free. My temper still simmered beneath the surface, and Bekka's magic had turned into a constant itch beneath my skin, always trying to break free. The energy I expended to keep it concealed gave me unwanted side effects. I balanced on the razor's edge of anger, quicker to tip over that precipice at even the smallest provocation.

But I tamped down on that fury as I entered the large, luxurious room, the mirror of my own. I scanned the interior and saw the goddess I sought standing outside on the balcony, overlooking the glowing Synbue River. I moved to join her, eager to speak with her, but uncertain how far I could take things with her. What could I tell her? I knew I could trust her with some things, but everything?

I had no clue. What I did know though? I had to do something. Bekka was counting on me.

Sylennia turned, seeming to sense me, and offered me a smile that didn't reach her eyes. I strode out to join her, resting my hands on the stone ledge of the railing. "Everything alright?" I asked. I'd never seen her look like that before. Not determined, flirtatious, suspicious, or even concerned, but sad.

She pressed her lips together and I turned to face her, resting my elbow on the rail. Her throat bobbed with an effort to swallow. "So, Bekka agreed to do it?"

I arched my brow. "You stayed for that conversation?"

She nodded. "And after too. I've been watching her today, Madwyn, I mean."

A dangerous thing to admit to, especially to me. I waited then, letting the silence stretch, needing it for just a moment. After a while, I let out a long breath, regret and worry plaguing me. I'd made promises to Bekka that I had no business making, and that I didn't know how to keep. The thought of that weighed heavy on my shoulders.

"Who is she to you?" Sylennia asked, breaking the silence as she searched my face for the answer. Before I could reply, she continued, "She's the Valerian creator, their princess, Gabryel's granddaughter, and you're a Moldizean prince, and a death deity. I know this thing between us is for show, but—" She swallowed, shaking her head, her eyes moving with some emotion I couldn't quite place. "But I care for you. Maybe more than I should, and I don't mean romantically. I just—why would the Valerian creator agree to risk the safety of her family and her realm for yours? And Moldize, of all places?"

I didn't know what to say, or how to answer her. Because that's what Bekka agreed to do for me. To risk disaster in Valeria to save me from the despair and grief she knew would destroy me if I lost everyone and everything I loved. Though gratitude lived inside me, I felt like a grade-A bastard for even asking that of her. I wouldn't have, had it been my choice.

I would have found a way out of it myself, and done everything in my power to keep the people she loved safe, along with my own. The thing was, she cared about my people, too. My parents, the Itorians, my sister. She'd grown to love them during the time we spent together in Moldize. They'd become hers as well.

Sylennia's eyes searched mine as though looking for answers. At last, I shrugged my shoulders and said, "We're friends. She saved Moldize, and I—"

"Sacrificed your freedom for her. Right?" Sylennia finished. "The rumors, they're true, aren't they? They've stopped since everyone thinks you spend your nights with me, but the ones I heard before I came here? They're true?"

I hesitated a long while, debating my next move, before nodding in confirmation. "There were other deities with us in hell that night too, but—" I shook my head. "Madwyn threatened to cut her and Remi to pieces, and send them back to Valeria." I opened and closed my fists, trying to relieve some of the tension that memory brought back. The bone-deep horror I'd felt at the prospect of my soulfused mate enduring that kind of torture? I couldn't describe it. After a long pause, I said, "I couldn't let that happen to her."

Sylennia nodded as though processing my words. "There's something you should know about me." I stayed silent and tilted my head, encouraging her to continue. After a long exhale, she did, "My brother was there that night. So, when you sacrificed your freedom, you didn't just save her. Whether you intended to or not, you saved him, too."

Unable to hide my surprise, my eyes widened. I scanned through my memory, trying to picture the others there, the male deities. Then I latched onto an image of a shadow deity holding a knife to Madwyn's throat. As I pictured the details of his face, it came into focus. I stared at Sylennia then and realized how similar they looked. "The shadow god?" I asked, brows cinching together.

She swallowed, nodding. "His name is Pietyr."

I swallowed, hand gripping the railing harder as I thought back to everything that had happened that night. "He fought well. He almost saved our skins, too. Bekka and I were in no shape to help. We'd been trapped in Bicaidian hell for too long, with too little food, water, and sleep, but he almost got us out. He and the time god. It was only Madwyn's leverage that saved her. She captured and threatened to kill his friends, so he surrendered."

She gave me another sad smile. "That sounds like Pietyr. He wouldn't have gone down without a fight, but that sounds like Madwyn, too. She always knows where to apply pressure." She looked down at the river, toying with a black, woven ring on her finger. "So, despite what you might think of me, I'm not Riven's lackey or hers. And the way I see it? You saved my brother, so I owe you a life debt. Madwyn might think I'm on her side, but Pietyr is my blood, and I won't forget what you did for him."

I considered what she said, and thought that she might eat those words soon, considering the payment I might ask for. But that could wait for the moment, so I nodded. "I'll keep that in mind."

"Good," she said, releasing the ring along with her breath.

I refocused on the river flowing beneath us and changed the subject. "There's something else we need to discuss. Riven came looking for me today. Davendrie is sick. He dropped into stasis sleep after that display on the training grounds. When he woke, he remembered nothing about what happened. Riven also told me that Davendrie had a high fever and a nosebleed the healers had trouble stopping. Then he asked me if I'd seen anything else out of the ordinary. Any similar, strange behavior."

Sylennia's eyes widened in surprise as she wet her lips. "What did you tell him?"

"Nothing. I wasn't sure how much you wanted me to divulge. You know more about what's happening than I do. Davendrie's outburst is the first I've witnessed like it."

She bit her lip. "Alright, I'll talk to Riven. Maybe I can reason with him and convince him to let me dig further into it." I gave her a skeptical look, and she shook her head, hair tossing from side to side. "Riven isn't a monster like his sister. You know that, right?"

I considered her statement, the skeptical expression still plastered on my face. But then, I thought about it more. He seemed worried about his friend; like he wanted to help him. Then I remembered that day in Quindale when he asked me how many I'd killed using our combined power. I remembered something like remorse in his eyes, along with the anger. "You think he'll help you?"

She shrugged. "He might, if he's worried enough about Davendri. When I first told him about my suspicions, he didn't believe me, but he still let me look into it. After I brought my findings to him, he told me to keep it to myself and warned me not to talk about it. So, I went straight to Madwyn, but she ordered me to stop digging too, and I didn't want to press it further with either of them. But if he's starting to see the evidence too? Outside of what I've presented to him? He might help keep Madwyn off our trail while we figure things out. She trusts him, and pretty much only him.

Though now that Ellarah is awake, he's been a little more preoccupied, which might make things more difficult."

"She's better?" I asked, letting Sylennia decide how she wanted to handle Riven. I knew without asking that she would keep me out of it. Our alliance could never seem like more than a fling, or it would lose its value.

"Yes, and you would think he'd be happy about it, but I can tell something's wrong. He won't admit it, though I'm sure he and Ellarah will make it through, whatever it is. They always do."

I didn't miss the bitter note in her tone. But then she changed the subject, steering things back to the other point of concern. "You know how I said I watched Madwyn all day?"

I nodded. "Did you learn anything useful?"

"I did, and I didn't. Partial information, not as complete as I'd like. But I learned Madwyn plans to ask the Valerians for a meeting to discuss a ceasefire and a truce. She's angling to have it in Valeria. Though I couldn't hear as much as I wanted to today, I can tell she doesn't want peace. That's just a pretense. Bekka's parents would be in danger if they agreed to meet with her, and so would Valeria. Not to mention Lilja."

I fought back the surprise that hit me at that last point. "Why Lilja?" I expected the rest from my knowledge of Madwyn, but my sister? What the hell did she have to do with anything? Hadn't I guaranteed her safety by getting Bekka to make the damned holo?

"Madwyn doesn't trust you, not when it comes to Bekka and the Valerians. She thinks you'll try to find a way around your orders, to stop her from whatever she has planned. So, she's going to take your sister along as a reminder of what's at stake for you, should you step out of line."

That familiar edge sharpened again, anger pulsing beneath my skin. What did Madwyn have planned that made her worry I would step out of line, and risk the lives of my sister and my entire realm? "Does she plan to start a war?" I asked.

Sylennia shrugged her shoulders. "I don't know, but whatever she's planning, it won't be good for the Valerians."

After a long pause that had us both falling deeper into contemplation, shadows grew around her. She turned, moving to the patio door, and gesturing for me to follow. I did, and she closed the doors behind me, drawing the curtains. "You never know—"

"Who's watching," I finished. "But you always seem to know who's listening." I offered her a crooked grin, gesturing toward the patio, referring to the conversation we'd just had out in the open.

She shrugged, a sly smile on her lips. "They'd have to get pretty close for that, and I would sense them before they heard a damn word I said." Her shadows grew deeper then, surrounding me. "So, are you ready to see Lilja?"

I nodded, and then we were gone.

24
TURMOIL

Bekka

A demon opened my door early that morning and released me from my cell. Disappointment filled every cell in my body that it hadn't been Arrick.

Instead, the creature led me down the hall to the bathing chamber. I showered, brushed my hair, and dressed in clothes provided by Madwyn. I could feel the silken, white pants brushing around my legs as I walked down the halls of my cellblock, the snug fit of the golden tank top a sharp contrast.

They wanted me adorned in house Daevos's colors so they could parade me in front of a camera to beg for ... something. I didn't know what they would ask me to say, but I could guess.

Lies? Definitely. Concessions? Probably. A peace treaty? I doubted Madwyn wanted real peace, but that didn't mean she wouldn't use it as an angle to ruin my family. They needed to be smart enough to see through it, and if not, I hoped Arrick would help them.

I also knew that Madwyn would expect me to pretend that the lives of my parents and everyone in Valeria weren't in danger. If I didn't, she would probably cut off one of Lilja's fingers to incentivize me. *All the better to manipulate Valeria*, I thought.

As I turned the corner, keeping my distance from the smelly, disgusting demon, another door sprung open. My heart leaped into my throat when I saw who stepped out from it—my sister.

"Remi!" I shouted, shoving past the demon and running for her without a second thought. It gripped my shoulder and tried to yank me back, but I twisted free, sprinting down the hall. Remi turned when she heard my voice, her crimson hair whipping around her shoulders. Her coffee-colored eyes, our single identical feature despite our twinhood, locked onto me and I could feel the threat of tears burning.

In less than a second, I crashed into her, wrapping my arms around her and squeezing. She did the same, her warmth and familiarity so comforting that I wanted to cry, but I knew I couldn't afford to do that. Not amongst my enemies.

"Rem!" I said, breathing hard from the run and the excitement of seeing her again. I released her and rested my hands on her shoulders to look her over. She did the same to me, but I spoke first, as usual, "You're OK. Well, of course you are. I mean, you look like shit, and when was the last time you slept? None of that matters. You're here, and that's all I care about!"

Dimples formed at the corners of her mouth as she offered me a sad, but genuine smile. Her porcelain skin looked smooth, except for the dark circles under her eyes. "Bekka, I don't even—" she broke off and looked away. Tears glistened in her eyes before she composed herself and refocused on me. "I can't believe it's really you." She gripped my hand hard, and I knew she had so much more she wanted to say, but unlike me, she'd never been great with the sappy stuff.

Before I could fill the brief silence, the demon shoved my back. "Move," it growled, its guttural voice echoing down the stone hallway.

I gave it my *die slowly* glare before I turned back to my sister and linked my arm with hers. We obeyed then, walking as directed, and I tilted my head to hers to whisper. "I can't believe you're here. How did they get you to agree? I didn't think you ever would."

Remi sighed and clutched my arm closer, as though afraid I might disappear. "Madwyn can be persuasive. She knows what buttons to push. It sounded like she did the same to you?"

I nodded, feeling my ire rise in response to the memory. Though Arrick had coerced me into making this holo, I didn't blame him for it. He'd been following orders. So, rather than get into the details, I nodded. "Yep. Did she tell you what she wants us to say?"

Remi shook her head. "Only that we're to make a holo for our parents. But it doesn't take a genius to guess what she wants from us."

I swallowed the lump forming in my throat. "Are we doing the right thing here?"

My sister's shoulders rose and fell as she took a long breath. "I think it's the least terrible of all our horrible options."

Remi had a way of putting a finer point on things. Of course, I'd told myself the same thing many times since Arrick's visit. I could still feel the warmth of his body on the calloused skin of my fingertips and I rubbed them together, thinking about the reason I was doing this—Lilja, his sweet, adorable kid sister, and all the rest of the Moldizeans I'd grown so close to in the months I'd spent there.

I couldn't bear to imagine her dead, nor any of the people I cared about in Moldize. Besides, Emorie was right. No way Valeria stayed out of Madwyn's war forever, but Lilja and the Moldizean mortals? They still had a chance to make it through this unscathed.

We fell silent, climbing the stairs that led out of the dungeons and into the Bicaidian palace grounds. Warmth and sunlight kissed my skin, and I inhaled, breathing in the sweet, floral scent of the fresh air. It had been so damn long since I'd seen the sun, or plants, or grass. It looked like heaven, I thought, trying my best to savor the moment, knowing it wouldn't last long.

My sandaled feet crunched on the gravel pathway that wound to the massive palace ahead. Flowering cacti and small shrubs lined the path, and I tried to focus on each step, my sister's arm still locked in mine. I didn't want to think about the possible ramifications of what we were doing because it felt like betrayal. I couldn't help but wonder—would my parents be able to handle it? Would Valeria? My instincts told me yes. Madwyn might have conquered Bicaidia, but she'd used the benefit of surprise to do it. My parents would know about her by now. They'd be ready. They would stop her.

A few minutes later, we skirted the palace courtyard, passing under the arched overhangs, and made our way through a large doorway.

I could still smell the warm, floral scent from the gardens outside as we crossed into the grand majesty of the Bicaidian throne room. My breath caught in my throat as I took in the crowded space. Deities lined the walls, some sitting in chairs and others standing, but they all went silent as their eyes landed on Remi and me.

My blood went cold as I hesitated, and the demon shoved me forward again. I resisted the urge to turn around and slam my fist into its face. But it didn't seem like the opportune time for that, considering how many

Nefarals hovered around us. So instead, I squared my shoulders, lifted my chin, and started walking.

Trying to settle my nerves, I focused on the rough-hewn wood and vibrant colors that permeated every aspect of the decor and the stunning paintings of Bicaidian history that decorated the ceiling and walls. It felt easier than looking at all Madwyn's allies, who stared daggers at us as we continued forward.

As we passed by them, I could hear whispered hisses whip through the grand hall, "That's the creator. It's her. We have her. She's ours now."

I wished I could show them just what a creator could do. Maybe disintegrate them all with a single thought? Or even better, disintegrate Madwyn and free Arrick. Though I knew that killing Madwyn wouldn't free Arrick from the binding, it still made me happy to imagine it. In response to my machinations, the rune on my wrist flared.

I hated that damn tattoo. If I'd thought it would help, I would have asked Emorie to carve it out with the dull spoon we received at mealtimes. But magic didn't work that way, and I had the distinct feeling that removing it through brute force would do little to dispel its power over me. I had to break the spell it had over my magic.

Deities still poured into the room from the open-air balcony, all dressed in formal attire with their sigils dangling from their necks. Not just Nefarals, I noticed, but from all Pillars of Power. All loyal to Madwyn, and from the varying arrays of styles and appearances, I knew these deities weren't just from Bicaidia. I took in the crowd and noted the white hair and golden skin of Quindaleans, along with the dark eyes and brown skin of the Perenelleans among the golden-tanned Bicaidians.

Flowing gowns, slick suits, and colorful clothing parted as all the deities crowded along the walls and I saw her—Madwyn. She sat on Thayne's family's golden laced wood throne, the grand chair molded to look like a large, sprawling vine of gem cactus. It meandered up the wall to the ceiling where large, golden Chamaelobivia flowers dangled. The stunning effect took my breath away, but not as much as when my gaze landed on Arrick.

He stood next to Madwyn, and when the green of his irises locked onto mine, I could hear my heart in my ears. I wanted to jump into his arms and wrap my body around him, feel the strength of his arms holding me, to know that we would be OK. That he would be OK.

But, just as in the cell, I could feel the tinge of pain and rage that he carried. That darkness seemed to have grown since the last time I saw him. What had happened since then? What other torments had he endured because he'd chosen to protect me? To protect all of us? Deep down, I knew, because I'd seen them. As much as I tried to deny that my nightmares were real, I could feel that they were.

Remi squeezed my hand then, and I tore my eyes away from him to look at her. Her hard stare let me know she had no intention of showing weakness or fear. She wanted to make sure that I wouldn't either. *Typical Remi,* I thought. She would never show fragility, no matter the circumstance.

I nodded, letting her know I understood and agreed. No weakness. But then a slight figure caught my eye, and I focused on the young goddess just over Remi's shoulder, not fifteen steps away from Arrick. Lilja, I realized. Her doe eyes watched me, wide with concern, as I saw her lips mouth my name.

I inclined my head ever so slightly, letting her know I saw her and tried to impart as much confidence as I could into my expression. She looked so young, so fragile, and the idea that Madwyn would threaten her made my fury rise again. She didn't belong there any more than Arrick did, I thought, hating our situation even more than I had five seconds ago.

Lilja fastened her teeth to her bottom lip, her concern obvious as a voice rang out from the throne. "There you are," Madwyn crooned, her words echoing from the lofty ceilings. "Come join us. We're ready for you."

25

THE HOLOGRAM

BEKKA

Madwyn gestured to two plain chairs that sat in front of the throne. I felt the heat of Remi's body next to me and knew she radiated with the same loathing as I did. We stood, shoulder-to-shoulder, glaring at the goddess who'd taken so much from us.

In unison, we stepped forward, toward those unadorned chairs. As I drew closer, I saw a holo device on a small table before them. The smooth black orb was little more than a blot on the raw-edged wood, and I tried to settle my nerves as it powered on, letters populating just above it.

I skimmed through the first few sentences and a pit formed in my stomach. Those were our lines, I realized, sickened by what I was about to do. No, by what we were about to do.

I felt like a fish in a bowl, all eyes on me, ready to tap on the glass and laugh as I floundered. My muscles tightened as I drew to my full height and made my way to the chairs. "Show no weakness," Remi whispered, just before we got within hearing range of Madwyn.

Then we were there, the demons pushing us with rough, clawed fingers into the chairs. I resisted the urge to stomp on their booted feet before they walked away, mostly because I thought it would hurt me more than them. Sandals were not the most effective shoe for foot stomping. So, I promised myself a rain check before I read the rest of the glowing words above the holo.

"You can't be serious," Remi spat, her attitude mirroring mine as she glared at Madwyn. "I'm not reading that."

"Oh, you'll read it alright," the chaos deity said, fingers tracing a golden vine on her throne. "You both know the cost of refusal."

My pulse quickened, and I looked at Arrick again, his expression dark, murderous. He didn't like being used as a pawn to manipulate me, and I could feel that reverberating off him even at this distance.

"Remi," I breathed, pulling her attention back to me. "We have to do this. Valeria is at the center of this fight. They're in it no matter what we do. But there are people here we can protect." If anyone could stop Madwyn, it was our family and the Valerian stronghold. She had to know that. And if they couldn't? I didn't let myself think about that possibility, because if I did, then I didn't think I could go through with this.

Remi's expression softened the barest fraction before she turned to the holo. She gestured at our lines, and hardened her features as she spoke to Madwyn, "I don't believe for a second that you want a truce with Valeria."

Riven stepped forward then, from his position on the opposite side of his sister from Arrick, and glared at Remi, "It doesn't matter what you believe—"

Madwyn raised a hand to stop him, and he snapped his mouth shut. Apparently, she liked to keep all her subordinates on a tight leash, even her brother.

"Riven is right. It doesn't matter what you believe. But just so you know," she said, rising from her throne and stepping forward, her hips swaying in her black silk gown. It pooled on the ground like water as she moved, a long slit slicing its way up her thigh. "We already have everything we've ever wanted. We have Bicaidia, we destroyed the governor chips, and we've conquered just enough of the Twelve Realms that we've weakened Valeria's position. Victory for them is uncertain now ... costly even. They'll have to negotiate with us. Believe it or not, I'd prefer to avoid an all-out war, if I can. So, look at it this way, you're going to be the ones to stop that war before it starts, and isn't that what you wanted all along, my dears? I can help you do that, and all you have to do is make the holo."

I stared at her, trying to tamp down the shock her words elicited. Conquered enough of the Twelve Realms? I again looked at the deities in attendance and realized what it all meant. Quindaleans, Perenelleans, Moldizeans, and—on that second look, I saw Crescendian colors along with their telltale silken, black hair and pale skin.

I understood why Madwyn had waited until then to strong-arm us into making the holo. She would force our parents to the table, and with so many of the realms on her side? The foregone conclusion of my family's victory felt a little less certain.

I hesitated, composing my features as I locked eyes with Remi. Her pale face showed nothing but iron will as she met my gaze. "She's lying, Bekka. She's a liar."

"I know," I replied, my heart aching, torn between two pieces of it. I didn't know what to do. Make the holo and risk my parents and my home or refuse and destroy my soulfused mate, not to mention Lilja and all my Moldizean friends. The stakes felt higher, knowing how much power

Madwyn had amassed. I thought my parents could handle her before, but now? I didn't know anymore.

I could feel Arrick's eyes boring into me, along with the spearing knife of fear slicing through him. Having him so close, I felt every emotion roiling through him. Guilt, fear, anger, despair, longing—I pushed them away as best I could. Not that I didn't care, but they were overwhelming, and I needed to think.

When I opened my mouth to say something to Remi, a blood-curdling scream tore through the throne room. I rose from my chair and sent it toppling to the ground as I spun toward that shriek. I recognized the voice and already knew what I would see when my eyes locked on Lilja. A deity I didn't recognize stood behind her, a knife pressed to her throat.

"Let me make this easy for you. I'll give you ten seconds to make the fucking holo, or she dies," Madwyn said, and my mouth dropped open. Fear flooded my system, panic rising as I saw Lilja's wide, terror-stricken eyes. The knife dug a little deeper into her flesh, a small rivulet of blood trailing down the slender column of her neck.

A tear slid down her cheek as Arrick roared, "Madwyn, stop!" He lunged forward, faster than I'd ever seen him move. Dark magic exploded from him, and he lifted his hand, the black mist already spearing in Madwyn's direction.

She spun, as though she knew how he'd react and was ready for it. She shouted, "Stop! Leash that gift and be silent."

He went still as stone, freezing in place as his magic guttered. I could see him straining against her invisible hold over him. Veins corded his neck as terror for his sister's life bucked inside of him, but it was no use. His eyes turned to me, and I could feel his desperation and despair.

I tore my gaze away from him and turned to the chaos goddess. I let the hatred and disbelief I felt show on my face. And why not? Did I think she wanted peace? Or to avoid a war? No, I didn't believe it for a second. But could I watch her slaughter Arrick's sister? Let her slaughter everyone left in his defenseless realm?

I already knew the answer as I bent, lifting the fallen chair from the floor and righting it. Remi stood too, her eyes wide with concern and still locked on Lilja. She didn't know what the young goddess meant to me, but she seemed to sense the resolve that had solidified inside of me like fucking stone.

"Bekka," she said, still standing as I sat on the chair and settled in front of the holo. "We can't. It's—"

"We don't have a choice, Rem. That's Arrick's sister, and it won't stop there. She'll kill everyone in Moldize," I whispered. "She's not bluffing. Now sit down before she gives the order."

Remi still hesitated, hands fisting on the small table as she glared down at me. "What about our people?" she hissed, voice low enough that only I could hear her.

"One problem at a time. They can handle themselves, but the Moldizeans can't. Trust me, they won't survive an attack."

"Your ten seconds is up," Madwyn said, cold eyes bright as glowing sapphires.

"We'll do it," I said, praying to the Ascended that I could get Remi to agree.

She stared at me for a moment, and I could feel the pain and fear rolling off Arrick, still frozen a few paces away. Terror—that we would change our minds, and the agony that speared him as he tried to fight through

Madwyn's hold on him, but he remained silent. As though he required every shred of focus to remain standing. I wanted to go to him, to make it stop, but I knew the best thing I could do was to make the holo.

At last, Remi relented, and she took the seat beside me. She muttered under her breath, "I hope you know what you're doing."

So did I.

At our compliance, Madwyn raised a hand. I shifted in my seat and saw the goddess behind Lilja remove the knife from her throat. An angry, red line remained in its wake, along with a trickle of blood. Lilja's hands flew to her neck, and she stumbled forward, trying to put distance between herself and her attacker.

"Better," Madwyn said, settling into her casual demeanor once more. "Charmelle, see to them, please." At the order, a goddess pushed through the crowd, and my sister sucked in a surprised breath.

Charmelle approached us, golden healing magic swirling around her fingertips, and she dropped to her knees in front of us. She raised her fingers to my cheek and touched it, the healing power flooding my veins and soaking through every inch of my body. The slight pain that remained in my hand from when I'd broken it released, and for the first time in months, I felt refreshed and rested.

She turned her attention to Remi, and as she raised her hand to my sister's face, Remi snatched her wrist in a white-knuckled grip. "What are you doing here?" she asked, glaring at the healer.

Charmelle cleared her throat, looking down, as though ashamed. "I can't—"

"Let her go, Remi," Madwyn said, rolling her eyes in annoyance. "What did you think? That everyone from the compound would choose imprisonment? Hardly. I offered some deities amnesty, depending on their gifts. Charmelle is one of the smart ones. She accepted, and now serves as a royal healer."

Remi's mouth opened before it snapped shut, and I saw the power that burned in her, despite the rune that flared on her wrist. Her body shook with fury, but rather than say anything, she released Charmelle's wrist, eyes pure fire.

When Charmelle's magic soaked her skin, her hands bathed in golden light again, she brushed her fingers over Remi's cheek. "Why?" Remi asked.

"I'm sorry," she said, ducking her head and rising to her feet. She hurried away, and I didn't blame her for it. Remi looked like she might incinerate her, given half the chance. But it begged the question: How many others served Madwyn out of necessity? How many would rally to the Valerian side, if given the opportunity?

With Charmelle's touch, the bags that inked Remi's under-eyes disappeared, and she looked healthy. A pink glow brushed her cheeks, and her pale skin shone with a rested sheen, but she didn't react. She didn't sigh or show any sign of relief, so I didn't either. The healing wasn't for our benefit, I knew. Part of the lie Madwyn would tell our parents, and yet another sign that we couldn't trust her.

"Now read," Madwyn said, pointing at the holo. "Don't make me ask again."

We did as she asked, my insides bucking at the order. I wanted to rip her tongue out and shove it down her throat. Instead, I read the damn holo. It felt like Remi's heart beat in unison with mine as we began.

Me: Hi Mom, Hi Dad. Remi and I are in Bicaidia with the leaders of the Nefaral Uprising.

Remi: They are treating us well and we are safe.

I resisted the urge to roll my eyes at that little nugget of bull crap.

Me: They want to meet with you and discuss conditions for a truce.

Remi: In return, they promise our safety and our care. Then, once a truce is secured, they will return us to Valeria.

Again, bull crap. Madwyn would be an idiot to send me, a creator, to any realm other than Bicaidia. My parents would have to be complete morons to believe that. Fortunately, I knew they weren't. As far as the truce went? I couldn't be sure what they'd make of that assertion. How much did they know about what had transpired in Bicaidia, or the other conquered realms? How much did the rest of the Twelve Realms know about what Madwyn and Riven had been up to?

The remainder of the communication proceeded much as expected. Lies and half-truths, along with promises and assurances that I didn't believe. The entire time I spoke, I kept my eyes away from Arrick, knowing that if I saw him, my emotions would betray me, and I'd have to go through this entire script again.

Even though I avoided him, I could feel his gaze on my face, and along with it, a pulse of anxiety and fear tugging within our bond. I knew why. He didn't know what would come next. He didn't know if he'd be able to stop it or mitigate any of the fallout, regardless of what he'd promised me in my cell the day before.

And the cold hard truth was, neither did I. I'd just have to trust that he would try, and that my family would be ready.

26
REMEMBER
Remi

A sour taste still permeated Remi's mouth an hour after that despicable holo she'd made for her parents. She'd barely been able to choke down the words. If she'd had any better options, she wouldn't have done it.

Not-Bekka hadn't appeared since that morning, but seeing the real Bekka? It had made her realize how similar her vision of her sister was. But also, how different. It was like a prequel to the current version of Bekka. A reminder of the goddess real Bekka been in the before time, the Bekka Remi felt like she knew. Because despite everything, she could sense that the sister who came back from Moldize had changed.

But before she could consider that further, she heard the quiet click of her cell door and then a slight breeze whooshed through her hair, tickling the back of her neck. She spun, staring in surprise as her mouth dropped open.

"Ellarah? What in the Twelve Hells are you doing here?" she asked, rushing toward her friend as she clicked the door shut behind her, silent as death.

Ellarah turned, depositing a ring of keys into the pocket of her loose pants and pressing a finger to her lips, and Remi realized she'd damn near shouted in shock. Remi snapped her mouth shut and Ellarah hurried forward, wrapping her arms around her. She squeezed Remi so tightly that her ribs compressed, and her breathing wheezed.

A second later, the energy goddess pulled away, resting her hands on Remi's shoulders, and peered into her eyes. "I remember everything, Rem. I mean, everything. Inauguration night, when Madwyn and Riven betrayed us, and how Madwyn stabbed me."

She stepped back, releasing Remi from her grip, and pressed a hand against her belly, where the poisoned dagger had sliced through her flesh. She shook her head as though she couldn't quite believe it. "Riven tells me he loves me, but how could he do what he did and still give a damn about me? And do you know the worst part? I'm just as much a prisoner here as you are. He lies to me, and he keeps me separated from everyone I love, not because he cares about me, but because he's scared. He doesn't want me to know the truth because he knows I'll leave." She paused, her shoulders heaving and her eyes welling with tears, as she fought to control her emotions.

Remi reached out and grasped her friend's hands, squeezing to comfort her. She understood the pain Ellarah must feel. After all, she still felt the sting of their betrayal, and the horrible events that followed, as acutely as she had that first night. And she'd only known Madwyn and Riven for a short time before everything went so wrong.

For Ellarah though? It would be so much worse. She loved Riven. Remi knew that. She should have felt awful for her friend, and she did, but something else overpowered that. Hope. A bright kernel of it bloomed inside her as she let the full weight of this visit, and what it meant, hit her.

Ellarah knew. She remembered.

Remi's heart pounded, and she resisted the urge to sob or scream. She didn't know which. They had an ally on the outside at last, someone who could help them escape this damned place. Or at least, she hoped Ellarah could help them.

Tamping down the elation, she gripped her friend's hands tighter. "I'm so sorry, Ellarah, I can't imagine what you're going through. I want to tell you everything, but I can't."

"You're bound, aren't you?" Ellarah asked, staring down at Remi's wrists as though trying to see the invisible ink, the evidence of Riven's binding. The one he'd forced her to agree to.

As a result, Remi didn't dare answer Ellarah's question. She couldn't, so she hoped that a stony, pissed-off silence would convey her meaning well enough. It did.

"That's what I thought," Ellarah said, eyes settling back on Remi.

Letting that pass, Remi asked, "How did you find me down here?"

"I snuck out after Riven left this morning and followed him. I saw the holo they forced you and your sister to make. After that, I followed you and those demons back here." Remi could see the sorrow in every line of Ellarah's face, but she shook her head. "I can't believe he did this to us. To me."

She pressed a hand to her stomach again and her lips thinned into a tight, angry line. "She almost killed me, and yet, he's still on her side. He's keeping me prisoner and lying to me on her behalf. As though I wouldn't find out? He's delusional, brainwashed, or something. I don't know how I didn't see it before." She strolled to the small cot and slumped into a sitting position. She dropped her head into her open palms, her despair palpable.

Remi could feel the weight of her anguish. He'd betrayed them all, Ellarah most of all. Yet she didn't seem broken. Hurt, but not destroyed. *Now, if only she could get angry*, Remi thought.

Rather than voice her thoughts, Remi moved to sit beside her. "Are you OK?"

"I don't know what I am," Ellarah said, "But I know I'm not OK."

"I'm sorry. I never should have gotten you caught up in my hunt for my sister. And I shouldn't have involved you in our insane plan."

Ellarah squinted and looked at Remi as though she'd lost her mind. "You? You're sorry? I'm pretty sure I'm the one who should be sorry. I trusted Riven. Though, I guess, to be fair, I paid heavily for that." Ellarah closed her eyes for a moment before waving a hand. "Let's not talk about that, though. There's enough blame to go around, and enough death and suffering that I'll never be able to wash the blood off my hands. But that's not why I came here."

"OK, then. Why did you come?" Remi asked, that kernel of hope growing.

"You need to escape. So do Thayne and your sister." She rose from the bed then and paced around, in full scheming mode, a posture Remi recognized well. Without warning, she turned and fixed an intense, golden glare on Remi. "Do you know who else is imprisoned down here? Anyone who can help you, if I can get you out?"

The hope Remi had been so careful to hold tight to her chest exploded into desperate excitement. Her heart skipped a beat as she tried to rein in her elation at the prospect of getting out of there once and for all. She couldn't let her emotions cloud her judgment, not yet. So, she swallowed them down, turning over her wrist to look at the cursed rune.

It flared as she spoke. "A goddess named Emorie is here, along with Thayne and Pietyr. Then there's another god named Rackham and two demigods, maybe, I'm not sure, who came with my sister."

"Demigods? Maybe? What do you mean?" Ellarah asked, confused.

"I don't know. Things got pretty hectic before we could make any formal introductions. I just know they aren't gods, but they aren't human either. Some combination is my best guess."

Ellarah nodded then, still looking a little confused. Demigods weren't a common thing in the Twelve Realms. "OK, that's good, I guess. Do they have power?"

Remi offered her a helpless shrug. "I have no idea. They didn't use any I could see. But they were in rough shape when we found them in Bicaidian hell, and I didn't get to see if Madwyn tested them. She inked me and Riven's demons took me to my cell first."

Ellarah's brows rose in surprise, but rather than ask for further explanation, she began to pace again. After a moment, she shook her head. "OK, it doesn't matter. You still have Rebekkah, Thayne, Rackham, Emorie, and Pietyr. Though, no idea who Rackham and Emorie are. What kind of magic are we looking at with them? Upper or lower-caste? Somewhere in the middle?" Remi opened her mouth to answer then, but Ellarah waved her hand, and Remi pressed her lips together, knowing it would be better to wait until Ellarah finished to reply. "You know, that doesn't matter either. You guys should be able to fight your way out with just the creator on your side, not to mention you, Thayne, and Pietyr." She stopped again and gave Remi a quick once over. "So, what are they using to suppress your magic? We'll need to make sure that's disabled before we make a break for it." She gave her a come-hither gesture. "Come on, show me what I'm working with here."

Despite the depressing answer to that question, Remi couldn't help but grin. It was the same Ellarah she remembered. Talking a mile a minute and barely letting her get a word in edge-wise. Despite only knowing her a short time before the shit had hit the fan, she still missed her. At last, Remi turned her hand over and showed Ellarah the rune embedded there. "Our caste and powers don't matter right now. I can't access my magic, and neither can the rest of us." The tattoo glowed golden on her skin, inky traces of black lacing through the pretty, luminescent surface of it as it flared to life.

Ellarah's brows stitched together in confusion, and she reached for Remi's hand, pulling her wrist closer and squinting as she surveyed it. After a brief second, something like recognition flitted over her face before she snapped her mouth shut and shook her head. "Well ... shit."

Taken aback, Remi gaped at her friend. "Wait a minute, do you know what this is, Ellarah? Have you seen it before?"

Ellarah pressed her lips together again, a serious expression sliding over her features as she considered. "I think I might, but let me check into it. This changes my plan, but it doesn't change the facts. We all need to get the hell out of here. Like yesterday. So, I'll make the arrangements." She held up two fingers. "Two nights, Rem. That's all I need. Expect me in the early morning hours of the second day."

"What do I need to do? What should I be prepared for? Do you think you'll be able to get this off me?" Remi asked, holding up her runed wrist as her mind whipped through every possibility.

Ellarah's lips twisted to one side in thought. "I'm not sure. If my recon today is any indication, there are a lot of Nefarals and demons around this damn palace. I'm going to do everything I can to get rid of that rune, but—" she shook her head. "Don't count on having your magic when we make a run for it. We'll have to plan around it."

Remi tried to picture what an escape plan without magic would look like. Or at least with just Ellarah's magic, and it didn't look too good. The best she could hope for was a quick get-away, but considering that all dungeons across the Twelve Realms didn't allow unsanctioned portals to be created in them, she didn't have high hopes for that. That left them with fighting their way out of the dungeons and then the palace, and into the heart of Helverta itself.

At last, Ellarah answered, "Look, just be ready to run and I'll take care of the rest." With that, Ellarah rose to her feet. "Riven will be coming for lunch soon. I need to get back before he finds me missing. He still thinks I'm bedridden and that I have no magic." She rolled her eyes and stared at the door, as though she'd rather stick around in the dungeon than return to the god she'd once loved so fiercely.

"So, you have your magic back then, right?" Remi asked, unable to hide the trepidation that filled her at the prospect of escaping with no power.

Ellarah winked and grinned a knowing smile. "Came back weeks ago. I need to get back up there, though. Two days," she said again, hurrying to the door. "That should give me enough time."

But before she could open it, Remi rushed forward and snagged her wrist. Ellarah turned, confusion knitting her brows together. Remi said, "Ellarah, he can't know or suspect that you remember." She thought about all the shit Davendri had put into her mind. She knew how easy it would be for someone as powerful as him to pluck that memory from Ellarah.

Ellarah shook her head. "He won't. I'm a good actress."

"Promise me you'll be careful and that you won't give him any reason to suspect you. You can't confront him, no matter what. He'll erase your memory." Remi tried to measure her words, to ensure she didn't trigger any negative effects of the binding. When no telltale sting came, she almost sighed with relief.

Ellarah's mouth dropped open. "He wouldn't do that."

Remi's brows rose in challenge. Even after everything that had happened, Ellarah still wanted to believe the best of Riven. "You want to risk it?"

Ellarah paused, her golden eyes scanning Remi's face, finding no trace of uncertainty there. "OK, I promise, I will take the secret to my grave. Believe me, Rem, I am motivated to get the hell out of here. I can't be around him anymore. Just looking at him makes me sick." She shuddered then and gripped the door handle harder, as though bracing herself for balance.

Remi wanted to reach out and hug her, but she didn't look like she'd welcome it. She seemed distant, traumatized. And who could blame her?

So, instead, Remi said, "Don't worry, we'll figure out how to pay them back for what they did to you. To all of us."

With one last mournful look, Ellarah sighed. "I know. Two nights, be ready."

Then she slipped out the door, clicking it shut behind her. As she left, Remi turned her attention to the apparition standing in the corner of the room. She'd appeared the instant Ellarah had opened the door. Not-Bekka watched her, arms crossed over her chest, looking smug.

Remi arched a brow in her direction, pursing her lips to hide the anticipation she felt pumping through every cell in her body. "Go ahead, say it. I know you want to."

"Told you," Not-Bekka said, her lips splitting into a wide smile.

"You never could resist the opportunity to gloat," Remi muttered, pretending to be annoyed.

"What can I say? I enjoy being right."

27

BATTLE PLANNING

ARRICK

"We've been summoned," Asthorea said, banging on the door to my chamber and yelling from the other side. I all but snarled at her as I paced my room like a caged wildcat. The fury that boiled inside me hadn't abated since that deity had held a knife at my sister's neck on Madwyn's order.

My soulfused mate's horror and fear, along with my sister's, had sent me into a blind fury. If Madwyn hadn't stopped me, I would have ripped her soul out without consideration of the consequences.

As it stood, though, a burn settled on my wrist, visible to the naked eye. A sign of my intentions and something Madwyn would never allow to stand unpunished.

Rather than rage at me, as I wanted her to, she refused to allow me back into the dungeons. I would never see whether she kept her end of the bargain and made the improvements she promised me. The entire exchange had me more irritable than usual, that burn of Bekka's power closer to the surface as a result. It grew more unbearable every day, and though I fought it with all my strength, it still dogged me every second of every day.

When I got my rage under control at last, I shouted, "By who?"

"Madwyn, obviously. Now hurry. She expects us all in the command room in less than five."

Her footsteps disappeared down the hall, and I suppressed the urge to hurl something at the door. It had been a full day since Bekka and Remi had made that holo. I knew Madwyn had already sent it to the royals—Sylennia told me as much. What neither of us knew was Madwyn's true plan. Grabbing a shirt, I pulled it over my head and slid my feet into my combat boots, letting their bulk cover the bottom of my leather training pants.

I all but slammed the door open and stomped down the hall, deciding to use this walk through the palace to calm my temper. It had become a living thing inside me, and I couldn't seem to shake it no matter how hard I tried. I'd never experienced anger like it before, and I didn't know what to do with it. It needed an outlet, and I needed to release Bekka's power, or I would explode.

But I couldn't. Didn't dare. Of course, I had one option. I chewed on my cheek as I considered telling Sylennia. She could mask my power with her own, but *could* wasn't good enough. She could also go straight to Riven and tell him about my newfound power, and I couldn't risk anyone discovering my secret.

So, I dismissed that idea, trying to think of another, and coming up blank for the thousandth time. As I reached the banquet hall, I turned a corner and headed toward the command room. The sound of foot soldiers' conversations and the clinking of dishes filled the hall, the scent of roasted meat tugging at me. But I didn't have time for that, I thought, turning down the corridor where I knew I'd find Madwyn and the other Diamanti.

As I approached its door, I cleared my mind, knowing I needed to focus on what came next. I could only assume that Madwyn wanted to prepare us for whatever she had planned in Valeria, and I'd made a promise to Bekka. I needed to do everything I could to keep it.

Pressing my hand to the lock, I sent a pulse of my death magic into it. The mechanism sprang free, and I strode into the room, scanning the round table at its center. A holo with a large map hovered over it, the topography familiar—Valeria, I realized. Within seconds of my arrival, the picture zoomed in to focus on one area. It had large hills, bordered by mountains, and a meadow at the center.

It was a giant bowl, and I knew without having to ask that it would be where I met Bekka's parents for the first time.

Madwyn sat in the large, green wingback chair that served as the only clear sign that she ran the show. The rest of her Diamanti crowded around the table. Our number had grown by one inductee, a god of war from Perenelle, and a strategist who rivaled my prowess. It seemed he'd been working with Madwyn before I arrived. Another punishment, I thought, trying not to wonder what they'd discussed in my absence, and what important pieces of information I might've missed as I strode to the last open seat, between Riven and Asthorea. I pulled out the chair in a smooth motion and sat down.

"Nice of you to join us, Arrick," Madwyn said, as I settled into the smooth, wooden chair. I gave the room one more once-over and noticed that Davendrie sat at the table, too. He must have healed since that incident a few days before, though dark shadows clung beneath his eyes and he had an unusual, drawn look about him.

I offered Madwyn a tight smile in response to her greeting, and she turned back to the holo, gesturing at the landscape. "Now that you're all here, I can tell you that the Valerian royals have accepted our offer to negotiate a truce. We leave for Valeria tomorrow night. This is the location the royals have provided for the meeting. It was non-negotiable."

I stared at the landscape, scrutinizing it further, noticing how strategically poor it was for us, and how good it would be for the Valerians, especially if they prepared before we arrived. I could only assume they would. "So," Madwyn continued, "We need to prepare a defensive strategy, as well as an offensive one that allows us to secure this location."

"Which one are you planning to use? Defense or offense?" I asked, rising to my feet to peer at the bird's-eye view and realized that I hated the meeting location even more at that angle. It was a fucking death trap. But then again, it meant that Bekka's family knew something about military tactics and that Gabryel had taught them well despite their near-millennium of peace. That could be a good indicator.

"Both, maybe. Maybe neither. Whatever the occasion calls for, we need to prepare for it."

I glared at her, unable to keep from pressing her despite the black burn on my wrist. "You don't intend to tell us beforehand?"

She lifted one delicate shoulder. "No." A rush of reactive sound filled the room, arguing and surprised shouts, but Madwyn raised her hands, and everyone went silent as purple smoke pearled around her fingertips. No one wanted to be humiliated by the power she wielded. "You'll all have your parts to play tomorrow." She looked at each of us. "Riven, you and

Davendri will stay here and ensure everything remains in order. Asthorea, Cerus, and Arrick, we can bring a small contingent of soldiers. A guard that you will lead in, as I said, whatever the occasion calls for. The rest of you will remain here and await your orders. Now, Arrick, Cerus, walk us through your recommendations."

Six hours later, Madwyn dismissed us from the command room. We'd ironed out all our plans for the next day and provided her with defensive and offensive battle strategies, which I'd crafted alongside Cerus. My diligence during our planning ensured that the formations left small openings where I could slip through if I timed everything perfectly. Though I had to keep the kinks in the armor to a minimum so Cerus wouldn't notice them. I needed him to see them as flexibility, rather than weaknesses.

After Madwyn had released us, I'd gone to the grand hall and the training grounds to gather fifty of my top soldiers. Once selected, I filled them in on our plans, careful to choose only those I trusted to obey my commands without question. To have a shot at keeping my promise to Bekka, I needed it that way and I couldn't afford to have any of my soldiers second-guessing me.

Once I finished my duties, Sylennia dropped me off in Lilja's room. I'd considered what to tell Sylennia, but decided against asking her for help, at least not yet. I didn't know how far she'd take that life debt, and I didn't think asking her to help me protect the Valerian Royals was the best place to start.

So, for the better part of an hour, I'd sat on the bed next to my sister, watching her sleep. Seeing her calmed that inferno inside of me, as it always did. She looked too damn peaceful to wake, but I needed to talk to her about what Madwyn planned to do. I needed to prepare her. For what? I couldn't be sure. But knowing Madwyn, I could be damn near certain that nothing would be simple. Or gentle either. Not after how easily Madwyn had almost killed Lilja yesterday.

The words *maximum impact* reverberated through my memory, and I recalled what she'd told me in one of her less guarded moments when she'd asked me to truly join her. She had said that she didn't need to burn it all down, she just needed to light the match, and they'd burn it for her.

So, turmoil gnawed at my gut as I tried to imagine all the ways she could accomplish that. The possibilities were infinite, but the most obvious stemmed from the secret the Valerians kept. About how they'd suppressed the magic of not just Nefarals, but Altruists as well, for almost a millennium. If I had to bet the last shred of my integrity, assuming such a thing still existed, I would say that she would publicize that to the masses. And if she did? All the defensive positions in the world might not be enough to save the Valerians from themselves.

Putting aside my dark musings, I refocused on the sleeping face of my innocent sister. It was time. I couldn't wait much longer or Sylennia would be back to collect me before dawn, and I'd lose my opportunity to talk to her. I sighed and ran a hand down her golden, curly hair. "Lili?" I whispered, not wanting to startle her. She stirred, her lips opening and closing, smacking sleepily as her eyes fluttered.

I felt the warmth that seeing her brought me, and let it wash through me. It was the nighttime that soothed the raw edges of my temper most. The time I spent with her fought back that familiar darkness that grew inside me and the unrelenting pain of Bekka's power. Her face, the innocence and sweetness of it, reminded me why I did what I did. It was for her and for all the people I loved.

When her eyes didn't open and she settled back into the pillows, snuggling deeper, I whispered, albeit a little louder that time, "Lili, I need you to wake up. We need to talk about tomorrow."

"Hmm?" She said, lifting one eyelid open and then the other. "What is it?"

I smiled down at her sleepy face. "Sorry to wake you, but something's happening tomorrow, and we need to talk." She blinked, trying to clear the sleep from her eyes as she rose to a sitting position, fluffing her pillows.

I examined her neck then. A small scab was the only sign that she'd almost had her throat slit the day before. The memory of it still had me on edge as she turned to face me, no small amount of concern in her eyes. "Why? What's happening tomorrow?" She still sounded sleepy, but she looked alert enough.

Pushing my fury at what had happened in the throne room aside, I told her everything. By the time I finished, her mouth drooped open before she snapped it shut. "I still can't believe Bekka did that for us, for me." She rubbed at that spot on her throat, a distant look in her eye.

I nodded, dragging a hand down my face as exhaustion tugged at me.

Lilja's mouth went tight as silver gathered at the edges of her eyes, though no tears fell. "She loves you, doesn't she?"

"Yes," I said, relieved at being able to tell the truth to another person. I'd kept Lilja in the dark since she'd come here. Our visits had always been light-hearted, and I'd never delved into more than the surface with her. I hadn't wanted to scare her or involve her, at least until that moment.

Before, I'd had a choice, but now? I'd made promises, and I had no one else I could trust. Besides, as innocent as Lilja might be, she was still smart, and cunning, and she knew how to fight, track, and hunt. She'd been trained by the best, our father, just like me. And while she may not have magic, she had other strengths. Add to that, she was small enough that she could slip out of sight amid battle, should it come to that, without drawing too much attention. All of those were skills we could use to our advantage.

"You love her too, don't you?" Lilja asked, shifting in the bed, the covers rustling as she turned to face me.

I rested my head back against the large, wooden headboard. "More than you can imagine. And I made her promises, Lili, promises I might not be able to keep on my own. So, tomorrow, I'm going to need your help."

"Mine?" she asked, the surprise widening her eyes. "You've never asked me for help before."

"I know, I'm sorry, but—"

She held up a hand to stop me, and I noticed the light of excitement in her eyes as she interrupted my apology, "No, don't be. It's about time you pulled your head out of your butt." My eyes widened in surprise, and before I could say a word, she continued, "I'm not helpless, and I'm not a little kid anymore, either. I'm eleven years old, and Dad trained me just as hard as he did you at my age. I can help. I want to help you, and Bekka, too."

The fierceness in her gaze, and the intensity of it? I recognized it as my mother's. Something she'd passed down to both of us. My sister, a warrior at heart, despite all we did to keep her away from the terrible realities of Moldize. Something like pride grew inside me as she asked, "What do you need me to do?"

And so, I told her everything I could without breaking any orders from Madwyn, and I didn't miss the gleam of anticipation in her eyes when Sylennia came to collect me. She radiated with purpose when she said goodbye, and I had a feeling she wouldn't get much sleep that night.

28
VISITOR
THAYNE

"That's it, Caden," Thayne rasped, rising to his feet and coughing as he sucked air. He wheezed for a few moments, getting his breathing back under control. "Nice work."

Pietyr grinned, as did Rackham, and a desperate hope seemed to permeate them both. He felt it too. The demigods had learned to control their magic and harness it as a weapon, which meant they had a chance. He turned to Deklan then and gestured to him—a signal to proceed. Deklan knelt on the stone floor and rested his palm on it. Vines began cracking along the walls, splitting the bricks before he commanded them back into place once more.

Caden and Deklan had been training for weeks since their gifts arrived. Their control had gotten better, and their magic had grown stronger. They could call their power as easy as their next breath now. It remained lower-caste in strength, but closer to the upper range of it. That was the best they would get, and they all knew it.

Thayne gave Deklan an approving nod, and Deklan's expression didn't change from stoic determination. Typical for him, but Thayne could swear he sensed a distinct pleasure within the demigod. Though, maybe that was just his imagination.

They had a plan, and it was risky. They all knew that, but it might just work.

"We're ready," Deklan said. "It's time."

Pietyr clapped a hand on his back and grinned broader. "About damn time. Let's get the fuck out of here!" Rackham let out a whoop and punched Caden's arm, who smiled too, swiping an arm over his forehead.

Thayne chuckled, enjoying the excitement that swept through the cell, but sobered when he said, "Let's go over the plan one last time. We need to make sure we have it down before we move forward. Any—"

"We know," said Rackham, "Any failure could lead to instant death. The protection the Moldizean bought us only counts while we're in Madwyn's care. We got it."

"I, for one, would prefer instant death over being stuck in this cage," Pietyr muttered.

Deklan pointed at Pietyr. "I'm with him." Caden nodded his agreement, and Thayne could see determination settle over them.

"Better to die fighting than live another second as a prisoner," Caden said.

Thayne nodded in agreement, his heart rate kicking up in anticipation. "OK then, in the hours before sunrise, we make our move. Now let's run through the plan one more time."

They sat on their cots; each bunk dragged together into a makeshift circle. They spoke in hushed tones, going through the layout of the dungeons from Thayne and Pietyr's memories, identifying the best possible weak points. At last, they selected the third escape path as their final decision when they heard the locking mechanisms slide in the door.

All five heads snapped up, each fixing their gazes on the door that had only opened once in all those months. Thayne's heart rate kicked up as the hinges creaked and the thick metal swung wide. To his utter astonishment, Madwyn stood there. Everything inside of him stiffened at the sight of her. She looked stunning, but then she'd never had an issue in that department.

She wore a deep purple, silk dress, its thin straps crisscrossing over her shoulders. Turning, she shut the door behind her, and he could see that the intricate pattern wove around her back, plunging low. Her smooth, golden skin and blonde hair glowed, as she offered them all a broad smile.

"Hello," she said, and he didn't miss the note of gloating in her voice.

"What the fuck do you want?" Pietyr said, rising to his feet, teeth bared. Deklan rose next, his cot screeching out from beneath him. Thayne reacted, rising as he clasped his hand on Deklan's shoulder. His bright, blue eyes snapped to Thayne's, and he gave him a tight shake of his head.

The demigods needed to keep their emotions in check. They couldn't afford to give any hint of the magic that settled beneath their skin. It was pure luck that their godly sheen only increased when they were wielding their power, and they couldn't risk any slipups. Not when they were so close. And while the demigods' magic might be powerful enough to help them escape, it wouldn't be strong enough to take on Madwyn.

Though no words passed between them, Deklan recognized the warning in Thayne's eyes. He ducked his chin in acknowledgment, his shoulders relaxing as he tamed that ever-present anger Thayne could sense rolling off him.

Madwyn spoke again, the tension so thick you could cut it with a blade. "Such excitement for little old me. I feel so special." She clapped her hands together and pressed them to her chest. He saw her slim muscles beneath the smooth skin and realized that she'd been training. She looked leaner, stronger, and maybe even a little sharper. As though whatever she'd been doing over the past months had given her an edge that hadn't been there before. He could only imagine what those things could be, none of them good.

Thayne stepped to the head of the group, Pietyr at his side, though one side-long look at the shadow deity had him stepping back too. They'd all allowed Thayne to take on the role of leader, since he had a natural knack for it, given his upbringing. It didn't hurt that he also had intimate knowledge of the Bicaidian palace and its dungeons.

"What is it you want, Madwyn? Why are you here?" Thayne asked. Her eyes fixed on him and every hair on the back of his neck stood at attention as his gut clenched. The depth of that look, everything about it, the intensity, the seduction, the greediness ... it threatened to wreck him, to tear him apart from the inside out, because he recognized it. It was a piece of the old Madwyn, the one he'd loved so damn much.

"I'm here to see you," she replied, her voice quiet. "I wanted to talk to you in private."

He didn't move, not daring to react. What could she say to him that he would want to hear? She'd tormented him with those fucked up dreams for months. She'd killed his entire family, ruined his realm, stolen his throne, and all for what?

He debated telling her to take whatever she had to say and shove it up her pretty little ass, but he hesitated. Part of him burned to know why she had done this to him. He wanted to know why she betrayed him after everything they'd been through. So, before he could think it through, he stepped toward her.

Rackham reached out then, grasping his shoulder hard, fingers digging in—a warning in his eyes. "Thayne, what are you doing? You can't trust her." Thayne turned then, his attention fixing on Rackham's earnest expression. He looked genuinely concerned for Thayne's safety, his grip tight to the point of discomfort. Rackham gave a warning shake of his head. "Don't go with her. Nothing good will come of it."

He scanned the faces of the four deities who'd become his friends, his confidantes, and the ones he would want fighting by his side when it came to that. They each witnessed everything he'd gone through those past months, and they all knew she had twisted him inside out with grief, guilt, and self-loathing. He'd never told them that, but he hadn't needed to. They already knew.

Pietyr spoke then, "He's right. Nothing she says will make any of it right, and you don't know what it is she wants from you. Don't go."

Thayne swallowed, already knowing what he wanted to do. But he spared a look at Caden and Deklan, who each shook their heads in turn. For once in her life, Madwyn stayed silent, waiting with hands on slim hips as she surveyed the scene before her. As though she already knew she'd get what she wanted without picking a fight.

"I know you don't understand, but I need to do this. I'll be fine," he answered, and with that, he crossed the room and stood beside the goddess he'd once loved so much that he'd almost sacrificed an alliance with Valeria for her. Maybe if he had picked her, things would have turned out differently. He supposed he would never know.

A small smile lifted the corner of her lips as Madwyn banged on the door and shouted, "We're ready!"

29
LOATHING
Thayne

A minute later, a demon pulled the cell door open from the outside. She offered a small smile and a delicate finger wave to the deities they left behind. Thayne heard Pietyr's shouted, "Fuck you, Madwyn!" before the door slammed shut.

He followed behind her as she led him down the same cell-lined hall Riven had, and he knew then where she was taking him. She validated his theory when they stopped in front of the same interrogation room door Riven had used. The metal precipice gleamed in the brightly lit hall, and he stared at it as she slipped a key into the lock. It clicked, and she slid the secondary mechanism, added protection for dangerous criminals, free.

She turned to the demon who followed them. "Lock us in and then wait at the end of the hall. I'll let you know when we're done."

She has a lot of faith that I won't get my hand around her throat and squeeze, he thought, as the demon obeyed her. They both stepped inside the small room and the door slammed shut, locking from the outside.

They stood shoulder-to-shoulder as Thayne took in his surroundings. A lone holo still sat at the center of the round, metal table, and he saw that the two utilitarian chairs remained as well.

He watched her from the corner of his eye as she stared at the table, her tongue sliding over her bottom lip. Her mouth, painted a deep burgundy that complimented her dress, looked full and sumptuous as his eyes tracked her tongue along its path.

Pulling his gaze away, he tried to focus his mind. To remember why he'd agreed to come with her, why he wanted to talk to her at all. He felt distracted, his mind jumping all over the place.

He kept seeing that mouth as it had been in his dreams. Trailing burning hot kisses down every rung of his abs, then wrapping around his rock-hard cock as she milked him dry. But then he could see it twisted in that malicious smile as she stabbed him through the heart with a black-poisoned dagger, and he sobered at the thought. The images collided and merged in his mind, and he shut his eyes, trying to clear them.

He took a calming breath before he focused on her again. "What did you want to say to me, Madwyn?" he asked, moving past her and to the table. She leaned her back against the door, her head dropping onto it with a thud as she looked up at the ceiling. He rested his hips on the table bolted into the stone floor, leaning back and crossing his arms as he surveyed her.

Her chest rose and fell, and he could see her thin fingers splayed against the cool metal as though she fought for control over some powerful emotion, one he couldn't place.

"I did it, Thayne," she said after a long while, her voice low, her eyes shut. "I'm meeting with the Valerian royals tomorrow. I fucking did it."

She opened her eyes then and stared at him. Thayne saw a mix of emotions moving in their depths, and everything inside him went cold.

He had thought maybe she wanted to talk to him in person instead of through that insufferable bridge, hoped that maybe she would give him some explanation for what she'd done to him those last months. To help him understand why she had done it, why she'd betrayed him, and maybe to show him one ounce of fucking compassion or remorse for it. But no, of course, that wasn't why she'd come for him after so many months of visiting his dreams. Instead, she wanted to gloat.

Thayne pushed up from the table and stalked toward her, her eyes bright with fury. Or maybe excitement? He didn't know what he felt as he prowled toward her, his own eyes gleaming.

"Why do you think I would give a good damn about that, Madwyn?" He stopped inches in front of her, glaring down at her. She just stared up at him with that same look. The one that made him want to slam her head into that metal door. "After what you did to me, and what you keep doing, why do you think I would care about your success?" He spat the words, letting the venom he harbored for her coat them.

Madwyn stared up at him, allowing his anger to wash over her. She didn't flinch from it, nor did she shy away. Instead, she faced it, examining him with the same determination she always showed in the face of opposition. "I told you, you're not allowed to hate me, and we both know you don't. Besides, you're the person I tell things to. You and Riven, but Riven—" she shook her head. "Things aren't the same between us since—"

"Since you stabbed Ellarah in the gut and almost killed her?" Thayne finished for her. She pressed her lips together, and after a small hesitation, she nodded in confirmation. "You know, Madwyn, I can't believe I have to explain this to you, but actions have consequences. When you kill or injure the people your friends or family love, then you break that relationship with them and the trust that those relationships are built on. You shatter it. You destroy it. That's what fucking happens. So, I suggest you find someone else to tell things to, because I'm not that person for you anymore. And you may think I don't hate you, but you're wrong because I don't just hate you. I fucking loathe you."

Without a second glance in her direction, he stepped forward and drew back his hand to bang on the door above her head. He wanted to call for the demon to unlock the door and return him to his cell. But she reached up and gripped his forearm with her fingers before he could slam his fist into the metal. Her burgundy-painted nails dug into his flesh, her strength far greater than his without his magic, and he slid his stare down to her face, letting every bit of contempt show.

"Let go of me, Madwyn."

"No," she said, tightening her grip harder, to the point of pain. He felt the skin break, the heat of his blood trickling down his flesh.

In a flash of realization, he recognized what that look on her face meant and why she'd really come. In reaction, his mouth twisted into a disgusted snarl. "You killed my family."

Her chest heaved, her breaths coming quickly. "Yes, I did."

"You destroyed our realm."

She nodded again.

"You trapped me in prison."

Another nod, her eyes never leaving his and her chin held high.

"You left me here to rot, and then toyed with me like a cat with its dinner."

She let go of his hand, red welts and bright streams of blood remaining where her nails had pressed into his skin. He leveled that same hand on her throat, pressing against her as he stared into her ice-blue eyes.

"You ruined my life, and destroyed so many others, too. Do you even have the decency to be sorry for it?"

She lifted her chin further, pressing her neck harder into his hand. Her heated gaze locked onto his and he didn't miss the defiance in them when she said, "No."

He slammed her back those couple of inches into the door as hard as he could, fingers tightening on her neck. And then he crushed his mouth against hers. It was a rush of passion, a rush of anger, of fury, of wanting to punish her. Of wanting to feel something, anything other than the bone-deep despair and self-loathing he'd felt since the moment she'd destroyed everything that meant something to him, and he knew what he needed to do to get it.

She opened her mouth for him instantly, her hands twisting into his hair, and he knew he'd read her correctly. He pressed his body flush to hers as he deepened the kiss. He didn't go gentle on her, biting her lips hard enough to draw blood. She gasped, his fingers digging into her hips as he trailed his other hand up her shoulder, tugging down on the tiny straps of the dress. She helped him, releasing her grip on his hair, and then slipping the other strap off her arm before she shoved the bodice of the liquid silk dress down to her waist where it bunched before he moved back a step and let it fall into his awaiting hand. He pulled it off her, watching her graceful legs as they stepped out of it. He gripped the slick fabric hard as he stared at the sight before him.

She was naked underneath that dress. All smooth skin, firm muscle, and softness in all the right places, and any doubt that remained regarding why she'd come there that night, dissipated. He rushed forward, pushing her back once more, her body hitting the metal while he gripped the familiar curve of her breast. He leaned down and fastened his teeth on her nipple, hard enough to make her cry out in pain. Then he swirled his tongue over it, and she moaned, letting her head loll to the side as he lifted one leg, pinning it with his other arm, opening access to her center.

But rather than plunge his fingers into the wetness he knew awaited him, he lifted his head from her full breasts and sank his teeth into her neck, biting and sucking hard as she raked claws down his back. He growled, pressing his fingertips harder into her hips, not wanting to be gentle. He wanted to hurt her, to punish her, to ruin her, the same way she'd ruined him, and he knew just how to do it. He knew what steps to take, and he'd take them, no matter what it cost him to do it.

She pressed two hands to his chest then and shoved him. He took a quick step back, allowing her to gain a foot of space between them. Their breaths became ragged as she dropped to her knees in front of him. Her finger slipped around the waistband of his pants, eyes hungry with anticipation. She worked at the button and zipper, right before he slammed his knee into her chin.

Madwyn gasped, teeth clacking together hard, the sudden strike catching her off guard as she sprawled back, falling right on her pretty little ass. Thayne didn't miss a beat. He lunged forward and using that discarded silk dress he still held in one hand, the only useful weapon in the room, he dropped to his knees and wrapped it around her neck. Moving fast, he wound it around his fists and crossed it, pulling as hard and tight as he could, cutting off her air supply, as he rose, lifting her off the ground with him, careful to keep a safe distance between them. She had her godly strength, and he didn't. He couldn't let her get a hit in or the fight would be over before it started.

Madwyn bucked, kicking her legs and making pathetic sucking sounds as she fought against him, trying to reach back and gouge at him with her sharp nails. He held fast. He might not be able to kill her like that, but he could weaken her. Maybe even injure her enough for them to escape in the chaotic distraction that would follow. To do that, though, he had to move fast and keep her too shocked to call her power. He also knew her binding with the Moldizean death deity wouldn't cover self-defense. No binding ever required you to let yourself die to uphold it.

With those thoughts in mind, he hauled her toward the table and wound the dress tighter before smashing her face into it. He did it again, and again, and again until blood seeped from her nose and a cut on her lip.

Then he leveled his boot straight on her back and pushed her neck into the edge of the table, forcing her to her knees once more, choking her with all his strength. She still reached back with her hands, clawing at him with her sharp, long nails. Trying to fight him without magic, panicking at the lack of air and the unexpected pain. *Exactly what I hoped for*, he thought right before he said, "That didn't go quite how you expected it, did it? I told you, Madwyn, you're wrong. I do hate you."

As though snapped into existence by his words, he saw the purple smoke seeping from her fingertips. Shit, he was running out of time. He moved her again. That time toward the two-way window and threw her against it, still using the dress like a choke collar and leash combined. The glass cracked on impact with her body, splintered as some shards clattered to the ground with her, cutting Madwyn's skin. But it didn't matter. It was too late. As he tried to lift her to her feet with the gown once more, magic burst forth from her like a torrent, hitting him square in the chest.

The silk fabric tore as he flew across the room. Part of the dress remained coiled in his hands as he hit the wall behind him with a bone-crunching crack. He saw stars, pain exploding in his head from the impact as he fell in a heap on the ground. Every part of him felt weak, agonized, and he didn't know how much of that came from her magic and how much from smashing into the unforgiving stone.

He watched, breaths stuttering as Madwyn rose, her naked body gleaming with sweat as her purple smoke danced around her, bright flashes of lightning snaking through it. The look of absolute fury on her face made everything worth it. Having to touch her to get her guard down, having to kiss her and pretend like he wanted her. It had been worth it.

She advanced on him, removing the severed fabric from her neck and tossing it to the ground. He smiled as he saw the red mark left behind from it. An hour of stasis sleep, and it would heal, but it felt good to hurt her. She'd been insane to think he'd want to fuck her. Delusional. But then, that's what she was. Maybe what she'd always been.

Another burst of magic whipped out from her, and pain shattered through him. He roared with it as wave after wave of electric chaos hit him. After what felt like an eternity, she relented. He gasped; ragged breathing painful as his entire body seized with agony.

She knelt before him, touching a gentle finger beneath his chin, and he hissed, drawing back. He would have spit on her, but he didn't have the energy. Instead, she forced his gaze up to her, and when he at last looked at her she said, "I guess that didn't go quite how you expected, did it?"

That time, he mustered the energy and spat blood on her beautiful face. *About time her beautiful exterior matched her hideous interior,* Thayne thought, before he said, "I'll never stop hating you, Madwyn. You may as well kill me."

She stared at him a long moment, his blood splattered across her face, before she said, "You know I can't, not when you're not an actual threat. But even if I could, I'm just not ready for that yet."

Then, with that last word, she rose to her feet and moved to the cell door, banging her fist against it. The loud, metallic thuds made Thayne wince just before the lock slid back and the demon entered.

Still naked and completely unconcerned with it, Madwyn commanded the demon, "Take him back to his cell." Then she stepped through the door and into the hall. When she left, he couldn't help but smile as he coughed and spat blood.

She might think that she won that round, but it didn't matter to him. He'd gotten to hurt her, and not just physically, either. Thayne knew his words and actions would have cut deeper than she would ever admit.

For him, agony already abating in the absence of her magic, it had been worth every bit of the sacrifice he'd made to achieve it.

30

NO MORE SHARING

BEKKA

"What's the first thing you want to do when we get out of here?" I whispered, snuggling beneath one of our new blankets and turning my head toward Emorie's new cot. Arrick had come through with his promise. We remained in our single room, but our accommodations had improved a lot since I made that damn holo.

I sat in silence for a moment, trying to push all thoughts of that disastrous day from my mind and hoping that Emorie wasn't asleep yet, or else I'd feel pretty shitty for waking her.

After a long pause, she answered, her deep, feminine voice devoid of sleep, thank the Ascended. "I want to eat a souffle, chocolate with a rasionberry drizzle. Then I want to find a sexy god or goddess, whichever, and let them do all kinds of naughty things to my body."

I snorted a laugh. "I'll share that souffle with you. Sounds scrumptious. The sex buddies, though, they're all yours."

"No, you will not! No offense, but I have zero interest in sharing anything once we get out of here." I could hear her new pillow rustle as she shook her head. I giggled again, and she joined in my laughter—the sound of hers throaty and rich.

After a few moments, we stopped laughing, and Emorie asked, "Do you think we'll make it out of here? That our plan will work?"

I shrugged, then realizing she couldn't see me, I said, "Hard to say. I don't know if Madwyn or her lackeys can kill us outright, but they can defend themselves against us. Also, I'm not sure what counts as under her care. Do we have to be inside a cell that she controls? Or just within a realm she controls? The binding didn't specify, but with the vague wording on that front, I think it's possible they could do anything they want to us once we're out of this cell." I thought about it a little more. "Or we could trip the defense systems in the dungeons or palace and die that way. Or we could end up in stasis sleep and right back in this cell. I doubt the binding's protection would cover any of that."

"Aren't you a ball of cheerful thoughts?" Emorie muttered.

I snorted. "I've had a lot of time to think about it."

"Too much time," Emorie replied. "We should have left earlier."

I sighed. It wasn't the first time she'd given me a piece of her mind on this topic. Arrick had gotten us more food, and I had convinced her to wait until she regained more strength. Just a couple of days. That was all she would need, and all she would agree to.

"I know," I said. "But you're stronger now, and we're more likely than ever to make it out because of that. You're worth the wait, Emorie."

"Yeah, I guess it would have sucked to get left behind, even though I know you would have come back for me. You love me too much to leave me here alone."

"I mean ... it would have been less urgent since you have blankets and food now, but I would have come back, eventually." A rustle sounded and then a pillow smacked my face. Snickering, I removed the pillow and adjusted it under my head. "Thanks. I needed another one of these."

"Remember what I said about sharing?" Emorie said, tone ominous. "You better give that back or it'll be my boot smacking you in the face next."

"So violent," I teased, taking the pillow and tossing it back to her. It sounded like she caught it, and I heard more shifting of sheets.

When she settled, she said, "Hey Bekks?"

"Hmm?" I asked, staring into the dark ceiling above me.

"What's the first thing you want to do?"

I thought through the possibilities. "Free Arrick, kill Madwyn, save Valeria, and free the Twelve, or Thirteen Realms, I guess, in the process." I still didn't know what Madwyn wanted to do with Valeria. What plans she had for my family or my realm, but I didn't buy that truce bullshit for one second and neither did Emorie. I also didn't want to leave the remaining Twelve Realms, including Moldize, to her tender mercies.

"There you go with the heavy stuff," Emorie said, sighing. "And all I wanted was some action and a delicious dessert."

I chuckled. "Heavy is the head that wears the crown," I said, an expression I'd heard every leader say in every realm—a truism I hadn't understood until recently.

"No shit," she said. "You know, I wish I'd known you before I discovered the governor chips. Before I started The Rising, and before everything went to hell. I think I would've trusted you enough to tell you about them, and you wouldn't have let it slide or brushed it under the rug. You would have stood up and done the right thing. So, when this is over, I'll help you. Whatever you need, Bekka, I'm yours."

My heart squeezed so hard I thought it might stop. Honored beyond words, I opened my mouth and then shut it, unsure what to say. I liked to think I wouldn't have kept things status quo, even before my power and before Arrick, but I didn't know that for certain. The distance from my family had changed me. And the old me? I didn't know what she would have done.

"You can say something, you know," Emorie quipped, and some levity broke through the heavy responsibility she laid on me.

"Thank you, Emorie. I won't take your trust for granted; I promise. I accept your pledge, and I will do my best to honor it."

"There you go, getting all sappy."

"You sure know how to ruin a moment, don't you?" I said, snorting back a laugh.

"Yeah, I've been told. Now, I have a more important question for you. What's the first thing you want to eat?"

After a millisecond to consider, I said the first thing that came to mind. "Tacos."

31
DANGEROUS HOPE
REMI

Remi paced her room like a wild, caged animal, her body humming in anticipation. Ellarah should be there any moment. It was time. Time to get out of her personal hell. Time to taste the freshness of free air. Time to rid herself of her tattooed shackles.

Hope was a dangerous thing, she knew, and as the time slogged by, she tried to keep it at bay and under control. She knew all sorts of terrible things could have happened since Ellarah's visit two days ago. Riven could have discovered her friend's plan. She could be in a cell. Maybe even the one next door to Remi, for all she knew.

The thought had a tremor of horror slicing through her, but she pushed it away. She had to trust her friend. If Ellarah thought she could trick Riven, then presumably, she could. Trust had never been Remi's strong suit, and after what had happened at her inauguration? She'd have a hard time relying on anyone for anything ever again. Dramatic, sure, but warranted in her view.

"She'll be here," a familiar voice said from across the room. Remi turned and saw Not-Bekka lying on her cot, hands resting under the back of her head. Her long, golden hair spilled over the pillow and off the side of the bed, tips nearly brushing the floor.

"You don't know that," Remi said, still pacing. "Anything could have happened to her in the last two days. What if she got caught? What if they found out what she planned to do? What if she's in this dungeon now, too? Or worse, what if Madwyn found a way to kill her like she threatened to do if I didn't make that fucking holo?"

Remi could hear the panicked sound of her voice, but she couldn't stop herself. She had such tenuous control over her emotions after everything Davendrie had done to her, a point that shamed her. She'd always kept herself on a tight leash, she'd had to, given the sort of power she wielded, but now? They had shattered that part of her.

"There's no reason to panic. At least not yet. She'll be here, Remi." *Hope*, Remi thought. She could hear it in every word Not-Bekka said, which meant that some small part of her still had it too, right?

Remi took a deep breath and turned to look at the apparition of her sister. "I'm scared," Remi admitted, and as though with that confession, her heart picked up its pace. "I wish I knew the plan. I wish I knew what was coming next. I wish I knew anything at all about anything."

Not-Bekka rolled onto her side, propping her cheek on a fist. Her coffee eyes swam with a combination of understanding and sadness. "She won't betray you. Not Ellarah, and whatever she has planned? Ellarah is smart. She won't be tricked again. Not by Riven and not by Madwyn either."

Remi let out a long breath, but a sound pulled her attention away from her sister. Or maybe not a sound, but a presence. A sense of tingling electricity.

Magic.

She'd know the feel of it anywhere—the power that radiated out of the gods like sweat did from a human's pores. She hurried to the door on the balls of her feet, careful to make as little sound as possible. Her heart slammed in her chest and she could hear it thrumming in her ears when the slight scrape of a locking mechanism jarred her. It was time. It was happening. Ellarah had come. The door swung open and for a second, Remi's breath caught in her throat as a tall, male deity stepped through.

32

DIE TRYING

THAYNE

He looked out at the nighttime sky in Helverta the next day. Stars blanketed the darkness and shone above him. He still sported some bruising and general discomfort from his fight with Madwyn, but most of the damage seemed to be magical. Once her power left with her, he'd risen to his feet and walked back to the cell with his demon guard. When he returned, looking disheveled and beat to hell, no one had asked him a damn thing. Nor had he offered anything.

It would change nothing. We have our plans, and Madwyn's distraction with the Valerian royals would only help us, he thought, cracking his knuckles.

As he took in the landscape, he let it soak in that Helverta had been his home since the day he was born. Then it had been his prison. *But it would be neither for much longer,* he thought, the pale, rainbow shimmer of the Synbue River dancing below them.

They'd made their decision. It was time.

As though in unison with his thoughts, a hand fell on his shoulder, and he turned. Pietyr's tall form stood behind him. Thayne peered at his friend, his expression grave. Not for the first time, Thayne wished they could all access their powers. It would make what they were about to do a hell of a lot less dangerous.

"You ready?" Pietyr asked, leveling his gaze on every male in the room.

Rackham cracked his knuckles and then his neck, readying for a fight. "Now's as good a time as any."

Caden nodded his approval. "It's a good night to get free or die trying."

In Thayne's opinion, truer words had never been spoken. He couldn't stand to spend another second in that prison.

Deklan and Caden both looked resolved, like warriors heading into battle. From what little they'd shared, he knew the brothers had seen more war and battles than any of the full deities present. And based on what they'd described of the Moldizean mortal realm? To survive there, you needed grit and determination. You had to fight for everything you had, your life included. It brought him some comfort to know that they would not falter in the face of what came next.

Deklan and Caden shared a look, and each moved into the positions they agreed upon when they'd settled on their plan. Caden stood behind the door, back pressed to the wall, out of sight should any demons come to interrupt them.

He closed his eyes, chest rising and falling with the calming breaths he used to call his magic. A second later, he glowed with power, a deep sapphire gleaming around the tips of his white hair and fingertips. He opened his eyes, and they shone bright, the glistening threads of blue in them a mirror of their natural color. When he used his magic, Caden looked no different from any other air deity, and that knowledge still surprised Thayne no matter how many times he saw it. He knew little about demigods. The same could be said for the rest of the deities in the immortal realm.

While gods mated with humans regularly enough, almost none of those unions produced offspring. He knew of precisely zero in all of Bicaidia. It made them an oddity. Pushing that curiosity from his mind, he hurried to the other side of the door while Pietyr and Rackham stood back a few feet.

With everyone ready and in position, Deklan stepped forward and placed a hand on the wall next to the locking mechanism. He may not wield any power over steel and iron, but he did over anything made from land, soil, and the roots of the plants that grew within them. That included the adobe bricks that comprised the ground and the walls of their prison cell.

Granted, he couldn't manipulate the exterior walls. Magic protected them against any use of power. But everyone in the Twelve Realms used some form of magic suppressor for the prisoners inside, so the interior walls and flooring didn't have the same level of protection. A chink in the armor that he'd be grateful for forever if their plan worked.

With a sharp inhale, Deklan pressed his fingers into the stone and glowed. The deep, forest green of an edaphopath scored his arms, traveling along the path of his veins, up his neck, and through his white-blonde hair. A rumble issued then, and they all braced themselves, praying to the Ascended that no one would hear or feel the quaking beneath their feet or the tremors in the walls before they could finish what they started.

In time with Deklan's measured breathing, the wall on his side of the door disintegrated. Slowly at first, the edges of the bricks crumbled into soft, powdery dirt. Then the progression quickened, and Thayne felt the anticipation of the fight that would come next humming in his blood.

The natural urge of his body fought against the rune at his wrist, trying to pull his magic from somewhere deep beneath the surface, but nothing came. No surprise there. He already knew he would have to fight without it. With his fists and blind rage—he knew he could do both when needed.

He'd trained for it before, and while it had been years since he'd fought hand-to-hand without the added boost of his power, he remembered the dance well enough. He saw a similar urge in the other two deities standing beside him. Rackham and Pietyr looked edgy with readiness, frustrated with their lack of magic as their runes also flared. But he knew that Pietyr, at least, could fight better than most.

He was an expert with weapons, not just his shadow magic. The customs of the shadow wielders, spies of the royal families, required it. That knowledge helped cut down on the fear he tried to keep at bay, though he didn't quell it entirely. Fear gave him an edge. He just couldn't let it overwhelm him.

As the wall continued to dissolve, he remembered black-poisoned blades that had nearly killed Ellarah and planned to relieve a demon of one as soon as he got the chance. It would be their best shot at defending themselves.

As the wall next to the door crumbled fully, disintegrating into dust, he thought—*We'll just need to be faster than the demons.*

33

THE UNKNOWN

BEKKA

"Remi?" The whispered name traveled beneath the door and had me jolting upright. Pitch darkness surrounded me, and I flung a hand toward Emorie's close cot to jostle her shoulder. Instead, I smacked her face, and her soft snores ceased.

"What the f—" she started, but I shushed her.

"Listen," I hissed, and she fell silent.

The whisper sounded again, and I tossed my feet over the side of my bed, rushing to the door. As I moved, I whispered to Emorie, "Did you hear that?"

Emorie had dropped into utter silence from the moment I shushed her. I could just barely make out her silhouette in the darkness of the cell. Her head bobbed up and down, and she rose from the bed, hurrying to my side. "Remi," the soft voice I didn't recognize whispered again.

I dropped to my knees then, pressing my cheek to the floor, trying to see through the minute gap between the door and the floor. I whispered, "Who's there?" Before I shoved my ear to the bottom of the precipice to see if I could hear any better.

Soft footsteps padded on stone, growing louder as they approached my door. "Remi? Is that you?"

I turned my head and pressed my lips closer so that my voice could travel. "No, but I'm her sister, Bekka." I hoped that whoever lingered outside our cell didn't mean us harm. I didn't know why she'd come in the middle of the night looking for Remi, but my gut told me she had to be there to help. She sounded too nervous and secretive for anything otherwise. "Who are you?"

"Oh, good, I was looking for you too," she said, voice still a whisper but closer now. I heard the mechanical slide of a lock, and my heart slammed into my throat. Leaping to my feet, I grasped Emorie's arm and pulled us both back. But Emorie, never one to be coddled, tugged out of my grip, rushed to my cot, and dropped to her belly. Reaching under it, she grabbed our weapons. She tossed one to me, keeping the other for herself.

We turned, ready to fight on the off chance that the presence on the other side of the door meant to kill us rather than help. I doubted it, but I figured one could never be too prepared.

My heart hammered with adrenaline as the door swung open, and I saw a tall, slender deity. A dim sheen of white magic coated her skin, glowing in the low-lit hallway outside. An energy deity? I wondered as a complete lack of recognition washed over me.

I'd never seen her before in my life, and I spared a glance at Emorie, hoping maybe she knew something I didn't. Based on the look of total confusion that crossed her face, she knew about as much as I did. But before I could open my mouth, Emorie did "Who are you?"

The goddess, dressed in the lightweight, magic-enhanced, golden armor and forest green fighting leathers of the Bicaidians, turned to peer back into the hall, a worried expression lining her face. As she did, I noticed the enormous sword, swirling with black magic, strapped to her back.

My mind whirled as I tried to process what I saw. The white magic glowing over her golden-tanned skin and light brown hair had to be energy magic. But the sword at her back? I would know that power anywhere. It had run through my veins since Arrick's soul fused to mine. It was death magic.

She grabbed the door and pulled it to, pressing a finger to her lips as she spoke. "I'm here to rescue you, but we don't have much time. My name's Ellarah and I'm a friend of Thayne and Remi's. Do you know where they are? I thought I could find my way back to Remi, but it's darker than I expected, and I got turned around. We need to find them before the window I created for us closes." She skirted her golden eyes between Emorie, the door, and me, and I could almost feel the urgency rolling off her. "Do you know where they're keeping them?"

Emorie and I shared a look that encompassed our utter stupefaction. Rescue us? Someone was there to rescue us? I'd given up hope that anyone would come for me so long ago that I couldn't quite process her words. I wanted to cry with relief, but I didn't think it was an opportune time for that.

Our rescuer seemed on edge, and I had a feeling that getting out of the prison wouldn't be as simple as walking out the front door. We would still have to fight our way out, just as Emorie and I had planned, so I needed to keep my mind clear.

In response to Ellarah's question, Emorie shook her head and then squinted. "Wait, you're the one we carried out on inauguration night, aren't you? The one Madwyn stabbed?"

Ellarah nodded her head. "Yes, I'm the one Madwyn stabbed, but we don't have time to get into that right now. Do you know where Remi and Thayne are?"

Emorie shook her head in response. "I've only left this cell to shower since they moved me into it, but Bekka might know. Do you?" She focused her intense gaze on me, her once beautiful curls dull and frizzing around her face.

Fidgeting with the metal pole in my hands, I thought back to the day of the holo. "I didn't see Remi leave her cell, but I think I know what direction she came from. I'll show you."

"OK it's settled," Ellarah said. "Lead the way, and hurry. I'm not kidding about that window. It took me longer to find you than I thought it would, and we're on borrowed time now." A shiver crawled up my spine, but I pushed that foreboding feeling aside and nodded, hurrying to the door.

Ellarah opened it to let me through first. "Be ready with those poles. I've avoided the demon patrols so far, but I don't expect us to remain that lucky for long, especially not with what comes next."

I tightened my grip on the weapon and turned down the darkened hallway, palms sweating as I wondered what the hell would come next.

34

BAD TIMING

REMI

"What did you say to Ellarah?" Riven growled, his usual slick, tailored suit disheveled. Remi could hear her heart drumming in her ears. He couldn't be there. Not then. Not when Ellarah was coming to help her, Twelve Hells, to help all of them escape. Her gut clenched in horror, but she tried not to let it show.

Her eyes caught the bottle of god's-liquor he held in his right hand. She could make out the outline of the golden liquid and saw that he'd drained most of it before coming there. Black misty magic leaked from his body, and dread pooled in her belly as an adrenaline rush flooded her. Why had he come? What did he plan to do? Would he leave before he ruined everything?

Composing herself, she squared her shoulders and glared her defiance. "I said nothing, Riven. Or don't you recall?" She held up her arm, where the tattoo of their bargain inked onto her skin, visible to only the two of them. "We made a deal."

"You found a way around it. I know you did," he slurred, his magic seeping along the stone ground, tendrils of death coming to claim her. She tried not to stare at it as she took a tentative step backward. "She hasn't touched me since you and Thayne left. Something's wrong. She knows something. I can feel it."

"I'm missing the part where that's my problem," Remi sniped, her anger rising inside her, outweighing the fear as she let his words soak in. "Did you ever consider that maybe she'd remember on her own? She doesn't need my input to hate you, Riven, you pathetic, traitorous coward."

He surged forward then, so fast Remi could barely register the motion without her heightened godly senses, as his magic exploded around her. It crawled up her legs, sliding down her spine as the icy fingers of death stroked every inch of her body. It left her gasping with terror just before he wrapped his fingers around her neck and slammed her back against the stone wall. The combination of the blow and his magic left her struggling for breath as she fought against him.

"Get off me," she hissed, injecting as much acid as she could into the words while she fought through the sheer pain of the blow. He'd lost his mind, and he was breaking the promise Madwyn had made to Arrick. She shoved and pushed, raking useless nails across his face. But he didn't react. He just squeezed his hand harder and smiled. His cruel, handsome face filled her vision, but she didn't stop fighting. She'd never stop fighting.

He leaned down to whisper in her ear. The musky smell of him mixed with the alcohol made her skin crawl. "Not so tough without your magic, are you?" His words slurred a little, and she knew he had to be wasted to come there and attack her. To defy the bargain Madwyn had made with Arrick.

She forced the words she knew would stop him from her lips. "You can't hurt me without hurting Madwyn." His face shifted then, as he noted his hand around her throat. On a snarl, he let go, the sudden release causing her to fall to her knees. She coughed, sputtering and hating the weakness of her muscles, her lack of magic. If she'd had her fire at her disposal, she'd raze the whole damn prison to the ground.

His lips pulled back into a snarl as she fought to regain her composure, knowing in her bones that Ellarah would be there any second, and they'd be screwed. Because Ellarah's magic would be no match for Riven's death power. Remi wanted to cry, to rail against the Ascended for letting him come there that night. *Why tonight of all nights?*

His velvet-smooth voice broke through her raging thoughts. "If you had never come to Bicaidia, none of this would have happened. If your family had left Thayne's well enough alone, he would have married Madwyn, and Ellarah and I would still be together. Instead, we got you. A useless, entitled, Valerian princess." He spat on the ground next to her feet, lips pulled back from his teeth.

Remi stared at him, stunned. He'd lost his damn mind if he blamed her for everything that had happened, and not his horrible sister. She recognized the denial for what it was, and knew he wanted to find some way to blame someone other than Madwyn and himself for Ellarah's suffering. Deep down, he knew, though. He had to know. Otherwise, why direct so much hate and blame at her?

A flutter of movement behind him caught her eye, and she sucked in a breath before she could school her features. He saw her expression change and spun back toward the open prison door. But when he saw nothing, he turned back to Remi, his magic still seeping around him like a misty fog.

"Expecting company?" he asked before he stalked to the still-open door. She pressed her lips shut, refusing to answer, even though she knew just how fucked they were. She knew they couldn't get out of this situation. He was too powerful, and he would stop them. No matter his feelings for Ellarah, she knew he wouldn't just let her walk out of the prison with Remi and the rest of them at her side. He reached the door and said, "I can feel you out there. You may as well show yourself before I make you."

He leaned a casual shoulder on the doorway, as though he hadn't a care in the world, and Remi watched as Ellarah stepped into the view. Riven's entire body stiffened as he took in the goddess he loved in full battle regalia. He stepped back as she raised a sword—no wait, his sword, the one imbued with his death magic—and leveled it at his throat.

"Hi, Riven," she said as Bekka and Emorie shifted into view at her sides. Without taking her eyes off her lover, Ellarah said, "Come on, Remi. It's time." Her expression remained cold as ice as Remi pushed to her feet and rushed past Riven, to stand behind Ellarah.

"What do we do about him?" Emorie hissed, her voice quiet. Riven's power had dissolved the instant he'd seen Ellarah, and Remi recognized pain and shock, laced with betrayal in his cool blue eyes.

His eyes flicked to the blade and back to Ellarah's face, pain etched in every line of it. "Would you really use that on me?"

Ellarah stepped forward then, pressing the tip of it to his throat.

He moved back and put up his hands. "Ellarah, that blade, it's poisoned along with my magic. If you cut me—" he trailed off, letting the sentence hang.

Ellarah's eyes burned gold fire as she said, "You betrayed us. You started a war, imprisoned our friends, and let your sister wound me to the point of death. I trusted you, Riven. I vouched for you. I loved you, but you destroyed that the instant you sided with Madwyn."

Desperation filled his eyes. "Please, Ellarah, let me explain." He reached out, as though to caress her face, and she shook her head, hardening her grip on the sword. He dropped his hand, and the bottle of god's-liquor slid from his grip, shattering.

"You don't get to touch me. You'll never touch me again."

Riven seemed to crumple then, falling to his knees before his lover. "Please, Ellarah, don't do this. Don't make me stop you." His magic seeped out from him once more and Remi reached for Bekka's hand, gripping it. She looked into her sister's wide, brown eyes, the mirror of her own.

"Cut him and be done with it," Emorie said, her voice dead calm and full of command. "His sister and her minions will find him before he dies, but you can't let him stop us."

Ellarah hesitated, and Remi understood the battle that raged inside her. She'd seen them together before that night in the control room when he'd destroyed everything. Ellarah and Riven had loved each other more than any pair she'd ever seen. It was probably why Riven had agreed to betray them in the first place. He'd assumed he could get Ellarah to understand and trust him again. He hadn't expected her to turn against him and side with his enemies.

Unfortunately for them, Riven saw the hesitation in his lover too, and reached out a tentative hand, moving his fingers toward her. "I love you, Ellarah, and even if you think you hate me right now, I know deep down, you still love me, too. You wouldn't cut me. And besides, Madwyn isn't here to find me right now."

"You're lying," Emorie said, tilting her chin up. "She wouldn't leave her city undefended."

He shook his head. "I'm not lying. She's in Valeria, negotiating your release and peace with your family." His eyes flicked to Bekka and Remi. "Which makes all of this quite pointless." Every hair on the back of Remi's neck stood on end at his words. Madwyn in Valeria? With her parents? Negotiating peace? Every fiber of her being told her that was a lie, and she felt a sense of doom as she thought through what Madwyn would do to her family, her home realm, once she arrived there.

"Ellarah," Remi hissed, seeing Riven's magic dance along the ground. "Cut him. We need to go. Now. He can't follow us, and we can't let him stop us. You know we can't trust Madwyn. If she's in Valeria, she's up to something and you know damn well it's not a truce. We need to get out of here on our own."

Remi scanned the room, worried that Ellarah wouldn't be able to do it. She saw Bekka watching in rapt attention beside her, and noticed the odd metal pipe in her hands as Ellarah continued to hesitate. From the tight expression on her face, Remi knew Bekka felt the same level of terror at the prospect of Madwyn in their home realm as she did. Their parents might be adept at hiding big secrets and betrayals, but they wouldn't break the bonds of a peace treaty negotiation. They had honor, and Remi knew Madwyn would harbor no such sentiment.

Then, to Remi's horror, Riven's hesitant fingers brushed the blade, pushing it aside. And then his magic exploded around him.

35
DESPERATE TIMES
BEKKA

The death magic hit us like a nuclear blast, throwing me out the door, along with Remi and Emorie. We slammed into the wall just outside Remi's cell before our would-be rescuer's magic burst from her like starlight. Black and white merged, blending and fighting for dominance as the death deity and the energy goddess charged each other.

I recovered quickly, and knew on instinct it had something to do with Arrick's death magic. Though I couldn't access it, the power still lived in my veins, a part of me. Turning, I saw the baton sitting at my side, within arm's reach. Behind me, the prison cell surged with a raging battle of magic. I could barely make out the energy goddess pressing forward, lunging with the sword, trying her level best to cut him. If only she'd acted sooner, I thought, grabbing my weapon and leaping to my feet.

Without giving it a second thought, I barreled into the cell. As I did, I heard my sister's scream chase me. "No, Bekka!" It didn't matter. The black magic would soon overtake the white, and without some kind of intervention, I knew we'd lose our opportunity to escape. Our only shot at getting out of there was if we could gain the advantage, and the energy goddess couldn't do it alone.

I would have to step up. I knew I couldn't kill him, weakened as I was, but I could distract him, I thought, as the first wave of their magic hit me. My whole body protested, and I gasped for air as it pulsed through me. But I kept going, fighting through it with every ounce of strength I had, careful to keep out of his line of sight.

The goddess fought like hell, slicing and attacking, trying to land a single cut. But the death god was fast, his magic more powerful than hers. And as I watched him, I could tell that he was holding back, as though he didn't want to hurt her, and a little ray of hope shone through me. It would be a handicap for him, and something I intended to use to our advantage.

So, I sprinted along the wall beside them, biting back a cry of agony as the death power nipped at my skin. But I pushed forward despite it, my weapon at the ready. I just needed to get one hit in and give Ellarah a shot at cutting him. I stopped just behind him, out of view, and waited. A second later, I saw my opening.

He stepped to dodge a blow and stumbled. I didn't hesitate. I lunged forward, swinging the baton down hard and slamming into the side of his head. The impact rattled through me, reverberating through my arms, almost making me drop the baton, but I held fast. He cried out, turning on instinct to assess the threat. His attention fixed on me for a split second as terror pulsed through me. *Shit, shit shit,* I thought, praying to the Ascended that Ellarah would take the opening I'd just given her. That she wouldn't hesitate as she had just moments before.

My eyes flicked to her, the blade already in motion. The death god saw it then, recognizing his error. He turned, blasting out his magic. It struck

Ellarah straight in the gut, making her cry out in pain, but not before the blade sliced through the disheveled, well-made suit and cut clean through the flesh on his arm. A deep wound opened, blood sliding down his hand and dripping onto the floor.

His eyes widened in shock, his magic evaporating as quickly as it had come. He staggered backward, looking down at the wound, and then back up at the goddess he claimed to love. I could see the utter stupefaction on his face as Ellarah's chest heaved with exhaustion.

He dropped to his knees then as the poison spread. He gasped for breath, slumping forward. "Ellarah," he said, reaching his hand for her, and she dropped the sword. It clanged on the ground, and I hurried forward to grab it, along with her arm. I pulled her, trying to tug her from the room, but she stood rooted to the spot, staring at the god she obviously still loved, complicated as that situation might be.

Remi and Emorie joined me then, all three of us yanking on Ellarah, trying to force her out of the room. She gave no ground and then whispered, "I'm sorry, Riv, but you chose wrong." Before she turned and ran, taking the sword from my hand, and shutting the door behind her.

We burst into the hall just in time to hear thundering footsteps and a loud roar. My stomach dropped to my toes as recognition clicked into place.

Demons. A lot of demons.

"And our window is officially closed," Ellarah said, as she grabbed Remi's arm and ran down, Emorie and I booking it behind them.

36
THE ESCAPE
THAYNE

Thayne wound through the halls of the prison, searching for Remi. He'd never seen where they kept her, her sister, or Emorie, but he leaned on his knowledge of the cells and of the goddess who trapped them here.

Madwyn would want them all deep in the center of the prison, far enough away from each other to make escape difficult, but still hidden from prying eyes. He relied on that knowledge and set them on a direct path to the cell blocks he'd have chosen, if he were a psychotic chaos deity with a grudge.

He turned the corner and halted, leaning back against a stone wall and gesturing to Pietyr, Rackham, Caden, and Deklan to do the same. Then he pointed at Caden and mouthed, demon. He slid a finger across his throat and made an expression as though gasping for air. Caden nodded and moved to stand in front of him. Still pressed against the wall, he angled himself to see the demon beyond them. Thayne followed suit.

Its pale skin and sharp teeth, mouth filled with black, tar-like saliva, made Thayne's entire body recoil. It carried one of the black-coated weapons. The ones that could poison and kill a deity, as it almost had Ellarah. The ones they needed to get their hands on as soon as possible.

Caden's body tensed beside him and the demigod's hands clenched into fists.

A second later, the demon clutched a sharp-nailed hand to its throat. It opened its horrible mouth, gasping for air. The leather and lightweight alloy of its battle armor groaned in protest as the giant beast dropped to its knees, still fighting for breath. A few moments of silent, tortured scrabbling later, and its body went limp.

Caden turned a grim face back to the group and nodded, letting them know they could keep moving. As they passed the creature, Thayne stared down at its wide, unseeing eyes in disgust. Pietyr picked up its discarded black weapon, and a deadly smile pulled his lips up as he twisted it a few times. "You'll get the next one," he said to Deklan, who glared at the weapon in what Thayne could only interpret as envy.

"I'll get the next one," Thayne corrected, fingers still itching for a weapon. The demigods had their magic, but he, Pietyr, and Rackham would have only the weapons they scavenged on their way out. But, begrudgingly, he agreed that the first one should go to Pietyr. He was the best fighter of the three of them, and while Thayne could hold his own, Pietyr had always been the better swordsman.

They continued on silent steps down the hall, the eerie quiet making Thayne's skin crawl. Where were the demon guards? He wondered as they passed bolted door after door with no one standing vigil. Thayne couldn't understand why. Had the halls been this devoid of demons the entire time? Or had something gone wrong? That uncertainty caused a foreboding sense of irrational dread to creep into his mind. Madwyn would never leave their prison, which held his and the future Peacekeeper's cells, so unprotected.

He picked up his pace as he felt Pietyr's presence at his side. The shadow wielder whispered, "Something's not right."

"No shit," he heard Deklan grumble in response.

"Where are all the demons?" Rackham asked, keen eyes scanning the halls.

Pietyr replied, shaking his head, "I don't know. Madwyn might be crazy, but she isn't stupid. Something must have happened."

As though in response to their questions, a roar sounded through the narrow hallway. It reverberated off the walls, and the floor shook, swaying a little as stone dust fell from the ceiling. They snapped their heads to the right, down the long cell-lined corridor, from where they'd heard the roar.

Another scream, higher and female, filled their ears.

"Bekka," Caden whispered, his eyes locking onto his brother's. Deklan acknowledged him just before they took off at a dead sprint straight toward it.

Without thinking, Thayne bolted, tight on their heels. *Remi!* His mind shouted. They hurtled down the hallway, the sound of their breaths and thundering footfalls dwarfed by the shouts and roars of demons. Thayne saw a bright, white light shine around a corner ahead, and then he heard demons squeal like pigs and shriek like falcons.

"Fuck, it's Ellarah. She must have remembered!" he shouted over his shoulder to Pietyr, who sprinted just behind him, black sword still clutched in his grip. "Run faster!" Thayne commanded loud enough to be heard over the deafening sounds of demons dying and magic thrumming.

Deklan, at the head of their pack, picked up the pace in response. A few more steps and they hit the crossroads, clearing it in seconds. As they did, their collective attention fixed on the hoard of demons crammed into the hall, and the four goddesses at the far end of it, a bolted door at their backs. Thayne clenched his fists, preparing for a fight, steadying his breathing.

Deklan never hesitated. Instead, he dipped his shoulder, charging at full speed, and tore through the first two demons in the hoard before them. A large, black-as-night creature took the brunt of the impact, flipping over Deklan's back and landing hard on the ground. Close on his heels, Thayne dodged the massive, sprawling form of the creature, giving Pietyr a clear shot with the blade. He used it without hesitation, slicing through the demon's neck, killing it instantly.

Deklan gripped the second demon by the shoulder joints in its armor and heaved it behind him. It flew through the air, landing with a thud at Rackham's feet, who ducked to his knees and grabbed its head, snapping its neck with adept precision. He snatched the blade the demon dropped from the stone floor beside him and tossed it to Thayne, who caught the hilt with ease, turning it in his hands.

Caden stepped behind them and summoned his magic. Demons further up the crowded mass dropped like stones, heads disappearing from the fray, suffocating and choking on the vacuum where the air used to be.

Rackham snatched a blade from another demon Pietyr killed and armed himself that time. Bright flashes of magic, white and vibrant, issued from down the hall. Thayne could hear shouts from the goddesses and grunts as they fought against the massive battalion of demons. Thayne scanned his surroundings as quickly as he could, trying to get his bearings, and as soon as he did, his stomach dropped.

This hallway didn't just dead end into a cell. It was also the most dangerous part of the prison. The exterior wall dropped straight over a cliff into the crystal-hewn Synbue River below. And with the magic that protected the external walls? They would never make it past them. Even if they could, they'd need their full strength and full power to survive the jump. But without it?

One problem at a time, he thought. They had to get through the demons and cut a path to Ellarah, Remi, and the others. He shouted ahead of him as Deklan fought hand-to-hand, dropping demons in his wake. "Deklan, use your damned magic!"

The demigod turned back to him, a little surprised, as though just remembering that he even had magic. He leaned to the side before a demon thrust a blade at him from behind, dodging it. Thayne could tell from that near-perfect spatial awareness that he hadn't underestimated Deklan. Though the demigod's fighting skills might be trained and honed to precision, he needed to use his fucking magic if they had any hope of saving the four goddesses pinned down at the end of the hall.

Deklan shuffled back toward him, dodging, weaving, and slicing with his own scavenged, poisoned sword. More demons fell as the hoard split, half fighting with Bekka, Emorie, Remi, and Ellarah, and the other focusing on them.

One more step and Deklan moved behind them, allowing Pietyr to lead the physical fight with Rackham and Thayne as he joined his brother. Thayne bellowed as he dodged a demon's jagged knife, slicing for his gut. He gripped its wrist, holding it still as he slammed his fist into the demon's face. Then, yanking that wrist hard, he gripped the back of its stringy-haired head and smashed that same face into the stone wall at his side before driving his new blade into its gut, ripping it free in a smooth motion. "Now! Both of you!" he shouted to the demigods.

His urgency ramped up as he heard a pained scream, and the bright white light ahead flickered. As though responding to his terror at the prospect of either Ellarah or Remi being injured, the ground shook beneath their feet. A small group of demons in front of them dropped, scrabbling at their throats and gasping for air. And he knew Caden had sucked the air from that portion of the hall, daring to let his magic work even closer to them. *Desperate times, and all that*, Thayne thought.

The demons dropped to the ground as Pietyr and Rackham advanced, still cutting and punching through the crowd of hideous creatures. Thayne hoped Caden could maintain control over the airflow and not suffocate either them or the goddesses while he unleashed his power.

The ground beneath him started to split and crack as Deklan's magic roared to life. Tiny threads of the vines within the earthen stones grew, directed by his hands, and wrapped themselves around the legs of the demons. They fell to the ground as the vines expanded, enveloping them like cocoons. The demons writhed and tried to break free as their swords clattered to the ground and holes opened up in the floor beneath them, revealing a drop at least fifty feet onto the cellblock beneath them. Deklan had broken through all the layers of stone that comprised the prison's floor. Thayne couldn't help but be impressed. He had tried to do it during training and failed. It seemed the demigods performed best under pressure. He hoped they would keep it up.

A demon stumbled back from the splitting ground, spinning to face them and lunging at Thayne with its black blade. Thayne dodged, kicking out and slamming his boot into its chest. It dropped its sword on the ground just before it fell into that gaping hole. Rackham and Pietyr followed Thayne's lead, kicking and shoving the demons into the gaping chasm. Dozens fell with bone-shattering cracks, as the building seemed to rumble with the impact. Deklan waved a hand and dissolved the stones of the cellblock floor below them into dust too, and they fell even further into the dungeon's belly. *Damn if they hadn't made it to the middle caste*, Thayne thought, wiping sweat from his brow.

Caden continued to suffocate demons, as Deklan dropped them from the hall, repairing the floor for them as they went, and they all pushed forward toward the goddesses still fighting like hell at their end of the battle. The gods cut and killed, and Thayne's magic itched at his fingers, wanting to be set free. He spared a glance at his wrist and noticed the high sheen and glow of the rune tattoo. It lit the surrounding area, as did Pietyr's and Rackham's, and he knew they must be feeling it too.

One more drop of demons, followed by a bone-shattering crack, and Thayne got his first unobstructed view of the end of the hall. Remi stood behind Ellarah, who glowed white with power, though he could see that it was waning. Bekka and Emorie stood on her other side, each wielding some kind of metallic pipe. They swung them out, striking at the demons, sweat slicking their skin and darkening their clothes. If Ellarah hadn't been there to defend them, he doubted they would have made it this far.

But, as it stood, he could tell that Ellarah was tiring. "Pietyr, Rackham, we have to push harder! Cut through! She can't hold them much longer!"

At the sound of his voice, Remi's gaze snapped up. Their eyes met through the haze of demons, magic, and battle. He saw the relief along with the fear and desperation in them. He pushed forward. Seeing her felt like home, like a fucking gift, if he were honest, and he'd be damned if he let her down. Not if he could help it. So, he pushed forward, a roar in his throat as he sliced his blade through the demons in his path.

Pietyr made quick work of them too, Rackham trailing behind, a little younger, and less experienced with his weapons. But to Thayne's relief, that didn't make him any less deadly.

They drew nearer then, close enough to see the whites of all four goddesses' eyes and the individual beads of sweat dripping from their temples. "Thayne!" Remi shouted as Ellarah glowed an ethereal white, power gathering and growing. Ellarah's eyes met his, a silent word passing between them as it had since their childhood, and he knew what she wanted to do. "Drop, now!" he roared, hoping that Deklan and Caden could hear him above the sound of demons dying and blades clashing.

He dropped to the ground, Pietyr and Rackham doing the same, as a flood of pure, primal energy burst from Ellarah's core. It blew what remained of the once large demon hoard back, peeling their skin from the bones of their faces and killing them all instantly. When it finished, Thayne jerked his head up to survey her. She sank to one knee, her shoulders heaving, and he hurried to his feet.

He ran the last dozen steps to get to her and skidded to a halt before her. Remi already knelt beside her, a hand on her shoulder. "Ellarah, are you OK?" she asked, and through her jagged breathing. The energy goddess nodded, wiping a small line of blood from her nose with the back of her hand.

After a few more moments of labored breaths, Ellarah lifted her head and locked gazes with Thayne. "And here I thought I was going to rescue you."

He let a grin slide over his features. "Was that your plan?"

She cleared her throat and nodded as she tried to get to her feet. She swayed, and Remi grabbed one elbow, and he gripped the other, hauling her up. He scanned her and his concern deepened as he took in the sheer exhaustion stamped on every line of her face, every movement of her body.

She waved them away, moving out of their grasp. "No, I'm fine. I can manage." And she did, steadying herself and squaring her shoulders. Behind her, he saw Pietyr and Rackham hugging Emorie, surveying each other as though checking for injuries.

Bekka was nowhere to be found. Unnerved, he spun and saw her wrapped in a tight embrace with the two brothers. Silver shimmered in her eyes, visible even from further down the hall. Caden rested an affectionate hand on her cheek before he jerked his chin toward the rest of them, and she nodded, turning and breaking into a jog. They dodged the bodies of dead demons, and Bekka knelt to grasp a sword as they went.

The demigods' faces held expressions as serious as death, and Bekka's did too. They seemed to know the battle wasn't over, and he could sense a current of rage beneath their stoic surfaces. And he had a feeling he knew why—the death deity who'd saved all their skins in Bicaidian hell. The one who'd made an unbreakable binding to protect them all and sold his freedom to make it happen. He wasn't there and wouldn't escape with them that night. Thayne already knew how the demigods would feel about that.

Pushing that thought from his mind, Thayne reached for Remi then, and she moved straight into his arms, wrapping her own around his waist and pressing her cheek to his chest. He wanted to lean down and kiss her, to spend plenty of time making up for the mistake of refusing her that last night they'd spent together. To wash any taste of Madwyn out of his mouth. He wanted his wife. But it wasn't the time, and they would need to do a lot of talking before that could happen. He knew that.

Remi pulled away for a second, her eyes staring up at him. "Thank the Ascended you came. But—" she said, her voice thoughtful, "how are you here? How did you get out?"

Pietyr answered for him, "The brothers have magic."

Emorie's brow wrinkled. "You mean, Madwyn didn't test them? Didn't rune them?"

"She tested them," Thayne said. "They didn't have it then, but now they do."

Rackham grinned, the expression youthful. "Turns out they just needed more time in the immortal realm. Maybe it's a demigod thing."

Pietyr cut in then, "Not that I'm not enjoying this reunion and all, but how are we going to get out of here? I'm guessing those aren't the only demons guarding this place, and we haven't been the picture of stealth."

"Right," Ellarah said, shaking her head as though to clear it. "I have a plan, but you need to trust me." She spun, turning toward the cell behind them. Thayne didn't miss the massive sword hanging on her back. *Riven's sword*, he thought, surprised as Ellarah said, "We just need to get this door open."

37

THE PRISONER

Remi

Remi turned a confused gaze on Ellarah. They all did. "You mean that's how we're escaping? From that cell?"

Ellarah nodded, her light-brown hair rustling in its ponytail. "I didn't think it would be locked. There's no record of any prisoner in here, and I dropped the keys I stole earlier during the fight. But—" she said, trailing off and her teeth fastening to her bottom lip in concern. A slight pang of unease rippled through Remi's gut.

"But what?" Bekka asked, her intense stare flicking from Thayne to Ellarah.

"It means that whoever is in the cell is someone my family wanted to keep a secret," Thayne answered. "And we only did that with the most dangerous criminals."

Emorie turned to Thayne. "Well, do you know who it is?"

He pressed his lips together and gave a curt shake of his head.

A silent hush pulsed through the group as all eyes landed on the door.

"Well, fuck," Deklan said, resting his demon blade on the ground and leaning on the hilt for support. "We couldn't expect everything to go our way, could we?"

Caden raised his brows at his brother. "You call this going our way?"

He shrugged a disinterested shoulder. "We're alive, aren't we?" he asked, and Remi saw Bekka's lips twitch in amusement. Amusement, for Ascended sake. They'd just fought themselves free of at least a hundred demons, their black blood still soaked all their clothes and skin, and her sister could laugh at a time like this? What had Moldize done to her?

"Deklan's right," Pietyr said, cutting in with clipped orders. "Search the remaining demons for another key now. We're wasting time."

Ellarah stepped forward, balance still a little shaky as she dropped to her knees and rifled through the demons' battle leathers, black blood coating her fingers as she did. "He's right. We need to hurry. We don't have much time left."

So many questions flooded Remi's mind that she didn't know where to begin, but it wasn't the time to ask them. Urgency spread through her veins as she and the rest of them kicked the dead bodies of the demons aside and rummaged through their clothing.

Well, all except one of the twin demigods. Deklan, she thought, but it was hard to tell. He stepped to the door and pressed a hand to the adobe brick walls on either side, where the earthen stone met the thick, metal barrier. He closed his eyes, lips set in a grim line as he concentrated, and she realized he must be the edaphopath.

But, nothing happened. He squinted harder and squeezed his eyes shut as he tried again. Nothing. "Something's blocking me," he said, shaking his head.

Ellarah knelt next to another demon as she said, "I already tried to blast our way in earlier. It's reinforced with protective power. It only affects the walls surrounding this cell. Thayne, you're sure you don't know who could be in there?" She asked before the demigod could reply. Remi paused her task of hunting for keys and focused on Thayne.

He looked haunted as he flicked his eyes to the cell and stared. "Does it matter? We have to go in regardless."

Pietyr kicked a guard over, and said, "You know who, don't you? You need to tell us."

Thayne growled. "No, I don't. I just know that if we kept a prisoner off-books, then it was for a good reason."

Emorie sighed. "Well, do you at least know why the interior walls have magic wards spelled into them?"

Before he could snarl a retort at Emorie, Remi examined the door and noticed the slight glow of something in the stones. Stepping back, she saw the rune. It shone brighter then, reacting to Deklan's power the same way the runes on their wrists did.

"Guys, look," she said, pointing to it.

Their heads snapped up in unison to peer at her, and Thayne gave Emorie a *there you go* look that left her muttering curses under her breath as they continued to search.

Bekka blew an exasperated breath, wiping the sweat from her brow with her forearm as she crawled to the next fallen demon in need of searching. "OK, so someone runed this cell, and only this cell? If that's the case, do you think Madwyn gave the demons the key to all the—oh wait! Here they are!" she exclaimed, leaping up to show them all a large ring of keys.

An old-fashioned security precaution, used to avoid magical tampering or remote hacking. *Sometimes, the old ways were best*, Remi thought again, the memory of her grandfather never far from her mind. He had always preferred the old ways. You couldn't trick a key, at least not these keys. Large and long, with complicated, non-replicable teeth, forged by ancient technology deities many millennia before.

Bekka jingled the keys in her upheld hand, pulling Remi's mind from her memories, as Ellarah rushed forward and grabbed them from Bekka before hurrying back to the door. "Look, I don't care if the fount of all evil is on the other side of this door. We're opening it. I chose this block because it's the most secluded. Almost no one patrols it and it's impossible to secure the exterior wall since it drops straight down a cliff into the river. I have a plan, and I need you guys to trust me."

Thayne moved to her side, placing his hand over hers as she tested the keys in the lock. She hesitated and looked up into his determination-filled eyes.

"The minute you open that door, step aside." She glared at him, annoyed, but he continued, "You're weakened after that last burst. All four of you are. You fought through how many demons and for how long before we got here to help thin the herd? The rest of you fought with no magic, and strength barely more than a human's. You're in no shape for another fight. Not yet." He gestured to Deklan, Pietyr, Rackham, and Caden. "We'll go in first."

Ellarah's teeth clenched. "Fine, but we're wasting time."

"She's right. Open the damn door," Pietyr said, grip tightening on his sword as Rackham, Deklan, and Caden pushed past Bekka and Emorie to stand at Pietyr's flanks, Thayne just behind them. Remi would have argued with their stupid masculine bullshit, but Thayne had a damned good point. They had fought for a long time before Thayne and the rest of them had shown up, and exhaustion tugged at her.

After so many nights with so little sleep and no exercise, every limb in her body felt like lead. So, with that decided, Ellarah tried three more keys before one slid in and twisted. She stopped, her eyes widening as she stared at them before she pulled open the door. She stepped back and Remi watched as all five gods rushed into the room, blades drawn.

They stopped as quickly as they'd started, still hovering close to the doorway, and Remi tried to peer around them into the room. Her mouth went dry when she heard Pietyr's voice, clear and deadly serious, ask, "And just who the hell are you?"

38
EXPLOSIVE
REMI

The gods eased further into the cell; blades still drawn as Remi stepped inside. Bekka and the rest of their companions filed in behind her.

Remi scanned the cell and shock filled every inch of her body. It didn't look like theirs at all. Rather, floor-to-ceiling bookshelves lined every available wall, all filled to bursting with leather-bound copies of books. Soft flames crackled from a stone fireplace at one end of the cell, an immense mantle fashioned from rough-edged wood above it. A small, but cozy-looking four-poster bed sat opposite the fire, and in the corner closest to them stood a desk and a well-worn leather chair.

A god sat in that chair, one ankle resting on the opposite knee as he read a thick book. His long, chestnut brown hair shone with smooth, untangled waves, and Remi noticed the bathroom then. She saw a rain showerhead, sink, and toilet visible behind an open curtain. He had a long, dark beard and wore simple clothes—a white linen shirt and a pair of soft, camel-colored pants. Old-fashioned, but well-made.

He looked up from his reading, fixed his stare on Pietyr, and then slid his attention to Deklan and Caden. Remi saw a moment of surprise register before he schooled his features. He surveyed them all as they stepped into the room.

Then, he leaned to the right in his chair and looked out into the hall littered with the bodies of the demons they'd slain. "I see you killed my captors. Are you here to end me too, then?" he asked, though he didn't seem alarmed by the prospect. That fact alone made Remi's blood run cold.

Ellarah pushed into the cell last, twisting the key and clicking the locked door closed behind her. Ignoring the prisoner, she said, "We don't have a lot of time here," and then rushed over to the barred window of the cell. "This window was the best option for us in the prison." She peered through the warded bars, careful not to touch them, and looked downward at the massive drop, as though preparing for something. What though? Remi had no idea.

Bekka snorted as she crossed her arms. "Why in the Twelve Hells is this guy's cell so much nicer than ours? I mean, a rain shower and a library? A four-poster bed?" She turned an accusatory glare on Thayne. "Who is he?"

Emorie shared the same angry expression as her sister and stared down her nose at the mysterious prisoner. It appeared they both decided he couldn't be that dangerous if they kept him in such luxury, but Remi didn't share their sentiment. Something about him made her feel on edge. She couldn't pinpoint what it was, though.

The stranger rose to his feet then, and Remi clocked the runes on his wrist as he pushed up his sleeves. He had six tattooed there, and she sucked in a surprised breath as they all glowed. What kind of power did he have that required six runes to suppress it? She rubbed the single one on her wrist as his nostrils flared, his powerful body taking up more space in the room than seemed possible. As though his very presence made the rest of theirs dim in comparison.

Thayne straightened, squaring off against the prisoner. He spoke in his commanding, high prince voice. The one that made deities, strong or weak alike, obey him. "Sit down. We're not here to end you, but you're not coming with us either."

He arched a well-shaped brow at Thayne, as though her husband's attempt at authority amused him. "Listen princeling. You're in my cell, and if you plan to go anywhere from here, then I'll be going with you."

Thayne's brows rose in surprise just before his expression hardened. Deklan and Caden stepped behind him, the threat clear in their glares, and again a shadow seemed to pass over the prisoner's face as he glanced in their direction. He shrugged it off though, and if Remi's attention had left his face for even one second, she would have missed it.

"How do you know who I am?" Thayne asked, expression darkening.

He lifted a shoulder in an apathetic shrug. "You look just like Rynard. I could only assume you're his son. Where is that son of a bitch, anyway? He hasn't been down here to see me in months."

Thayne gritted his teeth. "My father is dead."

The prisoner's eyes widened right before Remi heard a loud ripping sound from the other side of the cell. They all turned toward the window, where Rackham and Pietyr aided Ellarah in whatever plan she had. All three of them stuck small, fingertip-sized orbs onto the bars. They worked quickly, and Remi had to drag her gaze away to force it back to the prisoner.

He leveled a serious gaze on Thayne. "I'm sorry for your loss. Rynard was a decent deity."

Emorie balked then and stepped forward, arms still crossed. "You think your captor was a decent deity? You expect us to believe that? What's your angle? Who the hell are you?"

"Yeah, what she said," Bekka tossed in, and Remi had to restrain herself from shaking her head at her sister's blasé attitude, no matter how amusing she might find it under normal circumstances. Something deep in her gut told her they needed to treat this deity seriously.

Ellarah called out then, "Plug your ears!" Remi turned just in time to see the wall explode. Rippling magic pulsed around the stone walls where the window had been just a moment before. Pieces of rubble shot out from the gaping hole in the wall and down into the canyon below. Remi's mouth hung open, as did Thayne's.

"Twelve Hells, that was unexpected," Bekka said, pressing her palms to her ears and yawning, as though trying to clear them.

The twins looked almost bored when Remi turned back to the prisoner. Apparently, exploding walls happened on the regular in their world.

The prisoner also looked less than impressed. He cocked a brow. "Subtle," he said, lips twitching as though he meant to smile, but couldn't quite bring himself to do it. "But effective. I like her style."

"Shut up," Thayne replied, as Ellarah hurried toward them. She dropped another orb on the ground and rolled it toward the rubble, and bright, white energy pulsed from the hole. Swirling and morphing into a portal, the other side obscured by the sheer brightness of the energy magic.

"We need to go, now! Before the wards recover from the pulse bomb. Hurry!" The exterior walls of every major prison in the Twelve Realms contained magical wards meant to keep prisoners inside. Mostly, it could withstand the test of magic. But, with enough energy, you could take them down for a few minutes. Just enough time to escape, if you hurried, but no longer. Getting your hands on enough energy magic to accomplish it, though? Remi didn't know how Ellarah had managed it at all, let alone in such a short time.

Pushing that aside for the moment, Remi obeyed Ellarah's frantic waving, and ran toward the portal, grabbing Bekka's hand and tugging her along. Bekka fought, trying to tug her arm free, to turn back, but Remi held firm and pulled her forward. "Wait," Bekka hissed, digging her heels in, her eyes growing a little frantic. "Deklan, Caden! I won't go through without them!"

Remi spared them a glance over her shoulder. They stood close to the prisoner, weapons still poised to strike. He rose from his chair, his eyes fixed on the portal, and they bared their teeth in warning.

Deciding she'd tackle them next; she returned to her task and shoved her sister toward that portal despite her protests. Pietyr waited just at the mouth of its swirling winds, and she locked eyes with him, an understanding passing between them. She pushed her sister forward and into his arms just before he tossed her through, jumping in after her. Rackham went next, followed by Emorie.

Remi bellowed, "Caden, Deklan, go now!" The demigods turned their heads to the portal and away from the prisoner for a minute. Their white hair whipped, creating a halo around their dark skin. In unison, they looked back at the prisoner, hesitating. He appeared ready to follow them out; like he'd fight them to do it if he had to.

"I've got this," Thayne assured them. "Go with Bekka. Keep her safe. She is the most important thing right now." They spared one glance at the prisoner, and then back toward Thayne as though they didn't quite believe him. "Go," he said. "That's not a request." Though they both glared at him, they seemed to accept the wisdom of what he said. Nodding once, they each spun and rushed toward the howling wind. Seconds later, they charged through, one after the other, bodies disappearing within the blinding light.

Remi winced as she heard a muffled rustling amid the roaring wind of the portal, and knew that it was fighting to stay open against the wards. Ellarah's worried eyes locked with hers, just as the prisoner lunged. He slammed into Thayne, his body powerful, and Thayne stumbled back, sword tumbling from his grasp. The prisoner drew back a fist, taking advantage of Thayne's momentary disorientation, and punched it straight into his face as he continued to push Thayne backward, moving them both toward the portal.

"Thayne! We don't have time for this!" Ellarah yelled, her panicked voice rising above the whipping wind and the unfolding fight. Just then, a shrill shriek sounded from the other side of the prisoner's cell door, and Remi froze. Demons, she thought, as thundering footsteps pounded down the hallway close at hand.

"We can't let him out! We know nothing about him. He could be dangerous!" Thayne yelled.

"We've got bigger problems! This won't hold much longer!" Ellarah shouted, the desperation clear in her voice. The portal wobbled as the wards rippled, closing ranks on the flaw in their protection. The portal's bright white light shuddered before shrinking by a quarter.

"Thayne! She's right!" Remi called, just as the demons outside slammed into the door. The metal of it banged, flexing and warping from the pressure of creatures crashing into it. And then she heard a familiar voice ring out and everything in her went still with horror.

Davendrie's voice.

Chills snaked down her spine.

"Move, you useless abominations!" he shouted, and Remi knew their time had run out. She surged forward, gripping Thayne's upper arm and hauling him away from the melee with all her strength.

She shoved him toward the portal and Ellarah grabbed his other arm before he could right himself from the surprise of her attack. Ellarah pushed him through, the portal's light swallowing him, and then looked at Remi in question. "I'm right behind you!" Remi yelled, and Ellarah nodded, jumping through just as Remi heard the locking mechanism on the door begin to work. She spun toward her only hope of escape, mere steps away, and started running just when claws raked over her mind. She stopped, screaming, her hands flying to either side of her head, as she dropped to her knees.

Davendrie, she knew, tears swelling in her eyes without her permission. He wanted to get inside her brain, to see what was happening, and make her hallucinate.

But the runes. They protect this room from magic, she thought, growing frantic as desperation hit her hard. She threw up whatever walls she could manage without her magic, knowing she had mere seconds before he got what he wanted. *It must be the damage to the door and the bridge that already exists between our minds. It's the only thing that makes sense.*

She looked at the prisoner, the only one left in the cell with her, and his eyes locked onto hers. He hesitated in his hurry to get to the portal, staring at her as she let out a wild screech, clawing at her face and hair, trying to keep Davendrie out of her head.

Something shuddered over the prisoner's eyes as he watched, and she screamed again, those familiar claws raking her brain. She tried to shake it off, rose to her feet, and stumbled forward. But before she could make it two steps, she collapsed again, the pain of Davendrie's attack damn near unbearable.

Tears flowed down her cheeks, and she dragged her head up to look at the bright, white portal. It was so damn close. But it shuddered then, the light guttering for a moment before returning, but smaller that time. It was shrinking, the wards reforming in its place one piece at a time. Another hit to her mind and Davendrie's power pierced through. Her vision blurred for a moment, and she fell onto her side, gasping.

The cell door opened then, and she saw Davendrie's terrible smile through her blurry vision, his dark eyes looking at her like a lion would its prey. He stalked forward, his green and gold armor glowing with power, as the demons at his back charged past him with weapons drawn.

It's over, she thought. *I'm going to die here, and there's nothing anyone can do to stop it.*

Then, to her utter astonishment, she felt rough hands grip her under her arms before they yanked her to her feet. Her head lolled like a rag doll's, and she saw the prisoner's face, grim with determination, as he hauled her into his arms and ran for the portal.

She tried to look at it then, her vision going in and out under Davendrie's assault. The opening between worlds shrank at an increasing pace as her whole body went limp and useless. The prisoner ran faster. They were close, so close, and when they got within spitting distance, the prisoner tossed her through the light without ceremony, the hole too small for both of them to fit at once.

Remi burst through it, wincing at the tug of wind pulling against her body and ripping at her skin. She spun in mid-air, floating in the space between dimensions, as her eyes locked onto the prisoner's—nothing but dead-serious resolve in them.

He jumped through after her, body straight and arms stretched above his head, the portal still shrinking into nothing but a pinprick behind him, and all six runes on his wrists flared to life as he hurtled through it with her.

Behind him, to her utter horror, she saw Davendrie's body lunge through, just before the tiny circle of light closed.

39
VALERIA
ARRICK

I stood next to Madwyn, my stomach churning with a sickening combination of dread and anticipation. We'd arrived in Valeria at dusk with only twenty-five of the soldiers we'd chosen, along with Cerus, Asthorea, Lilja, and me.

I had to feign outrage when Madwyn informed me that afternoon that Lilja would accompany us as leverage. I'd sworn at her, called her all sorts of names, and issued a variety of threats.

It hadn't been difficult to fake the rage, because it wasn't fake. Anger had become a living thing inside me. Barely controlled, just as Bekka's magic had grown to a fever pitch beneath my skin. But I let Madwyn issue an order, and shut my mouth like an obedient fucking dog, leaving her with no trace of the plans Lili and I had plotted the night before.

I hadn't disobeyed a direct order by planning with my sister because I didn't tell her everything. Instead, I only shared a rough outline of the terrain and the promises I'd made to Bekka. She inferred the rest. Smart kid. She took after our mother that way.

As I scanned the valley and the high hilltops surrounding us, I noted the large thickets of trees at the edges, so dense one could get lost in them. Then I surveyed the guard we'd brought, checking their formations, and ensuring all looked in order.

After inspecting my selection of the full fifty soldiers, Madwyn had scaled it down by half. Instead, she ordered me to bring twenty-five of my most powerful demons. She didn't say why, but as I scanned the guard standing in full formation behind us, I understood. They made an imposing and terrifying spectacle, especially for deities who hadn't seen a death god in millennia.

Deities like the Valerians.

All my soldiers, both demon and deity, stood in their choreographed spaces; spread out enough to make them more difficult targets, but close enough to rally as a fighting force. The demons' skin colors ranged from a milky white to a depthless black, and their claws, spiky horns, and needle-like teeth were on full display as they snarled. Their hideous appearance and black-poisoned blades were all part of Madwyn's fear tactic. A strategy I knew would hit home once the Valerians arrived, I thought, wondering where they were. It was past our planned time. They should be here already. That thought alone unnerved me.

"You seem tense, Arrick," Madwyn drawled next to me.

I cut my gaze to Lilja, keeping up the pretense. "I'd be less tense if you hadn't brought my little sister here, and if I knew what you had planned."

Madwyn's lips lifted at the edges, cold amusement in her eyes. "Well, I brought her along as an incentive, and you know damn well why. That disobedience in the throne room? I can't have that again."

I clenched my jaw, biting back the loathing I felt. "And here I thought you wanted me to join you. Yet, you keep threatening the people I care about."

"Join me, and I'll stop threatening them," she said, still ignoring my comment about her plans. Not surprising. She'd been tightly wound since that morning, mouth sealed about what would happen when we arrived in Valeria.

I didn't know why she didn't want help planning it, but it had to be something big. Something terrible. I thought again about my suspicions. Would she release the truth and watch it all crumble around her?

"What makes you think I haven't joined you? I've served you for months," I said, clenching and unclenching my fists as Bekka's magic pressed closer to the surface. It always seemed worse with Madwyn nearby, and I wondered if Bekka's power reacted to the chaos magic flowing inside of her, taunting it to come out and show itself.

She chuckled. "Probably the fact that I'm not an idiot. You might fuck Sylennia every night, if that's even what you're doing, but it's clear you still love Bekka. So, this must be very hard for you, not knowing what my plans are and being helpless to stop them."

Ice slithered down my back at her comment about Sylennia and Bekka, and she turned then, looking at me as she smiled that charming, wicked grin. True amusement at my torment, and I schooled my expression into stone.

I fucking hated her.

But before I could say more, a bright light shone not twenty feet before us, a flare, followed by the hum of magic that shook the ground as a portal appeared. Then dozens more sprang to life in the valley, like stars against the darkening, dusk sky.

Deities stepped through them, the portals hissing shut behind them, and I could just barely see the edges of the famed golden city of Vyngale as they winked out. Within minutes, hundreds of deities stood before us, all adorned in the golden armor and soft white battle leathers of Valeria.

A portal formed just in front of us then, and Madwyn took a cool step backward to avoid it, all of us following suit, as a god and goddess stepped through. The goddess, tall and graceful with blonde hair braided in a crown, wore leather pants and a golden chest plate, a small circlet around her head. The god, tall with vibrant red hair, wore full Valerian battle leathers and armor for the occasion. I couldn't decide whether that was a good or bad sign.

The portal disappeared behind them, and they fixed their gaze on Madwyn, stone-faced and expressionless. Responding to the attention, Madwyn stepped forward. Her loose emerald tunic and black pants blew around her in the breeze as she closed the distance between herself and the royals.

Madwyn's clothing choice was a stark contrast to the rest of the host that surrounded her; casual, high-quality, and beautiful, but not meant for war. The rest of us wore battle attire, ready for whatever may come. Another clue that I quite couldn't interpret.

As Madwyn approached, the Valerian guard fell into ranks around their king and queen, in a formation of their own. They eyed our fighting force, their gazes settling on the demons in disgust and horror, but the tightness in their lips gave away the fear. It would be the first time they'd seen demons in, maybe ever. So, the automatic revulsion at the hideous creatures, combined with the jagged, enormous swords they carried, would unnerve even the most seasoned soldier.

I fell into step behind Madwyn, Asthorea moving too. Cerus stayed behind with Lilja, his orders clear. He was to ensure she remained unharmed, but if a battle started? I had little doubt my cunning sister could slip away without notice.

As we moved, my eyes scanned the wooded areas for threats, and I caught a slight movement, squinting as I peered up the hill into the forest. More Valerian soldiers? I wondered, knowing that higher ground would make any fight we might have there damn near impossible. But then I saw a break in the shadows, and the form materialized.

Sylennia? I thought, my mind racing. She hadn't been a part of the plan, at least not one of my making. Her eyes locked onto mine, and she pressed a finger to her lips before she disappeared in shadow again. I didn't dare react or show emotion as I moved my eyes along the tree line. Why had she come to Valeria?

"Hello, Madwyn of house Senagal," Bekka's father's voice broke through my thoughts. "I'm Lord Killian of House Daevos. We'd say welcome to Valeria, but under the circumstances, I think we both know that wouldn't be true."

Arrick could see a steady stream of glistening magic that emanated around both of Bekka's parents, a show of power and distrust. Another sign that they'd come prepared.

"Oh, come now, Lord Killian," Madwyn said. "No need to be rude."

Bekka's Mother's, the Valerian Queen's eyes hardened. They looked just like Bekka's. "I think the need for that is clear. You have our daughters, and you've attacked four of our allied realms."

"That's why we're here, is it not?" Madwyn retorted, a shapely brow arched as she surveyed the royals. Then she gestured to the small army that surrounded us, and to the field as well. "Surely, we can find more comfortable accommodations to discuss our business?"

Mackayla's hard stare never faltered as a white tent flickered into existence in the space behind them, between the Valerian royal's personal guard and the rest of the soldiers they'd brought. It shimmered into a solid form, a demonstration of the queen's power. Time was a fickle gift, especially in the immortal realm, and yet she'd just called forth what looked like a war tent from another time. I could tell because the air surrounding it seemed to vibrate, as though it didn't quite belong there.

It looked brand new, but I'd seen that tent before, and recognition flashed in my mind. It had served as Gabryel's war tent during The War of the Nefarals. He'd been photographed next to it so many times, it had become famous in its own right. I wondered how she'd done it, and why. It sent an interesting message. One I knew Madwyn wouldn't miss, either. If it came to war, then Valeria would be ready, and they'd win just as they had so many years ago. A not-so-gentle reminder of how things had turned out for the Nefarals the last time they let their power run too rampant.

"Much better," Madwyn said, letting not a single shred of surprise or sliver of admiration slip through her mask of good humor. "Shall we?" She gestured toward the large circular tent with an outstretched palm—dark, red nails almost black in the sinking sunlight.

Mackayla and Killian inclined their heads and turned to the side, careful not to present their backs to any of us. A wise decision, though I couldn't help but raise my brows in surprise as Madwyn strolled past them, behaving as though she hadn't a care in the world.

She snapped her fingers, "Arrick and Asthorea, you're with me."

The order pulsed through me and I moved without question, watching as two of what I assumed were Killian and Mackayla's Diamanti followed as well. So went the standard protocol for truce negotiations during a time of war. The ruling deities brought their most trusted advisors and warriors in to watch their backs and offer insight.

Royal blood in your veins didn't always make you smart, and kings and queens valued their advisors. I could only hope the beautiful, intelligent goddess I loved came from a family who knew how to handle someone like Madwyn. Or at least surrounded themselves with deities who did.

But then, Killian and Mackayla had both been young during the last war. They'd only ever experienced peace. Did it matter how intelligent they were? They'd never had to deal with outright cruelty, the raw desire for power, nor the will to take it. Madwyn had all three. The trifecta, or so I called it whenever I spent time in the mortal realm of Moldize. Lorus had had that combination, and he'd done incredible damage before Niko finally put him down.

Madwyn had also done a shitload of damage, and I knew she wasn't done yet. Sparing one last glance at the treeline, I wondered again what the hell Sylennia was doing in Valeria. Had it been part of Madwyn's plan, or had she come of her own accord? I had no idea. She'd said nothing to me about it one way or another the night before.

Concern burned in my stomach like hot acid, and I sped up my steps, catching up to Madwyn. I reached out, landing a hand on her shoulder. It was the first time I'd voluntarily touched her, but Madwyn didn't startle. Instead, she turned her head in my direction, looking uninterested. "A word, before we get started?" I asked, deciding to give it one more chance. I needed to take one more opportunity to burrow deeper into that mind of hers before everything started. Her eyes narrowed on mine, the irritation in them unmistakable. "It's important," I finished, not balking or flinching away from that glare.

She stared at me for a heartbeat longer, and then I saw it, curiosity mixing with her irritation, and I knew I had her; as though she couldn't resist the intrigue once it seeped deeper in her psyche. Perhaps it was the chaos magic flowing through her blood or maybe just an element of her personality. Either way, it was useful intel I filed away for the future.

Madwyn turned to the rest of the entourage and spoke directly to Mackayla and Killian. "You all can go ahead. We'll be right in. My bonded death deity requires a moment of my time." Mackayla and Killian's eyes narrowed, the suspicion clear. But before they could speak, Madwyn said, "We'll be only a moment. Use Asthorea as collateral, if you must. She's a trusted advisor and I would be very ... put out ... if anything happened to her."

Asthorea's lips twitched, her honey-colored eyes amused as she addressed the king and queen of Valeria without the slightest bit of ceremony. "She really would be. Put out, I mean. So, let's go, shall we?" She held out her hand, raising her arm as though to usher them into their own war tent. I couldn't help but be a little amused by the sight.

The royals and their two guards hesitated, before Asthorea dropped her arm, rolled her eyes, and strode past them into the tent. They shared quick, annoyed glances before Killian inclined his head to Madwyn in acceptance of the trade and entered the precipice.

Mackayla lingered for one second longer, as did the guards offering us glares that threatened to melt the bones from our bodies if we tried anything. Then she turned on her heel and followed her husband.

Once they disappeared inside, I led Madwyn away from them, out of earshot. Alone then, I surveyed her, my eyes traveling toward my sister and Cerus, where they stood at the head of our guard. "What are we doing here, Madwyn? What's your plan?"

She sighed, curiosity replaced by annoyance. "If I wanted you to know, you would. Besides, why do you think I have a specific plan?"

"Because if I've learned anything about you in these past months, it's that you're not reactive. You act first, and I have no idea what I should be prepared for, and you brought my sister here as collateral. So, I want to know where this is going."

She gave me a condescending look. "Well, we can't always get what we want, can we?"

"Madwyn," I said, using her name with none of the venom I usually injected into it. "I'm asking as your general, your ally, and someone who's served you well. Who's killed and bled for you, and who got you this meeting. Just tell me what's going to happen."

She considered for a moment, and at last relented, a gleam in her eye. She stepped closer, so close that I could feel the warmth of her body. "I order your silence on the matter."

The binding burned through my arm and down my back, the skin still raw from my disobedience in the throne room. I nodded, clenching my jaw. Sick as hell with the pain every order she gave me seemed to elicit.

"We're not here to negotiate a truce. I'm here to discuss the terms of their unconditional surrender."

My eyes widened as I noted the utter confidence in her assertion. "And how do you expect to accomplish that?"

That smile again, as she reached out and trailed a finger around the edge of my armored chest plate, tapping the seal of Moldize at its center. "Do you remember what I said about maximum impact?" she asked, eyes shifting back to mine, confirming my suspicions, my worst fears. Ascended be damned, she was going to use the information about chipping and caging the Altruists and force a surrender right then and there.

"I remember," I replied, stunned that she'd told me the truth. But then, what could I do about it so late in the game? Plus, she'd ordered my silence, so I would have to sit there and wait until all hell broke loose, and pray to the Ascended that my sister didn't get caught in the crossfire.

Fuck.

Without another word, she spun on her heel and strode back to the tent. When she reached it and I still stood there, frozen, she said, "Now, come along Arrick. We don't want to keep the Valerian royals waiting."

40

ASCENSION

REMI

Remi catapulted through the portal, with no idea where it led. She felt her mind break free from Davendrie's hold and spun within the vortex to look behind her. She could see the prisoner and the consciousness deity, the closing portal snapping at his heels. A dark part of her wished it would close on his body and cut him in two. That was probably too much to hope for. On the bright side, they would land in a place filled with her allies, and his enemies.

Maybe I'll finally get to kill him, she thought, exhilaration sparking within her before she remembered she had no magic. None of them did, except Ellarah, Davendrie, and the demigods, and Ellarah had already spent so much of hers. Dread pooled in Remi's belly at the thought, and she clenched her fists as she twisted to look ahead and saw the end of the tunnel.

She tried to discern where they were going and why the portal was taking so long to travel. Most portals worked instantly, but before she could riddle through it, she exploded from the opening and into a vibrant light.

Remi hit the ground hard, skidding across what felt like ... grass and rocks. She rolled, her near-mortal body bruised and burning. Sliding to a painful stop, she gasped for breath and struggled to rise to her knees.

At last, she sucked enough air to shout, her voice strained, "He's coming!" The prisoner shot through next, and everyone snapped to attention. Rather than skidding and slamming into the ground, he rolled and landed on his feet. Remi watched in amazement as his runes flared.

He lunged forward, back toward the portal as Davendrie launched through it next. The prisoner held out an arm, stepped to the side, and slammed it into the consciousness deity's throat before he could react. Davendrie's whole body jerked, head snapping backward before he hit the ground hard.

The prisoner wasted no time as he dropped his knee onto Davendrie's chest. Ribs cracked and Davendrie growled with rage, but the prisoner didn't hesitate. Instead, he wrapped his long fingers around Davendrie's neck and squeezed as the portal closed.

Davendrie didn't stay cowled for long though. He bucked, kicking out before punching at the prisoner's face. He made contact, the crunch of bone making Remi wince. The prisoner fell back against the full strength of his opponent, the true power they could all wield when they didn't have those damn runes on their wrists.

Pietyr rushed into the melee next, his lithe body delivering a lethal kick aimed at Davendrie's chest. But Davendrie's hands slapped his powerful leg aside, causing Pietyr to pivot, still keeping his balance. The shadow deity lashed out so fast Remi could barely see the blow as he slammed his other heel into Davendrie's exposed stomach.

The consciousness deity's breath puffed out in a heaving rush as he doubled over. Pietyr followed up with a palm to the nose and Davendrie stumbled. Rackham approached, the rest of them seeming to snap out of it and realize that they had a new fight on their hands. Rackham slammed his fist across Davendri's face, and the god's head whipped to the side.

The demigods charged forward too, along with Bekka, just as Davendrie let out a roar of rage. Only Remi, Ellarah, and Thayne remained frozen, each staring in disbelief as the rest of their allies jerked to a sudden stop. All their heads snapped up as their eyes rolled into the back of their heads. Remi's eyes went wide as Ellarah glowed, powering up her magic. Energy deities could use their magic for just about anything, and a blunt instrument was by far the easiest possibility.

Davendrie's attention fixed on her as he snarled. "Do it and I will unravel all of their minds."

Ellarah hesitated, and Remi realized something then. He hadn't wrapped them all up in his bubble. Thayne, Remi, and Ellarah remained awake and one hundred percent themselves. *They must be outside of his range to control,* she thought. He was powerful, but there were a lot of them, and he must have used plenty of energy, lots of his power just getting to that cell and trying to get into her mind through the runed walls. She looked at him closer, beads of sweat springing from his brow, a slight tremor in his fingers as he held them splayed. "Do it, Ellarah," Remi said.

But she hesitated.

"He's stretched too thin. He's bluffing. Do it!" Remi yelled, desperation seizing her.

Thayne's voice cut in then. "She's right, Ellarah, if we don't take him down, he's going to take us back! It's now or never, do it!"

Ellarah's body burned bright then, and the beam of pure white shot out of her, blasting through the air and hitting Davendrie straight in the chest. He grunted with the impact of the blow and went sprawling. Bekka and the rest of their allies dropped like stones, hitting the ground hard as they landed, limbs sprawled. Rackham, the closest one to Davendrie, convulsed. Remi ran forward, zeroing in on him. She skidded to a stop next to him and dropped to her knees. "Rackham!" she shouted, her heart pounding in her ears.

"Shit!" she yelled as Ellarah and Thayne rushed forward too, focusing their attention on Davendrie. Ellarah sent another blast of magic in his direction while she tossed Thayne Riven's sword from her back. Davendrie let out a pained scream as the energy magic ripped into him. Remi didn't bother to look as she pulled Rackham into her arms. Pietyr, who lay just to the right of Rackham, groaned, beginning to awaken, along with the others.

Remi stroked the young time god's cheeks. "Rackham, stay with me. Don't die!" The seizure didn't stop. Instead, blood seeped from his nose, and then his ears, and Remi stifled a cry. "No, no, no!"

Before she could say more, she felt a presence next to her. Looking up, tears swam in her eyes. Pietyr knelt on Rackham's other side. He gripped his hand. "Rackham, buddy, fight through it. You're gonna make it. Don't die!"

Rackham coughed, a spray of blood splattering Pietyr's face, but Pietyr didn't release his grip to clean himself. Instead, he looked into the eyes of his friend, and Remi remembered how Rackham had saved them. How when it came down to it, he'd helped them in Bicaidia after everything had gone to shit at the inauguration ball. He didn't deserve to die like this. Not when they were so close to escaping. Not when freedom was within their grasp.

He sputtered, eyes going wide before his body shimmered. He was going to ascend right then and there, and Remi's heart squeezed in her chest. She pulled her eyes away from Rackham's youthful, handsome face and looked at Pietyr's sharp, devastating one, and their eyes met. Pain traced every line in his expression. On instinct, she reached out with her free hand and grasped his before they both fixed their attention back on Rackham's still form. His body had already begun to dissolve, as Emorie crawled toward them, her voice groggy from Davendrie's power but still thick with emotion. "Rackham?" she croaked, moving closer, blinking as though she couldn't believe her eyes.

Then she saw the glittering lights that absorbed first his legs, then his torso. She rushed forward, a cry ripping from her throat that had tears budding in Remi's eyes. She reached for him and grabbed his hand just before it disappeared. "No! He can't be!" she screamed. "Rackham, no!" Pietyr's eyes fixed on Remi's once more as Rackham's body dissolved into pure, shimmering light and soared toward the sky.

He released Remi's hand and wrapped his arms around Emorie, whose tears streamed down her cheeks. He tucked her into his chest as she sobbed, "Rackham!" Everyone stood around them, Remi kneeling next to the spot where Rackham had lain only seconds before. She felt him then, the familiar scent of her husband filling her nose. Thayne dropped onto his knees beside her and pulled her into his arms, his hand wrapping around the nape of her neck and the other at the small of her back.

She inhaled once, and then twice as she heard him say, "Damnit. That son of a bitch." Tension tightened every muscle in his body, and she realized he was fighting back grief. She held him tighter, sorrow and regret burning in her throat.

After a moment, Remi brushed the tears from her eyes and tried to ignore the pain welling up inside her. "Where's Davendrie?" she asked, glancing amongst the remainder of their group, all present and accounted for, before her gaze flicked to Thayne's.

"He's gone," he answered, eyes burning with emotion and hand gripping Riven's black blade as he looked at her. "I killed him." Remi turned her attention to the spot where she'd last seen him. Thayne hadn't lied. He was gone.

Remi's icy stare fixed on the spot as she whispered, "Good."

41
RETRIBUTION

ARRICK

I followed Madwyn back toward the negotiation tent, dread pulsing inside me in time with Bekka's magic. The words *maximum impact* rang in my ears, and I didn't know what I could do to stop it.

I trained my eyes on the ground, running through every scenario of what would happen next in my mind, and that's when I saw it; a faint purple haze of power trickling over the field. I swallowed as my mouth went dry. Chaos magic was a tricky thing when you weren't looking for it. Pernicious, impossible to predict, difficult to perceive—and it coated every inch of the valley, the forest, and the hillside.

Dread coated my tongue before Madwyn stepped into the tent. With little choice, I chanced a look at Lilja and a scan of the treeline before I slipped inside behind her.

As I entered, I took in my new surroundings. The space seemed larger inside than outside. White canvas walls surrounded us, painted on two sides with stunning murals of battles and ascensions long since past. A tiger-skin rug adorned the floor, and a crackling fire burned to my left. Two cozy, red chairs, the color of blood, sat on either side of it, though they remained empty.

To my right, I saw a large, raw-edged, wooden table and matching chairs. Two on one side of the grand table, where Queen Mackayla and King Killian sat, and one sat opposite of them. Madwyn strolled through the extravagant luxury as though she'd been born into it. Despite not being a royal herself, she'd been the next closest thing—an upper-caste goddess with a powerful family descended from the Bicaidian creator who'd served as long-running advisors to the throne of Bicaidia. I could only imagine how they'd have burned with fury if they could see her now.

The Valerian royal guards and advisors stood behind the king and queen, legs shoulder-width apart and hands clasped at their fronts. Their soft, white leathers and golden-plated armor glowed in the firelight. A massive, jewel-encrusted chandelier hung above us, adding to the luminescent effect in the tent.

Energy magic, I thought, recoiling once again at how most of the Twelve Realms harvested that magic and how Madwyn had increased those same harvests since she'd taken over her segment of the realms. But I couldn't think about that. I couldn't let my mind wander to all the atrocities that happened in the Twelve Realms. Instead, I needed to stay focused and figure out what to do with what I knew would happen next.

The female, Valerian guard had dark hair drawn back in a tight braid, the angles of her features sharp and serious while the male's salt and pepper hair hung loose to his shoulders. Both all but sneered at Madwyn as she pulled the chair out and settled into the seat across from Bekka's parents. I moved to join Asthorea, who had filed in on Madwyn's righthand side, moving closer to the table. I took up the same position on her left.

Madwyn crossed a leg over her knee and leaned back, folding her slim hands in her lap. She looked polished, like a perfectly put-together painting.

The four of them eyed each other, each waiting for the other to speak first. Madwyn's sly smile let me know it would not be her. At last, Mackayla relented, "We want our daughters back."

Madwyn's grin spread wider. "That's why we're here, isn't it? To discuss the terms of a truce. You want your daughters back, and I, well, do you know what I want?"

"No, we don't. So, why don't you tell us?" Killian demanded as some scattered shouts sounded from outside. My gut clenched in warning, and I felt Bekka's magic rise in time with my death power. I pushed it down, the creation gift urgent to get out. To be used. I didn't know how much longer I could contain it, not with the turmoil roiling inside of me, and definitely not with Madwyn's magic coating the ground. I took a deep breath and did my best to focus on the conversation in front of me.

"Don't you think you should see to that?" Madwyn asked, pointing to the heavy canvas flaps that served as the door to their tent as more shouts sounded.

Mackayla never broke eye contact with Madwyn. "I'm sure everything is in hand. So, as my husband asked you, what do you want in exchange for our daughters?"

Madwyn pursed her lips, as though considering her options. "Perhaps I want you to leave me alone and allow me and my people to keep our newly gained territories. Maybe I want to divide the Twelve Realms between us. A stronghold for Nefarals and a stronghold for Altruists. Both free to live in peace wherever they please."

I watched King Killian and Queen Mackayla's reactions and thought about what they had done to their people. They were about to get their comeuppance, I thought, probably worse than they ever imagined possible. For Bekka's sake, I felt a pang of compassion for them. But that feeling extended only as far as Bekka was concerned because they'd done unspeakable things to me, my family, and my friends back home.

Despite wanting to feel that depth of regret, that passion to save them for their own sake, I couldn't. The Valerian royals had allowed my people to die in droves while The Burning wreaked havoc on my realm. Twelve Hells, they'd almost let our entire world get wiped from existence, all to punish us for the sins of the past.

I wanted to want to help them, but a part of me, the darker part I'd been fighting like hell to keep at bay, wanted to watch it all burn down around them and revel in that destruction.

My mind cleared when Killian scoffed, and I refocused as the shouting from outside grew louder yet again. And I knew without a doubt that the fallout had begun. Considering the suddenness of those reactions, I knew how she'd done it too. Only one way existed that would allow a secret like that to spread so fast.

She'd tapped into their feeds, or she'd used the team of technology gods she had back in Bicaidia to do it. They could too. Preva and her team had talent. All they'd need was one little entry point, past the wards of Valeria, and the Valerian royals had handed it to her on a silver platter.

In their arrogance, they thought Valeria served them as their seat of power. But they'd been wrong, so fucking wrong. There they were, strutting like big swinging dicks, and they didn't even realize they had already lost.

Killian leaned over the table, his posture menacing, as though he held all the cards. "We will never relinquish the Twelve Realms to the likes of you."

Madwyn threw back her head and laughed, shaking her hair back and forth. When she finished, she leaned forward, the gleam in her eye the only hint of the anger I could sense simmering beneath her polished surface. A scream pierced the silence in the tent, and that time, it was too loud to ignore.

"I really think you should see to that," Madwyn said, showing her teeth in more of a snarl than a grin that time.

Before anyone could react, a soldier threw back the curtain and rushed inside. "Majesties, we need to get you out of here now." He spread his fingers and fire licked up his arms as he turned to face Madwyn and me, the threat in his eyes implicit. "Step back, now!"

A second soldier hurried inside, the white battle leathers and golden-plated armor glowing with active defensive power. A sight that hadn't been seen in Valeria since the last war, I knew, as I watched as the two advisors ushered Killian and Mackayla to their feet, confusion plain on all their faces.

"What's happening?" Mackayla asked, still calm on the exterior, but I could sense the torrent of trepidation swimming beneath the surface.

"A feed started the instant they crossed into our lands. They broadcasted it across the realm, on every channel." The second soldier, a goddess, pulled her sword and electricity snaked up its blade. As the leather coat that covered her armor shifted, I saw the sleek energy detonator at her side. They'd not only brought their defensive armaments, but their weapons that amplified and channeled their magic as well.

I'd seen the swords adorned there and assumed them part of the normal attire for a soldier, but the detonators were a different story. Valeria probably thought we hadn't created our own yet, but they would be wrong. Like I said, Preva was damn good.

Mackayla turned, her sleek blonde hair whipping as she leveled a scathing glare on Madwyn. The kind of glare that only a born royal, used to power and influence on a grand scale, could muster. I'd seen a look like that before, from her father, in that terrible battle, before he'd sacrificed himself to save Bekka. Madwyn remained seated, legs crossed one over the other. She looked comfortable, as though she didn't have a care in the world.

She spread her hands as that dark smile crept across her lips. "I just showed them the truth. That's all," she purred, shrugging a shoulder. The words *maximum impact* echoed in my mind again. She didn't fuck around on that front. "How you've suppressed them their entire lives. Lied to them. Built this peace on the backs of their suffering."

Mackayla and Killian both went pale. "What are you talking about?"

"I'm talking about how you put governor chips in not just Nefarals, but Altruists, too. I'm talking about how you suppressed their magic, and never let anyone rise above their family's caste. We told them all the truth the minute you granted us access to your precious realm."

"Suppress them? We never did anything—"

"Shut your fucking mouths," Madwyn said, rising to her feet, palms pressed to the table, her glare menacing, unhinged even. "You don't get to lie anymore."

Mackayla's eyes hardened, going cold as ice. "You stupid child. You have no idea what you've done. You'll have nothing left to rule but kingdoms of rubble and ash."

"Better rubble and ash than a gilded cage," Madwyn said, the shouts growing more urgent, getting closer.

Killian stepped forward, his large frame towering over Madwyn. "We did what we had to do to stabilize the realms. And with this single, ignorant act, you've just turned the Twelve Realms into a tinderbox."

"Yes, I have. And now all we need to do is light a match," she said, her tongue sharp with venom. Then, without warning, she threw her arms wide, fingers splaying as magic burst from her.

42

MAXIMUM IMPACT

ARRICK

Madwyn's power rose like a sentient fog from the ground as purple smoke, lined with an electric current, erupted inside the tent, filling it in an instant.

It punched into Mackayla and Killian, along with the guards, blowing them back and causing them to hit the canvas with a loud thump. Then Madwyn's magic sliced through the tent's material, cutting it to ribbons as it shot forth into the shouts beyond.

I could feel the pull of her power the instant it hit me, the pulse of wild emotion it elicited, and I sucked in a breath to control it. Rage, boiling and hot, flashed red in my mind, and I watched as trickles of magic danced up Asthorea's arms, and a different kind of wind began whipping through the nearly ruined tent. I recognized it as Asthorea's dimensional gift roaring to life.

I didn't love the idea of her tearing holes in our reality and tossing people through so close to me. I didn't want to end up in one of her endless, empty dimensions by accident. So, I danced away from her, keeping my magic leashed, afraid of what that fiery rage fueled by Madwyn's power would do to my control. I could already feel the rising sting of Bekka's magic thrumming to the surface and understood why she'd had such difficulty controlling it at first.

It begged to be used, unleashed, and I knew then that I couldn't keep up this charade forever. I needed to release it and soon, or I'd explode. But that would be another problem, for another time. I couldn't let that happen, not yet.

So, I breathed deeply, fighting with everything I had to maintain some semblance of composure as Madwyn cleared our side of the room of her chaos magic with the sweep of her hand. I blinked, breathing fresh air, the red tinge that filled my world subsiding as the king and queen backed away from us, surrounded by deities who rushed through the ruined tent flaps to join them.

The strips of its shorn fabric rippled around us, open to the air, and for the first time, I saw what transpired beyond it. My demons stood with Madwyn's Diamanti and our hand-selected guard, unmoving, as the Valerian forces turned on each other. Nefaric gifts from within the Valerian ranks lashed out, as some Altruists joined them too.

I had a front-row seat to Madwyn's grand plan and watched as complete and utter chaos devolved on the battlefield. Our entire fighting force didn't have to lift a finger to defeat the Valerian stronghold. They'd do it to themselves. They'd rip each other apart. The full genius of Madwyn's strategy wasn't lost on me, and I knew what she meant when she'd said, depending on how things went. She'd foreseen the internal battle as a potential outcome. She must have had rock-solid proof for things to escalate so quickly and thoroughly.

Dragging my focus back to the Valerian royals, I watched as the male Valerian advisor stepped in front of his king and queen. One quick flick of his wrist and a barrier of raw, pure energy formed between us, surrounding the royals in a globe of white sparking light.

"Break that barrier! Don't let them escape!" Madwyn shouted, and Asthorea hurried forward, her hands moving as she went to work. Blackness, utter and complete, flowed from her fingertips. It gathered, surrounding one side of the protective barrier.

I felt the sting of Madwyn's order and sprang to action too, slamming my magic into the other side of their wall of magic. Madwyn took the front, focusing the brunt of her magic on it, purple and black power bearing down on their energy shield.

Through the darkness of our combined power, I saw a stream of light pierce through, rocketing straight for us. A detonator blast of amplified energy magic soared through the air so fast I barely had time to react. I spun, dodging just as another dozen blasts seared through the barrier right on the heels of the first one.

Asthorea, Madwyn, and I moved fast, bending, twisting, and blocking the blows with our magic, trying to avoid the beams of raw energy.

But we weren't quite fast enough. The edge of one sliced across my side, scoring straight through the smooth leather there, missing my spelled armor, and I hissed in reaction. I saw Asthorea take a glancing blow across her calf, and I smelled the raw burn of both our flesh as she stumbled.

The detonator beams stopped as suddenly as they'd started. But before we could recover our triple assault, a large blast of electric lightning boomed through the tattered remains of the tent, vibrating my ears and piercing straight for Madwyn. Madwyn had just enough time to lift her hands and loose her power. The lightning bolt hit her chaos magic and deflected, splitting through the tent and slicing out into the field beyond.

Not hesitating, I redoubled my efforts on the barrier securing the Valerian royals, Asthorea working in time with me. I breathed, calling my death power within seconds, and threw it forward. Recovering, Madwyn joined us then, her eyes hungry, like she wanted nothing more than to kill Bekka's parents.

But I made Bekka a promise, and Madwyn hadn't ordered me to kill them, only to break the barrier. So, I aimed for the guards, careful to avoid King Killian and Queen Mackayla. If I ended them, I knew there would be no coming back. Not for me, and not for Bekka, and then that darkness I'd teetered on the edge of for months would consume me. So, I threw my punches, doing my best to break through the guard's energy field without harming them. I would deal with what came next after that. I had no idea what that meant, or how I would keep my promise to Bekka. *One step at a time*, I told myself.

I heard shouts and screams of panic then, and the barrier protecting the king and queen flickered. Asthorea, Madwyn, and I advanced on them, pressing our magic deeper as the shield shimmered again, showing signs of faltering. We stepped forward once more, the energy power weakening and fading as we pressed.

One more step, and a few more seconds, and it would fail. I swallowed, anxiety rising as we kept pushing. I had no clue what I would do once it fell.

One more step forward and the energy field dropped, and at the same time, the Valerian royals disappeared. I blinked as no one except the female advisor stood before us. Time magic, I realized. Queen Mackayla's magic.

Madwyn meant to take them by surprise with her assault, to buy her time to chain them with the shackles she'd used on Bekka, Remi, and so many others. Or so I assumed. It would be the only way to control deities as powerful as them. Either that or she wanted to kill them. But it hadn't worked as she'd wanted. The Valerians had defended themselves faster than expected, and we'd had to improvise.

Madwyn yelled at Asthorea and me, gesturing to the lone advisor, "Kill her and then find the royals. We don't leave here until we have them in custody." Madwyn turned then, disappearing into a cloud of purple smoke. *Where the fuck did she just go?* I wondered, my mind flooding with relief.

Probably to hunt for the royals herself or to ensure that the rest of our guard was prepared to fight. Cerus had stayed behind to lead our soldiers, and I knew she would use him instead of me to fight the Valerian regiment if needed. The first conquest I wouldn't lead, and it was because she'd tasked me with hunting down Bekka's parents. Hate filled me once again, but I didn't have time for feelings.

The deity in front of us held two daggers in her fists, a detonator forgotten on the ground next to her. She hesitated, and I scanned my eyes over the valley and the forest that surrounded us through the shredded remains of the tent.

As I did, I caught the slightest pulse of bright white light rising within the purple smoke, far into the tree line. *Bekka's parents?* I wondered, refocusing on the last remaining advisor before she or Asthorea could catch on that I'd seen something. The binding tattoo burned with Madwyn's last order, and I drew my sword, but before I could surge forward and swing it down in an arching death blow, she disappeared into a puff of shadow. A second later, she reappeared behind me.

She wrapped an arm around my throat and spun, throwing me to the ground. Surprised, and acting on instinct, I rolled with the momentum and landed on my feet, rising as she lashed forward. Her knife, glowing golden, sliced toward me. I dodged, using my years of combat training to avoid her slashing blows.

After a few near-misses, I saw Asthorea from the corner of my eye. Her fist swung at the goddess's temple just as the shadow deity disappeared again. Asthorea's momentum had her stumbling forward, losing her footing just before the Valerian reappeared in the same spot a second later. She leaped, landing two kicks square in either of our chests.

I stumbled back, catching my balance before I fell, but the same could not be said for Asthorea. She crashed to the ground, the back of her head slamming hard on the grass, teeth clacking. The shadow deity dropped to her knees atop her, slamming down hard with both knives, the blow aimed straight at her heart.

I lunged forward then, launching myself between them and blocking Asthorea with my body as I rolled her away from the blow. The blade slammed into the back of my shoulder, cutting through the weak spot in my leathers, between the magical protection of my chest and shoulder plates. It slid through my flesh like butter and set fire to my insides. It felt like the knives had been dipped in hot acid and I roared in pain. Godsbane poison, or healer's poison, I couldn't be sure. Either way, I didn't have long before the effects took hold. Paralysis and agony, followed by prolonged stasis sleep. Without the cure, I wouldn't be long for this battle.

Fuck, fuck, fuck.

I rose to my feet, the effort costing me as Asthorea put herself between me and the shadow deity. She raised her black blade, twisting it in front of us, giving me a chance to recover. The Valerian charged, disappearing into shadow before reappearing next to us, knives slicing. She swung them fast, her body moving like a dancer's, only a hell of a lot more deadly.

Asthorea blocked and tried to counter to no avail as I fought to breathe through the agony that ripped through every cell in my body. I could tell the Valerian had the advantage of experience, and Asthorea couldn't hold out for long. So, without allowing myself to think, I charged her in a rush of fury, slamming my blade into her twin ones. The force of the hit caused her knives to clatter to the floor, and I wrapped a hand around the shadow goddess's throat. Gripping hard, I hauled her off her feet and threw her back a good twenty feet. I turned to Asthorea, "Make me a place to put this bitch. I'll hold her off until it's time." And then I charged the deity again, sword drawn.

Rage, a fire bright and hot, burned inside of me. I didn't dare to summon my magic. The pain lancing through my body made it impossible to separate one power from the other. I'd have to let Asthorea help me, or rely on my blade. Though, each time I thought my strikes would hit home, the goddess disappeared. She moved like a wraith, impossible to touch. Impossible to fucking kill.

But that's what we had to do, and once it was done, I needed to obey Madwyn's command and find the royals. I could feel the sting of the binding worsening with every second I spent there with the shadow deity. Add that to the fiery burn of the poison coursing through my veins, and I wanted to rip my mind from my body to escape the pure agony of it. But there was no time for that. I'd been in pain before, I reminded myself. I'd lived through it my entire life.

She reappeared behind me that time, knives back in hand, swinging like her life depended on it. I blocked her strikes one after the other, but I could feel myself flagging. I just had to keep her busy, tire her out, and hope she made a fucking mistake.

At last, she thrust forward, leaving herself exposed, and I brought the hilt of my sword down hard on her hand before I grabbed her forearm. She yanked, struggling to get free as she looked at me. I concentrated, gritted my teeth, and focused hard as I dared to let the tiniest fraction of my magic seep out. Black mist pooled from my fingers, and I could see terror flash in her eyes as the icy lick of my magic permeated her skin. She hissed, and I watched as she tried to translocate. Shadows gathered around her, but I gripped her tighter, my magic forcing her to stay. I was more powerful. My will would win, and we both knew it.

She bucked, trying to kick as a shout from Asthorea sounded, "It's ready!" I turned, dragging the Valerian forward toward the sound of Asthorea's voice, barely thinking about what I was doing. The endless dark of the portal Asthorea had created came into focus, and I didn't let myself consider my actions. I had to obey that order from Madwyn, and I wanted to punish the shadow goddess for poisoning me. It seemed like a win-win, in my rage-hazed mind.

Purple smoke I barely noticed coated the field outside the tent and swirled around my legs as my anger grew to new heights. I continued to drag her, kicking and screaming, to the endless black of Asthorea's portal. "No!" She screamed, "Please! Don't throw me in there! I yield! You hear me! I yield." But I didn't spare her a second thought. Instead, I gripped her shoulders and tossed her inside.

43
POISONED
ARRICK

Asthorea closed the portal a second later, and the advisor's scream cut off as though we'd flipped a switch. A hot sting burned down my torso, mirrored by the pain in my arm, where Madwyn's order still called to me.

Grunting in complete and utter agony, I continued forward anyway, and as I picked up speed, a sudden rush of fresh air blew across my face and filled my nostrils. I gulped it down, exhaling as my head cleared from that all-consuming anger that Madwyn's horrible power seemed to amplify.

I took a breath, then another, drinking them in like they'd be my last. I needed to find Bekka's parents while I could still stand. The burn of poison lanced through my arm, and I could feel a sharp coldness making its way further into my bloodstream. Through it all, the binding called to me, but so did my promise to Bekka. I thought about Lilja and everything we'd discussed the night before, and I knew what to do.

"We split up," I said to Asthorea. "They probably made a run for one of the thicker tree lines to figure out their next move. Madwyn would have locked down all travel into or out of Valeria. She never would have attacked without that precaution, so they'll be stuck here. You search there—" I said, pointing to an area far away from that energy flare I'd seen earlier. "I'll head that way." I pointed in the opposite direction.

Asthorea stared at me, hesitating for a moment, her dark hair and bronzed skin shining with sweat in the last of the sunlight. "But your shoulder—"

"I'm fine," I said, snapping at her. "Now go."

She gave me one last once-over before she shot out in the direction I'd commanded, moving fast. I said a small prayer of thanks to the Ascended that I'd done my job and made them trust me on the battlefield. Without hesitating, I peeled off in the opposite direction, stumbling as I ran to the outskirts of the skirmish, through the ensuing battle that surrounded us. While we'd fought the shadow deity within the confines of the nearly destroyed tent, the rest of the battlefield had descended into utter chaos, thanks to Madwyn's magic, I presumed.

Valerians fought each other, and our army joined in now too, the sounds of swords clanging and magic bursting filling the air. Shouted orders and screams of pain echoed through the fishbowl of a valley where the battle raged. I heard the cries of death and saw the sparkling mist of ascensions filling the air. Portals opened all over the field, and I couldn't tell where they came from, Bicaidia or Valeria, and I didn't care. I had to keep going.

So, I made a beeline toward the copse of trees where I'd told Lilja to slip away if a battle broke out. To the place I'd meet her, if I had the opportunity. But before I could make it there, a portal hummed to life between me and my potential salvation, its wind whipping hard as I stepped backward to avoid it. I saw the golden city inside it and sick dread coursed through me as a god stepped through. I could feel my broken breathing, the pain lancing through me, and my muscles weakening with every step I took.

But none of that mattered when the deity swung his blade, eyes locking onto mine. I saw red power glowing at his fingertips and knew he had to be a science deity. *Gravity-altering magic sounds shitty right now*, I thought, raising my blade to block him.

I tried to summon my magic but winced at the effort, the poison already working its way too deep into my system. Hand-to-hand it would be then, I thought, raising my blade as he lunged for me again, and I avoided the blow. My movements felt clumsy as I raised my sword to block his second blow. I fell to my knees with the impact, and the god's face alighted with the thrill of a near kill. But then a blade exploded from his throat, blood spurting as it coated my face.

The god gasped, dropping to his knees, his golden hair darkening without the portal's light shining on him. He opened his mouth as though stunned before he slumped over on his side. I looked up, staring at the deity who'd saved me. Cerus's long, dark hair obscured his face as he said, "You're welcome. Now get up and fight."

I rose to my feet as he turned, charging back toward the heat of the battle, and when he did, a small device fell from his leathers onto the ground a few paces ahead of me. I stepped forward, struggling for every moment of consciousness I had left, and bent to retrieve it. A portal generation device, I realized, rubbing a finger over the display. It still had one use left. I pocketed it, a plan forming in my mind, as I made my way to the forest not twenty feet away.

Breathing raggedly, I broke through the treeline, swiping at branches and dodging rocky, rooted undergrowth. A heavy canopy hung above me and a cool breeze brushed over my face as I turned deeper into the woods, looking around. "Lilja?" I rasped, making sure my voice was loud enough to be heard above the battle, but not too loud. "Where are you?" I spun and could feel the poison work its way deeper into my system with every single heartbeat, the sound pounding in my ears.

I waited for a moment before I started to worry. Did Lili get stuck in the battle? Had she been able to get free unnoticed? Dread coiled inside me just before I heard a soft, "Arrick? Is that you?"

Relief flooded me and I hurried to the sound of my sister's voice, my movements jerky and unsettled. I didn't have much time left. We'd gotten lucky. The flare I'd seen earlier, which I thought had to be from the royals and their energy deity guard, wasn't far from where we stood.

"Are you OK?" she asked, looking me over. I could feel the blood slithering down my body, likely rendered invisible by the black leathers I wore and the darkness of night.

"I'll be fine," I said, my voice hoarse.

"You don't look fine," she replied, worry etching every line of her face. Ceros had provided her with training leathers, and magic-enhanced armor, a measure of protection if all hell broke loose.

I felt a small pang of gratitude for that, and the favor he'd done me on the battlefield, as I gestured for her to follow me deeper into the woods. "We need to move. Now." Before we could make it ten steps, I heard a voice ring out above the fray.

It took a second for me to place it before I realized it was Madwyn. It was loud, loud enough to be heard across the entire battlefield. "Nefarals! My friends! And our Altruist allies! My name is Madwyn of House Senagal, ruler of Bicaidia, Perenelle, Quindale, Crescendia, and Moldize, and I put that broadcast on your screens today because you deserve the truth!"

Lilja and I looked at each other, and each moved without a word, closer to the edge of the forest but not too close. Just enough to see what was happening in the valley beyond.

The fight that had been raging mere moments ago had ceased. It didn't take a genius to see who'd won. Injured deities clad in white and gold littered the battlefield. Other Valerian soldiers stood aloft from Madwyn's host, not moving to attack our army. They wouldn't attack her, I realized, because they'd turned on their realm. The chaos magic and the world-breaking scandal Madwyn released that day had all coalesced into this moment.

I squinted, pain causing my vision to blur, but I could still make out the flare as portals dotted the entire valley, and Madwyn's army stepped through half of them. In the other half, I saw the golden city of Vyngale and other locations scattered among Valeria.

Our army marched through the portals into them, straight into the heart of Valeria, as Madwyn's voice rang out once more. "The Valerian royals betrayed you. They betrayed us all! We will no longer submit to their will, to their gilded cages! It is time for a new order! One where Nefarals and Altruists alike are free to use our powers and live our lives without their intervention. Join me, and you have my word that we will remove your governor chips, and none will ever enter your neck again! We will bring all the royals who violated and betrayed us, who manipulated us like puppets, to justice! And when that's done, we will be free."

We watched as holos sprang to life ahead of Madwyn, enormous renderings of city squares with her image at their centers, the deities in them watching her. I heard shouts ring out from the crowds. "Don't listen to her! She's a liar! Haven't you all seen what's happening in those other realms?" I heard more shouts. "Join her and we can be free! My name was on that list! So were my son's and my daughters'! They lied to us!" Round and round it went as each of the cities erupted into chaos and fighting.

Our armies swept through the open portals with little resistance then.

I stared until I couldn't anymore. Until white-hot pain seared through me. "We need to go," I gasped, gripping Lilja's shoulder. She nodded, and we moved back the way we'd come. As we hurried, I removed the portal generator from my pocket and reached out to Lilja, catching her arm and placing it in her palm. "Take this and use it if you need a quick exit."

She wrapped her fingers around it, nodding her head in agreement. I couldn't say more than that. We may have locked Valeria down for the royals and their allies, but one of our portal generators? Lilja could use it to take them to any of our allied realms.

So, I said nothing further and hoped she understood the weight of my words and what they would mean if we made it to Bekka's parents. She could take them wherever they thought it would be safest to hide. I had ideas, but I couldn't know where, and Lilja could never tell me. If she did, then Madwyn would find out, and I'd never let that happen.

Lilja nodded, looking me over, and I felt the blood seeping down to my hands and dripping onto the grass. Her eyes locked on the bloody pool beneath our feet then, and she gasped, seeming to realize just how badly injured I was. Her gaze fixed on the wound along my shoulder, a stab straight through the back to the front. She went pale, and I knew it must look as terrible as it felt. "You're poisoned, Arrick. You can't stay here! You need a healer!"

I coughed, tasting metal at the back of my throat, and shook my head. "It's not lethal. I need to make sure you find Bekka's parents before—" I broke off, coughing in heaving gasps as I tried to catch my breath. Shaking my head, I said, "I saw them come this way. Can you help me track them?" Sweat made my skin slick as I dragged a hand down my face.

Lilja nodded. "Of course, I remember what Dad taught us. I saw tracks that way the instant we broke through the trees. Broken shrubs and disturbed pine needles."

I smiled at her, impressed by her keen eye.

She looked at the blood dripping off my fingers again and pressed her lips together. "You only missed it because you've been poisoned."

She was right, but it wasn't the time for me to worry about that. "OK, hurry, Lili. We need to find them."

"Then what?" And I knew what she meant. What about me? What about Madwyn? I had no fucking idea. Maybe by then, I'd pass out, fall into stasis sleep, and save us the trouble.

"You use that portal, and I'll hold myself back as long as I can. Don't tell me where they're going, and move fast," I said, gesturing deeper into the woods. "Now let's go." I would have to hope I didn't get an even larger burn on my arm that would signal a new betrayal to Madwyn. Ascended only knew what she'd do if that happened.

To my relief, Lilja obeyed, turning, and I watched as she soaked in every detail of our surroundings, the way our father had taught us. The edges of my vision blurred, and I lunged forward, catching myself on a tree. I felt drunk, I felt sick, I felt fucking poisoned, and nothing in my body would let me forget it.

But I didn't stop. I followed her deeper into the belly of the forest until the heavy canopy overhead blocked out every trace of star and moonlight. We circumvented a large pile of rocks with an enormous tree growing from the top of it, and I felt it. The tang of magic, just before a blast of vibrant white exploded toward us. Reacting as best I could, I reached out, grabbing Lili's arm and spinning as I all but threw her back behind the rock and to safety. The magic hit me square in the back and blinding pain, unlike anything I'd ever experienced, sliced through me.

I collapsed, falling to the ground, face slamming into the unforgiving soil, rocks, and roots. I tried to roll over, my limbs heavy with agony. And as I did, I saw Lili, whose eyes went wide and round as she stared at me in utter astonishment. A second later, she was running for me. I tried to hold up my hand, to tell her to stop, when Mackayla and Killian stepped out from behind that same rock formation and the trees just beyond it.

Their bodyguard had a sheen of magic around him, the same potent energy power that had just knocked my fucking block off. Lilja skidded to a halt before she reached me, looking at the royals and their entourage like a scared rabbit. Her slim hand went to her pocket, where she'd slipped the portal generation device.

I blinked, my mouth feeling like it had cotton inside it, like I couldn't form words, and then another blast of power poured out of the god. It slammed into the massive, gnarled tree on top of the rocks, the resulting crack slamming through my ears. I wondered, *What the fuck and why?* just before the tree leaned. It crashed through the canopy, snapping its smaller branches against other trees, as it fell right toward the spot where I laid.

All I could do was watch in horror as my sister jumped out of the way, her eyes filled with terror before the tree crushed me and the world went dark.

A long time later, I felt hands grip my shoulders and heard someone saying my name. "Arrick, you need to wake up." Everything hurt. My head felt like someone had taken a dagger to it, and my whole body burned like my blood had been replaced with acid. I coughed, sputtering as consciousness fought against my need for stasis sleep. "Wake up. You need to get yourself under control before someone sees you."

At last, I opened my eyes and looked up at who'd been shaking me. Sylennia's face came into focus. Darkness and quiet surrounded me. The battle was either far off in the distance or long over. I had no idea which one.

I blinked, my vision clearing. Her shadow power surrounded us, the faint veil of it dancing around her. I turned my head then and saw the fucking enormous tree just to my right. She must have dragged me out from under it. She shook her head at me and said, "You stupid, stupid bastard. Why didn't you tell me?" Her eyes scanned down my body, a strange blue glow on her face.

I looked down then and saw what she meant. The blue glow? It came from me. My body was coated in it, Bekka's magic swirling through me. It had broken free. Panic speared me as I stared down at my hands coursing with that odd power. But it wasn't just that.

It wasn't just me I had to worry about.

Rising to a sitting position, I fought through the pain of the poison and the magic, and stared into the dark, empty forest. I squinted to see better, fear making everything more vibrant and sharper as I tried to rise to my feet but couldn't. I swore under my breath, words so vicious that even Sylennia's brows rose. Because the forest was empty. Lilja and the Valerian royals were gone, and I had no idea what had happened to them.

Or what Bekka's power might have done to them or anyone else nearby when it broke free.

44

WYNTHOREA

BEKKA

My sister's tears streamed down her face, and something cracked inside me, too. The time deity, the young one who'd come so close to rescuing us in Bicaidian hell, had ascended. He'd died to keep Davendrie from either unraveling all our minds or taking us prisoner. He deserved so much better than the death Davendrie had handed him.

And he earned so much more than the send-off we could give him. Our runes burned bright, shining in the surrounding forest, as we all fought to access our magic. To send tendrils of it up into the sky in a proper, honorable goodbye, but we couldn't. Madwyn had taken that from us.

I moved forward and rested a hand on Remi's shaking shoulders; her face still pressed into her husband's chest. Before I could say another word, Remi spun and wrapped her arms around me. Tears sprang to my eyes at the feel of her in my arms, the scent of her fiery hair. My sister, my twin. I'd missed her so fucking much. It felt unreal.

We'd made it out. After so many months of hunger and torment, we'd made it out.

"Bekka, we're free," Remi said, her voice choking with emotion. I could only nod in response, my eyes wet, and I realized tears streamed down my face too. "We're free. But Rackham—" she hiccupped, sucking in a breath and gesturing to the spot where the time god had passed. "He won't get to—" she broke off as though unable to finish.

"I know," I said, stroking a hand down her hair, like our mother did for us as girls. "I know, Rem."

Thayne looked pale, stricken. "He ..." he trailed off, swallowing hard. "Rackham was the one who kept searching, even when the rest of us had given up on finding a way out. He never did. He didn't deserve to die like this." The high prince faltered, shaking his head in disbelief.

Remi pressed her cheek into my collarbone, and I looked around at the rest of our rag-tag group of escapees. Ellarah and Thayne looked shaken, exhausted, coated with black demonic blood, their faces pale. The agony written in every part of Emorie's body let me know that she'd been close to Rackham. Grief reverberated from her while silent tears streamed down her face as the shadow god held her, also looking sick with grief. I wanted to comfort her, to tell her everything would be OK, but I knew it wouldn't. She'd lost someone important to her, and I knew better than anyone that that feeling didn't get better. Not anytime soon, at least.

My eyes landed on Caden and Deklan, and I saw ragged grief on their faces too. From the looks and sound of it, they'd spent their time in prison together, and Rackham was the one who kept them going. Thayne was right. It wasn't fair.

Deklan looked up into the sky, to where Rackham's fading light dwindled. Then his eyes landed on Thayne. "I wish I could have killed that bastard myself."

"Get in line," Remi said, tears still brightening her eyes.

The prisoner spoke then, his head tilted up, watching the time god's ascension. "You're all damned lucky he's the only one that the consciousness deity took with him."

Emorie heard that and shoved away from Pietyr, baring her teeth at him. "Lucky? You think we're lucky? Shut your fucking mouth before I rip your tongue out and feed it to you!"

The prisoner gave her a surveying look, as though considering her threat. "You thought you could escape from the Bicaidian dungeons, one of the Twelve Realms' most secure prisons, and all of you would make it out alive, in one piece? If that's true, you're either stupid or naïve."

Emorie lunged for him, her nails angled like claws, but Pietyr caught her around her waist and held her back. She snarled, urging forward, and trying to gouge his eyes with her bare hands.

The prisoner raised his palms in apparent surrender and had the indecency to look amused. "Fine. Forget I said anything."

In response to the fight, Remi pushed out of my arms and shoved her way between the prisoner and Emorie. I couldn't help the surprise I felt as I watched her. Emorie snarled and spat, but Remi didn't move. "Get the hell out of my way, Remi!"

Instead, she squared her shoulders. "Emorie, stop. He fought with us. Without him, we would have lost more than Rackham." She swallowed, her eyes going hard with resolve. "He got me through the portal. Davendrie almost stopped me. But he —" She looked at the prisoner, gesturing to him for emphasis. "He got me through. He could have left without me, but he didn't. I owe him my life, my freedom."

We all stared at the two of them. I couldn't believe what she'd said. He had been in a secret prison cell, locked away off-books, and apparently forgotten by everyone in Bicaidia, except Thayne's father. He could have made it through the portal without helping my sister. And yet ... he hadn't left her behind. He'd helped her. I looked him up and down and felt a familiar tug I couldn't quite place, but he didn't seem like a stranger. Not fully at least, and as I watched him, I noticed he watched me as well, like he might recognize me too.

Before I could make heads or tails of it, a shout sounded behind us. "Ellarah! Did you make it?" We all turned in unison, and I took in my surroundings for the first time. Sparkling teal water danced from a lake not far off, waterfalls rushing down at its far end. Large rock formations rose like sentinels around us, each lined with vibrant hues of purple, blue, pink, and orange amid the standard gray. Large trees, with twisted stunning limbs adorned with moss, surrounded the lake and rose in scattered dots through the meadow where we stood.

The grass beneath our feet, blanketing the ground, danced with wildflowers in every color imaginable. I sucked in a stunned breath at the unreal beauty of it as Ellarah called back, "We're here! We made it!"

"Where is here, exactly?" Thayne asked, resting a hand on Ellarah's shoulder to call her attention to him.

"We'll explain, I promise," she said, meeting his eye and then looking at the group. "All you need to know right now is that you're safe. They won't look for us here, and even if they do, they'll never find us."

Then, a deity broke through a thicket of trees near the edge of the water, her voice ringing out, "Thank the Ascended! You're much later than we expected. We feared they'd captured you!" Her low glow of energy power suffused the trees like white candlelight, and I wished again that we had our magic. If not just to give Rackham a hero's send-off, then to light our way too.

"No, they didn't. We're safe!" Ellarah said, and then winced as she realized the falsehood in that statement. Her voice sobered then, "Well, mostly." Emorie wrapped her arms around herself and stepped further from Pietyr. I could see the pain, raw and aching in her expression, and I knew she still wanted to rip that prisoner apart. But, out of respect for what he'd done for my sister, she wouldn't. I looked at her then, trying to catch her attention, but she just stared into the forest, toward the advancing goddess.

So, I did the same, watching as she approached, her long, white gown blowing in the wind, along with her dark curly hair. She looked like Ellarah, with deep-hued, rich skin and vibrant golden eyes. As she took in our collective appearances, she grimaced, though she tried to hide it. Her reaction made me look at myself for the first time.

My clothes, the same ones I'd worn when we'd made the sickening holo, were ripped and splattered with the black blood of demons. I reached a finger to my upper lip, and felt the tacky sensation of dried blood there, as though I'd gotten a nosebleed. From Davendrie, I realized, and then I looked at the rest of the group. They all had the same streaks of blood running down their noses, and then more blood trickled out from their ears.

The shadow deity, the one who'd been the second closest to Davendri, aside from Rackham, had streams of drying blood seeping from the corner of his eyes. Perhaps the prisoner had been right. It had been a miracle that more of us hadn't died.

"You all look like hell," the goddess observed.

Ellarah sniffed a hoarse laugh. It sounded raw and unnatural before she stumbled forward on shaky legs and wrapped the unknown goddess in her arms. She squeezed her eyes shut, and I could tell she was fighting for every bit of composure she had. "You have no idea how happy I am to see your face, Oni. Riven intercepted us along with his demons and a bastard of a consciousness deity. Not all of us made it out." She stepped out of Oni's embrace, and I could almost see her shudder, her legs wobbling.

"Come, let's get you back to the village, then we can talk more," Oni replied, slipping an arm under Ellarah's shoulders, and looping it around her waist, seeming to sense Ellarah's instability. Then she turned and spoke to our group, "You are all welcome here. This is a place of sanctuary and refuge for anyone who comes to find peace. Follow me, and let's get you settled."

Everyone hesitated, no one ready to move. I could tell that Emorie and the rest who knew Rackham didn't want to just walk away after what had happened to their friend. Ellarah seemed to recognize that, too. "We'll come back. I promise. When you've rested, and you've had your magic restored, we'll come back. Then we can pay him proper homage." Oni looked around at all of us, seeming to sense what Ellarah meant, and I could see genuine sympathy in her gaze.

Rackham's power, his essence, still tinged the air. It left an unmistakable sweet scent and tangy energy. "But until then," Ellarah said, raising a hand as a small, white orb glowed in her palm. She exhaled, closed her eyes, and sent it into the sky. The magic flowed up the same direction as where Rackham had ascended.

I watched Emorie tilt her head back, tracking the shining orb until it disappeared into the stars that sparkled overhead. She turned back to Ellarah and nodded at her in gratitude. "Thank you," she said, and Ellarah dipped her chin in acknowledgment. Then I watched in pure astonishment as Deklan and Caden did the same, small sparks of their elemental magic gathering in the air and lifting upward.

With that, we all fell into a loose group behind Ellarah and Oni and followed them through the forest. As we walked, Caden and Deklan drew closer to me and I looked at them, extending a hand toward Caden, knowing Deklan well enough to know he wouldn't want me to touch him. Not just yet, at least. Caden took it, squeezing, as his eyes filled with an eerie combination of sorrow and rage. And I knew without asking that it wasn't just because of what had happened to Rackham.

We'd also left Arrick behind, and I tried not to think about him. I tried to put him out of my mind. Because if I thought about him, about how far my soulfused mate was from me at that moment and how I'd abandoned him to his fate in Bicaidia, I might fall apart. And I couldn't afford that. I had to keep it together, to be the creator that everyone had gone through so much trouble to smuggle back into the Twelve Realms. I had to stay strong if I had any shot of getting him back.

Remi spoke up then, slowing her step to tuck in beside Thayne. She looked up at him, craning her neck in curiosity. "How did you all find us? We were on our way to you, and then the demons cut us off. They forced us to go on with our escape. I was afraid we were going to have to leave you behind."

She swallowed hard, and I could tell that her admission cost her. She hadn't liked the idea of leaving her husband and the rest of them behind in that dank, awful place. But we would have had a hell of a better chance of rescuing them from outside a cell than inside one. Especially after Ellarah had already blown any chance she'd had at freedom by cutting Riven with his own sword.

Thayne's lips tilted up then in a reluctant smile. "You did the right thing. You all did, and none of you should waste a moment of guilt over it." He looked at each of us, and I could tell in the deepness of his dark eyes, that he meant it. Then he continued, "As far as how we found you, I know that prison like that back of my hand, and I know Madwyn. I guessed where she might keep you, and then we heard the fight and ran to it."

Remi looked up at Thayne with such gratitude and genuine affection that my heart squeezed. *I want to see Arrick more than I want to breathe,* I thought, as a voice sounded behind us. The shadow god, I realized, "All that matters now is that we're out, and we have the next Peacekeeper with us."

He jogged then, squeezing between Remi and me, and I glanced up at him, really looking at him for the first time. He had tan skin, well-defined cheekbones, and a broad jaw, his silvery eyes sparkling in the moonlight. Handsome, I thought, unbelievably so, just before he extended his hand to me. "We haven't met yet. I'm Pietyr, leader of the Shadow Spy Sect of the Nefaric Pillar of Power in Bicaidia. Or at least, I was before Madwyn fucked all of us over."

My brows rose as I grasped his hand in mine. "Oh," I said, a little taken aback. It made sense, though. He had skill in combat, that much was plain enough. But I hadn't realized he was the leader of Bicaidia's spy ring. That could come in handy for whatever came next, I thought. Then I continued, "I'm Bekka."

"I know," he said, looking down as each of our runes flared. He released my hand and turned his attention to Ellarah and Oni, who walked several steps ahead of us. "Ellarah, do you have a solution for these runes?"

Ellarah and Oni paused then, as did the prisoner who'd positioned himself at the front of our group. They waited for us to get a little closer and when we did, Ellarah nodded, her eyes still filled with exhaustion and sorrow. She'd sacrificed a lot to get us out. I'd witnessed her fight with Riven and knew that they'd had something real. Or at least they must have, once upon a time.

"Short answer? Yes. You won't have to worry about the runes for much longer. Like Oni said, this is a place of sanctuary for the disaffected."

"What disaffected?" Deklan asked.

Oni replied, "We rescue deities from the energy fields across the Twelve Realms. We bring them here, where they can live in peace and sanctuary."

"Where is here, exactly?" Thayne asked, uncertainty lacing his words as he peered at the glistening forest. It was unlike anything I'd ever seen before. Beautiful, breathtaking, and so very unusual. Everything seemed to pulse and glow with a vibrant energy.

Oni gestured for us to follow, and said over her shoulder, "It's easier for me to show you than to explain." We broke through the treeline a few moments later, and a small hill rose before us. It was more of a mound coated in deep, green moss than anything, and she began walking up it. We all followed and when we got to the top, what I saw took my breath away.

I gasped at the stunning town that lay below. Shining white buildings, made from stone and fortified with magic, glowed between smooth, stone walkways. Bright, colorful flowers hung from windows and lush, glistening gardens settled between pathways scattered throughout the city. I could just make out the buzz and whir of machinery and watched with amazement as deities darted in and out of portals on the edge of the village.

"What is this place?" I asked, almost breathless at the beauty below.

"It's a dimensional fold," Oni answered, beginning to descend the mossy hill. We followed her as she continued to explain, "It's a secret dimension that we've hidden in the fold between the mortal and immortal realms."

We all gaped in utter astonishment. I'd heard of such things, but the Peacekeeper's Council outlawed them ages ago. My grandfather had deemed them too unstable after an accident that resulted in a black hole and a lot of death in both the mortal and immortal realms.

"How did you create this without anyone knowing about it?" Thayne asked, the first of us to recover from that revelation.

Oni let the accusation in his tone slide off her and answered with a placid geniality. "The deities who created this fold knew what they were doing. You'll find that many are willing to take risks when lives are at stake. There are a lot of deities, upper and royal-caste ones even, who don't agree with the energy fields. Using energy deities as batteries is despicable."

"I don't disagree with you," Thayne replied. "It's just that creating a habitable dimension without following proper protocol can cause even more death and destruction."

"Don't worry, young prince," Oni said, stopping at the edge of the town. "Like I said, we know what we're doing." She dismissed him as easily as she would have a small child, and I pressed my lips together, a little impressed despite myself.

Thayne's height and size made him a force to be reckoned with, but she didn't seem to notice. Or maybe she just didn't care, and a small part of me warmed to her. Then she said, "Now, come, it's time for you all to clean up, fill your bellies, and rest. You look like you all need it."

"Wait, what about our runes?" Pietyr asked again, rubbing his wrist.

"Yes, no need to fret. We're putting the finishing touches on the solution for that as we speak," Oni replied, as we approached a lush garden filled with vibrant pink, purple, and blue blooms. A white star jasmine grew along an old-fashioned picket fence, the scent filling my nostrils. She led us along a smooth stone path and then to a clearing in the garden. A small gate with a latch stood before us.

She opened it and said, "But before all that, welcome to Wynthorea."

ACKNOWLEDGEMENTS

The last few years have been rocky for my publishing journey. This book, in particular, has pushed me to the limit and tested my resolve to get it over the finish line. But, it's here and published and I couldn't be happier!

The Darkening took me longer than I expected to write. The story got bigger, the POVs expanded, and the world grew. This book stretched my capabilities, but I'm so happy I wrote it. I learned a ton, and that has helped me write the book that comes next: DoaD Book4 - The Dawning. And I can't wait to share that one either.

So, without further delay, I want to thank my husband who supported me during all of the difficult moments when this story got its claws into me and I just had to write. For all those late nights and busy writing days—Thank you.

This book would not exist if it weren't for my amazing plotting buddy and friend, Leoneh Charmell. Thank you so much for your invaluable feedback and keen eye for plot.

Another special thank you to Everly Taylor at Belle Ames Designs, who made the most beautiful cover art for this entire series! Also, thank you for your quick, thorough edit on this book when I needed it most!

Thank you to my sons, who inspire me to be more and do more. I hope to make you both proud.

And to everyone who continues to support me and who reads my stories, thank you. You make it all worthwhile.

ABOUT THE AUTHOR

Loryn Moore lives in Northern Florida with her husband and two young sons. She and her husband are avid DIYers, backyard gardeners, and devoted beach bums, when they can help it. The three men in her life are the inspiration behind everything that she does.

Loryn loves to read and write fantasy and paranormal romance/mystery stories because they take her into another place or time entirely. The idea of a secret world within our own, or any world filled with magic, makes her all warm and fuzzy inside. Add a little splash of forbidden love or just romance, period, and that is her happy place.

Sign up for Loryn's Newsletter or Follow Her on Social Media:

Join her newsletter and get a free download of behind-the-scenes details on the Diary of a Deity multiverse. She also shares updates on new releases, ARC (advanced reader copy) opportunities, giveaways, sneak peeks into her latest WIPs, writing insights, and so much more!

TikTok, Instagram, Newsletter:

https://linktr.ee/Lorynmooreauthor

Website:

www.lorynmoore.com/

OTHER BOOKS BY LORYN MOORE

Diary of a Deity Series

The Burning (Book 1)

The Rising (Book 2)

The Darkening (Book 3)

The Dawning (Book 4) – Coming Soon...

Jenna Torrence Series

Jenna Torrence Book 1- Coming Soon...

www.ingramcontent.com/pod-product-compliance
Lightning Source LLC
Chambersburg PA
CBHW020347010826
48973CB00005B/1309